Detective Inspector S.

TH.

LITTLE LIES

An addictive crime thriller with a twist
you won't see coming

GRETTA MULROONEY

JOFFE
BOOKS

First published in Great Britain 2019
Joffe Books, London

© Gretta Mulrooney

Please join our mailing list for free Kindle books and new releases.

www.joffebooks.com

ISBN 978-1-78931-241-6

With fond memories of Derry and Magee

Matis gasped.

There, stretched out on the ground at his feet, was a silvery alien.

Just wait till Filip heard about this. His jaw would drop. His family would never believe it. Matis had come to England hoping to find all kinds of things — a decent job, independence, a better life — but an extra-terrestrial was something else. He carefully stepped forward, a blur of images flashing through his mind: the headlines, his picture on the news, going viral, TV studios, interviews, a Hollywood film. Steven Spielberg. Money!

Yet, neither his family nor the press would ever hear about his incredible discovery.

CHAPTER ONE

Just before seven a.m. on a soft late April morning, bright after a night of rain. No one around. The ideal time for an angler without a permit to go fishing. There shouldn't be anyone by the river because British anglers seemed to stick to the rulebook, but it was best to be careful. When Matis Rimas first arrived in the UK, he couldn't believe that people caught fish and then put them back in the water. What a waste. You caught a fish, you cooked and ate it! But he was adjusting to life in Sussex and his English was improving slowly. He now understood when one of the guys at work said *Wanta cuppa?* Or *I'm just off for a leak*.

He was thinking of fat carp as he drove out of Berminster on the back road to the river. Carp were nomadic but they seemed to like a particular stretch of the River Bere, where the riverbed was silted, the water slow flowing. He could already taste the fillets, covered in mashed garlic and butter, then fried slowly in hot oil, the way his grandmother in Krosna always cooked them. He liked the cod and haddock that the British smothered in batter, but slow-fried carp were heavenly — and, most importantly, free. He sent a chunk of his wages back to Krosna every week and needed to keep to a tight budget.

He drove slowly past compact blackthorn hedges heavy with white flowers, looking for the lane to the left. He found it and then the little turnoff that led into a small patch of scrubby ground that ran along the western side of the river. Further along was the official entrance and the car park with the big sign that made it very clear that his type wasn't wanted. The dense woodland here was ideal because it was hard to access compared to others near the Bere. He'd found it all by himself a couple of months back and had been pleased by his ingenuity. The Polish guys knew about it too, of course. He'd seen one of them here, who introduced himself as Nowak. They'd given each other amused, furtive glances and Nowak had told him to watch out for the old guy from the anglers' club that he called 'Grandad,' who came to check up now and again. He'd also told Matis about a recipe for jellied carp. It sounded delicious but too complicated for his tiny kitchen. Instead he'd emailed the recipe to his sister.

He tucked the car in the shade of a riot of holly and buckthorn bushes. There was one other car parked there. He didn't recognize it. Probably one of the Poles who'd come with the same idea, but he'd approach the river carefully, just in case one of the club members was around. He checked his watch. He had about an hour. That should give him time to take his catch back to his small fridge before he was due on-site. Matis had been catching carp since he was four. As his grandmother had always told him, he might not be burdened with brainpower but he was pretty clever with a fishing rod.

He took his rod from the boot of the car, the only possession apart from clothing that he'd packed when he left Lithuania. He headed down the narrow, soggy path to the riverbank, brushing against valerian and stumbling over the odd hornbeam root. His jeans soaked up moisture from the grasses and the right leg snagged on a thorn. He pulled it free, forged on and then slowed as he drew near. He could see no one else at the river and he wondered where the owner of the other car was. Maybe they were walking in the woods. There would be mushrooms and young nettles to pick in the spring. The best time was after rain. That's what his grandmother would be doing on a morning like this: out with her woven basket, collecting fresh, juicy nettles to make soup. He could taste it now, sharp and peppery, and wished there was a pan of it waiting for him at home.

After just ten minutes, he struck lucky and caught a large carp, about six pounds in weight. One more would be plenty. Then there'd be one for him and one for Mrs Mazur. He liked to keep on the right side of Filip's mother. He'd landed on his feet at their place and it was clear she ruled the roost. But right now, he needed to piss or even *take a leak*. Too much beer last night. He put his rod down carefully and headed up towards a dense cluster of ash trees where he'd relieved himself before. He went to unzip his flies when his eye was caught by a flash of bright blue further back in the trees. Forgetting his urge to empty his bladder, he followed it, stepping slowly through damp ferns and leaf mould.

Matis's vivid imagination, fuelled by endless reruns of *ET* and *Star Trek*, ran wild. One of the first things he'd done on arriving in England was visit a Star Wars exhibition in London. Since his early teens, he'd been convinced that life forms from other planets were already visiting the earth. Back home, other adolescent boys spent their time searching the internet for porn. Matis crouched in his room reading websites with titles such as *Aliens — The Latest*, *Ancient Aliens*, *Aliens Are Here!* His sister teased him unmercifully about it, saying that if any aliens did discover us, they'd give us a wide berth as soon as they realized what a mess we'd made of our planet.

Matis peered short-sightedly. He'd broken his glasses a couple of weeks back but couldn't afford to replace them just yet. For now, the world was slightly out of focus until he was close up. So his first thought was that he was looking at an alien, a prone, spread-eagled form of shiny silver, shaped like a human, with silvery feet and hands and a blue-and-red head. Astonished and giddy, he drew nearer. Suddenly he understood what he was actually seeing, and his heart started hammering. He stopped in his tracks, crossing himself, and stared at the prone human.

She'd been cut savagely around the face and neck and was lying face up. Her head was thrown slightly to one side with one eye staring, the other torn open. The Lycra covering her body was spattered with blood. There was a photo lying on her chest. He halted, terrified, leaning against a damp tree trunk. For a moment, the world went misty. His hand went for the phone in his pocket but he stopped.

He had no licence or permission to be here.

He thought about the police, the questions. He'd watched cop shows and seen the small rooms they took you into for interrogation. His English was still slow and he might not understand them and they might think he was dodging the questions, had something to hide. They might get him to confess. His job. He might lose his job.

He stood paralysed with indecision, looking at the woman, who stared sightlessly back. But he had a sister, a sister he missed and loved dearly. What if something happened to her and the person who found her ran away and left her all alone?

He took his phone out and started to dial. He didn't hear the soft rustle behind him. A sharp, stabbing pain in the back of his neck made him cry out and stagger, and then another and another until his eyes were full of blood. He fell forward, his life seeping into the damp, fresh smelling earth.

In the minute it took him to die, as he drifted into his long sleep, he dreamed of a silver woman falling from the sky and settling under the trees.

The carp lay abandoned on the grassy edge of the river, its protruding mouth puckered, the golden tinted scales growing dull.

CHAPTER TWO

Siv woke early. She panicked. Where was she? Then she looked around. *Okay, calm down, you know this place. You chose it. Breathe.*

She lay for a while in the comfort of Ed's T-shirt. The three-quarter bed was pushed up against diamond-paned windows. She reached up and twitched back the curtain. The glass was rain-spattered, the sky washed and milky. Then she reached the same hand back to the shelf behind her head and looked at the time on her phone. 6.50. If she moved to the outside of the bed and stretched her other hand out, she could open the wardrobe. The compactness of this doll's house of a home was a strange delight. Four paces from the bedroom took her into the kitchen, two to the right from the kitchen into the bathroom. Another four led into the living room.

Monday morning. First day, new job. She started to panic again as the reality dawned. She was lying on her back but felt as if she was falling, spinning down a deep chasm, her heart thudding. Would she be able to remember anything? What if she walked in and everything was a blank? What if she made a crucial error that compromised an investigation? She stared at the wood-panelled ceiling, focusing on a knot shaped like a comma and concentrated again on breathing. She felt her pulse. It was steady enough.

She spread marmalade on her toast, listening to the River Bere flowing fast nearby. For the first couple of nights it had kept her awake but now she'd adjusted to the music of it, playing constantly in the background. It had moods: at times quiet and lazy, at times faster and murmuring. This morning, after the heavy rain, it was swollen and rushing. The rain had tumbled down for hours during the night, the wind whipping the trees, but now there was bright sky promising a warm spring day.

She wondered if it had been wise to rent a place at the bottom of a meadow, so near the water. In London, she'd looked at photos on a website and agreed a year's lease. There'd been floods in this part of Berminster five years ago. Her father had needed sandbags because of the stream that ran at the bottom of his garden. She stirred a teabag, watching the hot water darken to the colour of peat. Well, it would be the owners' problem if she came home and found her feet were damp. That was how she felt about things these days — let someone else deal with it. Apart from her job. That, she would have to deal with herself. It would at least keep her sane. Sane-ish. Or she'd be sent home when they realized she was incompetent, with a wet sponge for a brain. *Did you hear about DI Drummond? She only lasted a couple of weeks. Total nightmare. Reckon they'll find a way of easing her out now she's made a complete balls-up.*

She opened the fridge for milk. Someone — presumably the last tenant — had left magnetic Scrabble letters attached to the door. She'd left them there because they spelled out, *It can't get any worse.* Hopefully.

She cleared a space on the small fold-down table, opened her laptop and wrote the email to her sister that she'd been building up to. It would be evening in Auckland so she might even get a reply before she left for work. Unlikely, though. Weeks could go by before Rikka might send a brief response. She wasn't even sure why she was giving her sister her news. Rik had vanished to the other side of the world six years ago and rarely got in touch. She'd always been aloof, tucked tight into herself. At school, she'd been nicknamed *Clam*. Still, just putting it in writing felt like a validation. Something about linking the past and the future. Illusions could be a comfort, including the idea that her snotty sister gave a toss.

Hi, Rik. Happy birthday and hope you're doing well. I did send a card so hope it arrived.

Just thought I'd give you the heads up about me. I've moved back to Berminster, renting for now. Came down a week ago, pretty much settled in. I've got a new job, DI in the local cop shop. I'll see how it goes. Wasn't sure about the wisdom of returning but decided I couldn't face completely new territory. Drove past Dad's old house yesterday. Looks like a family living there now. Love, Siv.

She pressed *send* and then stood for a while at the narrow kitchen window, sipping her tea, watching the clearing clouds drift over the river and the tall, arching willow tree downstream. There was a light on in Corran and Paul's kitchen at the other side of the meadow. Her landlords lived in a beautiful converted barn, a place with wide, light-filled rooms. On the day she'd arrived they'd insisted that she come in for a coffee. She'd sat at the farmhouse table in their kitchen, absorbing the little details of their lives. They had five types of coffee beans, made their own pasta, wine, bread and preserves, grew their own vegetables, chopped their own wood in the two acres of woodland they owned bordering the meadow, and bickered amicably about who did the most housework. Both were allergic to cows' milk so they kept three goats. Corran rose early to feed them before he started his day's work weaving in the shed just beyond the house. Paul played the tin whistle and entertained her with a rendition of a jig. After an hour of their warm, embracing hospitality, she'd felt suddenly forlorn and had left abruptly, making some lame excuse.

She'd rented this trim home from them, a circus wagon that they'd bought on eBay. They'd worked on it between them, turning it into a bright, snug and comfortable home. Full-length oak doors at the front led to a decked area with a barbecue, table, chairs and tubs of shrubs and flowers. The wagon was a bit patterned for her taste, with throws and cushions made by Corran in contrasting prints and colours. She'd been alarmed the first night she slept there, wondering what she'd done, feeling strange and dislocated. But it was fine. It would do. It was quiet. A safe haven.

Corran and Paul had been delighted when she contacted them, offering to rent for a year. It had taken her just two days to unpack and sort the things she'd kept before consigning the rest to storage. This space forced her to be minimalist. She touched the top of the wood burner, fuelled by the free logs that Paul had left for her. The stove was still warm from last night and she put her arms around the pipe that ran up to the ceiling, absorbing the comfort. Poor substitute for a hug from Ed, but for now, it was the best she'd get.

She looked at her watch and saw that it was 7.45. She'd no idea where the time had gone. Mind wandering, it happened a lot these days. She'd emerge from a reverie and find that she'd lost an hour. She needed the discipline of work. She'd head there soon. Get a feel of things — the layout, the pecking order, how her desk was situated and the hot drinks supply.

In the shower, she thought about her meeting with her new boss, DCI Will Mortimer, who'd explained that the station was short-staffed. He'd clearly decided that a crisp, no-nonsense approach was best with her. Maybe he was frightened that she might dissolve in front of him and make a mess on his new-smelling, brown twill carpet. She was used to it by now. People being that little bit too cheerful, a bit too positive. It was the modern equivalent of wearing a talisman to ward off the contagion of someone else's sadness. He hadn't spent long on niceties, which was fine with her.

'So, DI Drummond,' he'd said, flexing his narrow shoulders and sniffing hard, 'settled in to your new home?'

'Yes, sir. Thanks.'

'You're from Berminster originally?'

'I came to live here when I was thirteen, sir.' *When my mother finally decided my sister and me were too much baggage to be hefted around.* 'I moved back to London when I joined the Met.'

'Ah, yes. Very good.' He'd tapped a key on his laptop and peered at the screen. 'Well, your last OH report recommends a full return to duties.'

'Yes, sir. I'm fine with that. It's what I want.'

'Good, because we'll need you to hit the ground running.'

'I understand.'

His sparse hair was dyed an intense shade of brown. It didn't go well with the inflamed, pinkish skin on his face. Rosacea, she thought.

'Yes, right. Good. Well, you come highly recommended re the work you did before, ahm . . . yes . . . anyway. Welcome aboard.'

She'd stepped out of his office on the third floor of the station, amazed that she'd conned OH and Mortimer into thinking that she was competent again. She didn't mind him being a bit wary of her and her history. It could work to her advantage.

She dried her hair and dressed in one of her work suits. They'd been in the wardrobe, unused, for months. She had four: navy, dark grey, light grey and black. Ed had always said they made her look the business. That was the idea. A woman needed armour to face the world. She had a dozen or so T-shirts to wear with the uniform in reds and greens, splashes of colour to offset the plainness. She'd go for fire-engine red today. Bold statement, not matched by the flutter in her stomach and the taste of anxiety at the back of her mouth. The waistband on the dark blue trousers was loose. They were going to rest on her hips for a while. She looked in the mirror. Nice enough face, shame about the pallid skin and hollow eyes.

She pushed her dark hair back. Clumps of it had fallen out when she'd been at her lowest. She'd paid a fortune before she left London and had it chopped into springy layers in an attempt to hide where it had thinned almost to baldness. The hairdresser had advised her on how to style it for maximum concealment. You had to make an effort. She was operating on the basis that if she acted like a fully functioning person, she'd fool herself and everyone else.

She drove the lanes into town, the Bere fast and brimming to one side, carrying a haul of branches and leaves from the night's mischief. The sun moved through the treetops, dappling the tarmac. Tractors were busy in the fields on her right, digging furrows for seeds. The seagulls and crows watched the tractors, seeking opportunities. She'd spent five years of her life in Berminster but she didn't know these roads on the southern side of the town or, as locals called it, *the posh end*.

Her phone rang when she was minutes from the station. DCI Mortimer, telling her two bodies had been found by the river at Lock Lane. Male and female.

'Who called it in?' she asked.

'Chap who found them, an Alan Vine. You're SIO. DS Carlin will work with you, along with DC Hill, and there are four other officers I'm attaching to you. As you know, we've staff shortages. Of course, if you need other help— I have to go. They'll fill you in at the station. Keep me updated.'

So much for getting a feel of things. She took deep breaths, rolled her shoulders. *Get through today. One day at a time.* That was the mantra.

She walked into the station, her expression neutral, the way she did before she entered an interview room. She had no idea if her new colleagues would know her history. It seemed inevitable that some details would have leaked out. All she knew was that she didn't want to be defined by what had happened.

She headed to her office on the first floor. Blank, musty, a gouge in the worn laminate flooring in front of the desk. There was a faint smell of stale food. The office had been partitioned off from the main room with a dark wood surround, inset with small windows and beige vertical blinds, drawn half across. A tall side window gave a view of the car park and a fine row of beech trees. Across the road was the museum and theatre.

She sat behind her desk, which was placed so that she looked out through the blinds into the room beyond. Someone glanced over at her. Others were busy on phones and at computer screens. One officer stood with his hands pressed against a window, as if he'd like to leap out. Sitting in here was like being in a shop window, exposed to public view. She rose, closed the blinds, and then looked at the empty desk and silent computer. Her mouth was dry. She could do this. She'd done it before. The therapy hadn't been much use but it had taught her that.

When you experience these anxieties, focus on how you've dealt with the issue successfully before.

The worst had happened. What else could the world throw at her?

CHAPTER THREE

The answer to that was a DS who never stopped talking in a broad Northern Irish accent that she had to strain to understand. Ali Carlin was a substantially built man, tall, quick-moving and wordy. He took up a lot of space in the car and his seat was pushed right back so that she had to turn her head around to look at him. He was squeezed into black jeans, cream shirt with straining buttons and black leather jacket with the collar twisted. Everything about him was a bit awry, as if someone else had dressed him in a hurry. His deep bronze hands on the wheel of the car were assured. He was a smoker, judging by the richly aromatic smell from his clothes. She reckoned he must just about pass his annual fitness test.

'Haven't had a murder for a while, ma'am, and then two come along at once.'

'Guv. Call me guv. Any IDs yet?'

'Aye, one, on the man.'

'What time was it called in?'

'Eight twenty. CSM and forensics already there.'

'Good work. Anyone reported missing?'

'No, guv. Not recently. Well, only an old man who absconded from a care home and we found him at the betting shop. First day here and a couple of murders, eh?' The prospect seemed to make DS Carlin smile. Maybe he'd been stuck on routine investigations.

'Who'd have thought it? Detectives investigating murders. DCI Mortimer informs me that we're short-staffed,' she said.

'Aye. Major budget cuts the last couple of years. Mortimer was like a bear with a sore head for a while. Then he went to a conference and heard that other forces are using volunteers. Essex did a successful recruitment campaign so he talked to them and cheered up a bit. We're using volunteers now in forensics, rape cases and even at crime scenes sometimes. Checking fingerprints and the like. When we questioned it, Mortimer told us that volunteering is a proud tradition and brings in valuable skills as well as encouraging young people to consider policing as a career. Waxed on about it as if it had all been his own idea. Makes you wonder why we bother training.'

'Brings a new flavour to work experience,' she said. 'We'd better be on the ball then, Sergeant, otherwise they might replace us with unpaid helpers.'

'Aye, well, plenty of people think they know all about solving crime these days. Everyone watches the telly and thinks they're an expert.'

She nodded, watching the road. She knew these routes towards the river. She'd gone to school near here, parachuting in part way through a term as usual, having to navigate being a newbie when allegiances had already been formed. By the time she was thirteen she'd been to eight schools in London, Surrey, Oxfordshire and Berkshire and in the most bizarre relocation, for six months in Biarritz. Each move had coincided her mother's latest whim, often a romantic interest, though at times just boredom and a need for constant change. The grass was always going to be greener just over another county border. Her mother's abandonment of her at thirteen had been a savage release. Sometimes she thought that's what made her a good cop. At an early age she'd got used to watching and reading people, working out their motives and back stories, understanding how frail and confused they were, finding a way in. 'Here we are. Pull in over there, by the fence.'

A uniformed constable was flagging them down, pointing into a potholed car park closed off with blue-and-white police tape. He moved the tape as they drove in through an open gate where a large sign with red lettering read:

Berminster Anglers Association. Strictly Members Only.
No fishing without a licence. We prosecute!
<u>*No Polish or Eastern European Anglers! Brak Polskich*</u>
<u>*Wedkarzy!*</u>
No dogs.

'How welcoming,' Siv said. 'I wonder if anyone's told them the "no Poles" bit is unlawful?'

Apart from the police cars, there were two other vehicles — a red Seat hatchback and a blue Volvo.

'We think the Seat might be one of the victims' cars, ma'am,' the constable said. 'The Volvo belongs to Mr Vine who found the bodies. The Seat's locked. We've had a good look through the windows but can't see anything immediate. We're running a check on the number plate and on a Honda found further up the riverbank.'

'Let me know as soon as you get names. Where's Mr Vine?'

'He's in our car for now. Not exactly lost for words.'

'Have you got his details?'

'Yes, ma'am. He's membership secretary of the Anglers' Association. Elderly gent but fit-looking. I've given him a bottle of water.'

'Good for you.'

'He keeps saying he wants to see the officer in charge. Very fidgety and tetchy.'

'He will, but he'll have to wait. Keep checking that he's okay, won't you?'

She and Ali donned coveralls and overshoes and then followed another constable along a well-kept gravelled path with the tape at either side. It led to the river, which was soon visible. The Bere broadened around here and a little further upstream there was a small island in the middle of the river, dense with weeping willows and alder. Siv saw two swans gliding towards the reeds below a wooden jetty, one at the front and one at the rear of their six cygnets who bobbed in a line between them. Rowan blossom scented the air and dangling yellow lamb's tails brushed her head as she passed by. A peaceful, pastoral scene. So far. The constable gestured to a wooded area just in front of them and to the side of the path, where two tents had been erected about three metres apart.

'That's the CSM by the nearest tent, ma'am. The pathologist, Dr Anand is *in situ*.'

In situ. She covered a smile, wondering where he'd learned that.

'*Guv*.' Siv heard DS Carlin murmur the correction to him as they headed to the nearest tent. The ground was damp from rainfall. The man outside the tent was checking his camera but stopped when he saw them approach. He was small, with shiny skin and narrow, darting eyes.

'I'm Steve Wooton, CSM. You DI Drummond?'

'That's right. Good to meet you.'

'Hi, Alistair, my man. How's it hanging?'

'It's hanging fine, Steve.'

'So, DI Drummond, you're the brand new kid on the block. Joined us from the mighty Met to share your expertise, have you?'

She wasn't taking to his hearty manner. 'Had the bodies been moved or touched at all when you got here? I'm thinking of the man who phoned in.'

He spoke in a rush. 'No sign of that and he says he didn't touch. We've got a nasty scene here I must say, pretty savage, so whoever attacked must have been—'

'Do you mind if I look at the bodies before we discuss it? I like to know who I'm talking about.'

He looked taken aback. Slight frown. 'Your call. Be my guest. The woman's in here.'

17

It was warm inside the first tent from the climbing sun. The scent of blood hung in the air. A tall man straightened up as they entered. He had a neatly trimmed beard and rimless glasses.

'Dr Anand. I'm DI Drummond. I'm sure you know DS Carlin.'

He nodded, his face still. 'Rey Anand. Morning. Though not a good one for this young woman, or the man.'

Siv stepped closer to the body and leaned down, taking in purple, red and pale pink tissue. Half of the woman's face was torn and damaged, the other half was a mess of bruising and blood. Her neck was a mass of wounds. She was slim and encased in a silver wetsuit, with matching neoprene shoes and gloves. Her head was covered in a close fitting blue Lycra cap with a narrow light stick attached to the side. A pair of goggles trailed around her neck. On her chest was a photo of a child, a head shot of a fair-haired girl of around three years old with bunches and a big grin.

'No immediate evidence of a sexual assault,' Anand said. 'Before you ask, for now I'd hazard time of death at between the early hours of this morning up to whenever this was called in. Rigor has just started in the face and neck. Usual cautions apply about waiting for post-mortem results. There are numerous wounds. The weapon split the skin and there are rough edges to the wounds. I'd say it could have been something like scissors.' He spoke precisely. Unflappable.

'I don't see any defence wounds,' Siv said.

'None immediately visible, nor on our other victim, although he is face down.'

'Looks as if she'd been swimming,' Ali said. 'I was reading a piece in the paper about wild swimming a couple of weeks ago. It's become very popular in lakes and rivers.' He had a warm, reassuring baritone voice.

Siv leaned down again, examining the woman's earlobes. She wore tiny gold stud earrings with a deep red centre. Siv didn't know much about jewellery but thought they looked expensive. 'Any sign of a bag or ID?'

'Nothing on the body. No pockets in her wetsuit. Your forensic colleagues have been searching the area.'

'She must have brought a bag, towel, car keys, something.' She nodded to Ali. 'Can you take a look at the male body and then talk to Wooton, check what they've seen?'

'He's a good sergeant, that one,' Anand said after Ali had gone. 'On the ball, even if I can't always understand his accent.' He was wearing a strong aftershave; the woody scent competed with the blood and losing.

I'll be the judge of how good he is. 'Pleased to hear it,' she said. 'Do you think she was killed here, in the trees?'

'I think so but I don't know for certain yet. I can tell you more when we move the body and once the ground around the river has been checked. The same applies to the male victim,' he said.

'Had she been swimming, or was she about to go in?'

'Her skin, general dampness and the slightly murky smell coming off her tells me she'd been in the river.'

'When will you do the post-mortems?' Siv asked.

'Tomorrow. I'll email the time when I've checked my diary.'

'Have you examined the other body?'

'Yes. He had a wallet in his jacket pocket, with a driving licence. Car keys also. Steve has them. I'd say he died around the same time as our female. Possibly after her, as rigor hasn't set in yet, but that's only a guess. Same weapon, same types of wound.'

'Okay if I take a photo of this child?' she asked.

'Yes, just be careful.'

She took her phone from her pocket, leaned down again and took a close-up photo of the child's smiling, happy face. There were smears of darkening blood above the picture. Nearer to the body, she could smell faeces and she turned her head sideways to breathe. She thanked Anand, went back outside and gulped fresh air. The green of the woodland was intense after the tent's foetid confines. The sun was hotter now, drying the riverbanks and shimmering on the Bere. A haze was rising off ferns and leaves. She entered the other tent. The young man was face down, his right knee slightly bent. He wore an old, dirty blue anorak over a sweatshirt and ripped, stained jeans. His feet were in shabby grey trainers. His hair was matted with blood and his neck a mass of gashes. Gazing at the dead man, she registered with relief and pleasure that she'd slid back into gear without thinking. Maybe it would be okay.

Ali was talking to Steve Wooton by the river and she walked down to them, skirting the cordon. 'Can I see the driving licence from the man's body?' she asked.

'Sure. It's a Lithuanian licence so it doesn't give an address here.'

'That means he's been here less than a year. Otherwise, he should have had it amended by DVLA,' Ali said.

'He's a Matis Rimas, aged twenty, from Krosna in Lithuania.' Wooton took the licence from his case and handed it to her. She looked at the purple-and-pink laminated card without removing it from its protective bag. It was headed *Lietuvos Respublika* and showed a photo of a young full-faced man with glasses and a neat moustache.

She handed it back. 'Anything else in his wallet to indicate where he lived or worked?'

'No. Thirty pounds in cash and a photo of an elderly couple. He had a mobile lying near his body but it's locked. We found a fishing rod by the river and car keys belonging to a Honda parked off the road near here just before you got to the scene. Nothing much in it except an old coffee cup and a map of Berminster covered in dirty marks. We're running a number plate check just to make sure the car's his. There are other fresh tyre tracks near the Honda, suggesting that another car was here very recently.'

'Where is this Honda?'

Wooton pointed. 'Up that way, through a jungle of bushes. Not the official entrance for a spot of fishing, so I reckon he wasn't a paid-up member.'

'Steve says there doesn't seem to be any blood here,' Ali told her.

Wooton nodded. 'That's correct, and there's no sign of the bodies being dragged the ten or so metres to the trees. There are a number of footprints around here and some leading up to where the bodies were found. It'll take time to sort those.'

'What about a weapon?' Siv asked. 'Dr Anand is thinking it could be scissors.'

'Nothing so far. Could be in the river. We've found no ID so far for the woman, no belongings. If the Seat is hers, there might be something in the boot. What I have got to show you is this.' He stepped back and pointed to a dead fish lying on the grass inside the cordon, next to a fishing rod. 'It's carp and pretty fresh. Eastern Europeans like their carp.'

Ali nodded. 'That's right. In Poland they eat them at Christmas.'

Wooton grimaced. 'I've eaten carp and it tastes like oily mud. And it's full of bones. Take my advice, if you ever eat it, make sure you're with someone who knows the Heimlich manoeuvre.'

'I'll bear that in mind,' Siv said. 'So it looks like Mr Rimas ignored the notice on the gate by coming in a back way, caught the carp and then for some reason, he went up to the trees.'

Wooton nodded. 'Looks like it. If you follow the tape that way, you'll find an overgrown path and a scrubby area where the Honda is. Be careful, we're still examining there.'

'Thanks. Can you bag that photo on the woman's body? I want copies made ASAP.'

Siv led the way along the tape to the path Wooton had indicated and they picked their way through thicker, still dripping vegetation. After a few minutes, they arrived at a churned-up area where a forensic photographer was taking pictures of tyre marks and a battered black Honda that was begging to be taken through a car wash. Siv looked around, memories surfacing.

'I know this place. Kids used to come here to swim. There's a lane up there off Hardwater Road leading down

21

to this sneaky way in.' She saw herself at fifteen-ish, on the back of a scooter on a summer's evening, necking beer passed to her by the boy who was driving. *Beer by the Bere*, she'd laughed. Her father thought she was doing homework at a friend's. What a habitual liar she'd been. Although, to be fair, not as brass-necked as Rikka. Rik lied about everything, almost as a matter of principle. *What do you expect?* she'd ask if challenged. *I've come from a broken home, I'm a damaged child.* On that evening, Siv had worn her swimsuit under her skirt. What was the boy's name? It was gone. Like that carefree evening.

Ali had his hands in his pockets and was leaning slightly backwards. 'You from round here then? I thought you were from London.'

'I moved here from London to live with my dad when I was in my teens.'

'Wow, that must have been a culture shock.'

He had a scrubby beard, as if someone had doodled on his chin with charcoal. She wondered if it was deliberate or he hadn't had time to shave. It went with his thrown-together look. 'For a while. But it's a lively town. There were compensations.' Including not having to live with her mother's foibles, getting regular meals and staying in one school for more than five minutes. 'What about you — when did you arrive?'

Ali feigned shock. 'You guessed I'm not local?'

'Yep. Powers of deduction.'

'I moved when I got wed. My wife's from here. I'm from Derry. Drummond's a Scottish name, isn't it?'

If you were Northern Irish, names carried a huge significance. One of her early boyfriends in London had been from Belfast. He'd explained how your name denoted religious and home background and often political outlook. She wondered if the time would ever come when that no longer applied and thought that Ali must have had an interesting time growing up as a mixed-race boy in that community. 'My great-grandad was from Edinburgh. Let's walk on up.'

Along the overgrown lane birds were busy, wheeling in the sun and singing loudly. There was a rich, earthy smell. Better than blood mingled with aftershave.

Siv nodded. 'This is as I remember it. You come on the back road out of town. I've swum in that bit of the river and over to the little island.' She didn't add that it had been a group of them skinny-dipping in the baking heat of a summer holiday. There'd been a lot of teenage fumbling and used condoms on that island.

Ali scratched between the greying cornrows at the back of his head. 'Has the town changed much since you were last here?'

'I'm still deciding. Yes and no. Definitely on the outskirts. There are new housing estates where there used to be fields and that huge new shopping mall, Bere Place. The centre of town looks the same, apart from a vape shop by the Guildhall, where there was a gentleman's outfitters. It was called Berminster Beau and had a dummy in the window in evening dress. One of my friends had a Saturday job there and every week he'd make an alteration to the dummy, like putting a rubber glove on one hand, or sticking on a monocle or false moustache or lipstick. I'd loiter outside in the afternoon, to have a laugh at his sabotage.'

He smiled. 'I'm reassured to hear you were a teenager with nothing better to do.'

'Oh yes, I liked a bit of anarchy. Maidwell estate is still the crime pocket it used to be?'

'Correct,' he said. 'We're up there most days.'

'I had a teacher who rented there temporarily when she moved to town. She went home to find all her clothes had been nicked from her washing line.'

'I'm surprised they left the line.'

Siv laughed. 'Okay, let's talk to Mr Vine.'

As they walked back, more memories came to her — smoking dope in the bushes around here and getting very drunk on cheap wine. Had Rikka been there? Possibly, although being older, she'd usually kept different company or hung out on her own in her bedroom. Siv realized she had no idea what her sister had been doing most of the time after the move to Berminster. Their lives had touched only at meals or passing on the stairs. They'd both been impossible teenagers, used to doing whatever they liked with almost no parental controls. Their father hadn't known what to do when they landed on him. They'd run rings around him. The poor man had assumed a mystified look that he wore to the day he died.

Ali was talking about the lack of staff at the station, the amount of overtime he'd done this month and the best places for a snack and a drink in the evenings. Siv let his voice wash over her, feeling oddly content despite the grim scene among the trees. There were two dead people with stories to be unpicked, a killer traced. This could be complex. She could feel the old familiar spark of curiosity and energy. Another tick in the progress box.

As they walked to the car park, Wooton passed them and gestured with his thumb to the tents. 'You had a double murder before?'

'No. With any luck there'll be a connection between our two victims. Have you?'

'No. The wild swimmer and the Lithuanian. Interesting.'

'Sounds like the title of an art house film,' she said. 'Something French and incomprehensible.'

He almost smiled.

CHAPTER FOUR

Alan Vine was a narrow, angular man, hunched in the seat. Siv sat beside him, guessing he was in his early eighties. She made the introductions, turning her body slightly towards him, and he twitched as she did so. He smelled fusty although his clothes were smart — an olive waxed jacket, a tie with a pattern of tiny world flags, smart dark green cords and peak cap.

'Thank you for waiting, Mr Vine. Investigations always take time.'

'I had no choice. This is dreadful, what's happened. I don't know what our members will make of it. We have a good reputation and something like this . . . well, it's extremely *unpleasant*.' His nostrils flared indignantly.

'Yes, it certainly is, and particularly for the dead victims of such a vicious attack. I understand you're the membership secretary of Berminster Anglers?'

'That's right. I've been the secretary for twenty-odd years. It's a *very* responsible post. I take my duties *most* seriously and carry them out to the best of my no doubt limited abilities. I believe that the club in general and the chairman in particular find my efforts satisfactory.'

He sounded as if he was being interviewed for a job.

'I'm sure. Can you tell me what happened this morning, Mr Vine? Start from when you got here.'

'But I've already told your constable, and in complete and *considerable* detail! I saw him writing things down, just as your sergeant is doing now.'

'I know, but now you need to tell me. Why were you here? Did you come to fish?'

'Of course not!' he said indignantly, rearing backwards as if she'd insulted him.

'Why "of course not?" This is an angling club, by a river.'

He blinked and cradled the water bottle he'd been given. It was sparkling water, the bubbles dancing on the surface. 'It's the *close season*, officer, and unlike those foreign gentlemen who flout our rules, I'm a responsible angler. As are all the paid-up members of our association. I come here every day to check on things.'

'What's the close season?'

He stared at her as if she was being deliberately dense. 'What *do* they teach at school these days?' he asked.

Siv was aware of Ali ducking his head to cover a grin. 'It's a while since I was at school and fishing wasn't on my curriculum. Please explain.'

He shook his head. 'The close season runs from March fifteenth to June fifteenth. There's a prohibition on fishing in the river between those dates. Anglers — *responsible* anglers — don't fish. The three-month season is there to protect coarse fish when they're spawning. It gives them a chance to replenish.'

'Are carp coarse fish?'

'They most certainly are, officer.'

'Okay. So, what time did you arrive? Take me from there.'

'I parked here just on ten past eight. The news headlines were ending.'

'Did you see any other vehicles on the road as you were driving here, or any pedestrians?'

He thought for a moment. 'Not along Lock Lane, no. There were cars on Minster Road, before the turnoff. That's a school run along there, it gets very busy. I can't understand why young mothers these days have to drive these huge vehicles. More like tanks than cars. I can tell you, it's always a relief when it's school holidays — takes me half the time to get here then.'

'Was the Seat in the car park when you drove in?'

'Yes, and I was annoyed because I thought it was one of those Poles. That's why I was here checking. They come and fish, especially for carp, *completely* flouting the rules,' he repeated. 'They don't pay for licences like the rest of us. There are good reasons for the regulations we have. I've given several of them their marching orders but they keep coming back. They ignore the notice, which states quite clearly that they're not allowed in here. They really have no—'

'Yes, yes, I see. And there was no other car here?'

'No. As I've already *told* your constable.'

'So you left your car parked. Then what?'

'I went down the path to the river, ready to give a barefaced Pole or one of those other ne'er-do-wells a piece of my mind. But before I got there, I saw the man on the ground, by the trees. I thought maybe he'd collapsed so I hurried over. As soon as I got near him, I could see . . .' Vine swallowed. 'I could see that he was all bloody. That he'd been attacked.' Vine undid the top of the water bottle. He took a sip, spilling some on his chin as it fizzed up.

'I know you've had a difficult time, Mr Vine. This is very helpful.'

He glared at her. 'I'm no "snowflake" or whatever they call it these days, officer. I'm made of sterner stuff than all that. I don't keel over as soon as things get difficult. I hope I know my duty as a citizen.'

'Of course. When did you see the other body?'

'I bent over for a minute to clear my head. I have angina and I do have to be careful. Then I saw the woman in the wetsuit, lying there looking terrible. My heavens! I could scarcely believe my eyes. This is such a *peaceful* place, quiet. A place to forget your worries and relax. We've never had a crime here — well, not until these foreigners showed up and started all their nonsense. If I had my way—'

'Mr Vine, did you touch either of the bodies at all?'

'*Certainly* not, officer. I knew better than to do that. I was in Kenya just after the Mau Mau rebellion. I've seen blood and corpses, plenty of them. Once there was a stack of them piled high with the flies feasting on them. Enough to turn your stomach, I can tell you. The Mau Mau gave no quarter. I know a dead person when I see one, and I knew they were both dead. I called the police *immediately.*'

'What did you do then?'

'I did as I was told. Followed orders. That's why we have rules, isn't it? To keep things orderly and make sure things happen as they should. I stayed where I was and waited.'

'You saw no one else?'

'No. I wouldn't expect to.'

'Because it's close season,' Ali confirmed.

'Correct. Although there's a lot of debate about whether or not a close season is really needed. Some scientists are saying that it doesn't really make much difference to stocks and a lot of anglers have been petitioning the government—'

'Yes, quite, Mr Vine.' Siv watched him closely as she asked the next question. 'Do you think you'd seen either of those people before?'

He shook his head resolutely. 'No.'

'Did you see what had been left on the woman's chest?'

'Not up close. It looked like a photo.'

Siv tapped her phone and showed him the photo. 'Do you recognize this child? Have you ever seen her around here?'

He tilted his head back and squinted. 'I don't. Don't know her. Never seen her. We don't like children coming here. In fact, we discourage it. We don't mind members bringing their children for the odd visit, as long as they're well behaved. We just don't want any noise and nuisance. There are plenty of parks for little girls like her. That's if I'm allowed to assume it's a *her,* what with all this transgender nonsense or whatever. I don't even understand it, all this confusion about men and women. It's been getting in a terrible muddle. When I was young, you knew a boy was a boy and a girl was a girl.'

Give me strength. Siv tried hard not to roll her eyes. Next thing, Vine would be saying that they should bring back National Service, the birch and hanging too. She shot a look at Ali.

He scratched his excuse for a beard and cleared his throat. 'The wetsuit the woman was wearing indicates that she was swimming in the river. Is that permitted here?'

Vine pulled a face. 'You wouldn't need a *permit*, if that's what you're asking. Technically she *was* trespassing. Common courtesy would indicate that you should contact the association to inform them and ask if there were any objections. And of course, if there were any members fishing, they wouldn't want a swimmer agitating the fish. But alas, common courtesy seems to have been forgotten these days.'

'Have you seen other wild swimmers here at any other time?'

'No. Wild swimming! When I was a youngster, you just called it swimming. And what's wrong with a pool? There's a state-of-the-art one in town; cost millions to build, and out of taxpayers' money. That's good enough for most people hereabouts. I don't know why anyone would want to swim in a river.'

'Different experience,' Ali said. 'How do you know you didn't recognize the man?'

'Come again?'

'He's lying face down.'

'Well . . . I suppose I can't be *absolutely* sure, officer, because of course you're correct, I didn't see his face. But no one who fishes here with a permit dresses like *that* — an old anorak, dirty jeans and cheap trainers. It's the sort of stuff the trespassers wear. Is he Polish?'

'We can't talk about that, Mr Vine,' Siv told him. 'You need to tell your members that the area will be off limits for now, close season or not. We'll let you know when you can access it again.'

'How long will it be closed for?'

'I can't say right now.'

'Well, I'll have to contact the owner of the land straight away and let him know.'

'Who is the owner?'

'Nick Shelton. He's the owner and the chairman of the association. This closure business is very annoying.'

'I suppose the two dead people might be a tad annoyed too, if they could feel anything right now,' Siv said sharply.

He reddened. 'I didn't mean to—'

'How many members do you have?'

'Well . . . let's see . . . at least thirty.'

She gave a silent groan. 'I'll need you to provide us with a list. Can you email it to us today?'

'I'll ask Mr Shelton to do that. I don't get on with computers.'

'We'll contact him. Did you know that there's access to the river from another path that leads up to Hardwater Road?'

'Oh yes. We've been arguing to get that closed off for a long time but the council won't agree. Claptrap about public access to woodland. I've lost count of the number of letters we've sent about it. Mr Shelton even went to a council meeting but he couldn't get anywhere. Got shouted down by a bunch of do-gooders. I know that's where the Poles get in, but you can't get anywhere with the bureaucrats. We can't put a sign up there because it's not Mr Shelton's land, *despite* the fact that—'

Siv cut across him. 'Has anyone told you your sign is unlawful? It's illegal to discriminate against anyone, including eastern Europeans. It's offensive at the very least.'

Vine bridled. 'No, I can't say that anyone has. As I've explained, this is *private* land, officer.'

'Doesn't matter. You can point out that it's private and say that trespassers will be reported. Then you should do so, and let the police deal with it.'

'As if you lot have got time to deal with stuff like that! You're hard pressed enough. When my neighbour had his car stolen it took ages for any of you to turn up, and even then you were about as much use as a bucket with a hole in.'

'I think you should take note of what I've told you.'

He touched the knot of his tie. 'Well, that would be a matter for Nick Shelton, not me. He put the sign up. But I'd have thought you'd have quite enough to concern yourself with, with those two dead people in there, instead of bothering about some politically correct *twaddle*. Yes, shouldn't you be concentrating on finding their killer?'

Siv looked at him steadily. 'I'll let that go for now, Mr Vine. You've had a nasty shock.'

He put his hand on the door handle. 'Can I go home now? I need to walk my dog, although quite frankly, I'm not sure I'm up to it after all this palaver.'

The two deaths were just a nuisance as far as he was concerned. 'Not just yet. You can talk to Mr Shelton about finding the bodies but I don't want you to give anyone any details about what you've seen here this morning, and you're not to mention the child's photo. DS Carlin here will arrange for you to give a formal statement. For now, you'll have to be taken to the police station. We need your clothes for forensic testing and we also need a DNA sample from you, just in case any of yours is found at the scene. Do you understand?'

'You what? My clothes? This is a very expensive jacket, Barbour. I'm not letting you lot mess around with it.'

'We'll be very careful with it. We need it to rule you out of the investigation.'

'It's the rules,' Ali said meaningfully. 'I'm sure you'd want us to do everything *by the book*, Mr Vine.'

He bristled but nodded. 'Yes. Understood.'

'Right,' Siv said. 'We'll get you to the station.'

'What do you think of him, *Officer*?' Ali asked as Vine was driven away. He'd gone to the car and was eating a banana.

'Apart from being a man who talks in italics and likes to air his prejudices? He's a useful witness in that I'd say he's got precise recall.'

'Hope you don't mind the banana, guv. I'm diabetic, need to regulate the blood sugar now and again. It's an uphill struggle all the way, to be honest with you. Why I'm going grey.' He grinned and unzipped another inch of banana skin.

'You're fine. My husband was diabetic.'

She saw the quick flash in Ali Carlin's eyes. So he knew. Well, that was probably for the best. No secrets. One of the constables hurried over to them.

'The Honda doesn't belong to Matis Rimas. It's registered to a Filip Mazur, address in North Road. And we have an owner for the Seat. Mr Ade Visser, 31 Spring Gardens.'

Siv nodded. 'Great, thanks. Quick work.'

Steve Wooton was talking to one of his colleagues. They were both laughing and she saw the man glance in her direction, then away quickly. She waited, checking a map on her phone, until Wooton had finished and then waved him over.

'We have an address for the Seat owner, so that may be where our female victim lived. Our killer had gone when Alan Vine showed up and he didn't see a car or anyone walking along Lock Lane. They must have had transport to get here and away. I reckon our best bet is around where Rimas parked, where there are other fresh tyre tracks. There might be other access points nearby, along the river. Can you check the whole area?'

'Will do. It'll take quite a while.'

'It takes the time it takes.' Siv felt the heat of the sun on her head. A wave of fatigue passed through her. A tiny prickling on her scalp sounded alarm bells. Six months away from work and she'd got into the habit of shaping her days to her own rhythms. She was unused to demands, decisions and expectations. She took a deep breath, aware that Wooton was watching her. She arranged with him that he'd contact the coroner and have the bodies removed to the morgue. 'I'll touch base with you later,' she told him.

'Your wish is my command, guv.' He said it innocently enough but she caught him rolling his eyes as her phone rang.

'Guv, it's the duty sarge here. We've just had a call from a man who's worried about his wife. He said she was going swimming at Lock Lane early this morning. He's arrived home from a conference and she's not there or at work. He can't raise her on her phone. I thought, as you've found a female, I'd pass it straight on.'

'Sure, thanks. What's his name?'

'Visser, Ade Visser. Address is—'

'It's okay, I know. What's the woman's name?'

'Lauren Visser.'

She rang off, turned to Ali and Wooton and gave them the information. She and Ali walked back to the car.

'Well, that's bad news for Mr Visser at Spring Gardens,' she said to Ali.

'Aye. We have both IDs, that's something.'

'Is it me, or has Steve Wooton got an attitude?' she asked.

'Ach, he's a wee man with a big head on him. Thinks he's forensics central. Sometimes I want to tell him to go and play with the traffic. I blame *Silent Witness* for his self-importance. We heading to see Visser now?'

'Yes, but can you drop me off? I can see Mr Visser and I'd rather you got on with finding out more about Matis Rimas. He might have family here who we need to inform. So, address, work place, anyone who can ID him. Delegate the legwork. Can you get someone to contact Nick Shelton about what's happened here? Confirm that we need a list of members. No details of where the photo was found to be shared with anyone. But first, get on to the mortuary. I want Mr Visser to ID the body today. If you need me to weigh in, let me know. Whatever they have to do to make Lauren Visser presentable enough, I want it done. I'd say get DC Hill . . . what's his first name?'

'Patrick. Patrick Hill. Generally called Hat-trick because he caught three burglars in three weeks last year.'

She'd tuned in to his accent now, got the hang of the cadences. She'd noticed that he'd slowed down when he spoke to Vine and liked the self-awareness. 'I'd say get DC Hill to do it, but Dr Anand is a fan of yours so you should be able to swing it.'

'Is he? How do you know?'

'He told me.'

'Right. How will you get back from seeing Visser?'

'According to Google,' she said, flashing her phone, 'Spring Gardens is only a ten minute or so walk to the station.'

'No wonder you look much fitter than me,' Ali said, gunning the engine.

No, it's not fitness. It's the way grief pares you down and leaves nothing to spare.

CHAPTER FIVE

Spring Gardens was a street of fine Edwardian houses not far from the town centre and just outside the conservation area. Siv walked up a beautiful tiled front path, treading on blue and terracotta lozenge shapes. The front door was inside an arched porch, the glass panels etched with pineapples. A honeysuckle trailed across a trellis along the top of the porch.

The man who answered the door was tall and striking-looking, with amber eyes and longish, caramel-coloured hair that curled damply on his neck. He smelled as if he'd just stepped from the shower. He looked past Siv, as if expecting to see her with someone else. His wife, possibly.

'Mr Visser?'

'That's right.'

She showed him her card. 'I'm Detective Inspector Drummond. I'm here about your wife.'

He licked his bottom lip. 'A detective inspector? Has something happened?'

'Can I come in? I need to talk to you.'

'Yes. Okay.'

He hovered for a moment, anxiety shadowing his face as he glanced once more over her shoulder, and then led her down a wide parquet hall with a racing bike propped against a wall, and into a sitting room. He gestured at a chair. 'Have you got news of Lauren? I've not heard from her.'

'Sit down with me, Mr Visser.' She waited until he was seated, leaning forward. 'I believe we've found Lauren's body. I'm so sorry.'

'You've found her? At the river?'

'Yes, at Lock Lane, but we still need to confirm her identification. Could you answer some questions? What colour wetsuit does your wife wear when she swims?'

He'd moved right to the edge of the deep, soft leather chair. He stared past her, out of the window behind. 'Ahm . . . she has two. I was with her when she bought them in that outdoor gear shop in town. One's a silvery colour, the other's dark blue.'

'And does she wear a cap?'

'Yes, just the one. It's bright blue.'

'I can confirm that the woman we've found is dressed in those things. I'm sorry,' Siv said again softly.

He gasped, coughed, and then started talking rapidly. 'I don't like Lauren wild swimming. Not safe out there on her own, in isolated places. You never know who's around. I've asked her not to go but she loves it so much . . . What happened to her? I had this feeling that something bad had happened, I just knew.' He clenched his fingers so tightly the knuckles were stretched.

Siv had been glancing at a photo of a young woman on the coffee table to her right. She was wearing the earrings. Now she watched Visser's face. He looked exhausted and racked with pain. She leaned slightly towards him. 'Mr Visser, the woman we found was dressed in the silver wetsuit and bright blue cap you've described, but she has no form of ID on her and little else to identify her. Tell me, did your wife wear earrings?'

'Yes. They were made in Antwerp for my grandmother. She gave them to Lauren when we got married. They're quite rare.'

'Can you describe them?'

'Ahm . . . small, gold, with red coral cabochons. Lauren wears them always, she loves them so much. Just takes them out to clean and puts them back in.'

She pointed. 'The ones in the photo?'

'Yes.' His voice dropped. 'The woman you found . . . she's wearing them?'

'Yes. Also, your Seat was found in the car park at Lock Lane. We will need you to identify your wife's body. Or, if you don't feel up to it, another family member can.'

He stared at her and shook his head. 'N . . . no, no. I'll do that. What happened? Tell me what happened. Oh my God, was she raped?' His horror seemed genuine.

She felt a twinge of nausea, made an effort to maintain the shield that kept her own memories at bay. 'I can't confirm anything yet, although there was no immediate indication that she had been raped. The woman we found was attacked with a blade.'

Visser got up abruptly and strode up and down. He stopped to touch another photo of his wife on the mantelpiece, and then straightened it. 'She's gone,' he whispered, sinking back into his chair.

'Yes. Can I get you anything? Some water?'

'No. Nothing. When can I see her? Can we go now?'

'We have to wait until the mortuary staff are ready.'

He stood again. 'No fucking way! I want to see her now. I want to see my Lauren!'

He was tall, muscular. There was something hard about the mouth that suggested a man who liked things his way and was used to getting what he wanted. Siv could see grief and anger building. She knew well how those emotions worked together.

'Mr Visser, please, sit down. Believe me, we will expedite your visit to the mortuary but it's not possible right now. When we find a body, there are protocols we have to follow. It would really help if you could tell me about this morning and Lauren's movements. Can you do that?'

He stared at her angrily for a moment and she held his gaze. He sat again, rubbing his thighs. 'What do you want to know?'

'When did you last see your wife?'

'Yesterday morning. I went away yesterday. Took the train to London. I organize equestrian events. I was attending a sales conference in a hotel there, the Raeburn.'

'On a Sunday?'

'Yes. That's not unusual. Events planning is a seven-day-a-week affair.'

'Why didn't you go by car?'

'Lauren said she might do some shopping and it's easier to get to central London by train anyway.'

'Did you speak to Lauren after you left yesterday?'

'I called her about half five yesterday evening. She said she was planning to go for a swim at Lock Lane early this morning.'

'Alone?'

'I think so. Sometimes she goes with other people but she's often solo.'

'What time this morning?'

'I don't know exactly. She usually went around six a.m. in the spring and summer, sometimes earlier. She's not a good sleeper, so she might go straight away if she woke up early. Sometimes I wake up and she's gone out. I hate that, finding the bed empty, but I know it means a lot to her to have that time to herself . . .'

'Wouldn't it still be a bit dark before six?'

'Yes but she didn't mind that. In fact, she loved to swim in the dark. She says the world's mysterious and silent then. And she always goes to places she knows and had checked out. She took a torch in case she needed it. When we talked last night, I said she shouldn't go because she'd had a cold. But of course, she thought the water and the exercise would be beneficial. We just chatted about this and that and then I attended an early evening event followed by dinner with colleagues.'

'Was that in the hotel?'

'Yes. In the restaurant.'

'Did Lauren usually swim in the morning?'

'Sometimes she went in the evening but it was usually in the morning. She's a morning person. Where you described, by Lock Lane, is a place she's gone before. She says the water's clean there and as long as there's no one fishing, the anglers don't seem to mind.'

She noted that Visser kept slipping in and out of the past and present tense when talking about his wife. That could suggest genuine grief. 'How did she sound when you spoke?'

'Fine. She was fine. Said she'd had a quiet day, gardening and reading. I stayed overnight with a friend and got the train back this morning. I'd left my bike at the station so by the time I cycled home it was around nine thirty, and I was surprised to see my car wasn't here.'

'Would Lauren not have used it to go to work after her swim?'

'No, she always walked to work, it's nearby. And the cats hadn't been fed or the litter tray emptied. Lauren always fed them first thing and cleaned out the litter. She'd never leave it, she was fastidious about it and the cats' comfort. She would worry it might smell. I tried her mobile but she didn't pick up. I had a shower and waited for a while but I was starting to worry. Then I rang Lauren at work and they said she wasn't in and they hadn't heard from her. I didn't know what to do. I thought maybe she'd had to go somewhere and forgotten to tell me or that she'd been taken ill or had an accident in the river and was stranded. I tried her mobile again and left another message. I kept looking out of the window, expecting her to turn up.'

'Did you ring any of her friends?'

'I tried Cora Laffin. She's the friend who got Lauren interested in wild swimming, and I thought maybe they'd gone together and Lauren was with her for some reason. But her phone went to voicemail. That's when I rang you.'

'Where does Lauren work?'

'At a nursery. Caterpillar Corner in Clarendon Street.'

It was warm in the room. Patches of sweat were blooming on Visser's pale shirt, spreading from his armpits, and his forehead glistened. He looked limp now, the fight gone out of him.

'Does the name Matis Rimas mean anything to you? Did Lauren know him?'

He shook his head. 'I don't know the name. Why do you ask?'

'His body was found near Lauren's. I believe he was attacked by the same person.'

'My God. This is crazy. Another person is dead as well?'

'That's right.'

'I've never heard of him.'

'Did Lauren have any connection with the Lithuanian community?'

'Not that I know of.'

Unless there were children with Lithuanian parents at Caterpillar Corner. 'Do you and Lauren have children?'

'No. No children.'

She took her phone out and showed him the photo of the child. 'Do you know who this girl is? Take your time.'

He blinked and stared at the screen. 'I've no idea. What's she got to do with Lauren?'

'I don't know. The photo was left at the scene.'

He looked closer. 'Unless it's a child at the nursery?'

'Perhaps. We'll check. Did Lauren have any children from another relationship?'

'A child? No, absolutely not. Of course not! None of this makes any sense at all — this dead man and this photo. What the hell's going on?'

'I don't know, but whatever you can tell me might help the police to find out.'

He sat back in the chair, his eyes vacant. 'I need a glass of water.'

'Let me get it.' Siv went down the hallway to a long kitchen painted pale grey. It had been extended at the back,

40

with a conservatory-type roof and folding patio doors. The doors were half open. Two Siamese cats were asleep on a small sofa under a window ledge. The kitchen was shiny and new, with a massive double Butler sink set into a wooden surround. A complicated coffee machine stood on a marble-topped side table. There was a framed wedding photo of Ade Visser and Lauren on the wall. She had blonde, wispy hair cut in a geometric slant, a full-busted slim figure and a closed-off smile. The coral earrings glowed. A shopping list lay on the counter by the kettle: *vegetables, almond milk and yogurt, buckwheat noodles, tofu, pumpkin seeds*. Beside it was a brochure — *Ethical Sole: cruelty-free footwear*, advertising leather-free shoes. Lauren Visser had been an organized woman if she'd left the place this tidy when she went out so early. Siv ran the cold tap, comparing this kitchen to Corran and Paul's. The rooms were about the same size, but theirs was hospitable and pulsing with warmth and energy. This place had a sterile, dead atmosphere, as if the Vissers knew what a home should look like but hadn't worked out how to imbue it with any personality.

She took a glass of water back to Visser and waited while he drank it in one go. He rubbed his forehead with the heel of his hand. The sitting room was south-facing and full of light, with a little shade from a tall silver birch in the front garden. Two of the walls were decorated with paintings and photographs of horses in various poses: galloping, racing and leaping hurdles. It was furnished with an eclectic mix of modern and mid-twentieth-century furniture, the armchairs in cream and light tan leather. Classy and costly, like the kitchen.

'Can you give me the details of where you stayed last night?' Siv asked.

'What?'

'I need to have the name of the friend you stayed with in London.'

'What's that got to do with what's happened?'

'We have to rule people out of our investigation.' It wasn't quite why she was asking, but he seemed to buy it.

'His name's Errol Todd. He has a flat in Earl's Court, near where the conference was.' He gave her an address and phone number. 'But Errol was flying to Valencia early this morning. He's a Buddhist and he's gone on a retreat there so he'll have switched his phone off. If I'd had my car I'd probably have driven back last night and this might never have happened.'

There was no point in going there. If he hadn't murdered his wife — and his shock seemed real enough — he was going to torment himself with all kinds of *what ifs*. 'What time did you leave your friend's this morning?'

'Half six, thereabouts. Errol had already gone. He'd ordered a cab for six.'

'And what train did you get back to Berminster?'

'The 7.10 from Victoria.'

'Can I contact anyone for you? Lauren's family?'

'What about them?' He spoke sharply.

'Is there family locally?'

'She's an only child. Her mother died three years ago, shortly before we met. Lauren never knew who her father was.'

'Why was that?'

'No idea. She told me her mother would never discuss it. Seems very odd to me, but I didn't know the woman so I can't give you any impression of her. I don't want anyone here.' He threw his hands up and gave dry, heaving gasps. 'This is all bullshit! I have to see her!'

'I understand. You will, and soon. Just for now, keep on helping me. Would Lauren have taken a bag with her? We haven't found one so far, although of course it might be in your car.'

'A small waterproof rucksack, a Kanken, dark orange.'

'Thank you. It's hard to be alone at a time like this. What about you? Do you have family nearby?'

'I'll contact them when I'm ready.'

'I'd like to arrange for a family liaison officer to come and be with—'

'I've fucking told you, haven't I? I'll contact anybody I want when I want. I don't want any busybodies here, making tea and fussing.'

Her phone rang. She took the call from Ali.

'The body will be ready for ID at five p.m.,' he said. 'I can take Mr Visser if you like. Pick him up at half four.'

It was tempting to let Ali do it, but she needed to bite the bullet and go back into a morgue again professionally. 'Thanks for the offer but I'll take him. See you soon.'

Visser was pacing again and rubbing his hands together. Siv stood. 'That was my sergeant, DS Ali Carlin. He's arranged for you to make an identification at five o'clock. I'll accompany you. I'll come and collect you at four thirty.'

He slumped against a wall. 'No need for that. I'll make my own way there.'

'I'd advise you to let me take you. You might not think you need the support but you do.'

'Oh, whatever. Do what you like.'

'Do you have a spare set of keys for your car? The Seat is still in the Lock Lane car park. We need to examine it before we can return it to you.'

'Yeah . . . in the kitchen.'

While she waited, she picked up a copy of *Horse & Hound* magazine from a stack and flicked through, glancing at glossy photos of lovingly tended animals. He came in, handed her the keys and leaned back against the wall.

'I'm sorry to have brought you such distressing news, Mr Visser. I'll go now. After the identification, I'll need to speak to you again. If you need anything, please call me.' She put her card down on the coffee table. He didn't look at it, just closed his eyes. She left him standing against the wall behind him.

She walked back towards the station, ringing Steve Wooton as she turned out of Spring Gardens into a main road.

'I've got Mr Visser's spare keys to the Seat. Can you ask one of the constables at the scene to come to the station in about fifteen minutes and pick them up? Mr Visser told me that his wife would have had a small waterproof rucksack with her, a Kanken, dark orange.'

'No sign of it so far.'

'Anything new?'

'Nope. Focusing on footprints right now.'

She stopped to buy a coffee, and then decided to get a selection of fruit, sandwiches, brownies and granola bars. It helped to get things off on the right foot if the new boss provided goodies, and this had all the makings of a long day.

CHAPTER SIX

Ali Carlin munched a hard-boiled egg as he drove. His wife, Polly, was a chef and no matter what hours she'd worked, every night she prepared a cool box of food for him. She knew that otherwise, he'd be filling up on bread, sugary drinks and the kind of snacks that should carry a skull and crossbones for diabetics. Today's box contained two bananas, two hard-boiled eggs, roasted chickpeas and aubergines and a small green salad. He tried to eat the eggs when he was on his own as the last time he'd had them in the office he'd been accused of farting. He was grateful for Polly's kindness and felt guilty when he accepted one of the sugary treats that circulated at work. The truth was that the stuff she gave him just didn't fill him up, but he could never bring himself to admit it. He ran a finger around his waistband now, regretting the biscuits he'd snaffled while he was arranging for the mortuary viewing.

He turned into North Road, looking for number 15B and opened a window to let the eggy pong escape. It was a down-at-heel area, a street of mixed residential and business premises. Polly brought stuff here from the restaurant for dry cleaning. He drove past betting, second-hand furniture and pound shops, a Kingdom Hall, a tanning salon, a Chinese takeaway, a removals firm and then saw the block of flats he wanted. He was working on the premise that Filip Mazur would know Matis Rimas. He'd got Patrick to check that the Honda hadn't been reported as stolen. It hadn't, so the car must have been on loan.

He left his car in the small car park at the side of the block, ignoring the half-mast Residents Only parking sign. Judging by the state of the sign, the litter strewn around and the scruffy appearance of the flats, he didn't think that anyone would be scrutinizing cars, unless to steal one. He flicked a few spots of egg yolk from his jacket and looked for 15B. It was on the ground floor, just inside the peeling wooden double doors that had been wedged open. Ali rang the bell. He could hear a baby crying inside. A plump middle-aged woman with dyed black hair, deep bags below her eyes and dangling earrings opened the door, keeping it on the chain. She looked like a woman who'd had a hard life and expected it to get harder. Back home, they'd say she had a face like a well-chewed chop.

'Yes?' Her accent was certainly eastern European.

Ali showed his ID. 'Hello. I'm looking for Filip Mazur. I need to speak to him.'

'He not here.' She looked wary.

'Where is he?'

'At work.'

The baby's crying was growing into howls of rage. 'Where does he work?'

The woman looked anxiously back into the flat. 'I not sure. Different places. I have to see to baby.'

'Are you one of his family?'

'I Mrs Mazur, mother. I okay here, have papers.'

'I'm not here about any papers. You're not in any trouble. Can I come in, please? I need to speak to Mr Mazur urgently.'

The woman was wearing a shapeless, short-sleeved dress. Her upper arms, fleshy and mottled, wobbled as, frowning, she undid the chain, saying, 'come.'

Ali followed her into a living room-cum-kitchen. It was sparsely furnished but comfortable enough. Something savoury and delicious was simmering on the cooker. The din from the baby was ear shattering. Mrs Mazur heaved the red-faced infant from a bouncing seat and sat with it sprawled precariously across her stout, slanting thighs, her skirt riding up to expose the tops of her hold-up stockings. She plugged a bottle into its mouth, holding its head in her other fat hand and a blissful peace descended. Ali thought that both she and the baby looked uncomfortable but they seemed happy enough with their arrangement.

'Why you want my son?' Mrs Mazur asked.

'I'm very sorry to tell you that we've found the body of a young man we've identified as Matis Rimas this morning.'

She gasped, her face and neck growing blotchy. 'Matis? No! How this happen?'

'You know Matis?'

'Yes, yes. He stay here, he rent a room. My son . . . he meet him at work. He like him.' In her shock, her hold on the bottle had slackened and the baby yelped, kicking angrily. She murmured something and raised the bottle so that the rhythmic sucking started again.

'Matis has been murdered near the river. We think he'd been fishing.'

Mrs Mazur nodded. 'Yes, Matis love to fish. He go this morning. He bring me fish to cook for family. How, how murdered? Who do this thing?'

'We don't know. Matis was attacked. When did you last see him?'

Mrs Mazur jiggled the baby. 'Last night. He have beers with Filip then he go to look at TV in his room. He say he watch film.'

'Did he like to go fishing in the morning?'

'He go morning, evening . . . when he can. He nice boy. Polite.'

'How long have you known him?'

'I not sure . . . Filip meet him, bring him here last year. October, I think.'

'Do you have any details for his family? Does he have family here?'

'No family here. In Krosna. Sister, I know. He call her. Send money for grandmother. Nice boy, good boy.'

'And do you have a phone number for them, in Krosna?'

'No. Maybe Filip have.'

She whispered something in her own language. Ali thought her English was running out under the strain. The baby gulped the last of the bottle, its eyes half closed in milky ecstasy.

'Can you tell me who lives here?'

'Me, Filip, Anka — Filip wife, Matis. Baby. All legal. No trouble. Anka back home just now. Her papa not well.'

Ali showed her photos of Lauren and the little girl. 'Do you recognize this woman or this child?'

Balancing the baby, Mrs Mazur fished in her pocket, and brought out a pair of reading glasses of the kind sold in supermarkets. The lenses were so greasy, Ali wondered that she could see anything through them. She dipped her head to put them on and then looked at the photo.

'I not know. Never see.'

'Okay, thank you. Could I see Matis's room, please?'

The woman nodded. She reached for a tea towel, slung it over her shoulder and hoisted the baby up, rubbing its back. Her earring tickled the top of its head and it gave a loud burp.

Matis Rimas's room was at the back of the flat, overlooking the bin area and the side of a timber yard. It smelled strongly of fish. Mrs Mazur showed him in and then stood in the doorway, patting the baby's back. Ali drew on protective gloves. It was small, containing a single bed with a crumpled duvet, a plasma TV attached to a wall bracket, a slim white melamine chest of drawers, a mini fridge and a one-ring electric hob with a dirty frying pan on top. The double socket by the skirting board held two adapters and a jumble of plugs, some with frayed leads. Ali frowned. The place was a fire waiting to happen. A collection of DVDs was stacked on the worn carpet by the TV: *Interstellar*, *E.T.*, *Star Wars*, *The Martian*, *Gravity*, *Inception*, *Alien*, *Blade Runner*. One of the curtains had detached from its track and a couple of well-worn hoodies and jeans were hanging from a picture rail.

He opened the drawers and found only a meagre stock of greyish underpants, socks and T-shirts. Under the bed was a large rucksack. It was empty, apart from the Lithuanian passport in a right-hand pocket. He flipped it open. The same young man from the driving licence stared back at him. Ali placed it in an evidence bag. One framed photo stood on top of the fridge on the chest of drawers. It showed the elderly couple from the picture tucked into his wallet. They were with a young woman with her hair in plaits and wearing a green embroidered waistcoat laced over a frilly white blouse, teamed with a long green-and-red woven dress and apron.

'Is this Lithuanian national costume?' Ali asked Mrs Mazur, who was still stroking the baby and crooning to it.

'Is tradition, yes.'

'And are you Lithuanian?'

'Is right. All of us.'

Ali opened the fridge. There were just two shelves holding a couple of pieces of fish wrapped in cling film, butter, a half-used bulb of garlic and a carton of milk. He stood and looked around. Matis Rimas didn't appear to have any paperwork in his life. He must have done his banking online. He thought of the young man lying by the river near his catch. It looked as if he'd been trying to eke out a fairly spartan existence.

'Did Matis have a computer? Laptop?'

'I not see one.'

'Can I have your son's mobile number? I need to speak to him about Matis.'

'My son, he not in trouble? He a good boy too. Very good boy. Work hard. Look after us.'

These two good, polite "boys." Well, maybe they were. 'No, he's not in trouble,' Ali said. He had no idea. Maybe Mazur had been up Lock Lane earlier on and killed two people.

Mrs Mazur bit her lip, nodded and walked back to the kitchen area. The baby had fallen asleep on her shoulder, its face flushed. Her phone was lying on the worktop. She brought up her son's number on the screen for Ali, who copied it and headed off.

He sat in the car and rang the number. It was engaged. Mazur's mother would be calling him. He waited for a couple of minutes, lit up a Gitanes and opened the window. He sat thinking about his new boss. Seemed on the ball if a tad edgy. Nicely turned out, well-cut suit. A strong face and good-looking in a knackered kind of way. Keen, dark blue eyes but kind of strained. As Ali's dad would put it, *lookin' fair wabbit*. He'd noticed the way she sometimes touched the little white scar on her right eyebrow. Too skinny but then Ali preferred well-covered women like Polly. A bit waspish, maybe. There was something about her, as if she had a shadow at her shoulder. But then, from what Ali had heard, that wasn't surprising. His last boss had been a sarky bastard so he was hoping he'd struck luckier this time. He tried the phone number again. A man answered, deep-voiced, shouting over background noise.

'Mr Filip Mazur?'

'Yes, who is this?'

'I'm a police officer. I need to speak to you urgently.'

'Police? For what?'

Don't give me that, he thought, *you know why*. 'It's about Matis Rimas. He's been murdered by the river. We found your car nearby.'

'When did you find him?'

'This morning. I need to see you now. Where do you work?'

He named a building site, St Jerome's, near the town centre. It used to be a hospital but was being converted into flats. Ali stubbed out his cigarette and rang the station as he drove, asking to speak to Siv, but was told that the guv was on the phone. He left a message to say where he was heading and that he should be back in about an hour.

* * *

The bright, cheery receptionist confirmed at the other end of the line that Mr Visser had attended a sales conference at the Raeburn yesterday and had been checked into the hotel's restaurant for an evening meal. Siv tried the number for Errol Todd but it went to voice mail. She left a message. Her phone pinged as she finished the call and she saw that she'd had an email from her sister.

Good luck in your new home. You deserve it. Hope whoever bought Dad's house has a happier marriage than he did! Rik

Minimal. Pretty much what she'd expected. Still, it was something. This had always been the dynamic between them. Siv sought her older sister's attention and affection. Rikka doled both out in small, unpredictable measures. She pictured her sister, as blonde as she was dark, her expression cloaked and just a bit smug, as if she knew something and wasn't going to tell. Another email popped up, this one on her work computer. It was from Nick Shelton, the owner of the land by the river:

I'm so appalled at what has happened at Lock Lane. Please give my condolences to the families. Attached is the list of members of the angling club. Can you let me know when the site can be opened to members again?

She saw through the glass partition that DC Patrick Hill had come in and was sitting at his desk at the other side of the office, a big grin on his face, chewing at a nail on his left hand and dancing his right thumb on his phone screen. She forwarded the email to him and went into the team room. There were a few other officers, busy on phones, clicking on their computer screens. She walked over to Hill.

'Hello. I'm DI Siv Drummond.'

He stood, straightening his tie. 'Hi. DC Hill. Nice to meet you. Double murder on your first day!'

51

'That's right. I need you to do something for me.'

He was gawky and all angles, like a teenager. Fresh-faced, freckled, his straw-blond hair short and spiky. A sharp dresser, in his narrow trousers and close fitting jacket. 'So, guv, I've been busy doing some checks on Matis Rimas for Ali.'

'I could see you were busy on your phone.'

The sarcasm passed over his head. He looked pleased and tapped the phone, holding it out so that she could see the Twitter feed on screen.

@DCBerminsterPolice. Pensioner & young mum attacked and had bags stolen last weekend town centre. Man arrested & charged. #keepingberminstersafe

'Did you make the arrest?'

'That's right, on the Maidwell estate. I like to keep my Twitter feed up to date every day. Let the public know we're fighting the good fight for them. DCI Mortimer thinks it's great.'

'Well done. Just now, I've two dead people who need us to fight the good fight, so can you take a look at the email I've forwarded to you? It's from Nick Shelton, with a list of the members of Berminster Anglers. I need you and another officer to contact all of them and ask if any of them were at the river at Lock Lane early this morning and/or if they know a woman called Lauren Visser or a man called Matis Rimas. And ask if they've ever seen a child there, a little fair-haired girl. I've attached her photo to an email.'

He ran a hand through his hair, lifting the spikes. His nails were chewed and ragged. 'How many names?'

'Thirty-ish. Let me know if you get any positives.'

She could see his face cloud. He was thinking this was grunt work. Nothing worth boasting about on Twitter. He'd need to learn to conceal his thoughts better. She went back to the empty desk where she'd left the goodies, picked up a chocolate brownie and brought it over to him.

'It's work that has to be done but just to sweeten it,' she said, placing it on his desk. 'Tell the others to help themselves.'

He put a thumb up. 'Ta, guv. But don't offer any of those to Ali. He's diabetic.'

'I know, so he's not likely to take one.'

He shook his head, spluttering on the brownie. 'That's the problem, he would!'

She was making her way to the hot drinks machine in the corridor when her phone rang.

'Hi, it's Steve Wooton. We opened the Seat. There was no rucksack, no phone and no personal belongings other than the usual glove compartment stuff: packets of tissues, bottled water, sweets and that. Tartan rug on the back seat.'

'Lauren Visser must have left her rucksack nearby when she went swimming. Maybe our killer liked the look of it.' Although she was sure that these murders weren't about robbery. The child's photo made this personal and Rimas's phone and wallet had been left.

'Kanken's an expensive brand. Dead cool. My son blagged one for his birthday. Maybe the killer just wanted to make sure we didn't get her phone and it was quicker to take the bag. Talk later.'

Wooton had a point about the phone. Maybe Lauren's killer had been in contact with her and had set up a meeting at the river. She punched the button for tea with lemon, imagining the scene. Someone had come to the river intending to kill. But to murder one or both of the victims? Rimas had been fishing. Had he heard a sound in the trees? Perhaps he'd had to die because he'd seen the killer. Both victims had been taken by surprise with no chance to fight back, given the apparent lack of defence wounds. And who took a photo of a child with them when they intended to stick a blade in someone? How did Lauren connect to the girl?

A thought crossed her mind. Back at her computer, she searched for Lauren and Rimas on the national database. She'd wondered if either of them had ever harmed a child but no trace came up. They were both squeaky clean as far as the police were concerned.

CHAPTER SEVEN

Siv was drinking her lemon tea when Ali arrived back. He chucked his jacket off, yanked a chair out and sat down heavily, catching at her desk to steady himself.

'I've met Filip Mazur and his mother,' he told her. 'They're Lithuanian too. Matis Rimas was renting a room from them in a social housing place. Illegal subletting, I suspect. You should have seen it — it was poky. And it smelled of fish. I think I do now.'

'I can only smell the fag smoke,' Siv said. 'What did Mazur tell you?'

'He works on a building site. He met Rimas last autumn on a housing development out at Harfield and they got friendly. Rimas was a plasterer. He was sharing a room with two other guys, so when Mazur offered him a room at his place, he jumped at it. That must have been a real dump if he thought Mazur's was an improvement. Mazur was really upset about the murder, said Rimas had become one of the family, played with the baby and so on. He had tears in his eyes.' He'd talked to Mazur, a giant of a man, in an overheated Portakabin. When Ali told him of his friend's death, he'd gone pale and seemed in danger of toppling over. It would have been like an oak tree falling.

'Why did Rimas have his car?'

'He wanted to go fishing this morning. He loved fishing and regularly contributed fish for the family's meals. I asked Mazur who would have known that Rimas was going to Lock Lane this morning. He said his mum knew but he didn't know who else might have.'

'Rimas could have told his other workmates. We need to check that out.'

'Sure. Mazur was getting a lift from a mate, so Rimas borrowed the car for the day. Mazur said he heard him leave about six forty-five. I spoke to Mazur's mate and he confirmed that he picked Mazur up from his place at ten past seven this morning and waved to his mum. Mazur said that Rimas was a bit of an innocent.'

'What did he mean? A learning difficulty?'

'No. I got the impression that he was just immature.'

'Did Mazur know where Rimas was working?'

'He said he was doing a month on a house extension on the Cherryfield estate. Small local builders, Johnstone. Mazur agreed to identify the body. I'll arrange that for tomorrow.'

'Did he have any information about Rimas's family?'

'Only that they live in Krosna, a wee town. I'll see if I can find any contact details for them this afternoon. I asked Mazur if he or Rimas knew a woman called Lauren Visser. He looked completely blank when I showed him her photo. Same response when I showed him the wee girl. Going by what Mazur said, he'd have arrived at the river soon after seven.' He stretched his arms and cracked his knuckles. His shirt rode up and Siv caught a glimpse of soft brown belly.

She leaned forward on her desk. 'This has to be about the child. She must be at the centre of it, otherwise why leave her photo? I wondered about paedophilia or some other child related crime but neither of them has any record on HOLMES. Lauren was a nursery nurse so she'd have had a DBS check anyway. This tea is weird, it tastes like cough sweets.'

'It all comes out of the same tube so who knows what the machine decides. What was Visser like?'

'Angry. A rigid man. Seemed genuinely upset. The hotel he was at yesterday confirms his attendance into the evening. He says he stayed at a friend's in London last night but said friend left for a Buddhist retreat in Valencia this morning and I can't raise him.' She glanced at her watch. 'I have to get going. I said I'd take Visser to the morgue. There's fruit here on my desk and sugar-free granola bars. Help yourself.'

'Ta, guv. Oh, Dr Anand emailed. PMs start tomorrow afternoon at two thirty.'

'Thanks. Conference meeting at nine tomorrow — can you tell the team?'

* * *

Climbing the four metal steps to her front door felt like a tremendous effort. Siv rested against the rail for a moment. It was almost dark but she could still make out the soft greens of the meadow and the pale clusters of wild flowers: agrimony, cornflowers, foxgloves, white campion and meadowsweet. Smoke was drifting lazily from Corran and Paul's chimney in the light breeze. She pictured them sitting at their big table, eating homemade pasta and discussing the day.

As soon as she was inside, her legs began to tremble. When she'd first trained in the Met, colleagues would talk about shaking leg syndrome, often experienced at or after post-mortems or vicious crime scenes. She threw her bag down and sank onto the sofa beneath the window. She closed her eyes and breathed, visualizing the shoreline of the sea: in, out, in out. The trembling slowly subsided. She wanted to stay where she was but if she did, she'd start thinking about Ed because this was the time, around sunset, when his shade joined the evening shadows. It wasn't cold in the wagon but she wanted the reassurance of a fire, so she made herself get up and light the wood burner.

Once the fire was crackling, she went into the bedroom, shrugged off her work suit and pulled on leggings and Ed's green sweatshirt. She sat on the edge of the bed and texted Ali Carlin.

Positive ID at morgue. See you tomorrow.

Visser had been silent during the drive to the morgue, where there'd been a forty-five-minute delay. He'd paced up and down, stopping now and again to rest his forehead against the pale green wall. Once he'd kicked it, his foot jarring. She'd watched him, glad to have the distraction of his prowling. She didn't want to think about the last time she'd been in a morgue. They'd done their best with Lauren but it was a difficult viewing. Visser had expressed no emotion as he looked through the screen, just confirmed that it was his wife. Siv drove him home, another silent journey. He got out of the car, and leaned in through the window.

'I'll give you two weeks to find who did this. If you've nothing by then, I'll take steps myself.'

She'd replied quietly, 'We'll find who murdered your wife, Mr Visser.'

'Take note. The clock's ticking for you.'

'I'll need to speak to you tomorrow. Will you be at home?'

'You've got my fucking car. Where can I go?'

He'd stalked away up his path. She'd never seen a back express so much fury.

In the kitchen, she reached into the fridge, took out a bottle of cold akvavit and poured a glass, relishing the kick of caraway and spices. One of the best things to come from Finland. She ate a handful of pistachio nuts and looked in the fridge again for inspiration. There wasn't a lot: a packet of serrano ham, flatbreads, tomatoes and olives and several bottles of akvavit. The awful realization struck her that this could be her mother's fridge, sparse on food but with a generous quantity of alcohol. So this was what had happened. On her own, left to her own devices, she was turning into Mutsi. The old adage about women morphing into their mothers was true. She laughed out loud, and then clamped her hand over her mouth. A sandwich then, maybe toasted.

She heard a tap at the door. It was Corran, holding a round foil package.

'Hi, Siv. Sorry to disturb you but we had baked potatoes for supper and as usual, I made too much so I thought after your first day back at work . . .' He held out the foil. He had small, deft hands, in keeping with the rest of his frame. She thought of him as pocket sized. He had a posh voice, courtesy of public school. Paul was from Liverpool and teased him about his drawn-out vowels. *At Corran's school, there was great emphasis on bowels and vowels*, he'd told her.

'That's so kind of you. Come in.' She was hoping he'd refuse and was relieved when he did.

'No, no. I have goat related things to do and I'm sure you're tired.' He turned as if to head down the steps, and then halted. 'Ahm . . . a lady rang today. She said she was your mother.'

She almost dropped the warm foil. It was as if by thinking of her mother, she'd unwittingly summoned her. 'What?'

He gave an embarrassed shrug. 'It was early afternoon. She wanted to speak to you. I told her I thought you were at work.'

'I see. Was that it?'

'She asked me for your mobile number. Said she'd lost it. I said I couldn't give it to her but I'd let you know she'd called.'

Siv knew her mother only too well. Corran wouldn't have got off that lightly. 'What else did she say?'

He glanced up at her cautiously. 'Some stuff about her youngest daughter living in a field, like a gypsy. Asked if I had the cheek to charge you for an old wagon. Said she'd had an uncle in Finland who used to keep chickens in one like it.'

'I'm sorry, Corran. I hope she wasn't too rude.'

'No, no, that's okay. Actually, I thought she sounded quite a character.'

Her heart sank. The last thing she needed was her mother trying to befriend Paul and Corran, even by phone.

They didn't deserve it. 'She is. Quite a character. But not in a good way.'

He nodded. 'Okay. No worries. Is she Finnish, then?'

'Yes. Siv's a Scandinavian name.' The same as her mother's, unfortunately.

'I know. Paul looked it up. Hope you don't mind, we'd never come across it before.'

'Of course not. Thanks for the supper,' she called again as he headed home into the falling dusk.

She locked the door and the world out, knocked her drink back and refilled her glass. As far as she was concerned, a taste for akvavit was the only gift her mother had ever given her. *Bloody woman, bloody interfering crap excuse for a parent*, she muttered as she unwrapped the potato. Her mother had lied, as usual. She didn't know either of her daughters' phone numbers and Siv hadn't told her about the move. She must have been looking at this place on the internet if she knew it was in a meadow, and had found Corran's mobile number.

Siv glanced out of the window, half expecting to see her mother outside, staring back at her with her ingratiating smile. How did she know her whereabouts and more importantly, why the attempt at contact? It was months since she'd last been in touch. Well, at least she hadn't tried to gate-crash the funeral. She'd sent a belated sympathy card with lilies and gold lettering on the front: *Sorry For Your Loss* and inside the trite handwritten message, *There will be sun after the storm. Love from Mutsi.*

She stuck the potato on a tray featuring scenes of the Sussex coast and sat with it on her lap by the stove. It was delicious, crammed with cheese, ham and grainy mustard. She hadn't realized how hungry she was until she started wolfing it down. When she'd finished she licked her fingers and put the tray on the wooden floor. She reached for the akvavit bottle — it was so handy having everything at arm's length, she didn't understand why she'd ever lived anywhere bigger than this — put it beside her and sat back with her feet up on the top of the stove. She buried her nose in the sleeve of her sweatshirt and sniffed. The scent of Ed.

She still couldn't quite believe that she was here, living this unexpected life. This time last year, she and Ed had been working in London, living in their flat in Greenwich. Content, full of plans. She was accustomed to the constant hum of traffic, the bumps and crashes from the cousins in the flat below who threw things at each other when they argued. There'd been long walks in the park at weekends, always stopping to chat to the deer, an afternoon visit to the Picture House on Sunday after a lazy brunch, stopping at a delicatessen to buy a diabetic-friendly dessert, usually almond torte. Ed calling her Sivster. He was forever misplacing things and his voice would echo from the hallway or kitchen. *Sivster, have you seen my keys/wallet/helmet/work pass/gloves/phone?*

She'd been promoted to DI. Ed had got a job as head of science at a huge academy school. They'd had a meal at a posh fusion restaurant to celebrate and a lot of wine. *It's all good, Sivster, it's all good*, he'd said, smiling and tucking her hair behind her ear.

Then, one Tuesday morning she'd had the call. Ed had been riding his bike to work along Romney Road when a lorry hit him. He'd died before the paramedics got there. He'd kissed her goodbye, tasting of toast and honey, reassured her that his blood sugar was on target and cycled out of her life for ever. The next time she'd seen him had been in the morgue, and that wasn't Ed at all.

Throughout the funeral, she'd sworn at him under her breath. Luckily, no one seemed to realize that her sorrow was half despair, half fury. *You wouldn't fucking listen, would you, Ed? How many bloody times did I ask you not to cycle in that traffic?* They'd talked about it so often. She'd pleaded with him, citing the number of fatal accidents on London roads, bus and lorry drivers failing to see vulnerable cyclists. He'd been reassuring, persuasive. *You know I'm really careful and it's great exercise for me, helps me deal with the stress of the job. I hate gyms and keeping fit's important for my blood sugar.* So she'd back off until the next horror story about a terrible accident. And then Ed was the story.

For months, she'd lived a kind of bewildered half-life. At times she raged at him and then she'd weep for hours. She'd tried to go to back to work but had panic attacks. Her scalp would start prickling and then the top of her head would feel as if it was lifting off. The first time her scalp started to lift, she was interviewing a man who'd murdered his brother and she thought she was having a stroke.

The doctor signed her off and kept signing her off. The skin on her forearms felt as if someone had scrubbed it with harsh soap. She developed a red rash on her chest, little whorls of bright colour. Her brush was suddenly thick with loose hair. She spent time sitting in stuffy rooms with occupational health nurses, never the same one. Some were useful, some not. One had a habit of murmuring sympathetically, which irritated her so much she wanted to grab the woman by the throat. They were all kindly and nodded a lot, handed her tissues when required and gave her flat-tasting water in plastic cups.

She began to think that grief was like a negative of falling in love: the same interrupted sleep, loss of appetite, racing heart and deep longing but paired with desolation instead of joy. When she woke in the mornings, her first thought was of how many days it had been since Ed died and she'd count aloud: *45 . . . 56 . . . 62.*

Other cyclists and friends of Ed took up arms. There were vigils and protests with banners. They kept telling her about these demonstrations, as if they thought that would help her grief. A white ghost bike was left at the side of Romney Road where he died. Bunches of flowers and candles kept appearing there. She felt as if by dying, Ed had become public property and was nothing to do with her any more.

She drifted around the flat, going out only after dark so that she wouldn't have to accept any sympathy. She didn't have many friends, had never been the kind of woman with a female coterie. It was something to do with all the moving from place to place as she was growing up. There was never time to cement relationships. Then she'd met Ed in London when she was nineteen and had just applied for police training. And that was it. He became the family she'd always needed — sibling, parents and lover all rolled into one. She thought she'd got too lucky, she didn't quite trust her good fortune. Turned out she was right not to.

Days and weeks merged. She couldn't concentrate to read or even watch a film. She felt Ed's presence all the time but it was no comfort. She was like one of those people who have a leg or an arm removed yet can feel the phantom limb, as if it's still attached.

She took up origami again and spent hours looking at designs, working out her own and folding paper. This was what occupational therapists did with people to help them, she thought. They got them to make things. If your hands were busy and your brain side-tracked from the usual thought treadmill, you found a kind of temporary peace. Doing something, focusing and losing herself in folding, eased the pain.

Finally, she knew that she couldn't stay in London. Ed was everywhere. She never knew when she would turn a corner and see a restaurant, pub, cinema or park they'd spent time in. The city was scattered with ghost bikes draped with flowers and she couldn't bear to see one more. She asked if there were any vacancies in Berminster, struck lucky, put the flat on the market, sent most of her things to storage and moved into her circus wagon.

She topped up her glass. *So, Ed. Here I am, living in my miniature world. Survived day one and didn't disgrace myself. But I'm ragged now. Two corpses and working with people I barely know. You wouldn't like the colour scheme in here, too busy. It's so quiet during the day but at night I can hear foxes barking in the dark and other sounds: yowls and screams of animals killing each other. I notice the weather more here than I did in London. I suppose because the sea's nearby. I can taste salt sometimes. Ali Carlin smokes Gitanes, so what with his diabetes, he's a bit of a candidate for heart disease. Funny how I hate smoking but I love the smell of Gitanes. What's that about? Ali's got a great expression, open and optimistic. I wonder if Lauren had a baby before she met Visser, one that she didn't reveal to her husband. Seems unlikely these days. That's the kind of secret women used to have to keep but not now, surely. Mutsi's on the prowl, sniffing around. She must want something. As if I haven't got enough on my plate.*

A log shifted in the fire. Her feet were toasting nicely. She reached an arm out to the fruit bowl and crunched an apple, then finished her drink. The taste of anise had increased with the warmth of the room. She felt desolate.

Sleep tight, she told Ed.

CHAPTER EIGHT

When the policewoman had left, Ade Visser paced around the house. His heart was pounding. His armpits were sticky. He stripped his shirt off. The feel and smell of his sweat disgusted him. He stopped in the kitchen and drank two glasses of water.

He was so *angry* with Lauren. He'd wanted to shake her there on that slab, shout at her. He'd loved her but God, she'd frustrated him! Aware of DI Drummond's gaze, he'd kept his emotions reined in.

When he'd met Lauren, she'd seemed so undemanding, pliable in a way he found soothing and reassuring. As time went on, he found that she had unfathomable layers. When he tried to reason with her, get her to see his point of view, she'd look as if she was listening, head slightly to one side, and then she'd go off and do what she liked. She had a way of being softly and subtly resistant. It was like pushing against air. He'd never come across a woman like her before. Sometimes he'd wondered if something was wrong with her. Yet at times he'd worried that she'd understood too much. She'd look at him with her deep-set eyes when he came home, and he thought she knew about his sickening secret. There was no way that she could, he was sure of it.

No one but him had ever known. But all the same, she had an expression that was both knowing and forgiving.

And now he was in this terrible situation, riddled with self-loathing and fury. And guilt. So much sickening guilt.

He showered again, lathering soap all over his body and using a hard loofah to scour his skin. The ritual of washing usually calmed him but after he'd dressed, his agitation was still intense. He took his bike out and cycled for a couple of hours, into town, through the harbour and out into the country lanes. Sweat and tears filled his eyes. Afterwards, he had no recollection of exactly where he'd been. He knew that he'd paused by the sea at one point, looking out over Minster Beach, the strong breeze rocking his bike. He'd seen a fishing boat heading out and longed to be on it, sailing into the horizon.

He was in the same emotional turmoil when he came home, but at least he was physically exhausted. He ordered a takeaway and showered yet again, scrubbing hard at every inch of his skin. He even did the soles of his feet. Then he stared up at the rushing water. He'd lied to Drummond and he didn't know if she'd find out. It depended on how sound a sleeper Errol was. He'd rung his friend and got his voice mail. He hadn't expected Errol to pick up.

He struck the side of the shower cubicle with his fist. Sometimes he felt as if he was rotting from the inside and people would smell a whiff of decay. It was why he showered as much as he did, up to four a day when he could. Trying to wash away the taint of revulsion. Maybe this turmoil in his life was a warning. If he'd been religious, he'd have believed it was God's way of getting him to repent. He struck the cubicle again and it shuddered, sending spray flying.

He was mad. Mad at Lauren for not listening to him, mad with guilt and grief and desperate because he knew he was going to be under a remorseless spotlight.

* * *

'The story so far,' Siv said, gesturing at the incident board. 'Lauren Visser, twenty-five, was stabbed, possibly with scissors, yesterday morning after swimming in the River Bere at Lock Lane. The photo of a child, a young girl, was left on her chest. Her husband reported her as missing when he got home from an overnight stay in London. He says he reached home at nine thirty a.m. yesterday and his car wasn't there. Lauren planned to go swimming around six or possibly earlier. I'm still waiting to contact Visser's friend to verify the information he gave me about his overnight stay. Matis Rimas, twenty, a Lithuanian man, left home to go fishing at six forty-five a.m. He was killed around the same time as Lauren — we're waiting on PM results — and with the same weapon. He arrived in the UK in July last year and was working as a plasterer. Lauren went swimming in the river at Lock Lane occasionally. Rimas went fishing there frequently and without a permit. To date, we have no connection between them. We need to look closely for one, through either place or people. The same with the child. The photo must have been left on Lauren's body because the little girl was linked to her in some way. She worked at a nursery so maybe that's a connection. Maybe Rimas had worked there as he didn't have children.' She looked at her colleagues. Ali was eating a pear, Wooton had his arms crossed and was staring up at the ceiling. Patrick Hill had got in at one minute to nine looking wild-eyed, as if he'd spent the night partying. The others were looking at the board or taking notes. 'Steve, can you update us?'

Wooton snapped to attention. 'Forensics are still processing shoe prints and tyre marks from the site. We're back there today. The fresh tyre marks near the Honda indicate that someone else was parked there at some point early yesterday. We've still got to examine the cars. Anand stated that they were both killed there, in the trees.'

'Rimas's phone?' she asked.

'I've sent it over for unlocking and scrutiny.'

'We need a search of the river, see if we can find the murder weapon.'

'I've already put in a request.'

'Filip Mazur said Rimas had a pay-as-you-go phone. No computer,' Ali said, picking up the thread. 'Mazur met Rimas through work and rented him a room. He moved in last October. Mazur loaned Rimas his car yesterday and his own early-morning movements check out. I contacted the police in Krosna. They were going to tell Rimas's family. I'm waiting to hear if a family member is coming over but in the meantime, Mazur is identifying the body later today.'

'Patrick and another officer were working through our list of members of the angling club,' Siv said. 'Patrick?'

'Guv. We got through eighteen so far on the list of anglers. Ten were contactable. None of them had been to the river recently — because of the "close" season — and none of them knew our victims or of a little girl. They all said kids rarely go there. One commented a bit tartly that "small children and fishing don't mix."'

The other officer raised a finger. 'Lisa Flore, guv. The close season thing means that it's much quieter at the river than usual.'

'So maybe that's why Lauren went there yesterday. Try to finish those calls today. The photo of the child is important. So far, no one we've questioned has recognized her. Visser said Lauren had no children but maybe she'd had one in a previous life and didn't tell him. Dr Anand will be able to confirm that. I want you to check the CCTV on roads around the area as well, see if we get any cars in the timescale. And I want someone to check out Alan Vine's background. I can't see him as a double murderer but find out about him. I want a door-to-door organized in Spring Gardens with uniforms. Maybe a neighbour saw Visser cycle home yesterday. Also, I want to know if anyone saw Lauren the night before she died or leaving the house to go for her early swim, or anyone visiting. Get a photo done of Rimas and show that round with the photo of that child. Maybe someone will have noticed Rimas in his shabby clothes, given that Spring Gardens is a genteel kind of street. And look into CCTV from yesterday morning. We also need to check Rimas's workplace, find out if there were any problems or if anyone there knew he was going fishing yesterday morning. Long list, I know. Ali, can you check who's doing what. Then I want you to come with me to see Visser. We're turning up unannounced. I just want to speak to DCI Mortimer about a press conference for later today, then we'll head off.'

* * *

Ade Visser looked washed out and subdued. He was tetchy and bleary eyed but fresh from the shower and dressed in chinos and crisp cotton shirt. The living room curtains were still drawn when they arrived just after half ten. He went and pulled them back as he led them in. The remains of a Chinese takeaway lay on the coffee table. Grief evidently hadn't robbed him of his appetite. Siv herself hadn't eaten much for months after Ed died. The smell of food had sickened her and she'd gone around lightheaded. But she needed to remember that everyone reacted differently to sorrow. There was no template.

She'd agreed with Ali that the sergeant would start off with general questions. 'He associates me with the bad news and the morgue. You might get more out of him to start with.'

Visser gestured at the mess. 'Sorry about this. I'll have to clean up later. My mother's arriving from Hampshire this afternoon. I don't want her to come and I tried to stop her but she insisted.' Visser was looking at Siv and seemed taken aback when Ali spoke.

'I'm very sorry about your wife, Mr Visser. I'm glad you've got someone coming to be with you. I know that this is a difficult time.'

'I don't need TLC, so save it for someone who does. What more do you know? What progress have you made?'

'We'll know more after the post-mortem,' Ali said. 'The weapon used to stab your wife might have been a pair of scissors. We need to ask you some more questions now, to get an idea about Lauren's life.'

His reply was a surprise. 'Have you found out anything about that man yet — the man who was found dead near Lauren? Rimas, wasn't it? Have you found out that she knew him?'

'We're making enquiries about Mr Rimas,' Ali told him, pulling out Rimas's picture. 'As yet, we haven't established that he knew your wife. Do you recognize him?'

Visser stared at the enlarged photo made from Rimas's passport. 'I've never seen this man.'

'Thank you. So, can you tell me how you met Lauren?' Ali said.

Visser gave a heavy sigh. 'February, three years ago. We met through mutual friends, Harvey and Jenna Seaton. I've known Harvey for a while because he rides and attends events. He sources new saddles and other bits of equipment through me. His wife, Jenna, owns the nursery where Lauren worked. It was Harvey's birthday and he had a party. We met at their house. We married six months later. I knew as soon as I saw Lauren that she was the one for me. She was so gentle and kind. My twin soul in life. She was such a caring person. I'd never known anyone who felt so strongly about nature and the environment. She worked as a volunteer with a wildlife conservation group in town, Minstergreen.'

'And her family? Where did she grow up?' Ali asked.

'Here in Berminster. Like I said yesterday, her mother died before we met. She never knew who her father was. There was no one else.' He rubbed at his head. 'Have you found her rucksack? I tried her phone again last night. Stupid, I know. It went to voice mail.'

Siv swallowed. She knew about ringing a dead person, listening to their voice over and over. *Hi, it's Ed. If you're not wasting my time, leave a message.*

'Not yet,' Ali said. 'Did Lauren have a computer or iPad?'

'No. She used her phone for all her online things. She had a little study upstairs where she did stuff for her conservation work.'

'We'll need to take a look in there and around the rest of the house. We haven't found her phone yet either.'

'If you need passwords for her accounts, I know them.' Visser rubbed his head again and then his eyes.

Ali nodded encouragingly. 'Can you tell us about Lauren's friends?'

'She had one close friend, Cora Laffin. They were at school together. Cora got Lauren into swimming in rivers and lakes. She calls herself a "life adventurer" and she's always surfing or climbing rocks. All very well if you're single, with no commitments and no one at home worrying about you. When we got together, I tried hard to persuade Lauren to give it up. Such a stupid craze, but she said it made her feel free. It worried me, her going off on her own so often to isolated places and swimming in water that might be dirty. Sometimes she'd be gone for hours. I told her it wasn't sensible. She'd get bad throats or stomach upsets and I'm sure it was from crap in the water. But I couldn't get through to her, no matter how hard I tried. I'd say to her, why can't you just use the swimming pool like everyone else?'

He sounded like Alan Vine. 'I suppose because everyone else would be using it too and she wanted peace and solitude,' Ali said. Visser had grown agitated as he talked about his wife's swimming, his eyes darting. 'How often did she go swimming?'

'Twice a week. More maybe when I was away. I travel quite a bit with my work. And, of course, that worried me because I wouldn't know if she was okay. We always spoke every day, but anything could have been happening to her while I was gone. It was all too much. At times, it seemed to me that it was a bit of an unhealthy obsession with Lauren.'

'You seem to have been very much against Lauren enjoying her hobby.'

'Only because it worried me so much. I mean, you hear about terrible things happening to women. There are predators out there and a woman on her own is so open to danger. You want to keep the people you love safe, don't you? She meant the world to me, she really did. I couldn't bear the thought of anything happening to her. And I was right. She'd be alive now if she hadn't been at the river. If only she'd listened to me, it'd be her sitting there now instead of you!'

Siv recognized his anger, knew that he was tasting it just as she had when she'd berated her dead husband. But there was an undercurrent she didn't like. His concern sounded more like, *I loved her so much I wanted to keep her under my eye and smother her.* He was a man who knew his wife's passwords. The kind who might end up bugging his partner's phone or putting a tracking device in their car. He was twisting his wedding ring round and round. His inertia had vanished and now he looked intense and angry. She nodded to Ali that she'd take over.

'How did Lauren feel about your dislike of her hobby? Did it upset or annoy her?' she asked.

'We just agreed to disagree. She pointed out that she didn't always like being at home on her own when I had to work away. So . . . you know. Sometimes you just have to accept things in the person you love.'

Siv didn't believe this grudging acceptance. He didn't seem the accommodating type. But would he have killed his wife because he objected to her swimming and she wouldn't comply? Seemed unlikely, but jealousy and resentment could reach a tipping point. 'How about Lauren's work? Was everything all right there?'

'Very much so. She was happy at the nursery. She looked forward to going in every day.' Visser got up and took a photo from the mantelpiece, ran his hand across the glass and handed it to Siv. 'That's Lauren with her nursery group. She was so good with children. We were planning to start a family next year.'

Siv scanned the photo but couldn't see the little girl. She passed it to Ali.

'She was always talking about the kids,' Visser went on. 'What they'd been saying and getting up to, their funny habits. She didn't allow herself to have favourites. She said you had to be careful not to show any preferences. Do you have children?'

'No, I haven't,' she said. 'Did Lauren seem upset or worried about anything recently? Any problems?'

'She seemed okay, and she didn't say that anything was worrying her. Apart from a cold last week, she was fine.'

'Did anyone else know that Lauren was going swimming at Lock Lane yesterday morning?' she asked.

'I've no idea. I suppose Cora Laffin might have known, or Lauren might have mentioned it to people at work.' He hunched in his chair. 'This is so hard. I can't believe . . . I feel so guilty that I was away overnight. Maybe there was something wrong and if I'd been here I could have intervened . . .'

'It's natural to feel like that when you're grieving. Going back to Sunday night, what time did you leave the Raeburn hotel and get to your friend's flat?' Siv asked.

'Ahm . . . it was about eleven when the meal ended. I walked to Errol's flat. It only took fifteen minutes and I needed the air and to walk off a three-course meal. So I got to his place around a quarter past.'

'Did Errol let you in?'

'He didn't need to. I've got a key. We go back a long way together and I sometimes stay at his flat when I've got business in London and it's a been late night. He'd said he'd probably be in bed by the time I got there because he had a very early flight on Monday. So I let myself in quietly. I went straight to bed. I was exhausted after a full on day.'

'Did you see him before he left for his flight?'

He shook his head. 'I heard the door as he was leaving but I didn't see him. I'd not slept well. Too much food and alcohol the night before, and my head was buzzing. I was hoping I'd secured a couple of promising contracts.'

'So Errol didn't actually see you at all on Sunday night or Monday morning?' Siv asked.

'No. But that's happened before when I've stayed over. He's an engineering project manager, works all over the world. Have you spoken to him?'

'I've left him a message.'

'Me too. As I said, he's at this retreat. Meditation and yoga. He goes there a couple of times a year, says it helps him de-stress and clear his head. The deal is that you don't have any communication with the outside world.'

'How long is he there for?'

'A couple of days, I think.'

Ali looked as if he was about to speak but Siv stood up. 'Let's leave it there for now. We'd like to take a look upstairs and in Lauren's study.'

'Help yourselves. Up the stairs, straight on.'

They went up, treading on deep cream carpet. The walls were lined with more photographs of horses. Reaching the landing, they pulled on gloves. It was sunlit from a side window etched in the same pineapple pattern as the front door. A reed diffuser on the window ledge scented the air. Siv opened the study door. It was a tiny box room and smelled of the same scent but much more strongly in the confined space.

'Jo Malone Pomegranate Noir,' Ali said, looking at the oil-filled jar on the narrow desk. 'That's more than sixty quid a bottle.'

'Are you into home scenting then?'

'My wife is. She's always trying to mask the lingering smell of my fag smoke.'

The room contained just the desk, a chair, a bookcase and one large framed poster, a stunning aerial view of a winding river with the slogan, *Keep it clean. Keep it safe. Keep it for all our futures.* The chair had a long yellow pashmina trailing over the back and a detachable lumbar support. Siv looked at the photo on the bookshelf, a selfie of Lauren and another woman, their arms linked, standing on a riverbank. She was wearing the silver wetsuit and the waiflike woman with her was in a black-and-orange one. The books were about swimming, wildlife conservation, birds and working with children. There were a couple of chick-lit novels. Nothing about Lithuania.

Ali was looking through the desk's single drawer. 'Passport, throat lozenges, emery boards, envelopes, couple of blank greetings cards and one from the nursery, *Congratulations on Your Wedding*, with lots of kids' squiggles. Posters and flyers for Minstergreen, about weekend clean-ups of the countryside and otter watching, etc. Piece of folded paper in the back of the passport. Take a look.'

It was in neat, rounded handwriting, the same as yesterday's shopping list in the kitchen. 'Looks like a list of passwords and pin numbers. Handy.'

Ali took one more look in the drawer. 'Nothing from or to Matis Rimas, unfortunately.'

Siv moved to the window. It overlooked a small back garden done in a Mediterranean style with pots of flowers and herbs and a gravel seating area covered by a jasmine-smothered pergola. 'We have to continue to look for a connection, but I'm not sure Lauren knew Rimas. My guess is he was in the wrong place at the wrong time.'

'Collateral damage — the murderer panicked?'

'That's my thinking,' she said. 'But that's still to prove. Let's look in the other bedrooms.'

The middle bedroom had a single unmade bed, fitted wardrobe and chest of drawers. The couple's bedroom was at the front, with wide blinds pulled halfway up at the windows. They stood inside the door, looking around. Everything was in shades of cream. There was a king-size bed with an oak headboard and matching drawers at each side, fitted wardrobes with mirrors inset into the doors and one upholstered chair. Two huge photos of horses that dominated the room provided the only colour. The nearest was a conker brown horse at full gallop along a sandy beach with the jockey standing in the stirrups, urging it on.

'That's Red Rum,' Ali whispered throatily. 'My da had some big wins on him back in the day. And the one on the far wall is Arkle. He's reckoned to be the greatest racer ever. There's a statue to him in Ireland.'

They looked in the bedside drawers and wardrobes but found nothing of note. On the way down, they heard a vacuum cleaner. Visser was busy in the living room. The rubbish had been cleared away. He showed them out, handing Siv a sheet of paper.

'Here's Lauren's passwords. Don't forget that your two-week clock to find this killer is ticking.'

Ali looked back at the house as they walked down the path. 'What's that crap about giving us two weeks to catch the killer?'

'Asserting himself. Flailing around. Sheer pain and confusion. Maybe he killed her and Rimas and it's a distraction effort, smoke and mirrors. Take your pick.'

'I bet he's a sulker,' Ali said. 'You'd get the silent treatment if he isn't best pleased. Mind if I have a drag?'

'Be my guest. I'd like him to see us hanging around. As yet, we've no proof of where he said he was late Sunday night into early yesterday. Put the pressure on in case he's got something to hide. What's your view?' Siv stood upwind, enjoying the sun on her face and admiring the well-kept houses.

Ali stood with his back to the car boot, inhaling deeply. His eyes had the faraway gaze of the addict getting their fix. His shirt was missing a button and he had a greasy smear of food on his jacket cuff. It looked unsightly. The sunlight glinted on his short cornrows. 'Not sure. He looks done in, as if he's genuinely sad. Definitely a control freak, though, and I reckon he's got a nasty temper. Maybe Lauren wanted to go swimming once too often and he snapped, but then you'd expect him to have killed her at home in a moment's rage.'

'It would definitely have been a lot more trouble for him to go to the river. Unless she was having an affair with Rimas and he thought he'd catch them there.'

'A river romance? That's possible. Plenty of space around there for al fresco shenanigans.'

Don't I know it. 'It's a masculine kind of house,' she said, 'dominated by Visser's equine interests. How many horse pictures does one man need? There's very little sign of Lauren except in the study. It's as if the smallest room in the house was the only space she claimed.'

'Or was allowed to claim?'

'Maybe. The elusive Errol's Valencian hideaway is a nuisance. If he doesn't contact us soon, we'll have to ask the Spanish police to help. In the meantime, I need to hear someone else's view of this marriage of twin souls, so I'm off to visit Lauren's workplace. There are twelve staff, so I've arranged for Patrick to join me later for interviews. You've got a stain on your sleeve, just there.'

Ali took out a used tissue and rubbed the spot. 'I'm a mucky terror,' he said. 'My wife's always asking if I was born in a hedge.' He glanced down at Siv with his merry eyes. 'Do you always look so well turned out, guv?'

Siv laughed. *You should have seen me four months ago, still unwashed and in my pyjamas in the afternoon.* 'Can't help it, Sergeant. Just comes naturally.'

CHAPTER NINE

Caterpillar Corner
Where Children Become Beautiful Butterflies

Siv stopped to look at the sign, painted in purple and yellow with multicoloured butterflies flitting through the letters. No doubt, many butterflies would emerge but she reflected cynically that some of the children would metamorphose into slugs and poisonous snakes. Given the well-heeled look of Caterpillar Corner, it would be white-collar crime. The odd murder, some domestic abuse, but mainly financial fraud and tax avoidance.

She pressed the intercom by the front door of the detached, double-fronted 1930s house and announced herself. The reception was furnished with a pale wooden desk, hard-wearing hessian flooring and rows of bright yellow pegs with children's names underneath. Gaily coloured mobiles of sunflowers, daisies, roses and birds dangled from the ceiling. The walls were covered in children's paintings and lime green plastic arrows supported signs pointing to Kidcave, Tigger Corner, Teddy Club and Rainbow Room. It was unrelentingly cheerful amid the blur of primary colours. She could hear children chanting a jolly song. She announced that she'd come to see Jenna Seaton, the nursery school owner. The receptionist took her through to a small office that looked onto a pretty walled garden.

Siv imagined a maternal, comfortable, middle-aged woman with rolled up sleeves. Jenna Seaton came as a surprise. She was tall and big-boned but slim. Her long hair was gleaming, the colour of almond butter and gathered loosely in an antique silver clip at the base of her neck. She had shiny hazel eyes. She wore a knee-length pale blue dress with a V-neck, which subtly exposed an impressive cleavage, and matching bracelet and necklace, made of teal glass discs. Her bare, tanned legs seemed endless. This woman didn't change nappies. Like the reception area, her office was busy with children's drawings and artwork. Wide shelves were stacked with trays of craft materials, glue, ribbon and stick-on shapes.

Jenna Seaton sat with her hands clasped on her desk. Her fingers were heavy with rings. 'This is a very sad time for us all, Inspector. The news of Lauren's death was a terrible shock. I can't begin to imagine what Ade is going through.'

'I'm sorry. It's very hard when a person you know suffers a violent death.'

Jenna shivered. 'I explained it to the staff and children this morning, as best I could. We're doing a letter for all the parents, printed copies ready for this afternoon and to email. The little ones might get distressed at home.'

'Yes, I'm sure you're doing all you can.'

'Would you like some coffee, Inspector?' Jenna asked in a low voice.

'Not just yet, thanks. I'd like to ask you about Lauren. Did you see her over the weekend?'

'No. The last time I saw her was on Friday, just before lunch. I asked after Ade and she said he was fine and going to a conference on Sunday.'

'Did she tell you she was planning to swim on Monday morning?'

'She didn't mention that. We really just passed in the corridor when she was heading out to eat a sandwich. I was busy with a delivery of new equipment.'

'You own and manage the nursery?'

'That's right. We opened about six years ago and Lauren had been with us for four years. She started as an assistant but she achieved an advanced child care qualification during her third year and was promoted.'

'Was she good at her job?'

'Excellent. So committed and kind-hearted. Really, Lauren was one of the most genuine people I've ever met. Perhaps a bit indulgent with the children at times, but that was her nature and of course, they all adored her.'

'Did she have problems with anyone here, or with any of the parents?' Siv asked.

'None at all. Lauren was a sweet woman, very caring. It would have been hard to pick an argument with her because she was so gentle. Our staff members are completely gutted about her death. We're all . . . well . . . stunned.' She fingered the discs on her bracelet, rearranging them.

These intense expressions of sadness felt disingenuous. Jenna did it well but she sounded mechanical. 'Do you know a Matis Rimas, or did you ever hear Lauren mention him?'

Jenna lifted an eyebrow. 'Can you say that name again?'

'Matis Rimas. A young Lithuanian man.' She showed Jenna the passport photo.

'I don't know anyone of that name and I don't know the face. I don't think I ever heard Lauren talk about him. It's not a common name. I'd have remembered it, I should think.'

'His body was found near Lauren's.'

Jenna put a hand to her mouth. 'Oh, good heavens! It said on the news that two bodies were found. This must be some kind of maniac, killing two people like that.'

Siv nodded at the computer on the desk. 'Can you search your database with his name to see if it's associated in any way with the nursery? Do you have that kind of system?'

Jenna Seaton looked flustered. 'Well . . . yes . . . I do . . . I suppose . . . it's an unusual request.'

'A double murder is unusual,' Siv said mildly.

'Yes . . . sorry . . . I'm still trying to come to terms with what's happened. Can you spell the name?'

She typed as Siv spelled it out, and then shook her head. 'I'm sorry. His name doesn't feature in any way, regarding either the children or the staff.'

'Okay. Mr Rimas was a plasterer. Have you had any work done on the building recently?'

'No. I had the premises completely refurbished when I bought it. I had to meet lots of regulations to open it as a nursery, you see. So, apart from the occasional odd repair, nothing. Certainly no plastering.'

'Tell me about Lauren and Ade. He said that they met through you and your husband.'

Jenna looked relieved at being back on familiar territory. 'That's right, at Harvey's birthday party. Harvey met Ade quite a while ago. Harvey rides, you see — well, so do I, but it's his particular passion — and Ade deals in all things horsey. We got friendly with him and his first wife — used to have dinner together regularly, socialize, you know.'

'Ade Visser was married before? He didn't mention that.'

'Well, given the circumstances, I don't suppose Melody was on his mind.' She sounded suddenly brusque.

'Of course. So what happened to Melody?'

'She died of breast cancer about a year and a half before Ade met Lauren. It was fast — just months from diagnosis to dying. So tragic. He went through a very bad time. That's why losing Lauren like this must be like a recurring nightmare for him. That poor, poor man.' She pressed her fingers to her temples. Her nails were smooth and beautifully shaped.

'That is sad. So would you say that Ade and Lauren's marriage was happy?'

'Absolutely. They fell for each other in a big way and they were devoted. We were so happy for Ade, after what he'd been through. We had dinner with them just a couple of weeks ago and they were in good spirits. Lauren was so different to Melody, who was gregarious. Ade and Melody used to clash sometimes because they were so similar. Both had strong personalities. Lauren was a quieter, calmer person, so she was good for Ade, especially after the turmoil he'd experienced.'

'You'd say then that Lauren was your friend, as well as your employee?'

The slightest hesitation. 'Yes, of course. As I said, we socialized. We could see that Ade thought the world of her, so we did too.'

'He made it clear he didn't approve of her wild swimming.'

Jenna nodded. 'He did struggle with that. I told him a couple of times that he should relax about it and he acknowledged that he needed to try harder. But you see, I suppose that, after what happened to Melody, he was over protective of Lauren. I could understand that.'

Maybe. 'Did Lauren seem worried about anything recently?'

'Not that I know of. She didn't indicate anything to me and when we chatted, she was fine. She'd had a cold — everyone here had it, it went around like wildfire. I had to buy in extra tissues.'

'Would you agree that Ade Visser has a temper?'

Jenna leaned forward, her cleavage forming a deep furrow. 'What do you mean?'

Siv was thinking that an expanse of cleavage, impressive though it was, seemed out of place in a nursery but perhaps it encouraged business among some parents and suggested maternal comfort. 'I mean that Mr Visser can get angry fairly quickly.'

'I've never seen him like that, no. Upset and despairing, yes, as he must be right now. I'm not sure what you're getting at, Inspector.'

'Nothing in particular.' Siv looked at the garden. Half a dozen tiny children had emerged and were milling about a wooden tepee, a huge table with a sand tray and a set of interlinking plastic dinosaurs. A tall bearded man with his hair in a ponytail was overseeing the activity and succeeded in stopping a boy who was trying to push another's head in the sand tray. He squatted down beside the aggressor, reasoning with him, while the intended victim dug in the sand with a plastic trowel. Jenna would never go out there. She might get grit in her cleavage. 'What attracted you to this job?' she asked.

Some people might have found the question intrusive but Jenna seized on it. 'I wanted to start my own business, be my own boss. I'd been in marketing and needed a change. I did my research and saw that there was a demand for good-quality preschool care in Berminster. We offer a holistic, child-centred approach and prepare all our meals on the premises from locally sourced food. We complete a daily report on the little people in our care for their parents. We have an excellent reputation and a huge waiting list. Parents put their children's names down here even before the birth. Blowing my own trumpet, I know, but I've achieved a big success with this venture.'

Child-centred. Holistic. A daily report. Siv couldn't help thinking of her own rackety childhood, with a mother who sometimes forgot to fetch her from school and had never attended a parents' evening or read a school report. Meals consisted of haphazard combinations — brie and marmalade quiche or chicken curry pie for breakfast, chorizo and pickles or haggis with gherkins for lunch, rye crackers with duck terrine for dinner. It had been a relief to have three square, home-cooked meals a day at her father's house. He'd done wonders with a simple roast chicken. 'I suppose it costs a fair bit to send a child here.'

'Quality care doesn't come cheap. Why are you asking? Are you looking for a nursery place?'

'Me? No, no. Just curious. I have another photo I'd like you to look at. Do you know this child?' She took the blown-up, A4-size photo from her briefcase and laid it on the desk.

Jenna picked it up and held it to the light. 'Pretty girl. I don't know her.'

'Could she have attended the nursery at some time?'

'Possibly.' She drew the word out slowly. 'It would be best to ask the staff. They have the day-to-day contact with the children.'

'I have another copy of the photo and one of Mr Rimas. I'd like you to put them up at the reception desk and ask all parents to check them when they're here.'

'If you like, I can scan them and attach them to the email I'm sending to the parents.'

'Yes, that would be helpful. Did Lauren ever give you any indication that she'd had a child? Perhaps a child she'd had adopted, for example?'

'Lauren? No. She was so young!'

'She was twenty-five. She could easily have had a child before you or Ade met her.'

'True, I suppose, but no, there was never any mention of a child. And for heaven's sake, Ade would have known! In fact, he was saying only recently that they wanted to start a family soon. You do ask some strange questions!' Her well-groomed eyebrows were raised.

'That's true. But people's lives are often strange.' The post-mortem would tell her what she wanted to know, but she'd been interested to see Jenna Seaton's reaction. There was a smugness to the woman that riled her.

Jenna's desk phone rang. 'There's a DC Hill in reception,' she said.

'He's come to help me interview the staff. We'll speak to six each. I'll use this office, if that's okay. Can you give DC Hill another room?'

Jenna looked irritated. 'He can use the staffroom. It's small but I think it will do. Will you be long?'

'I've no idea. Your hospitality is much appreciated. And now a coffee would be appreciated too.'

She spoke briefly with Patrick, checked that he had his staff list and returned to Jenna's room. She moved her chair, drawing it to the side of the desk. While she waited, she looked at the photo of Jenna and a well-built man — Harvey the husband, presumably — kitted out in riding gear and sitting astride a pair of enormous horses. The receptionist brought in a coffee and a plate of chocolate chip biscuits. Both were delicious.

All of the six staff she saw expressed variations of how terrible Lauren's death was and how much they'd miss her. None of them had heard of Matis Rimas or recognized his photo or that of the child. None of them except the deputy manager had noticed any change in Lauren or knew of anyone she'd fallen out with. They all said they didn't know she was planning an early-morning swim on Monday, although it was common knowledge that she regularly went wild swimming. All of them described the same kind of gentle, caring woman, wonderful with the children and so on. So committed to and serious about her voluntary work with Minstergreen. None of them had a bad word to say.

The cook, Simon Rochford, was a jowly, middle-aged man with a beak of a nose and a confident manner. He brought his own coffee in with him and started talking before she had a chance to ask any questions.

'I'll tell you straight up that I had some disagreements with Lauren. I could see that she was really good with the kids but I had a couple of forthright discussions with her about the menus here. We didn't fall out but we didn't agree about the food. I plan careful, balanced meals, catering for all dietary needs and preferences. We send the parents a copy of each week's menu in advance and we have regular consultation about the food we provide. Lauren thought I should use less meat and make most of the meals plant-based. I didn't agree and Jenna backed me up. We already have two meat-free days a week and I never use red meat. Currently, only two of the children are vegetarian. Lauren was vegan and I felt she wanted to push the kitchen in that direction. I did point out to her that hers was a minority diet and her response was that one day, everyone would have to be vegan because the planet would demand it. That's as may be. I'm dealing with the here and now. She was persistent, brought me in magazines about veganism, and left them in the kitchen. Trying to convert me, I suppose. I don't care what anyone's dietary preferences are but I didn't like the feeling I was being preached to.' He sounded amused rather than annoyed at the memory.

'It wasn't a dispute then? Are we talking raised voices and bad feeling?'

'Not at all. I'll cook anything for anyone if they pay me. If Jenna told me we were cancelling meat tomorrow, it would be a challenge but I'd rise to it. She's the boss so what she says, goes. But no cook likes someone interfering in their kitchen. Jenna told her to leave off in the end, and she did.'

By this time, Siv was beginning to think that Lauren had been a bit of a preachy bore. She was finding it hard to concentrate in the stuffy room. She opened a window and rolled her neck. Second day in, and her limbs and brain felt sluggish. She took a bottle of water from her bag and drank half of it.

The last staff member, Betty Marshall, was the deputy manager. A sturdy, competent-looking woman in her fifties with a country face and short brown hair flecked with silver. In her black trousers and navy tabard with deep pockets, she looked much more like Siv's mental picture of a nursery head. She volunteered all of the same sentiments expressed by her colleagues, adding well-mannered to Lauren's stockpiled virtues. Siv was just stifling a yawn when there was a shift in Betty's tone.

'I don't know if I should say this,' Betty said hesitantly, glancing around, 'but sometimes I wondered if Lauren was cheating on her husband.'

'What makes you say that, Betty?'

'Well, as deputy manager I spend time in all the groups, help out with any problems and I supervise the staff on a day-to-day basis. I know all of them well and their patterns and habits. You know, when they like a snack, when they take their loo breaks, if they've problems at home or illness in the family. Lauren rarely used her phone at work and then all of a sudden there were days when she made or took calls or sent quick texts. Never for long, but she often looked a bit flushed afterwards. Oh, dear, I'm not sure I should have told you that but I worried about her at times.'

Siv pushed the biscuit plate towards her. This was more like it. The virtuous Lauren's halo might be slipping. Betty had come to life a bit more, and there was a hint of disapproval in her voice. 'Have a biscuit. They're amazing. You're right to tell me about your concern, Betty. When did that behaviour start?'

Betty crunched a biscuit, holding her other hand out to catch the crumbs. She had fat, homely fingers. 'I'd say last autumn. I asked Lauren if everything was okay and she said yes and that she had an increase in her commitments to Minstergreen. But you see, I volunteer with them too and I hadn't noticed we'd got that much busier, so it didn't quite seem to add up. Although Lauren was on the committee, so I suppose she had more to do.'

Siv liked the way Betty left things implied and guessed she was practised at it. 'And did the phone use continue up to this week?'

Betty made a little gesture with her hand. 'Not as much, I don't think. Or not that I noticed.'

'Did she ever say anything to give you the impression that she was seeing another person?'

'No, never. I might be wrong. It's just that my husband cheated on me before he left and he'd have that same look. A bit sly and excited at the same time. Of course,' she went on hurriedly, 'Lauren did a lot with her conservation work so it might have been perfectly innocent.'

Siv looked at Betty's round face with its hint of a double chin and her quick eyes. Her instincts would be accurate and she'd have a nose for trouble. 'What you've told me doesn't chime with your colleagues' accounts. They've all indicated that her marriage was happy.'

'I can't comment on what other people might think. But her husband worked away a lot and she might have been lonely and wanting company. Loneliness can make you vulnerable, depressed even. You can start doubting yourself.' She stopped for a moment and Siv guessed she was speaking from her own experience. 'I suppose I thought that some man might be taking advantage of that. She did say to me once that she hated being on her own in the house, especially at night. Any creak or unexpected noise alarmed her.'

'Yet she went swimming alone, so she didn't mind her own company.'

Betty nodded. 'True, but that's different. An activity occupies the mind and the senses. Wild swimming would involve planning and focus in such a way that you'd forget yourself. And as I said, I might have added two and two about the calls and made five.'

Siv had warmed to Betty. She wondered how she got on with fashion mannequin Jenna. 'Have you worked here since the nursery opened?'

'Yes, I helped get it started. First time I'd ever been in at the beginning like that, building something up from scratch. It was great to roll up my sleeves and get everything just right. And such a lovely house, airy and well designed, with wonderful equipment. Everything here is carefully planned to be child-centred, which makes the job rewarding. I'd worked in a council-run nursery before and believe me, this is heaven compared to the tatty old premises that was in. It's a pleasure to come here every day.'

'I'd guess you must be invaluable to Ms Seaton. She looks like a woman who prefers to keep her nails clean.'

There was a glint of a smile but Betty kept her expression impassive. 'Well, of course as the owner and manager, Jenna has an entirely different role. She's the money and ideas woman. I focus on the welfare of the children, and the staff too. Good example from the top down is crucial in this kind of work. I wouldn't want to blow my own trumpet but I do ensure that the nursery runs efficiently from day to day. Jenna's part-time, you see, just three days a week, so I have the complete overview and she knows I'd always alert her if anything was wrong. She appointed me because I've so much experience in nursery management and she needed that. She's often told me she doesn't know what she'd do without me.' She gave a satisfied smile. 'And I have to agree with her, I don't know what she'd do!'

She was interrupted as Jenna Seaton opened the door. 'Sorry about this, but we have an open session for parents every week and Betty runs it. People are waiting and, of course, it's particularly important in the present circumstances.'

'Okay, that's fine. I'll take the opportunity to have a word with them and show the photos.'

'Is that necessary?' Jenna's nostrils flared, horse fashion.

'Yes. Betty can introduce me.' Siv nodded at Betty, who led the way to an airy room on the other side of reception. A group of parents, all young women, were seated in a semicircle, talking excitedly. *Absolutely appalling in a town like this,* Siv heard as she walked in. She sensed a slight air of feverishness. Murder always added its quota of drama to the everyday.

Betty clapped her hands, as Siv imagined she would do with the children.

'Hello to you all. This is Inspector Drummond from Berminster CID. I know that Jenna's told you the dreadful news about Lauren. The inspector would like to have a word.' She stepped back, nodding to Siv, who rested against a table at the front of the room.

A sea of interested, expectant faces awaited. 'I'm sure you've all had a bad shock. Could you pass these photos around? I'd like to know if anyone recognizes this man or child. The man's name is Matis Rimas. He was from Lithuania and worked as a plasterer.' She handed them to the woman nearest her who looked at them and passed them on. Siv watched as they went along the line but saw no sign of recognition.

A woman in the middle of the row with pink-and-purple-dyed hair put a hand up. 'What's the little girl's name?'

'I don't know and I'd like to. Thanks for looking. Does anyone think they recognize either of these people?'

They glanced at each other. A shaking of heads and little murmurs.

'Did any of you speak to Lauren recently, or think she was worried about anything?'

There was a silence, more glances around, more head shaking. A pale woman in a linen smock shifted in her chair and cleared her throat.

'I worked with Lauren, volunteering for Minstergreen,' she said. 'I saw her last Tuesday for a committee meeting. She'd had a cold but she was getting over that. She did have a difference of opinion with our chair, Mason Granger. He wants to broaden what we do and take on more challenges but Lauren thought we should focus on a few areas and do them well. It got a bit heated but, you know, we all feel passionately about what we do.'

'What was the outcome of that discussion?' Siv asked.

'We agreed to think it over and talk about it again next time we meet.'

'And your name is?'

'Cilla. Cilla Falkner.'

'Okay, thank you. And thank you all for your time. If you think of anything, please contact me.' She handed out a wedge of cards with her number and spoke briefly again to Betty.

'This difference of opinion with Mason Granger, did you know about it?'

'No, Lauren didn't mention it. I know Mason, of course, but only in passing. He does do some grunt work but he's more of an ideas person.'

'Okay. I'll let you get on with your meeting.'

A hubbub of talk broke out behind her as she left the room. Patrick was coming back through reception, thumb flying on his phone screen, as she headed to Jenna's office. She said she'd see him at her car in a minute.

'Was that a helpful session?' Jenna asked. She was standing in the doorway to her office with one hip forward in model pose. Her legs and hair gleamed in the light. Siv thought again that she was such an unlikely owner of a nursery school.

'Possibly. Betty seems very competent.'

'She is, yes. She can be a bit bossy at times. I think her private life is lonely, or at least I have that impression although she's never said anything. Sometimes she makes comments and I'm not sure how to take them, but I do rely on her to keep everything ticking.'

'Your cook mentioned that he'd had some disagreements with Lauren about the menus here.'

Jenna rolled her eyes. 'Poor Simon. Yes, Lauren nagged him for a while about adopting a meat-free cuisine. She could be unrealistic and a bit sermonizing on the subject of meat. Simon's a good cook and the parents like the meals he presents. Certainly, we never have any complaints. In the end I asked her to drop the subject and she did.'

'Did you ever have the impression that Ade Visser suspected his wife of having an affair?'

Jenna's mouth fell open. She looked astonished. 'Absolutely not! What makes you ask that? Has someone said something?'

'I just wondered.'

'I hope you're not going to start spreading hurtful gossip. Lauren would never have betrayed Ade's trust, not in a million years. I can't believe that you'd try to damage her like that.'

'I think the damage has already been done by someone else, Ms Seaton. Thanks for the coffee and biscuits but I didn't come for a tea party. My work involves asking hard questions. That's how we catch criminals.'

Jenna pressed her lips together and retreated into her office. A small table had appeared in the corner of reception, with a photo of Lauren in the centre of a group of children. A couple of soft toys lay beside it, flanked by cards with crayoned drawings. Siv stopped to take a look at the messages. *We will miss you. We love you, Lauren. With the angels.*

She glanced through the tiny window of the staffroom.

Patrick was still mid-interview. He glanced up, saw her looking and raised a hand to indicate he'd be five minutes. He'd been hearing about what a saint Lauren had been all morning. Now he was finishing with Jerry Wilby, one of the nursery nurses. Wilby sat very straight in his chair, almost to attention. He had a quiet, easy way of speaking if nothing very interesting to add.

'Lauren was terrific, really good with the kids. I just can't imagine why anyone would take her life.' He passed a hand over his eyes. 'My God, her husband must be gutted.'

'Did you socialise with Lauren and her husband?'

'No, but he dropped her off sometimes and she was so happy when they married. I suppose you've already talked to him.'

'Of course.'

'Does he have any idea about who could have done this?'

'I can't discuss that, Mr Wilby.'

'No, I understand.' He swallowed. 'Sorry — I suppose I'm just keen to hear that you have someone in custody. Everyone here is.'

Outside, Siv was waiting, leaning against his car boot. 'Let's sit in your car and you can tell me what you made of your interviews,' she said.

Inside, the car smelled strongly of shampoo. He slung a stuffed holdall into the back, and tapped the wheel with one hand as he glanced at his notes.

'They all seemed shocked and keen to help, and they all said they liked Lauren. She got on with everyone. She didn't seem worried about anything. None of them knew Rimas or the child. None of them saw her over the weekend. They all knew she went wild swimming but didn't know she was going yesterday morning. That last one said Lauren was dedicated to her job. To be honest, she sounded a bit boring, guv.'

'I got all that with a few exceptions. The deputy manager thought she might have been having an affair and one of the parents told me she'd had a disagreement with a Mason

Granger, the chair of Minstergreen. I also heard that Lauren and the cook had some conflict over the menus.'

Patrick's eyebrows shot up. 'That all sounds more like it.'

'Could provide motives. See you back at the station.'

As she started her car, she switched her phone on and saw a text from Ali Carlin.

Steve's sent a file of stuff downloaded from Rimas's phone. He'd emailed someone about Lauren Visser.

CHAPTER TEN

After the police left, there was a strained, flat atmosphere at the nursery. Once the children had gone home, Betty made tea for the handful of colleagues who didn't have families waiting. They milled about discussing what had happened. She didn't fancy heading back to an empty house herself. A shared pot of tea would be a morale booster. Jenna was busy on the phone in her office, reassuring parents whose childminders had fetched their children. Betty brought the tray of tea to the staffroom. She'd made it good and strong and had opened a fresh packet of biscuits.

'Here,' she said, pouring. 'We need this after the day we've had. I hope none of us ever has to go through anything like that again.'

Vicky Flynn, who headed up the infants' room, had been crying. 'I still can't take it in,' she said, shivering.

Jerry Wilby handed her a mug of tea. 'Get this down you. None of us can believe what's happened.'

'D'you think it might affect the nursery?' Alison Welsh, who was just eighteen and one of the assistants, turned saucer eyes on Betty.

'How do you mean, Alison?'

'Well, parents might take their children away. You know, because of the *scandal*. Jobs might go.'

In Betty's opinion, Alison was a silly girl who needed to grow up. 'No, I don't think it will affect the nursery,' she said repressively. 'And I think you need to be careful about what you say outside of these walls. Mrs Seaton has already asked us not to discuss it.'

'You're right, Betty,' Jerry said. 'We all value our work and we don't need to add to any gossip.'

Betty nodded at him. She had a thing about men with ponytails, thought they were a daft affectation, but Jerry was being sensible.

'I didn't mean anything, I was just saying,' Alison mumbled.

'I suggest you think before you speak, Alison, and take heed of what I've told you,' Betty said sternly.

Vicky looked at them with raw eyes. 'Poor, poor Lauren. She must have been so terrified!'

They sipped their tea. No one took a biscuit. Silence descended and they each sat with their own memories of Lauren. Not all were fond and regretful.

* * *

Natasha Visser could hear her son pacing in his bedroom. She'd told him to go and have a rest but clearly, that wasn't happening. Up, down, up, down, across the creaking floorboards. Ade had been like this when Melody died and now another wife was gone. How could he absorb this new grief?

She started the dishwasher and wiped down the already spotless sink. Everything in the kitchen was so huge and gleaming. The cooker took up half a wall and looked like a flight deck with banks of lights and buttons. The fridge was a larder type with double doors. She started to walk up and down herself. It was hard to read or settle to anything while that restless movement came from above. Her thoughts flitted around like small birds. There was a window box of herbs on the ledge: basil, mint, thyme and coriander. She felt the compost and it was dry so she watered them and then went to stand at the window, looking out onto the garden.

When she'd lifted the phone and heard her son's news, she'd felt an intense weariness. Her husband, Don, had been a difficult, crabby man, prone to mood swings. Her marriage had been challenging. She'd never been frightened of her husband but she'd allowed him to get away with too much early on in the relationship. Natasha was no doormat but by the time she'd caught up with what was happening, the dynamic was set. Ade was so much like her late husband and part of her resented having to be here. While she'd mourned Don, she had also felt a huge relief at escaping his overwhelming presence. Deep down, she felt she deserved time off now, a chance to breathe, but instead she was listening to the pacing overhead and feeling the familiar tightening around her jaw. Then she immediately felt guilty. What kind of mother was she, thinking of herself when her son had been widowed again?

She'd been so pleased to hear that Ade had met someone new after the tragedy with Melody. He didn't like being alone, needed the ballast of a partner. But when she met Lauren, her heart sank. This serious, softly spoken young woman who wore her heart on her sleeve had clearly been swept up by Ade, caught in his headlights. Natasha has been certain she'd never be able to stand up to his hectoring. As time went on, Natasha had been surprised to see that Lauren had a stubborn streak and stood her ground over her swimming. She suspected that like herself, Lauren had found space to breathe in her marriage by pursuing her own interests quietly and under the radar. Ade's frequent trips away would have helped with that.

Up, down, up down. Her son's pacing brought her back to the present. Something was troubling her son and it wasn't just his wife's murder. She knew him, knew that strained look and the belligerence that masked his true feelings. He'd barely spoken to her since she arrived. Her questions about the other body and what the police had said had gone unanswered. He'd merely mumbled something about stabbing with scissors. She was struggling to understand what had happened by the river and who this dead man was.

She decided to muster the energy and cook a meal. It was almost five thirty and it would give her something to do. This kitchen with its high tech gadgets made her feel stupid, but she couldn't bear to be idle. She looked in the fridge and saw vegetables in the salad drawer. She took out mushrooms, peppers, red onion and some sliced beef to make a stir-fry. She'd rarely visited the house, so had to search for a chopping board and a knife. She opened a couple of drawers, looking for cutlery, and saw a photo of Lauren and Ade on top of flyers and bills. She picked it up, looking into Lauren's candid, rather melancholy eyes.

As she replaced it, her fingers nudged flyers for a window cleaner and organic vegetable delivery. She saw a postcard lying beneath them. It was a plain white card with a cut-out of a pair of scissors glued on and red blotches of paint glistening like blood around the open blades. She lifted it out. White smears of dried glue seeped from under the silvery blades. There was no stamp or address on the blank front, just a couple of lines printed on a square of paper pasted to the back: *You will be the one to feel the pain soon enough.* She put it back quickly, shoving the flyers back on top, and closed the drawer. She felt hot and nauseous. She didn't know what to think and her mouth was dry and bitter. She picked up a pepper and rolled it between her hands, listening to the sound of her son tramping the floor.

* * *

Ali Carlin had attended Lauren's post-mortem with Steve Wooton earlier in the day. Siv went to Rimas's and watched through the screen as Rey Anand went methodically about his business. Wooton attended that one also and had smirked at her when she said she'd be in the viewing room. *Got a weak stomach, guv?* She'd ignored him. She wasn't squeamish. She simply thought that the dead suffered enough indignity when they were cut open, and anyway, she would learn anything of importance in the follow-up for both PMs in Anand's office.

Anand was a man who didn't allow dissecting bodies to get in the way of hospitality. A jug of coffee and a jar of sweets awaited when they sat down. Siv saw Ali look longingly at the sweets but he resisted with a sigh. Wooton took a handful and stacked them in a little pyramid in front of him.

Anand pushed his glasses up on his forehead. 'We're new to each other, Inspector. The way I usually play this is I give a summary of my findings and then my colleagues ask questions. That okay for you?' He spoke courteously, with a measured look.

'That's fine with me, thanks.'

He unwrapped a chocolate and popped it into his mouth. 'Something to sweeten the sour taste of death. I'll start with Lauren Visser. She wasn't sexually assaulted and there's no evidence that she had ever given birth. No evidence of drugs or alcohol. Mace was sprayed in her face. There were residues in her eyes and lungs. She'd have been temporarily blinded. She was stabbed from the front in the neck and face with a blade. Six incisions in all, and all with the same rough edges. At a guess, a closed pair of long, sharp scissors was used, or a blade very like that. No defence wounds. Because she was wearing neoprene gloves, there was no evidence available from the fingernails. She died where she was found.' He paused for a sip of coffee.

'The mace must have been used so she couldn't defend herself,' Siv said.

Anand nodded. 'The effects would have left her disoriented and unable to see the weapon. Whoever killed her was taller than her. Could have been a male or female attacker. The cuts indicate a downward thrust, as they do on Mr Rimas. Lauren was five feet six, Rimas just half an inch taller.' He consulted his notes. 'The only other possibly significant item is saliva on her neck. I need to run checks against her own saliva.'

'So if the saliva's hers we have no forensic evidence from the body to help us trace her killer,' Wooton confirmed.

Anand nodded. 'Moving on to Mr Rimas. Judging by body temperature, I would say that he died around the same time as Mrs Visser, but it's hard to be definite about that. All I can really say is that, like Mrs Visser, he died between the time he arrived at the river and when he was found. A healthy man, no evidence of drugs in his body although a level of alcohol indicating he'd had a lot to drink the night before he died. No mace was used on him but then he'd been stabbed from behind. The same blade was used. Again, no defence wounds, which indicates he didn't see what was coming. Five incisions in total, in neck and back of head. No forensic trace from anyone else on his body.'

Ali was nursing his coffee. 'You think the same person killed them both?'

'Correct, based on the fact that the same blade was used, the direction of the blade and the force used. If the saliva found on Ms Visser isn't hers or indeed Mr Rimas's, I can at least tell you if it's from a male or female. Whether or not that's your killer is your job to determine.'

Siv took a caramel. It was the same colour as Ade Visser's hair. She had a sharp pair of the type of scissors Anand had described at home, to trim paper for folding. Not unlike the ones she'd seen on a shelf in Jenna Seaton's office. She'd get Steve Wooton to have those collected for forensic testing.

* * *

At the station, Ali took her through what the techies had found on Rimas's phone. They sat at his desk, which was scattered with crumbs, food boxes and bits of cling film.

'He'd googled Lauren and looked at the Caterpillar Corner website. She's listed as a staff member. Then he visited her Facebook page and emailed someone about what she'd written. Take a look at these emails from a couple of months back.' Ali shuffled his chair aside and angled his computer screen so that Siv could read it.

From MatiRimas26@wingmail.com
To NowakB@quickword.com
21 February. 7.30 a.m.

Hey, have you seen this lady Lauren Visser wrote to Equality and Human Rights Commission about sign at river. She put poster up at Polska. She say can't be allowed. She get crowdfunding to do legal thing. You should talk to her. They might have to take sign down.

Siv clicked the attachment and saw a photo of a poster about a crowdfunding campaign with Lauren's email and mobile number on. Then she opened another email.

From NowakB@quickword.com
To MatiRimas26@wingmail.com
22 February. 8 p.m.

Hi Matis, Thanks for this and very interesting. I'll find out more. See you for a beer sometime.

'Do we know who this Nowak is? Sounds like a Polish name.'

'We're looking and I've sent him an email asking him to contact me. Polska is the Polish social centre in town so I'm going to call them to see if they know Nowak. In the meantime, this is Lauren's Facebook page and a link to the crowdfunding site. She'd posted regularly about the issue in recent months.'

Siv looked at the Facebook post from 30 January. It had a photo of the sign at Lock Lane. It had fifty likes and a dozen shares.

Berminster Anglers should be ashamed of themselves. Got this notice up, basically bracketing Polish and eastern European people with dogs. Disgusting. Bad enough that they torture and maim fish for sport! I don't agree with anyone fishing but at least eastern European people eat the fish instead of torturing and throwing them back in! I rang the owner who put the notice up and he said it's private land, they're trespassing so he's leaving the sign up. I contacted the police who said it's not their problem and directed me to EHRC. I'm waiting for their response. In meantime, I'm crowdfunding for a legal challenge. Please see link and give generously. #riversforall

She clicked the link to the crowdfunding page.

Lock Lane Appeal.

Thank you for visiting my page.

Please give to Lauren Visser's appeal to start a legal challenge against Berminster Anglers. This challenge is to force the angling club to remove a discriminatory notice, insulting and prejudicial to Polish and eastern European people. The club has refused to remove this notice and the issue has been raised with the European Human Rights Commission. Now I need to start legal proceedings so please give generously. #riversforall

£3,300 raised by *fifty-nine supporters.*

Siv sat back. 'So there's our connection between Rimas and Lauren. Perhaps they were lovers or bound up together with fighting this cause. Ade Visser didn't mention anything about this campaign of hers. Lauren had more of a link to the river at Lock Lane than just swimming there. Alan Vine didn't mention it either.'

'Maybe Vine didn't know. He's not the owner and I'd guess from the way he talked about computers that he wouldn't even know what crowdfunding is. By the way, I think the passwords Visser gave us for Lauren's accounts were out of date. The ones we found in her drawer are different.'

'So she felt the need to hoodwink him,' Siv said.

'Maybe she was frightened of him.'

'Does your wife know your account passwords?'

'Course not. That'd be like opening someone else's letters.'

'That's my view. I suppose some couples do share them but I bet Lauren didn't know his. Anything else of interest on Rimas's phone? Any direct communication with Lauren? We need to know.'

'The techies are still looking, should be in by the end of today. There are calls to Krosna and texts about work. So far, nothing to suggest he contacted Lauren directly. There's been no activity on Lauren's phone and no sign of her rucksack.'

Ali reached for a food box and took out a wedge of Gouda cheese, which he started nibbling. 'What did Jenna Seaton have to say about the Vissers?'

'Pretty much the same as all her staff. Wonderful couple, great marriage and Lauren was a saintly character, loved by all. He'd been married before, wife died of cancer. The deputy manager wondered if Lauren had been having an affair because of sudden and frequent phone activity from last autumn to fairly recently. But without her phone . . .' She looked up at the incident board and the photo of Rimas. His death was just as important as Lauren's. She needed to make sure he didn't get side-lined just because he might have been an unintended target. 'Are any of the Rimas family coming here?'

'I had a call from my police contact in Krosna. They can't afford it. Filip Mazur identified the body earlier.'

Siv rested her elbow in a tracing of crumbs. 'Rimas saw the poster at Polska so he could have met Lauren as well, either there or at the river. If someone resented this activity of hers, it could be a motive to get rid of her. But why the child's photo? I don't see how that would connect. Anything from the door-to-door?'

He shook his head. 'Nothing helpful so far.'

Siv glanced at Patrick's empty desk. 'How's Patrick doing with the list of members?'

'Not sure. He's been out for a while. I'll check in with him.'

She brushed off her sleeve. 'Do you ever come in and find mice dancing on your desk?'

Ali grimaced. 'I know, I know, I'm a mucky pup. I'm lowering the tone of the place. Every now and again, I get a disapproving note from the cleaners. I'll do a wee tidy now.'

CHAPTER ELEVEN

Jenna Seaton swung her Porsche into the wide drive of her house and sat for a minute looking at the front gardens. What a bloody awful day. She felt completely bushed. A niggling headache was pulsing behind her eyes. Harvey wanted her to sell the business. So far, she'd resisted. Jenna had little interest in children and had never wanted any herself. When she had to interact with them — and she kept that to a minimum — she treated them with a brisk efficiency. With Caterpillar Corner, she'd spotted a lucrative market need and supplied it with her usual business expertise. She enjoyed the success she'd achieved with it and she only worked there three days a week. Having a reliable Betty made that a breeze and things usually ran like clockwork. But after a day like today, she might give serious consideration to selling it.

The gardener had visited today and the laurel hedges had been clipped, the lawn mown, the flowerbeds tidied. New hanging baskets burst with trailing geraniums, lobelia, petunias and ivy. She wound down the window to inhale the scent of the grass. Last year, when she'd remarked on how she'd always loved the smell of freshly cut grass, Lauren had told her that it was a distress signal. Grass, Lauren preached, released volatile compounds while it was trying to save itself from the injury inflicted. It was almost as if the grass was screaming. Typical of Lauren — always so serious, always complicating everything. Going on in her soft, monotonous voice about the threat to wildlife, pollution of rivers, the hazards of plastic, how we needed to recalibrate our relationship with the natural world. She could never lighten up. Even when she came to dinner it was a headache, because she was constantly checking out what was on her plate. *Can I just make sure this is non-dairy milk? That there are no eggs in this sauce? That this hasn't got cheese in?* Jenna had always found her a bit of a drag but she was good at her job. The kids all loved her because she immersed herself in their world. She was able to absorb their inane, insistent chatter and respond to it. Jenna could see that Ade liked Lauren's subdued style and found it soothing. After Melody, who'd been a vibrant laugh a minute, he'd settled for a safe option.

Jenna had decided to say nothing to the inspector about Lauren being dreary. No point in being negative about the dead. The Drummond woman was hard to read. Some of her questions had been strange. She had a sort of lean intensity, sitting there, soaking everything up like blotting paper. Like a cat, waiting patiently outside a mouse hole.

She took another deep breath of the distressed grass. It certainly wasn't going to bother Lauren any more. On a warm evening such as this one, Harvey would be out on the terrace at the back, a pitcher of martini mixed, olives and nuts in bowls. He'd retired in his mid-forties after making a small fortune in software development and she liked the relaxed, softer version of Harvey she now came home to. They'd moved the month after he retired, to this seventeenth-century manor house on the southern outskirts of town. With it came an apple orchard, an orangery and a two-acre paddock and stables where Harvey kept their horses, a black Welsh cob for him and a chestnut Arabian for her. He spent his days riding, looking after the horses, lunching at the country club and booking little treats for them — weekends at boutique hotels, meals in top-notch restaurants, city breaks. It was Vienna in two weekends' time. She couldn't wait. She'd put up with years of not seeing enough of her husband while he grafted all hours and now she had her reward.

She walked through the house, admiring the delicate freesias that the housekeeper, Mrs Dexter, had arranged on the hall table. She'd also left something savoury and minty in the warming oven. Harvey was sitting where she expected to see him, glass in hand, his panama hat tilted back on his head to protect his thinning crown. He was a big man, over six foot, and chunky but without any fat. His skin was tanned and glowing from his ride and the fresh air. She felt a ripple of pleasure as he turned and got up to kiss her.

'Good day, darling?'

'Full on. Lots to do, as you can imagine. That's why I'm a bit late. Everything okay with you?'

'Oh, yes. Let me get you a drink.'

They sat and she watched him pour. The gardens were looking so lovely, coming into May. It was her favourite month, with the cherry and apple trees heavy with blossom, everything laden with promise. She sighed with pleasure at the first cold hit of martini and told Harvey about Inspector Drummond and her questions concerning Lauren.

'I could hardly believe it when she asked me if Lauren might have had an affair. Where did that come from? Someone must have been gossiping. I hope she doesn't say anything to Ade, you know how he can flare up when he's tense. Have you spoken to him?'

'I rang this morning. He didn't say much. Said he'd had to go to the morgue. Sounded in pieces. His mum was about to arrive. I suggested lunch or a coffee but he didn't want to.'

She put a hand on his, squeezed it. He looked distracted, worried. 'Ade knows you're a good friend, and that you're there for him, that's what matters.'

He nodded. The hat threw shadows across his face. 'What else did this inspector tell you?'

Jenna was halfway down her martini. Her headache was easing. What a day it had been, answering all those questions and dealing with the staff, parents' and children's emotions. Everyone had been off-kilter and upset. After the police left, there had been a strange atmosphere. One of the mums had become hysterical, sobbing in the middle of reception, going on about what an angel Lauren had been, and alarming the kids. Then a group of mums had started that thing you saw people doing on the TV all the time now, they'd clustered around, encircling each other with arms out, heads bent together. Drama queens, trying to make it all about them. Of course that'd set their kids off, so that the place had resounded with their bawling.

She poured it all out in a rush. 'She didn't tell me much at all. Lots of questions about what I thought of Lauren, how we knew her and Ade, what she was like at work, what her and Ade's marriage was like. I suppose all the stuff they have to ask. She asked if Lauren knew the Lithuanian man found dead too, that's the other body they talked about on the news. She asked all sorts of other strange things, like whether Lauren had ever had a child. She showed me a photo of a little girl. Then she wanted to speak to all the staff so I had to organize that and make sure everything was covered, as well as getting a letter ready for parents. Oh, and she asked if Ade had a temper.'

Harvey was fiddling with his glass stem. 'Sounds as if she suspects him. What did you say?'

'He's the husband, he will be a suspect, won't he? I said no, he hasn't and that they were happily married. It was all exhausting, to be honest.'

'I can imagine, darling. I'm a bit tired too. Had a long hack and then of course thinking about how sad it is about Ade. Worrying about him.'

They fetched supper from the oven — asparagus and mint risotto — and brought it out to the terrace with a bottle of Chablis. Harvey was quiet, saying and eating little. She didn't mind the silence, although it felt a bit odd, not like their usual companionable lulls. He would be taking this hard and worrying about his friend. She was hungry and had

105

seconds of the creamy rice. By the time it was getting dark, she was yawning and struggling to keep her eyes open. Scents from the terracotta planters behind her mingled in the air. She was reminded of a holiday they'd taken in Sicily, where banks of the herb grew outside the window of their room. One of the horses whinnied in the distance.

Harvey spoke finally. 'Are you going in to work tomorrow?'

'Of course, it's one of my days. Things have to carry on as usual. There'll be fallout to deal with, anxious parents and so on. I can't leave it all to Betty. Why? Is there something you want me to do?'

He was gazing at her anxiously. But then he shook his head.

'No, that's fine. I understand.'

'You always do. You're a darling. I'm lucky to have you.'

He reached for her hand and kissed it, looking over to the orchard.

She took a long, deep bath, nodding off in the steaming water for a few seconds. When she emerged from her bathroom, Harvey had showered in his and was sitting in his dressing gown on the end of their bed, nursing a glass of whisky. It was dim in the bedroom with just one lamp on but when she went to switch on another he stopped her.

'Can you leave it as it is, darling?'

'Of course. Are you okay? You're very quiet.' She rubbed moisturiser into her hands.

He cleared his throat, took a draught of whisky. 'Actually, there's something I need to tell you.'

His voice wobbled. She'd never heard Harvey make that sound. Alarmed, she sat beside him, placing a hand on the back of his neck. He had a good neck, strong and shapely, like a Roman statue.

'What is it? Are you ill?'

'Nothing like that. This is . . . is difficult . . . but I have to tell you. I've been working up to it all day. Been feeling sick about it.'

'Harvey, what on earth is it?'

'It's about Lauren. Me and Lauren.'

'What about you and Lauren?'

'We met up a few times. Had lunch, went for walks.'

Her hand fell away. She shivered, her skin dimpling. 'What are you talking about? When was this?'

He got up, went to the decanter on the dressing table and refilled his glass. Then he stood with his back to her, looking out of the window.

'It wasn't for that long.'

She stared at his back. Her brain had felt woolly with tiredness, martinis and wine, but now it was clear. 'What are you saying? Are you telling me you were having an affair with Lauren?'

'No, not that. It wasn't an affair. I didn't sleep with her. It's hard to describe.'

'Well, do try,' she said cuttingly.

He winced, drank some whisky. 'It was . . . I suppose I'd call it a *tendresse*.'

She felt a cold anger. 'A *what*? You think you can wrap it up as something innocent with a bit of poxy French?'

'Please, don't get angry. It was a foolishness on my part.'

'A *tendresse* and a foolishness. Well, that's okay then. All fine and dandy. How long was this going on?'

'Not long. We first had lunch last September and we agreed not to see each other again in that way in February. We were both worried that someone would see us. Lauren felt bad about Ade and I didn't want to hurt you.'

She snorted away the rush of tears in her eyes. No mention of loving his wife so much he had to stop the "foolishness." No mention of guilt. 'Why this confession now?' As if she didn't know.

He leaned his head against the window. 'Because there were calls and texts. The police will find out. I asked her to delete them from her phone and I deleted my history but they have ways of searching data. I've been worrying myself sick about it ever since we heard that Lauren was dead.' He turned his head sideways, glanced over at her. 'I'm sorry.'

He seemed old suddenly, diminished. She thought she had a glimpse of how he would look at seventy. She wanted to go to him and embrace him but she sat still. She was warm now after the first chill.

'Were you in love with her?'

'I don't think so. No.'

He wasn't sure, then. She saw her reflection in the mirror: elegant, trim, mature. She looked after herself, wore discreet make up, made sure her hair and skin always looked faultless. And he'd been fooling around behind her back with dull, virtuous Lauren with her thin hair and brittle fingernails. For God's sake, the woman wore those clumpy vegan shoes! If he'd been romancing some glamorous type like one of the women at the country club, she might not have felt so shocked. 'How did it start? *Why*, Harvey? Christ's sake *why*? Were you bored with me? Are you now?'

He faced her and slumped onto the window seat. 'I don't honestly know why it started. I was at a loose end one day. I know I have a full life but there are times when the hours drag a bit. You were working. I was in town, in the bookshop, and Lauren happened to be there, looking at the nature section. She had a day off and Ade was away. There's a café on the top floor of the bookshop so we went up there and started chatting. She was different. Refreshing. I'd always thought she was a pale imitation of Melody, but then she started talking so passionately about her work with Minstergreen and I found it fascinating. Since I retired, I miss that buzz of ideas flying. I don't know . . . If you can have a crush in your forties, I suppose that's what I had. Pathetic, really, having a crush on a woman half my age.' He poured another whisky.

She would be looking in the fucking nature section. She was coming to work, knowing she was canoodling with my husband. Sneaky little bitch. I'd never have thought she had it in her. 'Sorry my business doesn't bring me home with ideas flying,' she said coldly. 'Sorry I've been so boring. No causes, no passion, just making a roaring success of my business and making lots of dosh. Oh — and giving your girlfriend a job and promotion.'

'Don't,' he said wearily. 'That's not what I meant at all. It was just . . . a silly bit of romance. Hand holding, soppy little kisses. Lauren got a bit lonely when Ade was away. She liked my company, said she felt at ease with me. We spent most of the time just chatting.'

'I'm so pleased for you both. How many times did you meet for your little flirtation?'

'I can't say. I suppose a dozen or so times.'

'Always when I was at work and Ade was away, I suppose.'

'Yes. I know why you want to make it sound tawdry but it wasn't. It was just a simple sort of attraction. A fond friendship.'

Oh God, I might start howling. She felt queasy and stupid. How could she not have known that her husband's attention was roaming elsewhere? 'Did anyone else know? Did Ade?'

'No. I don't think so.'

Lauren would be the type who might blab. Confession cleansing the soul crap. Another thought occurred to her. 'So when she sat at our dinner table a couple of weeks ago, scrutinising her beetroot and mushroom burger in case I'd hidden meat in it, you two were presumably still exchanging fond glances?'

'No. I told you, it wasn't like that anymore.'

'Didn't you feel awkward, knowing that you'd been fooling me and Ade?'

'Well . . . yes, a bit. But I knew I'd done the right thing in the end.'

'Bully for you.' She could imagine Lauren's earnest tones, turning something mean and underhand into a virtuous cause: *we have to stop seeing each other, Harvey. No matter how fond we are, we have to do the right thing, stick to our principles and keep our marriage vows.* She wished now that she'd put raw steak in the bloody burger.

'I'm so sorry, Jenna.'

'Yes. Did you kill her?'

The glass almost slipped from his hand. 'What? No! Of course I didn't kill her. I couldn't kill anyone!'

No, she thought. *I could but you wouldn't have the guts.* He looked so pathetic with his dressing gown trailing, his bald patch just visible in the dim light. She had no idea if she believed his description of an innocent romance. It sounded ridiculous enough to be true, and he was a sentimental man. But for now, what she believed didn't matter. Her headache was back, pulsing, stronger. She wanted to take a sleeping tablet and crawl into bed but she knew she'd have to take charge of this. Damage control.

'Contact Inspector Drummond first thing. You need to talk to her before she finds out, because she will and then you'll be her number one suspect. I'm not having the police coming here. You can ask to see her at the police station.'

'All right. What am I going to tell her?'

'For God's sake, Harvey! What do you think? The truth. All of it. Exactly what you've told me.' She stood. 'And, of course, anything you haven't.'

CHAPTER TWELVE

The press conference finished just after six p.m. Mortimer had let Siv carry it, opting to speak at the end, saying that he needed to reassure the public that they were putting all their efforts into finding the perpetrator of these terrible crimes. Siv was just glad that the two photos of Rimas and the child were out there. Afterwards, she'd updated Mortimer on the investigation and the main lines of enquiry. He'd told her it sounded as if she had things on track. He could have sounded more enthusiastic.

Afterwards she walked to the Talisman cinema where Cora Laffin worked. The roads were busy with office workers heading for home. She was relieved that unlike many British towns, Berminster's handsome centre hadn't been meddled with and uglified. There were streets of Georgian buildings and Victorian terraces lined with mature trees. As she approached the centre, narrow cobbled lanes with Tudor houses and tiny fishermen's cottages sloped down, opening out onto the harbour. Berminster was a large town and had once been a thriving seaport, important for trading from Roman Britain to medieval times. It was now five miles from the English Channel. A combination of storms, silt and human intervention had changed the course of the

River Bere, and the town had been an inland harbour since the thirteenth century. It still maintained a steady fishing industry.

The Talisman was an independent cinema, housed in a pale stone building on the east side of the small harbour, facing out to the placid water. It had started life as a dance hall in the nineteen twenties, then transformed into a major chain cinema, then to a bingo hall, until it had been turned into a cinema again. When Siv was a teenager, it had been on its last legs as an Odeon, with grubby, broken seats, litter-strewn aisles and a pervasive smell of junk food and ripe socks. She remembered going there with friends to see *Titanic*, choking back tears as the doomed hero slid beneath the icy waves. Now she walked into a white-painted foyer with oak flooring, a scattering of sofas and chairs, an aroma of fresh coffee and film information written on chalkboards. There were two small screens, the Monroe and the Poitier, and a café on the ground floor. Siv waited in the café for Cora Laffin, sipping a coffee and studying posters for a Kathleen Turner season. A young man in a striped apron emerged from behind the counter with an ice-cream tray supported by a neck strap.

'Choc ice, strawberry, vanilla or mango tub?'

'Not just now, thanks.'

He headed off towards the auditorium upstairs, humming the theme from the *Godfather*.

Cora Laffin came in at a run. She was so slight she made underweight Siv feel like a giant. Her outstretched hand was small and soft. She had china blue eyes and strawberry blonde hair flowing down to her waist, completing the doll-like look. She wore denim dungarees, and the voice from her little frame was surprisingly deep and robust, although Siv could detect the nasal tones of recent tears and she looked pale.

'Is it okay if we talk in the Monroe? There is an office but we're having windows and flooring repaired and it's a right mess in there. The Monroe's having some seats replaced so that's empty tonight, but it's okay to sit in.'

'That'll be fine, as long as it's private.'

Cora led the way to the empty auditorium. It contained around fifty seats with several rows missing a few, like a mouth with gaps in the teeth. There were tall, framed photos of Marilyn on the walls, including the one from *Some Like it Hot*, where she was poured into a figure hugging dress, and the iconic image of her standing over a grating with her skirt blowing upwards.

They sat in the front row, Cora with her ankles crossed. She wore round toed biker boots with straps. They looked like the ones in the cruelty-free catalogue that Siv had seen in the Vissers' house. Music and voices reverberated faintly from the Poitier upstairs.

'I'm very sorry about your friend,' Siv said.

Cora nodded. Her eyes were red and watery. 'Thank you. I still can't believe what's happened. I should have been there. If I'd gone swimming with her, she might still be alive.'

'Do you mean you'd planned to swim with Lauren on Monday morning?'

'We talked about it the night before, but there's been so much to do here I had to give the river a miss. I've got staff off sick so everything's down to me, and there's all this work going on that I have to keep on top of. I haven't even got time to grieve for my best friend.'

'I'm sorry. That's hard.'

'Yeah. I hadn't seen enough of her recently and I feel so bad about that. The last couple of months have been frantic workwise and I was away for most of March, climbing and bouldering in Cornwall. We hadn't had a good catch-up for ages.'

'Did Lauren often swim at Lock Lane?'

'Not often. Just now and again. It's clean around there so it's a pleasant spot, but she didn't go more frequently because of the anglers. I swam there with her once.'

'Did you see anyone else around when you were there?' Siv asked.

'No. It was just me and Lauren.'

'How long would Lauren swim for?'

'About an hour, usually.'

Siv showed Cora the photos of Rimas and the little girl. 'Have you seen this man or child at Lock Lane or anywhere else?'

The lights were on but they were low. Cora took her time. 'No, I don't know them. Who are they?'

'The young man's body was found near Lauren's. His name is Matis Rimas. He was Lithuanian. Did Lauren ever talk about him?'

'No. That doesn't mean she didn't know him but if she was friends with him, I think she'd have mentioned the name.'

'Okay. I don't know who the girl is, that's why I was asking.'

Cora looked as if she was about to say something else but then just sighed.

'We haven't found Lauren's orange rucksack,' Siv said. 'Where would she leave it when she went to Lock Lane?'

'We usually left our bags somewhere accessible but safe. Best place is hanging on a tree branch — hidden but dry. I think at Lock Lane we left them in one of the trees just up from the river.' She closed her eyes, pain written on her face.

Siv waited a couple of beats then said quietly, 'Tell me about your contact with Lauren the night before she died.'

Cora hugged her knees. 'We didn't talk for long. She was cooking quinoa with grilled vegetables. Ade doesn't like quinoa. She was vegan, and meals with Ade could be difficult. He's keen on hearty meals and likes his meat, so she was indulging herself in simple food while he was away. She asked me if I wanted to come round and share it but I was too bushed. Too tired that night and too busy the next morning. I let her down.' A few tears slipped down her cheeks and she brushed them away. 'Sorry.'

'Take it slowly. What time did you speak to Lauren?'

'About seven thirty. I was driving home when she rang me.'

'How did she seem?'

'Like her usual self. A bit tired, maybe. She did say there were some things she wanted to talk about but she'd wait until we could meet up. She asked me how I was, told me not to work too hard, talked about things the kids had done at the nursery. She felt so much responsibility for the kids, as well as helping nature recover from all the damage we inflict. We both volunteer with Minstergreen and we discussed a bird count at Harfield Country Park planned for next weekend. And she talked about Ade. He was hoping to get a deal from some conference he was at in London, and she was concerned about it going well for him.'

'Do you know Ade well?'

'I know him but not that well. Lauren and I usually met up on our own.'

'The way you say that makes me think you don't care for him much.'

Cora was a hair fiddler, touching and smoothing the length of it. She reached behind and pulled it over her right shoulder. 'I'm not Ade's biggest fan. Lauren loved him so I didn't say anything, but I thought he was possessive, over-bearing. The few times I met him, I could tell he didn't like me. I thought he was jealous because Lauren and I had been friends since school. He's one of those men who like to manage everyone, or try to. And he didn't like it that I'd introduced Lauren to wild swimming and she'd become a self-confessed addict. She'd get restless if she hadn't been for a swim. I could see that Ade didn't want her going off and enjoying herself without him, although he dressed it up as being concerned for her safety.'

'Did Lauren ever say she was unhappy in her marriage?'

Cora straightened her back, her eyes wide. 'Do you think Ade killed her?'

'Do you?'

'Haven't a clue. I suppose he could have . . . I don't know.'

'So — back to my question. Did Lauren ever talk about being unhappy with her husband?'

'She was a very loyal person, so no, she didn't. She wanted so much to get married, you know. She'd had a lonely sort of childhood, just her and her mum, and then her mum died when she was twenty-one. She was still living at home with her mum up to then. She wanted the security of marriage and lots of kids. Sounds old-fashioned, but then she was kind of old-fashioned — in the nicest way. Dependable, and so kind. Her mum was completely devoted to Lauren. She never worked after Lauren was born, and was always cleaning, polishing and baking. Whenever I went round there, the place was sparkling but really homely, too. We had big homemade pies and delicious cakes.'

Siv thought how amazing it would have been to have swapped her own flaky, flighty Mutsi for Lauren's stay-at-home mum. 'Ade Visser told me that Lauren never knew who her father was.'

'That's right. Her mum would never talk about it and Lauren learned not to ask. I reckoned Ade was a bit of a father figure — you know, eight years older than her and telling her what she should do, disapproving of things he didn't like. When they met, I think she took him for some sort of tragic hero because his first wife had died of cancer. She cut him a lot of slack when he fretted about her swimming, because she said he'd been traumatized by that bereavement and it made him over protective. I don't know, I thought he just liked pontificating.'

'But Lauren didn't always go along with what Ade said — concerning the wild swimming, for example.'

Cora laughed knowingly. 'The swimming, and other things.'

'Such as?'

'Lauren mentioned it on the phone the other night. She was running a campaign about a horrible notice at Lock Lane. You must have seen it when you found her — it's really offensive about people from eastern Europe.'

'I've seen it. Anglers are supposed to have permits to fish there, but I agree that's not the way to try to enforce the club's regulations.'

'Right. Well, Lauren phoned your lot, the police, about it but she was told it was a civil, not a criminal matter. She'd found out how much it would cost to make a legal challenge and she started a crowdfunding page. Lauren was quiet and unassuming but once she'd got the bit between her teeth about something she was determined, and she had a strong sense of justice. Ade didn't know about it. He'd have disapproved. He didn't mind her volunteering for conservation work because that's acceptable — fashionable even — and Minstergreen gets good publicity. But he's dead against things like crowdfunding, says it's a form of begging and if people want money for something, they should earn it. He's a snob, really. Likes to spend his time with the horsey, county set, goes on hacks with his mate Harvey Seaton, who thinks of himself as a kind of squire. He wouldn't have liked the idea that Lauren was involved with immigrants who fish in rivers that should be free to all of us. No one should own parts of rivers, it's ridiculous.'

Siv took a breath. 'Was Lauren friendly with any of the eastern European anglers who fish at Lock Lane? It sounds as if she might have discussed this campaign with them.'

'She didn't mention any but she might have come across them at the Polska centre in West Street. She'd put a poster up there, informing about her campaign over the sign. Ade wouldn't have liked that. He'd have reckoned she was slumming it.' She adjusted her hair, pulling it to her left shoulder. A few strands detached and floated through the air.

'Seems a bit odd. Contradictory. I mean, Lauren objected to fishing but she was defending the right to fish at Lock Lane.'

'It was a matter of principle, wasn't it? Lauren might not have agreed with the fishing but she'd oppose discrimination where she saw it.'

'And maybe she thought that if she caused enough problems for the angling club, the owner would cut his losses and close it down?'

117

Cora nodded. 'We agreed that would be the best outcome — if Nick Shelton decided to stop the fishing there.'

So, a controlling man and a wife who was a lover of causes and who'd decided to do things behind his back. 'Was Lauren worried that Ade would lose his temper if he knew about the crowdfunding?'

Cora screwed up her mouth. 'It wasn't so much that. She wasn't frightened of him. But he'd be kind of heavy and scathing. Censorious. She just preferred to manoeuvre around him.'

'And that wasn't too hard because he worked away a lot.'

'Right.'

Cora would know about the passwords. 'This manoeuvring included changing her account passwords without telling Ade.'

Cora gave a watery smile. 'She changed her passwords and pin numbers regularly without telling him.'

Her voice had become muffled. She was pulling her hair across her mouth and pressing a strand to her lips. Siv felt a sudden, familiar sense of detachment drifting through her and moved her shoulders up and down, refocusing. 'So, Ade wasn't in the habit of checking up on her.'

'Suppose not. I think as long as Ade *thought* he had the upper hand, he was happy. And he just didn't know Lauren as well as he thought. He made assumptions about her. He mistook her mildness for meekness. They're not the same thing. Lauren had strong convictions about cruelty to animals, the environment, justice and fairness.'

'Did you ever think that Lauren might have been seeing someone else?'

'What — you mean like an affair?'

'Yes.'

'No way! Not Lauren. She valued her marriage, and she was just this deeply reliable, loyal person.'

The soundtrack surged upstairs. The seats were comfy and Siv had sunk down into hers. She blinked, suddenly tired. After months of comparative inactivity, her brain was struggling to process so much information. It seemed unreal, sitting in an empty cinema, surrounded by Marilyn's curves and smiles and discussing how a murdered woman had outwitted her oppressive husband. Or thought she had. Maybe she'd made her own wrong assumptions. She sat up straighter, thinking of the possibility of an affair.

'Did Lauren have any other close friends — maybe in Minstergreen?'

'Not really. She never had much of a social circle. She spent most of her time with her mum until she died and then she met Ade soon after. When she wasn't with Ade, we hung out. She liked a woman she worked with at the nursery — Betty someone.'

'Betty Marshall is the deputy manager,' Siv said.

'That's right. She reckoned Betty was really committed to the job and the kids. And Betty does regular litter-picking, so they shared a concern for the environment. But I don't think they socialized as such.'

'Going back to Minstergreen — were you at a committee meeting last Tuesday?'

'No. I'm not on the committee, don't have time. Lauren was.'

'Did she talk to you about a difference of opinion she was having with Mason Granger, the chair?'

'Oh yeah, she did mention that. I got the impression she didn't have a lot of time for Mason. She thought he was self-important. He likes giving interviews to radio and TV. Lauren reckoned he was empire building. He wanted to expand what we're doing, but it would be hard to be effective without way more volunteers than we have now. What was it she said? That's right, she laughed and said Mason had ambitions to be a minor celebrity.'

According to Dr Anand, Cora was too small to have stabbed her friend and Rimas but the question had to be asked. 'Where were you on Monday morning between six and eight thirty a.m.?'

'Wow! That's a bit below the belt!'

119

'I know.'

'Yeah. It's okay, I get it. I was in bed with my boyfriend. We got up at seven thirty, had breakfast. We both left for work at half eight.' She yanked her sleeve down and dabbed at her eyes. 'Lauren was my friend for so long, I don't know what I'll do without her. I can't believe she won't phone me any minute.'

Siv felt a ripple of sadness. She sat silently with the grieving woman for a couple of minutes, struggling with her own memories, then thanked her and left the cinema.

The light outside was strong and vibrant, striking her eyes and making them water. The sun was pure gold on the harbour and the bunting that had been installed for the May festival. She crossed to the harbour and stood at the railing, looking out across the fishing boats to the ivy-covered Martello Tower. Gulls swooped and screamed across the sandbanks and shingle. A cruiser puttered through the harbour mouth and manoeuvred into a berth. She thought about mild but not meek Lauren. Cora had given her more of a sense of the dead woman, still a gentle sort but with grit and always ready to push her causes. She still had no understanding of where Matis Rimas fitted in. It seemed unlikely that he and Lauren had been having an affair. Surely she'd have mentioned it to Cora. She kept thinking that Lauren had been the primary victim, because of that photo, but what if she was wrong? Best not to get hung up on it. She found the phone number for Filip Mazur and rang it. When he replied, she could hear a baby crying. He said grumpily that it was okay for her to call by.

* * *

Mrs Mazur, the mother, was dishing up the evening meal when she arrived and insisted that Siv sit with them and have some.

'Eat! Eat! You so thin! You want a beer?'

She said no to beer but accepted a meat pie sitting on top of a potato pancake. The small living and kitchen area was very warm and Mrs Mazur drew a thin, rose-patterned curtain against the sun. Mazur dwarfed the small table, Siv's knees almost touching his huge thighs. He wore a paint-stained T-shirt, jeans and a beanie hat. His mother saw Siv looking and clicked her tongue.

'I tell him to shower and change before dinner but he don't listen.'

'Leave it be. I have the boss telling me what to do all day. I washed my face and hands,' Mazur muttered. His manner was rough and ready but his tone to his mother was affectionate. He held the baby in one arm while he cut his pie. The large infant sucked on a cherry-coloured dummy and stared intensely at its father. It was going to take after him in size.

'I'm very sorry about your friend Matis.' It was hard to talk through the dense, tasty food. The pie was packed with lamb mince and thick, herby gravy.

'Any idea who killed him yet?' Mazur asked.

'Not yet. I understand that you got to know him last year?'

'That's right. We were working together for a while, got chatting. Nice bloke, interesting, although his head was full of nonsense about aliens and space ships. His English wasn't great so I helped him with a few things he was struggling with, about tax and insurance. He didn't like where he was living and we had a room, so he moved here.'

'We've been able to take a look at his phone. He did know or know of Lauren Visser, the woman who was murdered around the same time. She was campaigning about a sign at the river, warning eastern European anglers to stay away. Did Matis mention that to you?'

Mazur swallowed and lifted his bottle of beer, downing half of it. His face was sun-reddened, his eyes bloodshot. 'He said something about a sign once. He laughed about it, said it didn't stop him fishing where he wanted. That was it.'

'He didn't mention a campaign to go to court about the sign?'

Mazur shook his head. 'You mean something legal?'

'That's right.'

'No. He just caught fish and brought them home.'

'Lovely carp,' Mrs Mazur agreed. She watched Siv keenly as she ate.

The baby waved an arm and grumbled. Mazur rubbed his stubbly chin gently over its head and it smiled.

'Can I just show you these photos again?' She showed Mazur and his mother the photos of Lauren and the little girl. 'Are you sure you've never seen them?' They both shook their heads. 'Did Matis ever mention someone called Nowak?'

Mazur shovelled the remainder of his pie into his mouth and his mother immediately popped another one on to his plate. 'Don't think so. I don't know a Nowak. Common Polish name. Could be someone he worked with. Lots of Polish guys in building.'

Mrs Mazur had finished eating and leaned over to take the baby from her son. 'Maybe he meet this Nowak at Polska centre. He go there sometimes. He like Polish beer. You have another pancake?'

'No, thank you. This is delicious. Had Matis argued with anyone?'

Mazur shook his head. 'The other police guy asked me that. I don't know anyone he fell out with. He was too busy working and fishing to argue. Sending money home. No time to have rows.' His phone rang, vibrating on the table beside him. He glanced at the screen, said it was a call about work and went into the hallway.

The baby spat its dummy out. Mrs Mazur dipped her little finger into the gravy on her plate and nudged it into the baby's mouth. It sucked greedily.

'Boy or girl?' Siv asked.

'A boy. Filip. Like his papa.' She repeated the move with the gravy, glanced at the hallway and looked at Siv. The grooves around her eyes and mouth were scored deep. 'You okay, you and the other policeman. Polite. We here four years now. Much better life. Good work. Happy. Settled.

Filip and his wife work. I look after baby. Don't want no trouble.'

'I understand, Mrs Mazur. I'm doing my job. I know you'll understand that.'

She nodded. Mazur came back in and fetched another beer from the fridge.

'You talk to Matis's family?' Mrs Mazur asked.

'My sergeant, Ali Carlin, talked to police in Krosna who spoke to his family. Unfortunately they can't afford to come here.'

'Sad,' Mrs Mazur said, with a faraway look. 'Sad to come so far from home and someone kill you. So far from people who love you. Your own people.'

'It is very sad. All I can say is that we will find who did this.'

Mrs Mazur gave Siv what seemed to her an unbelieving, pitying look, then she asked if Siv would like *pyraga* cake. 'Is good, much fruit. I make today.'

'No thanks. I'd better be going. Thanks for the food.'

Mrs Mazur saw her to the door. 'Is okay if I use things in Matis's fridge? Nice carp in there. Pity to waste.'

A pragmatic attitude to death. Mrs Mazur would be a woman used to making the most of what she had. 'Yes, that's fine. His catch might as well get cooked.'

A decent dinner. The young man hadn't left much of a legacy. She walked to her car, full of pie and potato. What Ed would have called a good plate of artery fur.

At home, she donned Ed's sweatshirt and sat for a while out on the decking, drinking akvavit and watching the sun vanish. The goats were bleating. Corran had explained that they got talkative at this time of the evening. They sounded uncannily like children screaming. She wondered again about that little girl and what she had to do with Lauren Visser. The killer had left them a message, or had wanted to signify a meaning to her death.

She cradled her glass and checked herself out. Today had been Okay-ish. No shaking legs at least. She was tired but

123

too wired to sleep. Nothing about these murders made sense so far. Cloud was building and the night was growing cool. Bats flitted to and from the trees by the river.

Her phone rang, breaking the silence. 'Hi, Patrick.'

'Guv, I had a call from Nick Shelton, the guy who owns the land at Lock Lane. We'd left him a follow-up message about the victims. He met Lauren Visser once, at his home. Said she contacted him about the notice and he agreed to talk to her.'

'When was this?'

'Beginning of February. They couldn't come to any agreement. He said he hadn't heard from her since.'

'Okay, thanks for that. I'll get Ali to talk to him tomorrow. Can you put that little girl's photo out on Twitter, ask if anyone recognizes her?'

'Will do. Night, guv.'

Inside, she lit the wood burner. She went into the bedroom and took the paper shape she was working on from the wardrobe. She'd designed the piece herself, a multifaceted geometric fold of wall art in grey and blue. She was shaping it from Korean duo paper, based on twenty-two icosahedrons. It would take weeks.

She poured another glass of spirits and sat on the floor in the living room. She'd started paper-folding when she was eight, around the time Mutsi had introduced the third "uncle" since she'd divorced her husband. She'd seen a presenter fold on a kids' TV show and it caught her imagination. She was good at maths, which was the basis of her understanding and proficiency. She'd started with newspaper, making a simple "fortune teller," the creased envelope many children make with predictions about love or future careers written under the folds: *you'll be a doctor, you'll have four children, you'll marry an astronaut.* She grasped it easily and became hooked, progressing quickly through simple birds, boats and flowers to more complex structures — sea monsters, human shapes and complicated stars. Her father sent her boxes of quality Japanese paper and books of patterns for birthdays and Christmases.

By the time she was a teenager, her room was full of paper creations and her friends would ask her to make them one or she let them watch her as she constructed an intricate form from a single sheet of paper. Folding was her port in a storm. The rules and constraints of the art helped lend some order to her chaotic childhood. She'd turned to it when her mother dumped her and Rikka in Berminster and hoofed it back to Finland to marry the equivalent of a baronet. She'd constructed a globe on a stand after her father died and in the months after Ed's death, she made an intricate series of trees.

A couple of years ago, her folding had taken off in a new direction. A friend who knew someone who ran a music shop off Regent Street had told him about Siv's talent and shown him photos of her work. He'd commissioned her to make a group of paper musicians for a window display. She'd provided a tiny orchestra of violinist, saxophonist, drummer, horn player, clarinettist and flautist in ivory and forest green. Other orders followed as news of her work spread. This geometric piece was the first commission she'd accepted since Ed's death and was destined for a Danish furniture shop in Highgate.

She worked on, head bent, absorbed. When she was folding, she tuned out reality. Time became suspended. And while she focused on the paper and her fingers, she processed thoughts and feelings, trying to make sense of the world, as well as the geometry of paper.

CHAPTER THIRTEEN

Errol Todd still hadn't been in touch. Siv left instructions for Ali to contact the local police in Valencia and set out just after eight to see Visser.

Despite his truculence, she felt some sympathy for him. Two bereavements, two wives dead. *How would you deal with that avalanche of agony?* That morning, she'd woken from a brightly lit dream of Ed. The content had eluded her but he'd been smiling at her, that crinkled, daft smile of his. Yet again, she'd awakened only to feel the ache of knowing that now he existed only in her mind. It had taken her some time to ground herself in the here and now and gear up to the day ahead.

Something about Visser niggled at her. Was it the desire to control, the anger he carried in him? She needed to give him the post-mortem results and she wanted to apply some pressure.

When she rang the bell at Spring Gardens, a woman answered. Silver hair in a bob, flat but pleasant features. Inquiring but strained smile.

She showed her badge. 'I'm DI Siv Drummond, from Berminster CID. I'd like to speak to Mr Visser.'

'I'm Natasha Visser, Ade's mother. Do come in. I think he's still in the bathroom.'

She followed the woman into the living room. It was spotless, the window thrown open. Mrs Visser smoothed the top of a chair before sitting in it. She wore a pale green skirt and striped green-and-white shirt with a pretty sky blue scarf at her neck.

'Do you have any news about Lauren, Inspector? Anything about how she was killed, or the person who did it? We're desperate to know.'

'We haven't yet found the person who murdered Lauren. The post-mortem is complete. I can confirm that Lauren was stabbed, most likely with scissors, as was the young man who was found with her.'

Mrs Visser blanched visibly and clutched at her elbows. 'Scissors! That's so horrible.'

'Yes. I'm very sorry.'

'I've never heard of anyone being murdered with a pair of scissors,' Mrs Visser said faintly.

'Any blade can be a weapon, I'm afraid. Were you close to your daughter-in-law?' She seemed an approachable woman and having lost her own mother, Lauren might have confided in Ade's.

Mrs Visser seemed to make an effort to focus. 'Well . . . ahm . . . I was very fond of Lauren and I think she felt the same way. I didn't see them that often, just a couple of times a year. Young people have their own busy lives and I live in Hampshire, so I'm not exactly on the doorstep.'

'Had you heard from Lauren recently?'

'No, not recently. We last spoke on the phone a while ago. She told me about her latest work with Minstergreen, clearing scrub and checking moss species in some woods. She was devoted to that.'

'I wondered if her husband ever felt a bit left out, what with her wild swimming and conservation work, as well as her job at the nursery.' She asked mildly enough but could see that Natasha Visser understood the question's subtext. Her reply was intelligent.

'It was a modern marriage, Inspector. Two partners working. Ade fully supported Lauren's conservation work and he thought the world of her. He's very busy with his own business. I'm sure they had their own modus vivendi. I didn't poke my nose into their marriage. I've seen parents do that and it never goes well. Would you like tea or coffee?'

'Coffee would be great, thanks.'

'I'll let Ade know you're here.' She moved towards the door and then stopped and turned, clasping her hands before her like a supplicant. 'He's hardly slept and he looks terrible. I hope you'll forgive him if he's a bit scratchy. Not his usual self. This has been a terrible blow for him.'

Siv didn't respond to the plea. 'I do need to speak to him. It's necessary for our enquiries.'

Visser appeared within minutes, arriving at the same time as his mother brought in the coffee. A miasma of peppery scent surrounded him. He was wearing clean jeans and a T-shirt with soft moccasins on his bare feet. His face looked raw and haggard. Mrs Visser placed a tray on the low table, pressed her son's shoulder and left the room.

'How can I help you, Inspector?' he said. 'Have you got the post-mortem results?' His manner was placatory. Siv wondered if his mother had warned him not to be antsy.

'The post-mortem has been completed. Lauren was stabbed and the weapon was probably a pair of scissors. There were no defence wounds, but she'd been sprayed in the eyes with mace and would have been temporarily blinded. There had been no sexual activity.'

'Thank God for that at least.' He placed his hands over his eyes for a moment. 'Mace. So she wouldn't have had any chance to fight back.'

'No.'

'What a coward. What a shit way to come at someone. She must have been terrified.' He picked up his coffee mug, spilling some on the coaster. 'I've been wondering about that photo you showed me of the child. Where exactly did you find it?'

'It was left with Lauren's body,' she said.

'That's so sick. Who'd associate a child with murder? It must be a real sicko who did this. Maybe there's some weird person working at the nursery who hated Lauren. Is that a theory you're working on?'

'We consider all motives, but so far there's no suggestion that anyone connected to the nursery bore any animosity towards Lauren.'

'I reckon that must be it. That's why the photo was left. It's something to do with the child, surely.' He ground his teeth. Tension hummed around him.

Siv clicked her pen to focus him. 'Were you aware that Lauren was running a crowdfunding campaign about a discriminatory sign at Lock Lane?'

His head went back in surprise, his eyes widening. 'No, I wasn't.' He sighed. 'When did that start?'

'Recently. She wanted to fund a legal challenge against it, as it's prejudicial against people from eastern Europe. The issue clearly concerned her greatly, yet she didn't tell you about it.'

He shook his head wearily. 'She'd have known I wouldn't approve of crowdfunding. It attracts cranks and weirdos. People who like to hover around causes.'

'So there might have been other significant things going on in her life that she didn't share with you.'

'I suppose,' he said. 'How would I know?'

'When we spoke before, you didn't mention that you'd been married previously.'

'Didn't I?'

'No. I wondered why.'

'I have no idea. I can't remember everything. I suppose it's the shock. It's hard to know what you're saying when the woman you loved is lying dead, hacked to pieces.'

'I understand.' *More than I can express.*

'Do you? I feel as if I'm going mad. Nothing makes sense. A Lithuanian guy and a child's photo . . . and now you're telling me Lauren was involved in stuff I knew nothing about. I'm like a broken record, I keep thinking if only I hadn't been away Sunday night—'

'Have you heard from Errol Todd?'

'No. But then I wouldn't expect to.'

'You do understand that's it's important that we speak to him. Verify your whereabouts on Sunday night.'

His expression was rigid. 'What are you implying?'

'I'm not implying anything.'

There was a silence. Then he erupted, shot from his chair and stood with his hands gripping his head. His voice trembled. 'My wife has been murdered. She's been cut up like a piece of meat. I've had to look at her poor mangled body and you dare to come here to my home talking about verification! Why aren't you out there catching whoever did this to Lauren and that young man? You should have everyone at that bloody nursery under the microscope.'

Siv watched him. She'd seen this kind of performance from people under pressure before. Usually when caught out in a lie. But the man seemed genuinely tortured. 'Mr Visser, please calm yourself. I'm sure you know how police enquiries work. We have to question and check everyone and everything. That's our job.' *And believe nobody* she could have added, but for now she didn't want to needle him too much. Just enough. 'Is there anything else you want to tell me about Sunday night?'

He gave her a disgusted look but sat back down. He closed his eyes and took a breath, struggling for control. 'I'm not stupid, and I am able to remember what I was doing the night before my wife was murdered. That's all I can tell you.'

'You told me that you cycled home from the railway station and got here at about half nine on Monday morning. Is that right?'

'Yes.'

'Did you meet anyone you knew on the train, or chat to anyone?'

'No and no. I don't chat on trains. I get my laptop out and work.'

'Did anyone see you arrive back?'

'I've no idea. Not that I know of, and I didn't speak to anyone. The people living around here are professionals, out at work. There's no old biddies peeping from behind net curtains. You've had officers on this street asking around so you'll know that. Seems like time-wasting to me. I thought the police used more sophisticated techniques these days, but maybe you're the bargain basement team, the remedial class.'

He couldn't maintain the mannerly act for long. What had Lauren's life with this man really been like? He drummed his fists on his knees and then was on his feet again, thudding up the stairs. His mother appeared, with a quick glance upwards. She'd applied some lipstick, her mouth now pale apricot. Siv thought it was the wrong colour, it aged her.

'Is Ade all right?'

'He's finding some of my questions very upsetting. This is a difficult time for him. It would help if he could try to stay calm.'

His mother bit down on her lip. 'Yes, I know. I'll speak to him.'

'Mrs Visser, can you take a look at these photos for me? The man is the other person who was murdered, and the child's photo was left at the scene. Have you ever seen either of them before?'

'I'm sorry, no.'

The photos trembled in her hands. There was a peculiar tautness to her too. It was hard to read. The atmosphere in the room radiated with it. When she'd pressed her son's shoulder, Siv couldn't tell if it was a gesture of comfort or caution.

* * *

131

Natasha watched the inspector drive away. She took the tray back to the kitchen, rinsed the mugs and then dried them thoroughly with a tea towel bearing the slogan *Plant Flowers. Save Butterflies*. She stood and listened to the washing machine humming. There was no noise from upstairs but she could feel her son's torment weighing on the house. Something was terribly wrong. She longed to be back in her own small, peaceful home, living her daily routines. Unexciting, but she was past the age where she wanted excitement. She didn't want to deal with other people's problems. This one had fallen on her from the sky. She should be taking her puppy for a morning walk and dropping into the café for a latte and cinnamon bun. Instead, she was in a strange kitchen, listening to her son's restlessness upstairs. Now and again, she went up and crept along the hall to stand outside his room but she didn't dare go in. It reminded her of when he was a baby and she'd check that he was still breathing. The extraordinary relief every time she confirmed that he was. But now she couldn't get near him.

She crossed to the drawer and looked again at the garish picture of bloodied scissors. She kept being drawn back to it. Now that she knew how Lauren had died, she couldn't have felt more frightened if she'd found real scissors covered in blood. Who would think of making such a macabre image? A couple of times she'd opened her mouth to tell Ade about them but then stopped. He looked so forbidding and remote. She should tell Siv Drummond, the woman who looked as preoccupied as she felt.

But if she did tell, what might it mean for her son?

* * *

The team was meeting. Steve Wooton had a dental emergency so had sent an email update. Siv was glad he wasn't there with his sarky, clever-clogs manner. She'd brought coffees in from a café she'd found around the corner, a tiny Italian place called Gusto with steamed-up windows, tables

132

crammed in and trays full of wonderful pastries. Not wishing to torment Ali, she'd eaten a *bombolone*, a baked doughnut filled with vanilla cream, while standing at the counter. She watched as the chef took savoury tarts from an oven and placed another batch of focaccia in to cook. She breathed in the aromas of oil, rosemary and vanilla. It was a relief to take pleasure in food again, to feel her mouth water. She bought a bowl of mixed nuts for the office to go with the coffees.

Ali was tucking into cashews while Patrick added chocolate powder to his coffee with a shaker he'd fetched from his desk. He saw Siv watching.

'Basically, I like to turn my hot drinks into a pudding. Gives me energy.'

'Whatever keeps you ticking along,' she said. Staff who worked in offices always tried to domesticate them, mark out their territory. It was why hot-desking messed with people's psyches. 'Let's just recap what we know about Lauren and Matis's movements on Monday morning. I think we can assume that she was murdered first. She went swimming around six a.m. Her friend Cora said she usually swam for about an hour and would have left her rucksack hanging from one of the trees near where she was found. So let's say she exited the river around seven a.m. and walked up to the trees to get her rucksack. Someone was waiting, sprayed mace in her face and then stabbed her from the front and placed the child's photo on her body. Matis left home about quarter to, so would have reached the river soon after seven a.m. He'd had time to catch one fish before he went up to the trees for some reason.'

'Probably needed to have a pee,' Patrick said. He was tapping his knee with a pen. He was always tapping, either with his fingers on desk tops or with pens on mugs, plates, computer screens or parts of his body. It was distracting.

'Possibly. I propose that when he arrived at the river around seven ten, he blocked the escape route of our killer, who couldn't get back to their car without attracting his attention. So the killer waited among the trees and either called to him or, as Patrick says, Matis went up to the trees. Then he was attacked from behind. Neither of them had defence wounds. The only connection we have so far is that Matis Rimas had emailed someone called Nowak about Lauren's campaign against the sign at Lock Lane. Ade Visser says he knows nothing about that and doesn't recognize Rimas or the child. To date, no one we've interviewed has recognized the child.'

'Rimas had few social networks, maybe because he'd not been here for long, so there's little to look at with him. What's eating Visser, apart from the obvious?' Ali asked.

'Don't know. There's something there. But I wouldn't bet money that he killed his wife, despite his unconfirmed alibi. His grief seems genuine to me. That dazed look.' She'd seen it on her own face in the mirror every day. *This can't be real. Somebody tell me it's a nightmare.* 'What did the Valencia police say?'

'They're sending someone to the Buddhist place today, so hopefully we should hear something soon,' Ali told her.

'There's no forensics pointing to Visser for now,' Patrick said. He'd been rubbing his eyes. Now and again he shook himself like a dog after being in water.

'I know. There's no forensics pointing to anyone. No unidentified blood or DNA. The saliva on Lauren was her own. Our killer was careful. What have you got for us, Patrick?'

'Okey-cokey. We've looked at traffic cameras and no result. Problem is, the nearest one to those residential lanes around the river is on the middle of Minster Road. We couldn't spot Rimas's Honda or any other car within a mile of Lock Lane or Hardwater Road. It's possible to drive there and avoid cameras if you plan the route. Slightly more positive news — we know that Nick Shelton met Lauren Visser. We've spoken to all the members of the angling club now. I stayed up till almost midnight working on it with Lisa.'

His eyes were certainly crusty and tired. 'Thank you both,' Siv said. 'So that's why you look done in. You can tweet something to that effect, Patrick, saying you were burning the candle at both ends to contact witnesses. I'm sure you'll make it sound snappier.'

He nodded, preening slightly. 'Apart from Shelton, all members of the club except one said *no, niet, nada, rien* to ever seeing Lauren, Rimas or a little girl. The one remaining, a Rob Price, said that he'd seen Lauren once at the river. He called her the weirdo mermaid. Said she "waxed on" about the sign, saying that it was offensive and she was going to do something about it.'

'When was this?' Siv asked.

'Beginning of February,' he said. 'Price said he'd told her it was nothing to do with him and she should talk to Nick Shelton. He also told her that she was disturbing his fishing and she responded that torturing fish was a crime and that one day there'd be a law against it. He reckoned she was a bit of a nut. Price didn't kill her, by the way. He'd just got back yesterday from a holiday in Tenerife and I checked with the hotel there.'

'Thanks for that. We badly need something on this child in the photo. What about the door-to-door?'

Lisa checked her notes. 'That's still ongoing. Nothing to report. No one saw Lauren on Sunday evening or Monday morning. Haven't found anyone who was at home on Monday morning at the time Visser says he got back. I'm still waiting to hear from the railway station about their CCTV, but the manager told me that there isn't any at the side gate where some people exit from the London train. And guess where the exit for the bike lockup is . . . so I think we're stuffed on that.'

Siv went through Wooton's email. 'Shoe prints from the river up to the trees match with Rimas's trainers and Lauren's neoprene boots. Rimas's prints have been found by the Honda and on the path from there to the river. There's some other footprints along that path and to and from the trees. Whoever made them was wearing shoe covers made of carpet material, which suggests it was our killer, but we

135

have nothing identifiable. So, definitely a carefully planned operation. Nothing back yet on car tyres. Anything else from Lauren's Facebook?'

Ali shook his head. 'Nothing that looks significant. I'm ploughing through. Lots of stuff about Minstergreen. They seem to do shed loads of counting — birds, badgers, foxes. Even flies! How do you count flies, I wonder? Every now and again, she promotes a "Hit Squad," which is a small group that targets a particular area, like cleaning a bit of the riverbank, litter-picking or helping with coppicing. Cora Laffin does lots of likes and supportive comments but no one else pops up regularly. No sign of anyone called Nowak. He hasn't replied to me yet and although they know of him at Polska, they don't have a contact number or address. He's not on the electoral register. I'm still searching. The techies finished with Rimas's phone. No direct contact from him to Lauren, so if she was playing away, it doesn't look as if it was with him.'

Siv sipped coffee. 'A parent at the nursery and Cora Laffin told me that Lauren was on the committee of Minstergreen and had a difference of opinion with the chair, a Mason Granger, about their strategy. According to Cora, Lauren would never have had an affair, but the deputy at the nursery wasn't so sure. I've been thinking that the calls and texts Lauren was getting might have been to do with the campaign about the sign at Lock Lane. The timing coincides. The disappearance of her phone is frustrating. So far, people, we have no motive. So we keep digging. I want you to check out all the nursery staff, find out if any of them have any previous convictions or history of dispute with Lauren and establish where they were Monday morning. Lauren and Simon Rochford, the cook, had some disagreements over the menus. Not a big issue according to him and Jenna Seaton, but look into him. Ditto all the members of Minstergreen. I'll talk to Mason Granger. Someone needs to check Cora Laffin's alibi with her boyfriend. Ali, can you speak to Nick Shelton, find out what Lauren's contact with him was and his whereabouts on Monday?'

Siv's phone rang. 'Guv, there's a Harvey Seaton in reception, asking to speak to you. Shall I get him to make an appointment?'

Never turn down someone associated with a victim who volunteers information. 'No, that's okay. I'll be down shortly.'

'Right, I'll tell him to wait. One more thing, guv — a couple of members of the public have phoned in with tips, including a Mr Wilby who says he worked with Lauren Visser. Seems everyone at the nursery is in bits and he thought it might help if he could reassure his colleagues with any news. He also mentioned something about Ms Visser saying a man had been watching her when she was swimming.'

'Okay, thanks.' She turned to the others. 'One of Lauren's colleagues just phoned, asking about progress. Said he's remembered something that might help. Patrick, get his details from the desk sergeant and talk to him. In the meantime, Harvey Seaton, husband of the nursery owner and Visser's pal, is here to talk to me.'

'Maybe he's going to confess and I can tweet we've solved the case in just days,' Patrick said, punching the air and grinning.

Siv really wanted to tell him to grow up but held her tongue — for now.

CHAPTER FOURTEEN

Harvey Seaton sat in a small, bare room containing a plastic table in the centre, with beakers and bottles of water and four orange moulded chairs. The air was stale and there was one large, desiccated ficus in a corner. His fingers itched to winnow the dead leaves and water it. He checked his tie knot and swallowed. He'd dressed in black jeans, ice white shirt and linen jacket. Casual smart, but not looking as if he was trying too hard. He needed this inspector to believe him. He'd never spoken to a police officer before. A look of respectability would surely help. Not that it had helped with Jenna. Since he'd told her about Lauren, she'd hardly looked at him and had barely spoken. She'd asked him to sleep in a spare bedroom. He hated that. They'd never slept apart before, never been a couple who had cool silences.

Leaving the house, he'd said, 'I'm going to the police station. I'll give them the full picture.'

She'd grimaced. 'What do you want, a medal?'

He hadn't said what he wanted to say to her, that if she'd sold her business, as he'd asked her to, the foolishness with Lauren wouldn't have happened. He would have been out with her, not wasting a morning in town on his own. He liked retirement but still hadn't quite got to grips with it.

In his forties, he'd encountered the problem faced by many people twenty years older: what to do all day? His uncertainty reminded him of the empty, anticlimactic feeling after exams. There'd been a big buzz and some hubris about being able to retire comparatively young. He liked the fact that people envied him. He might feel like the local squire when he was out riding but once he climbed down from his horse, his feet were back on the ground in more ways than one. It was hard sometimes to listen to Jenna talking animatedly about work and watch her racing around, trying to fit everything in. The pace of their lives was mismatched these days. Truth was, he'd been feeling passed over and ignored. Life was duller, and Jenna didn't notice.

Then he'd bumped into Lauren and poured all this out to her in the bookshop café. She'd listened carefully with her habitual grave expression, giving him her full attention. The next time he saw her, on a walk through Halse woods, she'd asked why he couldn't start another business. There was nothing to stop him and if retirement hadn't brought contentment, it was an obvious solution. That was when he'd kissed her. Not so much because he fancied her but because she'd taken him seriously and understood his feelings, made him feel as if he could be a player again. That was a potent mix. He didn't tell her that it was impossible because Jenna would hate the idea. Jenna liked her husband's role of leisurely lord of the manor, owner of pasture and orchard, man of status at the country club. She'd see it as losing face if he started work again.

The woman who walked through the door with a folder and notepad reminded him a bit of Lauren. She had the same concentrated way of holding herself. But Lauren's eyes had been gentle, a bit dreamy. This one held you bang in her sights.

'I understand you want to talk to me, Mr Seaton.' Her voice was quiet, controlled. 'I'll probably make some notes as we speak.'

'How is your enquiry going? Ade said you hadn't found Lauren's rucksack or her phone.' He'd been so relieved when he'd heard that.

She looked at him with a little smile. 'I think you came to give me information, not the other way around.'

'Yes, of course. I want to talk to you about Lauren. Poor Lauren. Her death is terribly shocking.'

'You have my sincere condolences. I believe she and her husband were good friends of you and your wife.'

'That's right. Good friends.' He couldn't think of how to go on now that she'd referred to both Ade and Lauren as friends. He was going to sound like such a sneaky bastard and it hadn't been like that all. He waited for her to say something but she just sat looking at him. 'This is a bit difficult. A bit embarrassing, really.' He gave her the engaging grin that usually brought one in return, especially from women, but she remained impassive.

'I see. Take your time, Mr Seaton.'

He shifted in his chair. 'Ahm . . . I'm retired, you see. I was lucky enough to make a lot of money from my business. I say lucky but I worked long hours, sweated the deals. So I retired early. I keep horses.' He thought that if she knew the context, she might understand what had happened.

'And do your horses keep you busy?'

He felt ambushed, as if she'd got straight to the nub of his dissatisfaction. 'Up to a point. But at times, I have felt a bit aimless. A bit lonely, I suppose. I ahm . . . you see, I had a friendship with Lauren and I thought I should let you know.'

She nodded. 'Yes, you've already said that you were friendly with the Vissers.'

Was she deliberately making this harder? He couldn't tell. 'I mean . . . what I mean is that I saw Lauren on my own a few times. We met up, just the two of us.' He felt a flush on his neck, ran a finger around inside his collar.

'Go on.'

'It was nothing much, you see. I don't mean that to sound as if I wasn't fond of Lauren because I was. But it was a fond friendship. Tender. Walks and talks. A kiss now and again. As I said, nothing much.' Oh God, it was all coming out wrong and she was so deadpan.

'Have some water,' she said, unscrewing a bottle and pouring him some. 'Tell me about your tender friendship. When did it start?'

'Last September. We bumped into each other in the bookshop by St Mark's church. We just started chatting, went to the café. I felt as if I'd never really got to know Lauren. I'd never seen her on her own before. When she was around Ade, she was quiet, a bit low key, let him lead and do most of the talking. She told me a lot about her conservation work. She lit up in a way I'd never seen. Her face was sort of lively. We saw each other now and again after that. Really, we spent our time talking.'

'Where did you meet?'

'At Halse woods, various places by the river. Once, when the weather was bad, in a pub out at Little Godstone. We met when Ade was away working and of course, Jenna was at work. I know this sounds awful, as if we were going behind their backs and it was cheating but believe me, it was the most innocent kind of cheating.'

'"An innocent kind of cheating." That's an interesting viewpoint.' Her level, slightly amused tone did make it sound as if she was turning the idea over rather than being sarcastic. 'Would your spouses have thought of it like that?'

He drank some water, longing for a chill martini. 'No, I don't suppose they would.'

'So, I presume they didn't know.'

'No. Jenna does now. I told her yesterday. I explained that I had a "tendresse" with Lauren. She knows I'm here to tell you.'

'Did you and Lauren have sex?'

'Absolutely not. We kissed and held hands. That was the sum of it.'

'Did you want to, though?'

This took him aback. 'That's a very personal question.'

'Is it? Well, murder is very personal, you see.'

He thought of lying but the sceptical look on her face stopped him. 'I was tempted, yes. But I knew Lauren didn't want that. She made it clear. She liked being with me because I talked to her about her swimming and her conservation work and I didn't disapprove. Ade wasn't always very understanding about her interests. And Lauren appreciated that I've found it hard to adjust to retirement. I have plenty of things to do, but they don't always seem that important. It's hard when no one depends on you for decisions any more, or throws ideas and proposals at you. It was just so good to be able to express all that. We were close and warm. I'd kiss her lips and her hand. Truly, Inspector, that was all. A great fondness. On the days I saw Lauren, I went home feeling younger and invigorated, like I was walking on air. I suppose you think I sound like a dirty old man because I was older than her.'

She poured some water for herself and stretched her legs out, her tone more conversational. 'I'm not sure I take that view and anyway, it doesn't matter what I think. You were both adults. People cheat on each other all the time. I'm only interested if it leads to crime. Did it? Did you kill her and a man called Matis Rimas?'

He pressed his hands together on the table. 'No! I would never have harmed a hair on Lauren's head, and I've never heard of this Rimas. You must believe me.' He couldn't tell what she believed. She made a note, underlined what she'd written.

'In all these heart-to-hearts, did Lauren tell you about her campaign to take legal action regarding the sign at Lock Lane?'

'She did, yes. She talked about that quite a bit. She was keeping it from Ade, so I think she was relieved to be able to discuss it. I gave her a contribution towards her crowd-funding for it.'

'Did Lauren mention any members of the Polish community who were helping her?'

'She might have. I'm sorry, I really can't remember. We'd be talking non-stop. She said so much about so many subjects it's hard to recall everything she said.'

Siv tapped her pen against her chin. She took two photos from the folder and placed them in front of him. 'Have you ever seen this man or this child?'

'No, never.'

'And had you seen or talked to Lauren recently, after your special friendship ended?'

'No — or at least, not just the two of us. We stopped seeing each other in February. It was difficult, but the decision was mutual. We both began to feel bad about our spouses and we were worried that someone might see us. We agreed we'd have to settle for the friendship we had before, as married couples.'

'Sounds very neat. Affairs don't usually end so tidily. Someone is usually left feeling angry, sad, upset.'

'I told you,' he said. 'It wasn't an affair.'

'So you say. I suppose it depends on your definition. And you're sure Ade Visser didn't know?'

'He's shown no sign of knowing. We've been out riding together recently and he was fine. Will he have to know now? Will you tell him?'

'It depends. How has your wife taken it?'

He hesitated. 'She's angry. I tried to explain the nature of the friendship, that it was affectionate.'

'Where were you between six a.m. and eight thirty a.m. on Monday the twenty-ninth?'

This was the question he'd been dreading. Jenna had already been at pains to point out that he was up shit creek where Monday was concerned. She'd turned that into an accusation as well, as if he should have known he'd need an alibi. He felt the sweat collecting down his back. 'I went out for an early hack. I left around six forty and got home around eight fifteen. Jenna had gone to work by the time I got back.'

'Did anyone see you on your hack? Did you talk to anyone?'

'No, I'm afraid not. I was on bridleways. I saw no one else. That's one of the pleasures of riding, the peace and solitude. Just being part of the natural world. That was why I could empathise so closely with Lauren's love of wild swimming, because that's what she craved. But the route I took went nowhere near the river and I was always miles away from Lock Lane.'

'So, just to be clear, when did you last speak to Lauren?'

'A couple of weeks ago. She and Ade came for dinner. I can check the date. I was relieved because it was our first gathering as couples since we'd agreed to stop meeting, and it was okay. No real awkwardness.'

'Did you know she was going swimming at Lock Lane on Monday morning?'

'No. How would I? I hadn't seen her since that weekend dinner.' Which was true but not the truth.

She sat up, suddenly brisk. 'Given what you've told me, it's unfortunate that you were out alone during the time Lauren was murdered and no one can vouch for your where-abouts. I need you to provide an accurate route of exactly where you were riding on Monday morning, from start to finish. I'll get someone to bring you a printed map of the area. Try to remember if anyone saw you. Also, I would like you to allow us to keep your phone for a while, so that your history can be checked. You'll get a receipt.'

He stared at her for a moment, on the verge of object-ing, and then handed it over. He waited, finishing the water, while a constable brought a receipt and another came in with a map of the town and surrounding area. She handed him a red pen and watched while he traced out his route. He felt like a schoolboy in detention being observed by teacher. He couldn't think straight and his hand was shaking. This was turning into a nightmare.

He could only hope that some of his lies stayed buried.

* * *

Siv went to find Patrick. He was on his phone, deep in con-versation, tapping his temple with a pen. She heard him men-tion medication and prescriptions. He rang off as soon as he saw her, looking flustered. She relayed the interview with Seaton and gave him a copy of the route that he'd drawn.

Then she asked him to drive the roads around it and ask if anyone had seen Seaton riding on Monday morning.

'Try farmhouses, places where people might have been outside and seen him. And around Halse woods.'

'I'm onto it, guv.'

'And by the way, Patrick, I'm all for positive publicity about what we do on Twitter and the like, but the investigation comes first and that's what we focus on. We're not here to feed social media.'

'Sure, guv.'

He nodded, frowning slightly. She wasn't sure that he'd got the message. He was making another call as she left to step outside for a breath of air in a small courtyard at the back of the station. The station was an old listed building, previously part of the corn market. It had rained again during the day and the courtyard was pleasantly cool. Ali was also outside, sitting on a bench, smoking and checking his phone. He looked up and smiled broadly at her. Siv went over and joined him. She liked his solid presence.

Ali held his cigarette away to one side. 'How'd it go with Seaton?'

'What a smarmy piece of work he is! As soon as I walked into the room I realized that I knew his dad, Colin Seaton. Harvey's a dead ringer for him. Colin was head teacher at my school for a couple of years. He had a reputation for getting just a little too close to the prettiest girls.' Colin Seaton was a handsome, well-built man and some of the girls had liked his proximity, played up to him. Not Rikka. She'd jabbed him in the chest with a ruler after he'd breathed in her face. Harvey had his father's boyish grin and thinning hair. 'According to Seaton, he had a "fond" friendship with Lauren. They swapped confidences about things their spouses didn't understand. No sex, just lovely chats and walks. A bit of fondling. All dressed up by him as a "tendresse." Judging by the shame on his face when I mentioned his wife, I'd say she made him come to see me.'

Ali pulled a face. 'He sounds a complete eejit. Did Visser know Lauren was playing away?'

'There's the question. Seaton says not. He says he's only just told his wife, but either Ade or Jenna might have found out somehow before now, which would give us motive. Seaton reckons they saw each other from last September to February and then stopped. Mutual guilt.'

Ali blew a smoke ring. 'And Seaton might have a motive himself. What if he's lying about the mutuality of the friend-ship ending? What if Lauren didn't want it to end and was being clingy? Maybe she was threatening to blab.'

She watched Ali's smoke ring curl away and fade. 'He says he was out on his own for a hack when she was murdered, and he didn't see anyone. I've asked Patrick to check out his route. So now we have another possible explanation for the calls and texts Lauren was getting at work, plus both the husband and the fond friend with no alibis for the time around her death, but no forensics to place either at the scene.'

In spite of herself, Siv had to admit she felt some satis-faction that Lauren wasn't as wonderful as painted and was certainly capable of a deception her best friend wouldn't have believed. The only person who she felt any real sympathy for was young Matis Rimas, who'd only been caught up in it because he'd got in the way of someone's plan.

She looked down, her attention caught by Ali's right foot. She tried not to smile. 'Your sock's on inside out.'

'And there's me, calling Seaton an eejit.' Ali slipped off his shoe, turned the sock the right way so that the diamond pattern on the ankle showed. 'I've been out to the Cherryfield estate,' he said, 'talked to Rimas's workmates. They knew about his fishing but not when or where he went. They also know a Bartel Nowak. He's a roofer and did some work at the site recently. He's moved on now but the head guy gave me his phone number. And Nowak is also an angler, so we've a few more jigsaw pieces.'

'I'll speak to Nowak and I'll try to clarify what time Jenna Seaton arrived at work on Monday morning.' She felt a fuzziness descend and leaned forward, closing her eyes.

'You okay, guv?'

She nodded and looked up at Ali. His warm eyes were a comfort. 'I'm fine. Just a bit tired.'

He nodded. 'Maybe get an early night? There's not much a good night's kip can't fix.'

'Are you always so annoyingly optimistic?' She grinned.

'Aye, that's me all right, blessed with a hopeful nature. Glass half full, but then I know I'm lucky.' He lowered his voice although there was no one else around. 'Just to say, guv, hope you don't mind . . . I know about what happened, that you were widowed. Mortimer told me but only me. He thought I should know.'

'It's okay. I understand.' Funny, she didn't think of herself as a widow. It seemed to be a word for a much older woman, someone who'd had a long life and memories of years with her husband.

'Just wanted to say. You know. Must be tough at times. Anyways . . . I wondered if you'd like to come for a drink on the bank holiday weekend. My wife Polly's a chef at Nutmeg, a place in town, and some of us meet up there once a month. You can have a meal if you want or just a wee drink, it's up to you.'

Siv fought a surge of anxiety. These days, any questions about how she spent her weekends, or offers of hospitality had this effect. If anyone asked her about her personal life, she might open her mouth and no words would come out. Ali was smiling at her expectantly.

'I'm not sure. I might be away then. Can I let you know?'

'Course, no worries. Just a chance to chill out with each other. A bit of craic.'

She watched Ali head over to his desk. Then she put her head back and stared at the light-drenched sky. More than anything right now, she wanted it to be dark and she wanted to be on her own, the rest of humanity securely outside her locked door.

CHAPTER FIFTEEN

The evening litter pick at Minster Beach was in full swing. The afternoon had been showery but now the sky was brighter, although it might not last. Betty Marshall rubbed her aching back and looked out at the funnel shaped clouds. Far out at sea there was a charcoal block of sky. A dramatic sky, one for an artist to capture. Terry, her runaway husband, had tried his hand at watercolours and although she'd offered words of encouragement, she never thought he had much talent. She wished now that she'd told him straight out that he'd been rubbish.

She moved on over the shingle, allowing her mind to wander. She'd always loved this beach. Her parents had brought her here as a child, and she and Terry had come regularly with Erica. She'd loved the sea, loved running in and out of the waves on her plump little legs, shrieking and dancing on the shingle. She hadn't minded the sharpness under her bare feet at all and would kick off the beach shoes Betty had bought her. Helping to maintain the beach, keeping it clean, was a way of honouring her memory.

A pair of abandoned shoes sat at the top of Betty's orange garbage bag, in a nest of crisp packets, condoms, cans, sandwich and chocolate wrappers and fag ends. Maybe someone had decided to walk out into the waves. She'd felt like doing that in the months after Terry buggered off. But then she'd found reasons to carry on, and had seized control. She'd found resources in herself that she'd never been aware of. She'd got the job at Caterpillar Corner, which meant better money and working conditions. Life had gradually taken shape and meaning again, especially since she'd met Julia.

She smiled involuntarily at the thought of Julia. It was lovely to establish such a good friendship in her fifties. They were both on their own and that was a relief. It was hard being friendly with women who had husbands. They were only available when the husbands were otherwise occupied, and then they would take calls from their spouses when they met up with her. When she was with Julia, she had her full attention. Julia was such a powerhouse, so energetic, always making plans. She was on lots of committees, sang in a choir and went to aerobics twice a week. One of that invisible army of women who formed the backbone of organizations and got things done, Julia claimed that the more she did the more she found time for. When Betty was with her, life felt full of possibilities. They met for a meal in town every week, their regular treat. She was going to help Julia run the stall by the harbour on bank holiday Saturday, and on Sunday they were having lunch and a wander around the May festival.

Betty's thoughts shifted to Inspector Drummond. She'd liked her voice. Even and reassuring. The inspector had phoned her earlier and Betty had told her that Jenna had been at the nursery when she'd arrived there at eight on Monday. Jenna opened up at seven Monday to Wednesday, she'd added, and she did the same on Thursday and Friday. She knew why the inspector was asking but she was surprised that Jenna was a suspect. For the life of her, she couldn't work out why the inspector would think Jenna had anything to do with it. She made sure she got on with her boss because she loved her job and the environment at the nursery, but the woman had no real interest in the kids. She was all about the money and her own reputation. She could talk the talk though, you had to give her that.

Betty looked down at her task. Despite the constant tramp of feet, the shingle beach supported lots of flowering plants: red valerian, slender thistle, silver ragwort and tree mallow. Betty knew them all because last year she, Lauren and a couple of others had surveyed them. Her favourite was the sea heath, with its delicate pink flowers. Lauren had loved starry clover. People dropped their rubbish in among the plants, or the wind whipped it into them. She used her grabber now to extricate a clump of wet wipes from a viper's bugloss.

It was strange not having Lauren here this evening, but a relief as well. One of the keenest members of the group, Lauren was always so intense. She always wanted everything done by the book, which was okay but not when it made you feel you could have achieved more by other means. These people were volunteers, after all, giving up their time. They'd roll their eyes at each other behind her back. Betty always ached for hours after a litter pick, but Lauren would be urging them on to do a bit longer. Funny how she seemed so mild, yet more than once Betty had thought she was quite selfish.

During these times on the beach, she'd listened to Lauren speak about her marriage. Heads bent together as they harvested litter, the young woman had confided in her. Her husband had turned out not to be the man she thought or hoped he was. She felt suffocated by him. Betty knew all about husbands who didn't pass muster but she never passed comment. Besides, Lauren never asked Betty how she was — her job was to listen. She'd probably known Lauren better than anyone, but what she knew stayed with her. She wasn't going to break that trust now, not even to Inspector Drummond. Of course, she had told Julia a few things, but she knew Julia would never tell a soul. And she'd only told the inspector that she'd suspected an affair because she was sure she recognized the signs and she disapproved strongly of such behaviour. If Lauren was that dissatisfied in her marriage, she should have left, not started carrying on with someone else — who was probably someone else's husband. She'd been on the receiving end of that sort of nonsense, and knew it led to nothing but pain and misery.

Some of the others had suggested having a drink in the beach café when they finished their work, to raise a glass to Lauren. They were a bit subdued tonight, each working in their own separate silence. Betty'd said she couldn't. She didn't want to sit with other people and think about Lauren and the way the world was now without her.

She carried on with her work, her anorak rustling in the sharp breeze. Grab and lift, grab and lift. She liked the monotony of it, found it soothing. After a while, she paused to take a breather and stood watching a couple of dogs racing along. If she narrowed her eyes, she could still see Erica running at the water's edge on that August day, spray glistening around her. The next morning she'd complained of not feeling well and in the blink of an eye, they'd been sitting in front of a consultant. *Brain tumour. Inoperable.* She died days before her fourth birthday.

She should be walking on the beach with an adult daughter now, someone who provided company, shared memories. Maybe there'd be grandchildren. All those things other people took for granted.

A man stood at the shoreline, gazing out to sea. The tide had started to come in and tiny waves licked at his shoes. She recognized Ade Visser. He'd dropped Lauren off at work a couple of times. He rocked on his heels and from the way his shoulders moved, she thought he was crying.

* * *

Ali's trousers were too tight. The waistband cut into him as he drove. No matter what he did, and despite Polly's valiant efforts , the weight still crept up. He'd lost his waist a while ago and he wasn't sure he'd ever find it again. He tried not to look in the mirror when he stepped from the shower. The nurse at the diabetic clinic would give him the evil eye, he thought. Smoking was supposed to be an appetite depressant, the only possible benefit from polluting your lungs. It wasn't with him.

Minster View was the unoriginal name of the bed and breakfast run by Nick Shelton. Several miles from the sea, it didn't have a view of anything much except fields, but the sign outside said No Vacancies, even this early in the season. It looked smart and welcoming. Shelton was outside cleaning the windows when he arrived. He put down his extending brush and wiped his hands on a flannel hanging from his belt, as Ali crossed the drive towards him.

'My wife says we should get a window cleaner but they never do a thorough job. If you want something done properly, do it yourself.'

Ali nodded, although he'd never been tempted to clean a window. He followed Shelton inside. The hall smelled of fresh paint. Shelton took him through to the small private flat at the rear of the building. He was a small, mild-mannered man with a jaunty roll to his walk. He took off his peak cap and offered coffee and biscuits, which Ali refused — *one small victory*. They sat in a living room furnished with chintzy, striped fabrics.

'I want to talk to you about Lauren Visser, the woman who was murdered on Monday morning. Her body was found by the river at Lock Lane, on your land.'

'Dreadful, that. One of your colleagues and Alan Vine told me but of course at that point, I didn't know the dead woman's name. As soon as I heard it on DC Hill's message, I rang and spoke to him. I gather the young chap Alan found was Lithuanian.'

Shelton had such prominent front teeth that Ali reckoned he'd be able to eat an apple through a tennis racquet. 'That's right. But staying with Lauren Visser for now — did you know her?'

'I wouldn't say I knew her. As I told DC Hill, I met her once.' He picked up an iPad. 'I got this stuff ready because I knew you'd be asking me about her.'

'When did you meet her?'

'To be strictly accurate, and I always do like to be if I can, I spoke to her on the phone first. She rang me in January. I can't remember the exact date. I'd no idea who she was. She was haranguing me about a notice I'd put up at Lock Lane.'

'Yes, we've seen the notice.'

'Okay. Well, she was going on about it, saying it was racist and I should take it down. I told her that I had every right to put the notice up as it's private land. The members of the angling club pay for the privilege of fishing there and I maintain the land and the river along there. I was fed up with those Polish and other guys just rocking up whenever they felt like it, leaving fag ends and rubbish around. Alan keeps a general eye on it and he told me he'd had to warn some of them away and they just laughed at him. Called him "Grandad," that sort of stuff. So I told Lauren Visser that they were trespassing. She wouldn't listen, said she was going to take "further steps." I told my son about it so he looked at her Facebook page and said she was campaigning about it and crowdfunding. So I rang her at the beginning of February and offered to meet her. I was hoping that if I talked to her in person, I could get her to see my point of view.' He pulled a face. 'Fat chance.'

'It didn't go well?'

He switched his iPad on. 'You could say that. She came here on 15 February, a Saturday morning. My wife was here and we gave her herb tea and biscuits — although she said no to the biscuits because she was a vegan. My wife's done mediation courses so she knows all about trying to find ways of sorting out disputes. I went through it all with Lauren again. That land has been in my family for almost a hundred years and we look after it, maintain it. I told her I have every right to stop trespassers and thieves. In fact, I've considered taking out an injunction against them. She wouldn't listen. She was insistent. Solemn young woman, never cracked a smile. After she'd gone, my wife said she needed to get out more. The real cheek of it was when I asked her how she knew about the sign and she said, cool as a cucumber, that she went swimming there! I pointed out to her that that was technically trespassing too, so then we had a sermon about rivers and the countryside belonging to everyone. Bollocks — pardon my French. Anyway, we got nowhere and she went off saying she was going to go through legal channels. I just told her to bring it on. I've heard nothing more from her since. I thought she'd decided to drop it or more likely, hadn't raised enough money.'

Ali took out the two photos. 'Have you ever seen this man or this little girl?'

A shake of the head. 'I don't know them.'

'The man is the one whose body was found near Lauren Visser's. His name was Matis Rimas. It looked as if he'd been fishing that morning.'

'Well, I'm sorry. I've no idea why he was murdered or who could have done it.'

'Where were you on Monday morning between 6 a.m. and 8.30 a.m.?'

'My wife and I got up at a quarter past six. I was here, helping her with breakfasts and the other morning routines, between then and eight o'clock. We're full and it was busy. I drove my son to school at Bere High just after eight and came back here. Am I a suspect?' He said it in such an upbeat way that he clearly didn't consider it a possibility.

'We have to ask people these questions. Did any of your members know about Lauren Visser's campaign?'

He sucked in air through his teeth. 'I don't think so. I didn't tell any of them and no one mentioned it. I didn't want any of the members getting rattled and as I said, I was hoping it would all die down. Sorry, that's probably not the best turn of phrase in the circumstances.'

Ali closed his notebook. 'That sign you've put up is unlawful and offensive, Mr Shelton. I'd advise you to remove it and replace it with one that simply states "No Trespassing."'

Shelton scowled. 'Everyone is so busy taking offence these days, banging on about other people's rights. Well, what about my rights? I'm only sticking up for myself because you lot can't be bothered.'

Ali headed back to the station. One of the anglers could have got wind of Lauren's campaign and, fed up with her and trespassers, killed her and Rimas. But that didn't explain the child, and he agreed with the guv that the child had to be significant.

As he came into town, he saw that more green-and-white bunting was being put up for the May festival, "Minster Magic," which ran through the month. There'd be music, book readings, folk dancing, steel bands, street theatre, cooking demonstrations, a small traditional funfair. It kicked off over the bank holiday weekend with a concert at the harbour and an open-air food market. And the forecast was good, unlike last year when there'd been downpours. Ali loved the general air of festivity and the way people came out of themselves.

Thinking of that, he hoped the guv would come to the restaurant for the get-together. She looked as if she could do with a good night out. He'd never seen anyone freeze at an invitation like that. He couldn't begin to imagine what it would be like to lose Polly, but he knew he'd hate being on his own. He got edgy and miserable if he ever went more than a couple of hours in his own company. Polly laughed at him because on some evenings when she was working and he was home alone, he dropped into Nutmeg for a drink and to read the paper. Just to be around people, with something going on, noise and voices, the clatter of dishes.

The guv seemed more the self-sufficient type. Just as well, in the circumstances.

CHAPTER SIXTEEN

Siv left the station after eight o'clock. She'd got through a long list of tasks but seemed to have made little progress. Errol Todd still hadn't responded to messages. The Valencia police had been dealing with a major road crash and hadn't yet been able to contact the Buddhists, who had no landline. After speaking to Betty Marshall, she'd phoned Jenna Seaton and asked her what time she'd arrived at work on Monday. Jenna had been icy, saying that she arrived and opened the building at seven sharp. There was CCTV outside the front door and the police could look at it if they wanted to verify that. Siv had emailed Patrick, asking him to follow it up, but it seemed that Jenna couldn't have managed to get to Lock Lane and commit murder before arriving at work.

Siv had got hold of Bartel Nowak but he said he was working in Pevensey. She'd arranged to meet with him at Polska the following morning. No further forensics had come in. She'd looked at the route drawn by Harvey Seaton, along bridleways, cutting across lanes, skirting farmland. It took him south of town and through Halse woods, far from the westerly reaches of the River Bere at Lock Lane. If that had indeed been his route. She'd googled bridleways around Berminster and saw that there was a network of them leading to the west of where the Seatons lived and joining Lock Lane about a mile from where Lauren and Rimas had died. Then she looked up how fast a horse could canter. Twelve to fifteen miles per hour. That would have given him the time he needed, but there were no hoof prints reported at the scene. She emailed Steve Wooton to double check. The thought of Seaton cantering to the river with a pair of scissors in his pocket seemed ridiculous.

Just as she was shutting down her computer, an email arrived at her work address.

You'll be wondering how I got hold of your new landlord. He sounds very top drawer. I phoned your landline in London last week and a woman answered. She said you didn't live there anymore and your mail is being redirected to Berminster. She was kind enough to give me your new address. I googled it and I guessed that you'd got a job with the Berminster police. See, you're not the only detective in the family! So I had to find out where you'd gone from a stranger and not from my own daughter. Rikka was always difficult with me but you were a much kinder girl, Sivvi. Why on earth are you living in a field like a gypsy, and what made you move back to that hick town? You must miss London. I hope you're not moping. Don't forget, you only have one parent left and I always tried to do my best for you, even when things were tough.

Love Mutsi xx

She read it twice. It was classic Mutsi: self-serving, nosy, persistent, insensitive, manipulative. Her own special airbrushed version of the past. *I hope you're not moping.* She started a reply but deleted the email.

She drove away from the station, thinking that so far in this case she was learning all about carp fishing, the close season and horse speeds but not much else. Hunger pangs steered her towards Minster Beach where the Horizon café did wonderful fish and chips. She sat on their heated terrace, drinking a glass of white wine and making her way through a large plate of cod and chips. As she ate, she googled Mason Granger. There were lots of hits concerning Minstergreen. He featured on Twitter, Instagram and Facebook, as well as popping up on local radio and TV. She watched a film clip of him talking about how to volunteer and the kinds of work the group did. As well as speaking well and easily, he was enthusiastic and friendly. He had a Minstergreen column in the weekly free newspaper, *Berminster Herald*. She read the most recent about migrating birds arriving at Bere Marsh nature reserve. It was witty and engaging. She wondered if sober, plodding Lauren had been jealous of his easy manner.

She put her phone down and finished her meal. The tide was rushing in, rattling the shingle, and there was a milky haze out at sea. She watched and listened. Tears pricked her eyes and she brushed them away.

Their father had brought her and Rikka here the day Mutsi put them on a train from Victoria and then phoned him after it had departed. He'd met them at the station, touched them both on the head, put their bags in the boot of his car and driven straight to the café for an early dinner. The café had been revamped since but the owners were the same and the food as excellent as it had been back then. Her father had eaten little, probably through shock, but she and Rikka had wolfed down dinner and pudding because their mother had forgotten to give them any money and they hadn't eaten since breakfast.

'Where's your mother gone this time?' was the only reference he'd made to her.

'Helsinki, to marry Bjork von Essen,' Rikka had told him.

'He's a baronet,' Siv added. 'She met him at a reception at the Finnish embassy.'

'It won't last, even though she's really desperate this time. The men never do last. Like you, Dad,' Rikka said bluntly.

Their father had stared out to sea. He was a bony, pale man with an androgynous, otherworldly look, and dealing with his ex-wife accentuated his mystified expression. Truth was, they hardly knew him. Mutsi had run off with another man when Siv was two, taking the girls with her, and their father had spent much of the intervening years working in

Dubai. Since he'd moved to Berminster, they'd visited once and seen him twice in London.

When they'd got back to his house that evening, they'd tried to find enough pillows and bedding to make up beds but had to settle for a mixture of sheets, cushions and sleeping bags. *We'll get things sorted. I'm not geared up for visitors*, their father had said, standing in a muddle of crumpled linen. She and Rikka had looked at each other without much optimism. His house was a time warp from the 1970s, with high-ceilinged rooms decorated in oranges and sludge browns. It had been a vicarage until their father bought it and there was a hint of incense in the air still and the shape of a crucifix imprinted on the living room wallpaper.

That first night Siv had watched in wonder as her father made the cocoa in a saucepan, slowly mixing powder to a paste and then carefully adding milk and sugar. His steady movements and patient stirring reassured her. She'd rarely seen her mother use a cooker. After a huge mug of creamy cocoa and biscuits, Siv had climbed into a torn sleeping bag with a dusty corduroy cushion for a pillow. The ridges rubbed at her cheek. She'd gazed around at the wallpaper, patterned with ochre and green circles. Her stomach was full and a glance in the kitchen cupboards had shown that they were satisfyingly full of tins and packets of food.

As she'd drifted off to sleep, she'd thought she must be dreaming but if she was, she never wanted to wake up.

The waiter dragged her back from the past, asking if she'd like anything else. She paid the bill and then walked down to the narrow strip of shoreline left untouched by the tide. She wandered along, her shoes crunching the shingle, thinking about Lauren Visser's childhood and the father she'd never known.

* * *

They'd decided to have a curry tonight. They were tucked into a booth in World of Spices, sipping lager. Julia loved fiery food and was having lamb madras. Betty had gone for a milder chicken korma. Julia'd had her hair dyed a lovely dark blonde with golden highlights and as usual looked assured in grey jeans and a soft blue linen shirt. With her stringy neck and pinched features she was by no means a pretty woman, but she made the most of what she had. Betty thought she should get something done with her own salt-and-pepper mop of hair but lacked the courage. What if it didn't turn out well and they sniggered behind her back at work? She wished she didn't care so much what people thought, but she'd always been that way. After Terry left, she'd gone into hiding for months, not wanting pity and remembering what a woman at work had said about a friend whose husband had strayed. *There's always two sides to every story. He must have gone after what he couldn't get at home.*

'She talked to everyone,' Betty relayed, 'including some of the parents. Wanted to know all about Lauren.'

Julia scooped up fluffy golden rice. 'Did you tell her you suspected Lauren was seeing someone else?'

'I did mention it. I thought that was the right thing to do.'

'Oh yes, you did the right thing. You have to be frank with the police.'

Julia was always so sure about everything, so cut and dried. Betty was slightly in awe of her friend's calm resolve. Her pragmatism made life seem simpler. She liked the way Julia was always so neatly turned out and in charge of herself. She'd told Betty about her husband's sudden death at fifty-eight. They'd been sitting watching TV. He'd eaten a slice of cake, sighed, clutched his arm and died of a heart attack. Julia said that although it had been a terrible shock, in some ways being widowed had been the making of her. It had forced her to look at the world with clear eyes, and mirrored her own experience after Terry left.

'The inspector's coming to Polska. I presume that's about Matis Rimas, because he used to call in now and again,' Julia said, cutting into the lamb. 'So I'll meet her myself.

People have been subdued there this week. Matis was such a pleasant young man, very cheery and friendly. We've started a collection for him, just a gesture for his family in Lithuania.'

'It's all so sad. I was with my Erica when she died. Held her, told her I loved her. It must be terrible to know your loved one has been murdered hundreds of miles away,' Betty said.

Julia arranged her cutlery on her empty plate. 'All pointless death is dreadful. All young death is dreadful. You were kind and supportive to Lauren. I hope she appreciated having you in her life.'

'I was fond of her, although sometimes I did feel as if she took me a bit for granted.'

Julia raised her large, pale eyes and nodded. 'That's certainly true. Think of all the support and advice you gave her about getting qualified at work, as well as listening to her marital woes. She never even bought you a bunch of flowers by way of a thank-you.'

'No . . . well, I didn't do it for the thanks.'

'Still, some appreciation goes a long way. Matis was always polite. Lauren seems to have lacked manners. Oh dear, I suppose I shouldn't say that about someone who's died.'

Betty leaned in. 'I think the police suspect Jenna Seaton. They've been checking up on her.'

'Interesting. Maybe they've found out some background we don't know about. From what you've told me, the Seatons and Vissers were friendly. Friends can fall out. Anyway, enough of sad events. Are you looking forward to the festival?'

'I certainly am. I've bought a new dress to wear. Not my usual kind of thing. I took your advice, went a bit upmarket, made a braver choice.'

They talked on about the festival, looking at a programme between them. Betty pictured her new dress. It gave her a less rounded, more fluid look. She was tired of appearing comfy and maternal, a motherly type with no one to mother. She thought she might approach a makeover in stages. Wear the dress and then tackle her hair, maybe try a new lipstick.

* * *

Siv climbed the squeaking stairs in the tall, narrow house. On the first landing, she stopped to look at the view of the harbour from the side window. Light white clouds were moving fast out to sea and oystercatchers were wading in the muddy foreshore. There was a stall selling fish near the road and she could make out the grey, white and brown sheen of their skin and the bright green of samphire. So much fish in this case, she thought. She carried on to the flat on the third floor.

Mason Granger opened the door as soon as she pressed the bell and let her into a light-filled converted loft with a panoramic view over the town. A couple of deep armchairs were arranged in front of the wide plate-glass window. The brick on the internal walls had been left exposed and painted white. The wall to the right of the window had a massive indoor vertical garden made with six wooden pallets and featuring different succulents. She gazed at colourful large-leafed plants, interspersed with smaller pale grey and green varieties. It was a stunning mixture of colour and shape and she wondered if she could work up a similar piece of origami.

Granger was a tall, stringy man in his late twenties with short black hair and smoky lensed glasses. He invited Siv to sit down and checked the laptop on the dining table before closing the lid and taking an armchair.

'I haven't noticed a TV in here but you don't need one with this view,' Siv said.

He nodded. 'I have a TV in my bedroom but I don't use it much. As you say, sitting here and looking out, there's never a dull moment.' He had a wide smile, neat teeth and perfectly shaped, symmetrical eyebrows.

She couldn't see his eyes behind the tinted lenses. 'I need to ask you about Lauren Visser.'

'Lauren — my God, that was savage. I couldn't believe when I heard about her.'

'How did you hear?' she asked.

'Cilla phoned me. Cilla Falkner. She's in Minstergreen and one of her kids goes to the nursery where Lauren worked.'

'Where were you last Monday morning between 6 and 8.30 a.m.?'

'Here, working. I work from home.'

'Was anyone with you?'

'No. I live on my own. I got up around eight fifteen and started replying to emails. Some from the States come in overnight.' He shrugged. 'I thought you'd ask me that. No one can vouch for me, I'm afraid. Is it a problem?'

'For me or for you?'

'Could be for me, I suppose, if I was a murderer. Which I'm not.'

'I'll note that you told me that. What do you do for a living?'

'I'm an animator. I work mainly on games. I usually go up to London a day or so a week for consultations. Otherwise I'm working here.'

He looked out of the window most of the time, so that she was seeing his profile. She wanted to turn the chairs around and get him to take his glasses off.

'Tell me about how you knew Lauren,' she said.

He crossed his ankle over the knee of the other leg, foot pointing outwards. He wore soft yellow and black trainers with orange laces. He looped a finger through a lace and played with it. 'I met her a couple of years ago when we set up Minstergreen. She was on our committee, so I saw her regularly — usually every week. We worked on strategies, publicity, campaigns, all that kind of stuff.'

'How did you get on?'

'Okay-ish. We had different styles and approaches.'

'Elaborate for me.'

'Okay. Let me see.' He rested his chin on the back of his hand, in thoughtful pose. Grandstanding. 'I thought we needed to take a longer term view with our work, plan ahead more. I wanted to broaden the Minstergreen agenda, keep it in the public eye. I'm pretty skilled in networking and strategic positioning. That's partly why the members agreed that I should be chair. I'm an ideas person, if you like. I understand that you have to work hard at engaging people and making conservation fun. Lauren could be a bit of a drag sometimes, to be honest, a bit of a virtue signaller. She was keen on keeping our focus small, sticking to what we know. Our volunteer numbers have been dropping and we need to get more people, especially younger ones, working with us. I wanted us to go into schools, colleges, workplaces, anywhere you get numbers of people, and do presentations about us, but Lauren argued that would distract from our main task of hands on conservation.'

She could see that he liked the sound of his own voice. He was getting into his stride. 'I understand that you had a disagreement at the committee meeting the week before she died.'

'Yes, and it wasn't the first time we'd seen things differently. But that's how it goes in all organizations. People have strong feelings. I thought Lauren was too plodding. She could be kind of dogged and I'd had feedback that some volunteers were put off by her tunnel vision and her insistence that they keep to the hours they'd offered. We had to take her off managing the rota because if volunteers couldn't make a session, she'd be on the phone to them, telling them off. You have to work flexibly with volunteers, not guilt-trip them and manage them as if they're in paid employment. Lauren bludgeoned people with facts. Like I said, what we do is serious work, but you don't want to frighten people all the time. Fear can paralyse rather than inspire action. You have to make conservation enjoyable or helpers fade away.'

'And how about the other committee members? Did they agree with you or with Lauren?'

'There are six of us on the committee and I'd say most of them agreed with me. Lauren could be very persuasive and she worked hard so she was well respected. But I think my lead on our strategy was weightier, given my expertise. Plus I've put massive effort into cultivating media outlets to get our message out there, and I've built up valuable contacts. Overall, the committee members recognize my background and my CV. We agreed to take a final decision on the issue next week.'

He hadn't said *and Lauren was only a nursery worker with limited talents* but he might as well have. 'Did Lauren seem worried or upset in any way the last time you saw her?'

He glanced at her and then back out of the window. 'Not that I noticed. But I didn't actually know her that well. I wouldn't have chosen to socialize with her. She'll be a real loss to us though. She certainly grafted.'

Siv wasn't sure if he'd added that at the end because he'd revealed too much dislike of Lauren. She showed him photos of the child and Matis Rimas but he said that he didn't recognize them.

'Have you got a car, or do you borrow one?'

'No. I have a licence but I don't drive. Carbon footprint — I practice what I preach. I cycle or walk around here or take the train.' He gestured to a fold up bike propped by the door to the stairs.

She left him, reflecting that he and Lauren seemed to have been polar opposites in terms of personality and style. They must have clashed more than he was willing to acknowledge. She drove away, unsure of what she thought, except that Granger was full of self-importance.

* * *

Patrick was driving the lanes around Harvey Seaton's route. He'd downloaded a photo of him from the country club website to prompt people's memories. He'd stopped at a couple of farms with no luck, but he'd been thrilled when the woman at Honeywell House had asked him if he knew the detective who was on Twitter. He'd confirmed that it was him, and she'd told him that she thought what he wrote was terrific. It was good to see the police being proactive and getting positive feedback instead of being criticized. He'd got her permission to quote her and left with a swollen head, wishing that the guv could have heard her. In the car, he'd tweeted:

@DCBerminsterPolice. Thank you to lady @ Honeywell House who's just told me we're doing a terrific job. Good to get public support when we're busy fighting crime.

#keepingberminstersafe.

His phone rang. Jerry Wilby, returning his call. He pulled over to take it, nodding as he took notes, feeling increasingly deflated. The man had little more than a vague recollection that didn't amount to much. Patrick drove on to Halse woods, wishing they had more leads. He wasn't sure where this case was going with no forensics. His money was on the husband or this Seaton bloke, but it seemed messy. Patrick liked things cut and dried, which was why he preferred working burglaries. Burglars were usually stupid enough to leave DNA or repeat known methods. Or there'd be witnesses, descriptions. Driving around the countryside tracking a bloke on horseback was weird.

Patrick entered the woods through the main entrance, a pair of tall iron gates that led into a car park with several timber huts, including a warden's office and toilets at one end. He parked by the warden's office and knocked on the door. There was no reply and it was locked. One of the windows was covered in notices and posters about the woods: seasonal bird visitors, a pond called Frog Central, the butterfly haven, the sensory garden and various flora and fauna. There was a Minstergreen poster advertising activities over the bank holiday. He walked around the back of the office and stood watching the sun playing on the leaves. He'd never been much of a lover of the great outdoors and disliked getting wet and mucky. When had he last been here? Probably on a school trip, eating soggy sandwiches amid drizzle and wasps and avoiding the boys who liked to find branches to use as weapons. One of the reasons he was wary of Steve Wooton was because he would have been one of those in your face, aggressive boys, jamming sticks in your ribs.

Hearing a rattling sound, he walked towards it. A woman in jeans, wellies and a denim jacket was moving around a copse of trees, filling bird feeders. He called to her and showed his badge. She stopped and shaded her eyes. She was one of the most attractive women he'd seen in a long time, with long russet hair framing an oval face and a curving mouth.

'I wonder if you can help me, Ms . . .'

'Kitty. Kitty Fairway. I'll try, DC Hill.'

'Were you here on Monday morning?'

'Yep. I'm the warden.'

'What time did you get here?'

'Around seven. Loads to do at this time of year.'

'Did you see this man? He was riding through the woods around that time.' He showed her the photo on his phone.

She scratched her nose. 'I saw a guy riding up by Bluebell Corner, where the bridleway tracks the edge of the woods. I can't tell you if it was this man. He was in the distance. Biggish guy, big black horse with hooves like white socks. Reminded me of a cat I had once with white paws.'

'Do you know what time that was?'

'Not exactly. That's one of the nice things about this job. I don't have to clock watch. I expect you do.'

'Too right.' She was flirty, smiling at him. He wondered fleetingly if he might ask her out for a drink, but something was bound to happen at home with Noah and he'd almost inevitably not be able to make it. She'd be pissed off with him before they even got started. That had happened with Lisa Flore a couple of times and she'd finally told him he was a nice bloke but not her type. He smiled back. 'Rough time, then?'

'Say about half seven. Why are you asking?'

'It's an ongoing investigation. Sorry, I can't tell you any-thing more.'

She was looking past him and tapped his arm suddenly. She put a finger to her lips and pointed, whispering, 'Look, over there! A willow tit!'

He followed her finger and saw a small bird with a white breast and greeny-yellow plumage. It busied itself at a high feeder before fluttering away. He was aware of her soft breathing. She smelled like the woods: fresh and grassy.

'That's terrific,' she said. 'I must record seeing it. It's become rare, the numbers have declined dramatically.'

'Why's that?'

'Us, probably. Humans. Mucking around with their habitat. But seeing that one gives me some hope. These woods go back centuries, you know. There are over thirty ancient plants and trees here.' She bent to pick up a bag of bird food, and then looked up at him again. 'Is this about Lauren's murder?'

'You knew her?'

'I met her quite a few times. She was in Minstergreen, and they do a lot of conservation work with us here. Like me, she was passionate about these woods and maintaining the legacy we've been left. She'd have been absolutely thrilled to see the willow tit. So sad, all that youthful energy and promise ended. You know, I saw her here once with a big guy who might have been the one in that photo. Must have been last winter. They were walking along one of the paths, deep in conversation. Holding hands. Is he her husband?'

'The man in this photo isn't, no.'

'Oh. Must have been someone else then. I wonder if that's who she was waiting for last Sunday.'

This was one of the things he loved about police work: the casual remark that pulls at a thread. 'Lauren was here on Sunday? Did you talk to her?'

'I saw her late afternoon, about four, in the sensory garden. It's a secluded area with high hedges, all little nooks and cosy corners. I was cutting through. She was sitting on one of the benches, just staring into the distance. I wasn't going to disturb her because people go there for peace and quiet but she heard me and looked over. I said I was on my way to fix some fencing. She told me she was waiting for someone but she reckoned they couldn't make it and she might as well head home.'

'How did she seem?'

'A bit flat. I thought she was disappointed because she'd had a wasted journey. She started off to the car park after we spoke.'

'Where is the sensory garden?'

'That way, five minutes' walk.'

'I'll take a look. Thanks for your help, Ms Fairway.'

'Any time, officer.'

He felt himself blush. She had a direct, teasing look. He turned to glance back at her as he headed up the path, but she was busy with the bird feeders, standing on tiptoe to fill one. For a moment, he envied her her job. It seemed straightforward, stress free. Though he'd die of boredom here in the woods with just a willow tit for excitement.

As soon as he saw the sensory garden and its conveniently hidden corners, he reckoned that Lauren must have arranged to see Seaton. It figured. Her husband was away that day. But according to Kitty, Lauren's expected friend had failed to turn up. He headed back for his car, calling the techie to ask what Seaton's phone had revealed. What he heard made him smile.

CHAPTER SEVENTEEN

Polska was a mixture of social and welfare centre run by older women, most of them volunteers. Siv reckoned that if every volunteer decided to stay at home, the social fabric of the country would begin to fall apart. She sat with Bartel Nowak in the bar at noon, drinking tea. He was downing a foaming pint of beer and making his way through a plate of pierogi. He was bald, with a long, reddish pointed beard and wore three earrings in each ear. He looked more like a biker than a roofer, rough at the edges and pugnacious, but on meeting her had kissed her hand and called her *madame*. That was a first for a police officer.

'Did you know Lauren Visser and Matis Rimas?' She showed him the photos.

'I met Mat at the river and we had a drink in here sometimes.'

'You didn't think to contact the police when you heard Lauren and Matis Rimas been murdered there?'

'I didn't know they were dead until you told me. I've been working in Pevensey the last two weeks and staying there with a mate. Long days and I don't watch much news. All too depressing. After work I have dinner, a beer and go to bed.' He wiped froth from his lips and burped lightly.

'You were in Pevensey on Monday morning?'

'That's right. I'm happy to give you a contact number for the friend I stayed with. I understand you'll want to check up on me.'

'Yes, I will. Let's start with Matis. When did you meet him?'

'Around November last. He was fishing, so was I. We chatted a bit. Very sad, what's happened to him. He was a nice guy, straightforward. He was there at the river a couple of other times. We'd watch out for each other in case this old guy we called "Grandad" was around.'

'Because you were trespassing on private land.'

'Just catching fish, Madame. Not doing anyone any harm. No great crime.' He looked at her mischievously. 'Mat and I exchanged emails and met in here a couple of times for a beer. He was kind of naïve, always going on about extra-terrestrial life.'

'Did he ever say he was in any kind of trouble?'

He wolfed down his last pierogi and patted his beard delicately with a napkin. 'Nope. He'd moved in with some Lithuanian family and he was happy about that. He seemed fine the last time I saw him, around mid-February. He emailed me to tell me that this woman, Lauren, was complaining about the notice at the river and crowdfunding about it. He knew I was angry about the notice.'

'How did Matis know about Lauren?'

'He spotted her poster on the wall here and emailed me a photo of it. I texted her to say if she wanted any support, I'd be happy to give it but I didn't want to go public. I contributed to the crowdfunding.'

'Did you meet her?'

'No. She just texted me back, gave me a few updates on how the campaign was going. I didn't know anything about her personally.' He gave her a twinkling smile. 'I keep my head below the parapet, don't cause any waves. I've lived here for eight years and I find that's the best way to get along.'

She couldn't help liking him. 'Some people might say that illegal fishing wasn't exactly keeping a low profile.'

171

'Touché, *madame*, but we all have our little ways of rebelling, don't we? I bet even "Grandad" is naughty sometimes.'

'Perhaps, Mr Nowak. Have you ever seen this child?'

He looked at the photo of the little girl. 'I haven't, no. Who is she?'

'I wish I knew. Do you know if any other "rebel" anglers met Lauren at the river?'

He threw his hands up. 'I don't know. I haven't come across any. Matis was the only other bad boy I met down there. None of us stay too long at Lock Lane, because we're not welcome. Quick and dirty fishing. Do you think they were killed because of Lauren's protest?'

'I don't know at this stage. Thanks for your help. Here's my card. Contact me if you think of anything else.'

He tucked the card into his wallet, finished his beer and they got to their feet. 'I suppose this is a horrible and very difficult time for you,' he said.

For a split second, she was nonplussed, wondering how he knew about Ed. She felt herself pale, touched the scar over her eye. Then she understood. 'Investigating murder is always hard and it can be distressing, but it's the job.'

He nodded, took her hand and kissed it. 'Madame, you are a fine woman. Your shirt is a beautiful colour. Is it that shade called coral?'

'Quite possibly. I'm never sure if it's orange or red.'

'Would you care to take tea with me sometime?'

He'd wrong-footed her a second time but she shook her head, smiling at him. 'Perhaps. Not just now.'

On her way out, she stopped at the help desk and showed her ID to the woman who was staffing it. Her lapel badge showed the name Julia.

'I'm investigating the murders of Lauren Visser and Matis Rimas. Did you know them?'

'That was dreadful news. We've all been so upset here. I knew Matis. He'd been in a couple of times when I was on duty. We gave him information about the area, how to find a GP and dentist, things like that.'

'Did he ever seem troubled about anything, or did he fall out with anyone here?'

Julia was long and lean, with a narrow face and large, soulful eyes. She reminded Siv of a greyhound. 'Matis never looked worried and he got on well with people. He was quite shy. We get the odd troublemaker here but Matis was never involved in anything. He was a polite young man.'

'And how about Lauren?'

'I didn't know her. She came in once when I had a day off and asked if we could put up a poster concerning a campaign she was running. She left it with the staff. I wasn't sure about it at first because we don't like to get involved in anything controversial. When I realized it concerned a discriminatory notice I was appalled, so I agreed to have put it up.' She gestured to a pin board with the poster about the crowdfunding on it. 'I think some of our visitors contributed. I suppose I should take it down now, given what's happened.'

'Do you know if Lauren came here at other times?'

'I don't think she did. I'm the salaried manager so I'm here most of the time and I didn't see her. We have volunteers who help out. I can ask them, if you want.'

'Yes, please, and can you ask them and your visitors about this child?' She showed Julia the photo of the little girl. 'This photo was left at the crime scene and we need to establish the child's identity. Do you know her?'

She held it up to the light. 'No, sorry, I don't. That's very strange, surely — leaving it where people were murdered.'

'Yes, very strange. You can keep that copy to put on your notice board.'

'I might see you over the May festival,' Julia said. 'We're running a stall with all things Polish, and there's music, too. Do come along and say hello.'

* * *

Siv was parking at the station when she glanced at the car next to her and saw Patrick. He was fast asleep, his head

173

propped against the window. She knocked on the passenger side window, gently at first and then louder when she failed to rouse him. He started up and looked around. His eyes were heavy and puffy. She made a window down gesture.

'Are you okay? You know we've a meeting due now?'

'Yeah . . . sorry, guv, don't know how that happened. Be with you in a minute. Got an update for you about Seaton.' He grabbed a bottle of water.

She went into the station, glancing back once. Patrick was combing his hair and yanking at his shirt. This wasn't the first time she'd noticed that he looked tired and distracted. She wondered if there was a problem. She opened the cheese sandwich she'd grabbed on the way in and ate it while she examined the incident board. There were too many question marks. The others arrived and sat around, Steve Wooton clutching a box of tissues and a nasal inhaler.

Siv chucked her sandwich wrapper away. 'Right, let's have an update. I spoke to Mason Granger, the guy who's the chair of Minstergreen. He says he was home alone on Monday morning, working. He and Lauren disagreed on the direction Minstergreen should take. He's so full of himself she might have got on his nerves big time. I definitely got the impression she was a thorn in his side, but I can't believe it would be a reason to kill her. However, he has no alibi. He says he hasn't got a car so we need to check that.'

'We've spoken to all the Minstergreen members now,' Ali said. 'They all have alibis for Monday morning. No one seems to have had a beef with Lauren but a couple of them mentioned the tension between her and Granger.'

'I tried Todd's number again,' one of the other officers said. 'Went to message.'

Siv sighed. 'Okay. After the meeting I'll follow up with the Valencia police.'

'The nursery staff are all clear except for Simon Rochford,' Lisa Flore said. 'There's a report on file from September 2015. A neighbour called us at two in the morning and reported hearing a blazing row, shouting and screaming. Two officers visited the house but Simon and Lynda Rochford were both okay. They acknowledged there'd been a row over money but they'd cleared the air. That's it. They divorced in 2017, so it looks like the rows continued. Nothing else on him though. But he has no confirmed alibi for early Monday morning. He lives on his own and says he woke at eight and left for work at nine.'

'Okay. We need to talk to his ex-wife and then to him again. He did have a disagreement with Lauren about her views on his menus, so I want to know if his temper ever went beyond the verbal.' Patrick was looking lit-up and waving a finger. 'Patrick, what have you got?'

'I've just been around Seaton's riding route and met the warden at Halse woods.' He told them what Kitty Fairway had said. 'I've just had the details on Seaton's phone and the news is that they found deleted text messages from last Saturday that prove he's a lying toerag.' He scrolled on his phone. 'Here we go. Lauren to Seaton at 11.15:

'*Can we meet tomorrow @ Halse woods? Want to discuss something. Need advice. Ade's in London.*

'Seaton to Lauren at 13.00: *Not sure that would be wise. What's the problem?*

'Lauren to Seaton at 13.45: *Can't talk now. Please, could we meet? Not for long. Just feeling worried.*

'Seaton to Lauren at 15.00: *Okay. Sensory garden, half three tomorrow. Make sure you delete all messages.*

'So Seaton lied about when they last arranged to meet, but Ms Fairway said he was a no show. Must have been too worried.'

'Or couldn't get away from his wife,' Ali said.

Siv thought that was the likely reason. 'But we have a sort of confirmation of where Seaton was on Monday morning. Seems unlikely that another man of similar build was riding where he claims he was, so I think we can marginalize him as a suspect. That leaves us with what was bothering Lauren and what she needed advice about.'

Lisa pointed to the board. 'Why wouldn't she have told her friend, Cora Laffin? If she was worried, I'd have thought she'd have turned to a woman friend.'

'Maybe that was a ruse she was using to try to get Seaton involved with her again.' Ali stretched his legs out, his chair creaking under his weight.

'Playing the needy woman? Possibly, but that's not the impression I have of her. Cora told me she'd been busy recently and hadn't seen much of Lauren, so maybe Lauren didn't want to bother her. We need to talk to Seaton again.'

'I checked in with Cora's boyfriend. He confirms her account of Monday morning,' Lisa said.

Siv nodded. 'Anything else from Seaton's phone, Patrick?'

'So far, nothing else to or from Lauren since 10 February, which fits what he told you. One more thing. I spoke to Jerry Wilby. About a year ago, Lauren met him on the way into work and said she thought a guy had been staring at her while she was swimming. But then she thought she might have startled him. That was it. Nothing about what this guy looked like, or where it happened and she never mentioned it again.'

'Hardly helpful,' Siv said, shrugging. She looked at Steve. 'What have you got for us?'

Steve Wooton had a heavy cold and had been blowing his nose and coughing throughout the meeting. He sucked on a lozenge as he gave his update. 'CCTV for Caterpillar Corner nursery shows Jenna Seaton opening up at 7 a.m. on Monday morning. Forensics back on the scissors from the nursery reveal no blood. No weapon found in search of the river. No hoof prints around the Lock Lane area, confirming what Seaton's told us. Results are in on the car parked near Rimas's on Monday morning. The tyre prints show wearing on the outer edge of the front left tyre. They were all Michelin. I'd say that was our killer's vehicle. If we can find the car, we can match that front left tyre.'

'Big if,' Ali said through Steve's new coughing fit. 'Haven't you heard that coughs and sneezes spread diseases? You should catch yourself on and go into quarantine.'

'It's not as bad as it sounds,' Steve wheezed.

'Yeah,' Ali said dubiously. He turned to add his piece. 'I talked to Nick Shelton, owner of the angling club and the land at Lock Lane. He met Lauren about her campaign over the sign and tried to reason with her. He and his wife had her round for a cuppa in February but she wouldn't budge. He painted a picture of a moralizing, solemn woman, but then he was never going to take to her. He gave his movements for Monday morning. He was at home, catering to his B&B residents with his wife or driving his son to school.'

'Anything in from the media release of the child's photo?' Siv asked.

'Nothing,' Patrick told her, lowering the iPad stylus he'd been playing with. 'Not even any weirdos.'

Siv updated them about her meeting with Bartel Nowak. 'He says that he never met Lauren and as far as he knows, neither did Rimas. He was working in Pevensey on Monday morning and says he stayed there Sunday night.' She got up and stretched. 'Right, tasks. Ali, can you see Seaton and question him about this proposed meeting that he bailed out of? Check the colour of the horse he rides as well. I want someone to verify Bartel Nowak's whereabouts Sunday to Monday and verify that Granger doesn't own a car or didn't hire one for Monday. Also revisit Rochford and the ex-wife. Steve, I think you should go home. You look as if you've got a temperature.'

* * *

Every evening, the cleaners opened the internal window blinds of her office. She had no idea why. Judging from the undisturbed layers of dust, it wasn't to clean them. She closed them as she walked into the office and reached for her ringing phone. She'd eaten her sandwich too quickly and had given herself a fit of hiccups. She swallowed some water as she answered.

'Inspector Drummond? This is Errol Todd. You've been trying to reach me.'

'Finally! Are you still in Spain?'

'Just. I'm at Valencia airport, waiting for a flight to London. I'm sorry I haven't been in touch sooner but I've been at a retreat and my phone was switched off and locked away in a safe.'

'Okay. At least you're in contact now. I need to speak to you about Ade Visser. Can you talk now?' She reached her desk and swung her chair out.

'Yes, I've about fifteen minutes until the gate call. Ade's left me loads of messages. He said Lauren's been murdered.' He sounded nervous, his voice strained.

'That's correct. She was murdered on Monday morning. Have you spoken to Mr Visser yet?'

'No. I thought I'd better ring you first, like you asked.'

Too right. 'Mr Visser said that he stayed at your flat on Sunday night and that he had a key.'

'That's right. Ade stays now and again, usually when he's working in London and it's a late one. I gave him a key ages ago.'

'Did you see Mr Visser when he arrived at your flat?'

'No, I was asleep. He said he'd be late and I wanted an early night because I had to get a flight first thing Monday morning. He knows where everything is.' He'd started to squeak and cleared his throat.

It would be hard to come out of days of quiet meditation and find you'd been bombarded with calls concerning a murder. 'Mr Visser stated that he didn't see you at all but that he heard you leaving to catch your flight. Did you see him?'

There was a long pause. 'Look . . . this is really difficult. I don't know what to think. This has all come as a real shock, actually.'

'Okay. Take your time. I can understand that. It's important that you're honest with me, Mr Todd. This is a murder enquiry and another person died as well.'

More throat clearing, some rustling noises and the line faded, as if he was on the move.

'Mr Todd? Are you there?'

'Yes. Sorry, I wanted a bit of space. Bit public here. Okay. Ahm . . . is Ade in trouble or something?'

Siv took a breath. What did he bloody well think? 'Mr Visser's wife was stabbed to death so he has certainly got troubles, wouldn't you say? I'm sure you can see that I have to clarify his whereabouts. It would help if you would just tell me what's on your mind. Clearly, there is something.'

'Yeah. I didn't sleep well Sunday night. I never do before a journey. I'd taken a sleeping pill but it didn't knock me out fully, just made me hazy. I, ahm . . . I heard Ade get up about three and he went out. I looked out of the window and saw him get in a cab. I didn't know what was going on. I thought maybe he wasn't well and just wanted to go home.'

'At three in the morning, with no transport?'

'I thought maybe he was getting the cab all the way to Sussex. People do those long journeys by cab sometimes. I almost phoned him to see if he was okay but I didn't want to make a fuss and I was feeling groggy from the sleeping pill so I crashed out again.'

'What time did you leave to catch your plane?'

'My cab came at six.'

'Mr Visser hadn't returned before you left?'

'No. I looked in his room and he wasn't there, and his overnight bag was gone. Look, I don't want to get Ade into any trouble. I expect he was just feeling rough and wanted his own bed.'

'That's fine, Mr Todd. You've been very helpful. I'll need you to make a formal statement when you get back. Are you going to be in London for the time being?'

'Yeah, for a couple of weeks. What do you mean, a statement?'

'We'll contact you. Please don't phone Mr Visser now. Just get on your flight and come back. Do you understand?'

'Yes, okay. But what's happening with Ade?'

'I can't discuss this any further at the moment. I'm instructing you not to phone him. Now just board your flight and I'll talk to you again when you're back home.'

She ended the call, hoping he'd do as he was told, and sped into the main office. Ali was out and Patrick was texting on his phone.

'DC Hill! Put the phone down. I want you to take a uniform, find Ade Visser straight away and arrest him on suspicion of the murder of Lauren Visser and Matis Rimas. Got it?'

He shot up. 'Yes, guv.'

'Phone me as soon as you have him with you.'

As Patrick hurried out, she rang Ali. 'I spoke to Errol Todd. Visser lied. Todd saw him leave in a cab at three in the morning on Monday. I'm bringing him in. Get back here, please. I want you to interview him with me.'

She leaned over her desk and googled trains from Victoria to Berminster on weekdays. The earliest left at 4.15 a.m., arriving at 6.15 a.m. Earls Court to Victoria wouldn't take long by cab, not at that time. Visser could easily have got back in time to kill his wife and Rimas, although she wasn't sure he could have cycled to Lock Lane that fast. Perhaps he'd got a cab to drop him somewhere near there, but then how did he get back to fetch his bike? The jigsaw piece wasn't right, it didn't seem to fit.

CHAPTER EIGHTEEN

Visser looked washed out but calm — almost accepting, Siv thought. He'd have known that this might happen but would have been hoping that Errol hadn't clocked his absence. He'd accompanied Patrick quite willingly and had said no to a solicitor, which surprised Siv. She'd have thought he'd be a stickler for his rights. Ali poured three beakers of water and Siv flipped her notepad open.

'We need to clarify a few things with you about Sunday night. You told me that you stayed at your friend Errol Todd's flat in Earls Court. You said you arrived around 11.15 p.m. and left at 6.30 a.m. on Monday morning.' Visser was looking down at the table and rubbing the tops of his thumbs together. 'Is there anything else you want to tell me about that night?' She could see him trying to work out what she knew.

He looked up finally. 'Have you talked to Errol?'

'Just answer my question. Do you need to alter what you told me in any way?'

His right foot jiggled on the floor. He reached for his water. He had beautiful hands, strong, with well-shaped nails. She supposed you might need capable hands to control a horse. She'd never sat on one, although she'd often thought it would be a great way to get into the landscape. Mutsi had once taken up riding because one of her boyfriends owned a stable, but of course Siv and Rikka had never been invited. This case seemed to be full of active people spending their time outdoors swimming, horse-riding, fishing. The long silence extended. She was happy with that. Silence could speak volumes. Ali was rubbing at his knee with a finger and she wanted to reach over and grab his hand to still him. Someone hurried along the corridor outside, talking rapidly into a phone.

'I don't know what to tell you,' Visser finally said.

Ali cracked his knuckles. Little explosions. 'Give it a try, why don't you?' he said. 'You're doing my head in. You're the one who's given us two weeks to find the person who killed your wife. We're sitting here with you listening to ourselves breathe instead of being out there getting on with the job.'

Visser flinched. 'This is a nightmare. I can't . . . I don't know if I can do this.'

Siv gave him an understanding smile. 'It does sound as if there's something you want to tell us. As DS Carlin has pointed out, time's wasting while we're in here.'

He shifted his chair and looked around the room. He tensed and for a moment, she thought he might make a run for it but then he sank back.

'Okay. I panicked when I talked to you. I've been in such a state of shock, I couldn't think straight. I didn't stay at Errol's until half six. I couldn't sleep. I called a cab and left around 3 a.m.' He drank more water, licking his lips.

'Right. Now we're making progress. So where did this cab take you?'

He shot a glance at Siv. Embarrassed, shifty. 'This is very difficult.'

'I'm sure. Where did you go in the cab?'

'Look . . . could I talk to DS Carlin on my own? Please? I'd find it easier.'

'Why would it be easier?'

His neck was reddening. 'It just would. You know, man to man. It's very awkward. I feel so uncomfortable talking about it in front of you.'

Siv lost all patience and snapped at him. 'Mr Visser, you've lied to us and as such you might have seriously hampered our enquiry. If you've got something to say, say it to both of us and make it quick. I haven't got any more time to waste.'

Ali thought she sounded like Ms Moynihan, the only teacher he'd been frightened of at school. She'd been firm and kind but the minute you crossed her you wished you hadn't. *Don't give me that old nonsense, Ali Carlin. I wasn't born under a cabbage.*

Visser put his hands to his face and then started mumbling. 'I took the cab to a flat in Pimlico. I, ahm . . . there's someone there who I visit now and again. About once a month. I was there from half three until half six. I did catch the 7.10 from Victoria. That was the truth.' He seemed to deflate in front of them.

'Go on,' Siv said coldly. 'Who do you visit in Pimlico?'

'Her name is Serena Davis.'

'I can hardly hear you, Mr Visser. Why were you visiting Ms Davis?'

As if she didn't know. Once a month in the early hours of the morning. Not for tea and biscuits.

'She's . . . we have a long-standing arrangement. She supplies . . . ahm . . . she supplies "activities."'

'Activities. What kind? Ludo? Scrabble? Basket weaving?'

'BDSM,' he whispered.

'So you're changing your story. You were with Ms Davis for three hours while you engaged in these BDSM activities.'

'Yes.'

'What's her address?'

'Eighteen Bancroft Street. Flat five. Does anyone else have to know this? It won't become public, will it? There's my job . . . my friends. Errol . . .'

He looked terrified but Siv had little sympathy. 'If Ms Davis confirms what you've told us, there's no reason why anyone should know your private business. It would have been so much easier if you'd informed us of this straight away.'

'I'm ashamed,' he whispered. 'I've always been ashamed. It started in my teens. I've tried to stop so many times. I feel so filthy afterwards. I feel filthy all the time because I think about it and when I'll next be able to do it. It's like needing a fix. I didn't want it to come out. It's so sordid. I let Melody down. I was going there when she was dying. Lying to her and saying I had a work commitment when I was indulging myself in London and she had only weeks to live. And now I've let Lauren down.'

Ali felt a peculiar mix of shock and excitement. Visser's revelation fascinated and disgusted him. The guv hadn't batted an eyelid.

'Did Lauren know about your visits to Ms Davis?' It wasn't relevant but Siv was always intrigued by the secrets people kept from each other — or were willing to accommodate.

He flinched. 'God, no! No one else has ever known. Although sometimes I wondered if she knew I was keeping something from her.'

Well, she was certainly keeping some things from you. 'We'll need to verify your story, Mr Visser. You'll stay in custody until we've spoken to Ms Davis. We'll inform your mother.'

'How long will you keep me here?'

'We can detain you for twenty-four hours initially. Are you sure you don't want to see a solicitor?'

'I'm sure. I've told you the truth now.' He looked ill. Sweaty and chalky.

Ali handed him back to the custody officer, grabbed an apple from his desk and then joined Siv in her office, tossing it from hand to hand.

'Now we know why he isn't asking for a solicitor,' Siv said. 'He wants as few people as possible to know about his secret addiction.'

'I wonder what exactly Serena supplies him with?'

184

'I think I can tell you that.' Siv was busy tapping on her keyboard. 'Here you are. Serena of Pimlico. A curvaceous blonde.' She read from the screen.

My name is Serena. I do what I love and love what I do. I live in a world of rich sensations. Pain and pleasure are my exquisite weapons. I can be subtle or strong. I can make you laugh, scream or cry. I can take you to extremes. I can take you to heights you've only dreamed of.

'Then there's an extensive, eye-watering menu of all the things Serena can do for you. Or to you. I suppose that's how Visser finds a release for his controlling nature. I can see why he'd feel so guilty about his wife. He was regularly playing in Serena's world of rich sensations. Bit of a difference from the worthy Lauren and her causes.' She wondered if he enjoyed the guilt, if it was another form of masochism.

'Expensive too, I suppose. Couple of hundred quid a month?' Ali said.

'Are you thinking you can't afford Serena on a sergeant's pay? She might offer special rates for public servants.'

Ali laughed uneasily and bit into his apple to mask his discomfort. 'What do you make of it though, guv? A man like that with a wife, a lovely house and a beezer job wanting to play sex games.'

She looked at Ali, naïve and sheltered from the big wide world in a cosy marriage, with amusement. 'I don't make anything much of it. I could cite a number of famous men who appear to have it all but wander off-piste for other delights. It's Visser's life and he can do what he likes with it. What I can't stand is his hypocrisy. Lying to his wives and not wanting to talk about it in front of me. As if I care if he wants to pay to be tied up or spanked or whatever. Right, can you get on to the Met? I want someone to call on Ms Davis and verify Visser's story. Careful you don't choke on that apple.'

* * *

Patrick took the call from Mrs Visser while the guv and Ali were interviewing her son. She sounded hesitant. She'd answered the door when he'd gone to arrest Visser and her anxious face had upset him. She reminded him of how his own mother looked after Noah had the stroke. He thought she was going to enquire about what was happening with Visser but she had something else on her mind.

'I've found something and I've been so worried about it. I think I need to speak to Inspector Drummond. It might affect what's happening with my son.'

'She's not available right now.'

'Oh, I see. Well . . . I suppose it can wait. It's just that I was hoping to go home tomorrow morning. It's my fault. I should have contacted you before now. Are you the policeman who was here earlier?'

'That's right. What have you found?'

'Well . . . I found it in a drawer. It's a postcard with paper scissors glued on and paint that looks like blood.'

'I'll come round, Mrs Visser. Don't touch the card. I'll be with you in ten minutes.'

Patrick hurried out to his car, squirting some water on his face and wiping it off with a tissue. God, he was tired. Noah hadn't gone to bed until after midnight and then had a restless night, calling out in his sleep. At 2 a.m., he'd needed the loo and fallen on his way there. He was like a ton of bricks to lift. Patrick had dozed in fits and starts after that. Then the carer had arrived late again this morning, rushed and apologetic, so that he hadn't even had time for a shower. He sniffed his armpits, hoping he'd remembered deodorant. Just in case, he reached into the glove compartment for a roll on, undoing a shirt button and dabbing it on quickly. This was life nowadays. All fits and starts and making do.

When Mrs Visser let him in, she said, 'Why have you arrested Ade? I don't understand. He wouldn't have killed two people.'

'He's helping us with enquiries. That's all I can say for now.'

She pressed her lips together, her mouth drawing down. She looked haggard. 'You'd better come to the kitchen.'

He followed her into the airy, gleaming room. She pulled open a drawer. 'The card is in there, just below the leaflets.'

He pulled on gloves and took the leaflets out, exposing the postcard below. He removed it, looked at both sides and then placed it in an evidence bag. He took a photo of each side with his phone. 'When did you find this?'

'On Tuesday evening. I was looking for cutlery. I have touched it. I took it out to look at it and then I put it back. I know I should have called you straight away.'

'Why didn't you?'

Instead of answering she said, 'Will you have a coffee with me?'

It was like a plea. 'Okay, thanks. Black for me.' It would help keep him awake. 'I just need to make a call.'

He stepped out into the hallway, closed the door behind him, and called the guv. She was at her desk, so he sent her a photo and filled her in on what Mrs Visser had found.

He went back into the kitchen and sat at the glass-topped table looking out to the manicured garden. The house was so shiny and uncluttered, so quiet. He'd love to live somewhere like this, in an elegant street. The messy semi that he shared with Noah fronted the busy road leading out of town to the beach. The living room vibrated every time a bus went past, and having the windows open meant you tasted diesel fumes. The coffee was proper stuff in a cafetière that Mrs Visser brought to the table on a tray with mugs and a plate of biscuits. She put two placemats down. Despite her agitation, she was being a polite host. He thought she'd be the kind of woman who always held things together. Bit like the guv, from what he'd seen of her.

He took two biscuits. He hadn't had time to eat yet today. 'Did you tell your son about finding the postcard?'

'No. I wanted to but I just couldn't find a way. He's been so distraught and I didn't know what to make of it. It's such a peculiar thing. It didn't come through the post. Do you think Lauren might have made it herself?'

He thought it unlikely. Maybe Visser had, threatening her with what was to come and maybe his mother had thought that. Mrs Visser was chewing her lip. 'Are you frightened of your son?' he asked.

'What? No! That's not why I didn't speak to him about it. I felt confused. This has all been so hard to deal with. But after you asked him to go to the station with you, I realized I had to. What do you think it means? Was someone threatening Lauren?'

'I don't know. We'll have to send it for forensic testing. That might tell us something. Why didn't you contact us straight away?'

'I'm not sure. I was shocked. I couldn't think clearly but I've been worrying about it, knowing I should have. I'm sorry.' Mrs Visser looked out to the garden. The sky had darkened and it had started to rain, a light drizzle. She spoke angrily. 'Sometimes I really do wonder if everything is just random and pointless, whether there's any meaning to anything in this life.'

He stared at her profile and took a long drink to steady himself. It was strange to hear those raw sentiments from this well-mannered, carefully dressed woman with her Home Counties accent. He had often had those exact thoughts himself since what happened to Noah. He tried to keep them at bay with work but in quiet moments, they crept into his mind.

On the way back to the station he called in to check on Noah. It wasn't a day for the social centre so his brother was on his own for part of it. He was calling in because at four o'clock that morning he'd wished Noah dead. The medics had said that he might have another stroke, that if you'd had one, there might be more. Lying half awake in his bed, Patrick had wished that his brother would have another stroke that would finish him off, liberating both of them. He might live for years, slowly deteriorating and becoming more dependent. Patrick's life would continue in its current rut, a pattern of juggling work, tending to Noah and trying to keep the house afloat.

Noah was sitting in his adapted chair in the living room, amid the usual tide of clutter that always spread around him. They had a cleaner who came for a couple of hours a week but she only had time to touch the surface. The house always smelled a bit ripe, like an animal's burrow, and the kitchen was a minefield of sticky patches and dropped foods. As Patrick came through the front door, he spotted a piece of toast and jam on the carpet that must have escaped from Noah's tray in transit.

Noah was reading a book on his iPad, which was sitting in a special arm attachment on his chair. A soap opera was flickering on the TV screen with the volume low. The kind of programme Noah would have mocked not so long ago, saying that daytime telly was for saddos. He looked up as Patrick came in and gave his lopsided smile and a slightly mistimed, floppy high five.

'Crime novel,' he said indistinctly. 'Page sixty. I've already guessed who did it.'

'Glad you have, bro, 'cause I haven't a clue about the murders we're working on. You okay?'

Noah grimaced. He'd been the good-looking one of the two brothers but now his face was chubby and his neck was vanishing into folds of flesh. 'Sorry I woke you up last night. Naff.'

'It's okay. Don't worry about it. What time did the carer leave?'

'Just gone nine. Didn't have time to give me a shower because of running late. I managed a sort of wash so not too pongy.'

Patrick felt a flash of annoyance. 'That's not right. I'm going to complain.'

'Oh, don't sweat it. I'll survive a day unshowered. Love a cuppa though, managed to spill most of the last one.'

A lorry crashed its gears outside and the window rattled. Noah was smiling. How did he stay so cheerful, sitting here day after day trapped in his own body, listening to the traffic grind its way to and from the coast? He used to take his surfboard there, run the path to the headland. He'd been a lean, fit machine until the evening someone found him collapsed on the coast path. The GP had told their weeping mother that *it was just one of those things.* She'd said it wasn't fair that this should happen to a fit young man who looked after himself but Patrick knew life didn't work like that. He'd been a police constable for a while by then and he'd seen plenty of decent people whose lives had been shattered by random events.

He glanced at his watch. The carer wasn't due for another two hours — if she was punctual, which was unlikely. He didn't have time. The guv would wonder where he'd got to. 'Okay. Camomile time of day for you, right?'

CHAPTER NINETEEN

Siv looked at the time and rang Patrick. She was curt with him, asking where he'd got to. How long did it take to bag an item and bring it back? He was on his way, he said jumpily.

Siv had spoken to Visser again. When she showed him the photo of the postcard and told him where his mother had found it, he looked as if a truck had hit him. He said he'd never seen it before and had no idea what it meant. She'd believed him and sent him back to his cell. Now Ali was perched on the corner of her desk, swinging a leg, while she finished the call to Patrick.

'He sounds knackered,' she said. 'Is there something going on with him? He looks unfocused at times and I saw him asleep in his car the other day.'

Ali fingered his beard. 'He has a tricky time at home, guv. He lives with his brother, Noah. Noah had a stroke a couple of years ago and it left him pretty disabled. So Patrick has a lot of caring to do.'

'No one else around?'

'They lived with their mum but she died six months after Noah had the stroke.'

'It would have been helpful if someone had told me about this.' Mortimer should have told her.

'Sorry, guv. Noah has carers going in and some days he attends a centre, but it's still a big responsibility for Patrick.'

'Okay. Thanks for telling me now. So — this postcard. I think Visser was telling the truth when he said he knew nothing about it. Either Lauren made it herself, which seems unlikely, or someone gave it to her or posted it through the letterbox.'

'If she came home and found it, why not tell anyone and why keep it in a drawer?'

'I can imagine she might do that out of shock. People shove red bills, debt letters and other post they don't want to think about in drawers. Out of sight, out of mind.' Mutsi used to until their father or a new man with a healthy bank balance bailed her out. *What I don't see I don't worry about.* They'd twice been threatened with electricity disconnection and on one terrible morning, the bailiffs had turned up. It was why Siv was always so careful to pay all her bills on time.

'Interesting that she didn't tell her husband.'

'Along with other things. She certainly kept him out of the loop when she wanted to. But now I think this might be what she wanted to talk to Seaton about when she asked to meet him. He says they'd been close, confiding in each other, and maybe she missed that. We can now say with some assurance that the weapon used was scissors and that Lauren was definitely the primary target. Can you let Steve Wooton know about this and tell him we're sending the postcard for testing? Here's Patrick at last.'

He came in, perspiring and holding the evidence bag out like a peace offering. 'Sorry, guv. Mrs Visser wanted to talk and then the traffic was bad.'

He had a husky voice, a catch in his throat. He sounded more like a smoker than Ali did. Siv examined the card on both sides. Homemade, a bit messy. She read out the message. '*You will be the one to feel the pain soon enough.* The underlined "You" implying that someone else had felt the pain before? So perhaps this was a revenge killing.' She passed it to Ali and turned back to Patrick. 'What did Mrs Visser have to say?'

'She found the card on Tuesday evening when she was looking for cutlery. She was frightened by it. Sort of frozen, I'd say. She looks as if she can't believe what's going on. She said she didn't tell Visser about it because he's been so upset. I got the impression she tiptoes around him.'

'If he was a difficult husband then he's probably a difficult son,' Ali said.

'I asked her if she was frightened of Visser but she said no. She contacted us because we'd brought him in and she realized this might be important evidence. Maybe she wonders if he did it and thought she was protecting him.'

Siv glanced at him. He was holding onto the back of a chair. He looked hot and rushed. That had been a good question to ask Mrs Visser. A strange detachment seized her. She had a sensation of being outside herself and regarding the three of them talking. It had happened a couple of times in the last few months but not recently. She licked her dry lips, aware that she was speaking a little too loudly. 'Thanks, Patrick. Ade Visser has now told us that he went to visit a sex worker in London in the early hours of Monday morning and reiterated that he didn't get back home until nine thirty. We're asking the Met to check out Ms Davis, the sex worker. If it all adds up, he can't have stuck the scissors in his wife and Rimas. Ali, can you get this evidence over to Steve?'

Ali took the hint and left the office.

'Sit down a minute, Patrick. Take a breath. I understand that you help to look after your brother.'

He blushed. 'Yeah, guv, that's right. Who told you?'

'That doesn't matter. I'm glad I know. You look tired sometimes.'

He sat up straight. 'Yeah. I do a good job, though. I don't slack, guv.'

'Okay and I'm not suggesting you do. But it can be hard when you're pedalling furiously below water to stay afloat.'

He bristled. 'Who says I am?'

'I do. I know because there are times when I am too. It takes one to know one, Patrick.'

He shot her a surprised look but said nothing. He was behaving like a suspect under questioning and she half expected a *no comment*.

'That was good work today. This isn't a pep talk or a guilt trip. We all limp along in life in our own ways. I'm acknowledging that we can carry burdens, but there's a demanding job to do. Okay?'

'Okay, guv.'

'Right. If there's anything I need to know about regarding your home situation or anything you think I can help with, let me know. Now, can you get back to Mrs Visser and tell her we need her fingerprints to check against the postcard. I don't want her going home without that happening.'

In the main office, Ali nodded to Patrick. 'You okay?'

'Yeah. Guv knows about Noah.'

'I told her. She asked about you, wondered if you were all right, so I thought it best.'

'Right. I don't need her sympathy.' He chewed at the edge of his thumbnail.

'Hey, big lad, ease back. I don't think she's that type. If anything, she can be a bit sharp. Look — she was widowed last year so she knows it can be tough.'

Patrick nodded. Truth was, he felt relieved that the guv knew. She'd been okay. The previous guv had been a bristling macho type and you could never show weakness. It had encouraged Patrick to stay wound like a spring. He reached for his phone to ring Mrs Visser. Then he was going to get on to the care agency and give them hell.

* * *

The dog had been fed and was in his bed, dozing. Monty was getting old, like him. Now it was his turn to eat. There were seven days in a week, so Alan Vine had seven dinners: beef stew, ham and eggs, pork chops, fish and chips, roast or casseroled chicken, macaroni cheese and shepherd's pie. He varied the sequence so as not to get into too much of a rut.

He'd read all the stuff in the papers about keeping active and healthy in old age, and that included the brain. He dreaded losing his marbles and being carried off to some old folks' home where he'd be fed baby mush. Tonight was pork chops, with mashed potatoes and frozen peas. He'd never married and had always been competent at looking after himself. That's what the army did for you. Set you up for life. His one-bedroom bungalow was spic and span, everything in its place and as it should be, each task with its allotted time. 5.45 p.m. was time to start dinner.

He seasoned the chop ready for the oven, then peeled the potatoes and put them on to boil. When he told people he cooked proper meals for himself every day, they seemed amazed. He couldn't afford convenience food but he wouldn't want to buy it even if he could. He liked to know what he was eating. He watched the woman over the road when she came back from the supermarket, heaving bags full of frozen stuff into the house. Pizzas and the like. No wonder that whole family was fat. They all had legs like tree trunks. He saw the kids puffing along the pavement and shook his head. He didn't say anything, of course. You weren't supposed to express opinions these days. Might hurt someone's feelings. Alan prided himself on being fit for his age, despite the angina. He walked miles every day, in all weather.

He sat at the table with his dinner and a glass of milk. He had the paper by his elbow but ignored it, looking out to his patch of garden. All week, he'd been thinking about those bodies and the photograph. The most peculiar thing had been seeing that kid smiling up from the dead woman. As if someone was playing a horrible joke. It had made him feel queer. He'd taken a good look at the photo before he phoned the police. Something had stirred in his memory and he'd wanted to think about it.

That inspector had rubbed him up the wrong way, keeping him waiting and interrupting. And then she'd got on her high horse about the sign, talking down to him as if he was some kind of idiot. He'd noticed her sergeant trying to cover a smile now and again, making fun of him. He knew what these youngsters thought of him, that he was a boring old fart. The oldest of the fat kids across the road, the spotty one, had called him that a couple of weeks ago when he'd told her to pick up a chocolate wrapper she'd chucked on the pavement. If Drummond could take her time then so could he. He'd mull over what he'd seen, and she needn't think she could needle him into telling her anything he didn't want to either. People always underestimated him now he was old; he might as well be invisible. Well, he could turn that to his advantage. The Drummond woman thought she was so smart, let her solve the murders if she could. And then she'd turned on the fake concern, saying he'd had a nasty experience. Hilarious. He'd seen too much of death to get fussed about those bodies by the trees. The dead man was just riff-raff, probably an illegal, and that woman had no right to be swimming where she wasn't wanted.

He'd seen the woman at the river last year and given her a piece of his mind. They'd had a real barney, with her going on about wild places belonging to everyone and saying that angling was a cruel sport and should be banned. He'd wanted to hit her then. He'd had two abiding loves in his life: the army and fishing. It was as if she'd spat on him, the way she'd ranted on about anglers: *You men and your casual cruelty. Fishing is just another blood sport. Have you any idea of the pain you cause? Would you do that to your dog, stick a hook in his mouth and half suffocate him, traumatize him?* He'd yelled back *Don't you insult me! You don't know anything about me. I love nature as much as you do and by the way, fish don't feel pain!* He'd had to walk away in the end because he thought he might smack her, and he'd never yet raised his hand to a woman. He'd been shaking and when he got home, he'd had to have a rest. So she'd get no sympathy vote from him.

While he'd twiddled his thumbs in the back of the police car, he'd had time to think things through. First day in the army he'd been given the mantra *keep your eyes open and your mouth shut,* and had decided to ration what he'd tell the police.

Enough to keep them happy. Nick Shelton's family might own the land at Lock Lane but as far as Alan was concerned, he was the true custodian. Nick had said at the last AGM that he didn't know what he'd do without Alan staying on watch like the true soldier he was. They'd given him a round of applause. He fished most days, except of course in the close season, and by the end of it, he was fidgeting to get his rod out again. He visited Lock Lane every day to check the place over, clearing any litter that had been left, doing a bit of weeding, observing the state and flow of the river. Sometimes he walked there and took a sandwich and a flask of tea. He'd sit by the riverbank and watch the water. The day he couldn't go there any longer, his heart might as well stop beating.

He peeled an apple. One portion of his five a day. He took pleasure in keeping the skin unbroken in one long curling ribbon and then coiling it on the plate. As he drew the sharp blade carefully along the soft pink skin, he thought again about a skinny little thing with bunches, narrowing his eyes to look down the tunnel of the years. He'd been trying to bring her into focus all week. The image sharpened as the peel lifted off and bingo! There she was. Must have been more than twenty years ago, so his memory was doing okay. She'd been down by the river with her dad. That was unusual — kids weren't encouraged — so maybe that's why he'd remembered. What was the dad's name? James somebody. Didn't come to the river that often. A right snob with a clipped accent, always talking down to you and boasting about the size of his catch. Like some of the loud-mouthed officers he'd had to put up with in the army. He'd avoided the man when he could. Then James had left the club suddenly. Something had happened but Alan couldn't remember any details. He could see the girl, though, sitting on the grass and playing with her soft toys, chatting to them and pretending to give them a picnic. Sophie — that had been her name. He reached for the notepad and wrote it down: *Sophie*. He'd said hello to her and she'd smiled at him. A pretty, light little fairy of a thing, not like those tubs of lard across the road. He remembered her dad calling over to her. *Sophie, come and see this big fish I've caught!*

He shared the inspector's interest in the child's photo. Sophie's photo. He could tell she thought it was important when she showed it to him. Why would anyone have left it there? The more he mulled it over the more his interest grew. It was something different, a real-life puzzle instead of the ones he completed in the newspaper. He thought he'd call into the Boar's Head tomorrow lunch time and have a chat with Nick's dad, Mike. Mike always called him Viney in a matey way that reminded him of being in barracks. He was always there with his pint at around half twelve, getting nicely pissed. Mike had been a sergeant in a tank regiment but he never pulled rank. He was always up for a bit of a yarn, particularly stuff about the club, and he'd be interested to hear how Viney had given a DNA sample. He'd enjoyed that bit. It had made him feel important. He'd buy Mike a drink and drop in something about the little girl and her dad. Mike would know what had happened, he had a razor-sharp memory, and now that he'd handed over the land and business to his son, he liked to reminisce about the old days.

If he could find out the details about Sophie and her dad, he might get the police a lead on who'd committed the murders. That would give the inspector and her sergeant a shock, if he walked into the police station and told them *he'd* got them crucial information. He'd like to see their faces when the boring old fart came up trumps.

He finished his apple — core and all — and washed and dried up. He set his place for breakfast: bowl, spoon and cereal in a Tupperware container. He'd read that the Queen kept hers in one and if it was good enough for HRM, it was good enough for Private A. Vine. Then he sat in the armchair by the window. Satisfied that he had a plan of action, he picked up his history of the Suez crisis and listened to the dog snoring, his tail thumping as he dreamed.

CHAPTER TWENTY

The Met report had come in. It said that Ms Serena Davis had confirmed that Ade Visser had been with her in the early hours of Monday morning. They'd sent a voice recording. She sounded a confident, upbeat woman:

I've known Ade for years. He's one of my regulars. We have an arrangement about once a month. Sometimes he rings in advance, other times it's impromptu. He rang me around half two in the morning and said he was in Earl's Court. I could tell he badly needed a session so I said I had availability for a couple of hours from half three. He arrived about then and left at half six. The session was two hours but it was strenuous so he needed to have a shower and rest for an hour before he left.

They'd released Visser, which meant that Siv had to head to the top floor and report to Mortimer that their main suspect was in the clear and out of custody, and that the other suspect's whereabouts at the time of the murders was still being checked but seemed firm.

'We're following every lead, sir. It's hard to believe that no one recognizes the child in the photo.'

He rubbed his inflamed face. 'Well, you need to push on. Push harder, make sure everyone's pulling their weight.'

That was a lot of pushing and pulling. 'Okay, sir. I understand.'

'Good. This is all very unfortunate.'

She wasn't sure if he meant for her or the corpses in the morgue. She didn't stay around to ask.

* * *

Jenna Seaton was fed up to the back teeth. Mrs Dexter had gone down with tonsillitis and within a day the house had started to look untidy. Harvey had been moping about ever since he'd seen the police. They'd barely spoken since his confession. All he'd told her was that he'd spoken to Inspector Drummond and she'd made him draw a map of his route on Monday. When Jenna had pressed him, he'd turned on her, yelling, *I don't bloody know if the police bloody believed me so can you get off my bloody case!* He'd never shouted at her before and she'd locked herself in her bathroom and wept. This was the thanks she got for being his rock!

She found herself distracted at work, constantly replaying the past months as if they were a film she was pausing and examining from different angles. She tried to recall if Harvey's tone had been different or if he had seemed inattentive, but couldn't spot any signs that he'd been hand in hand with Lauren. Her stomach churned. In the middle of the night, she'd realized that the worst aspect of all this was that she now knew that her husband was a good liar. She'd have said she trusted Harvey with her life and here he was, just another phoney who cheated on his wife with one of their friends because he was bored. Then she thought that no, there was an even worse aspect — she didn't know if she'd ever want sex with the pathetic two-faced bastard again. Hunky, sexy Harvey had dwindled to a pigmy overnight.

Then Ade had turned up half an hour ago. He was the last person she felt like seeing. He and Harvey were sitting out on the terrace, not talking. She'd made a pot of coffee and put biscuits out but they were untouched, apart from the odd fly dive-bombing them.

She glanced out at them, both sitting slightly hunched like two old men with hours to waste and nothing to say to each other. She didn't think Harvey had showered today and his skin looked dingy. Ade might look terrible but at least he was scrubbed and smelled nice. He always did look newly minted. She took her fruit tea out and joined them, another hunched and silent figure. The late-afternoon sun was mellow and clumps of bluebells were flowering at the edge of the orchard. Many a time they'd sat out like this, chatting and laughing. Lots of horse talk, inevitably. It had always been better if wet blanket Lauren wasn't there with her serious face, because of course she'd objected to horse racing, saying it was cruel and wrong. She'd dragged on for ages about the Grand National. She might as well be here today because she was certainly still putting a dampener on everything.

'How are you managing, Ade?' Jenna asked at last.

'I don't know. I don't know what to think. My mother found a postcard in the kitchen drawer and gave it to the police. Cut-out scissors glued on with paint that looked like blood and a threatening message. Horrible.'

Jenna put her cup down. 'Sent to who?'

'No name on it, or address.'

'It hadn't been posted?'

'No. There was no stamp. The police wanted to know if I'd ever seen it and I told them I hadn't. My mother didn't tell me about it — she phoned the police instead of talking to me.'

Jenna looked at Harvey but he ignored her gaze, completely withdrawn. *He knows something.* It was as if someone had stolen the man she knew and left a malfunctioning replica. 'But how did it get in the kitchen drawer?'

Ade shrugged. 'No idea. Lauren must have put it there. I've found out that there were all sorts of things she kept from me. She was organizing a protest of some kind about a notice at Lock Lane, calling for crowdfunding and such. I'm starting to think I hardly knew her. I felt like a complete idiot when the police brought that up and then when they showed me the postcard.'

'I'm sorry. That's hard, finding out that someone's been keeping secrets. Isn't it, Harvey?'

Harvey looked into his cup and made a noncommittal noise. Jenna wanted to kick him hard.

Ade stirred his coffee and drank it down. 'Sorry, I haven't come here to burden you. Jenna, I wondered if you'd help me with arrangements for Lauren's funeral. I have to wait for them to release her but it would be good to know I've got some support. I just can't think straight about anything.'

Jenna pictured a large wreath with SLUT written in flowers in the centre. 'Won't your mother want to help you with that?'

'She's gone home. I told her to go. I didn't want her around. I felt she'd betrayed me by looking through the drawers and ringing the police without informing me about the card. You expect your close family to have your back, don't you?'

'Yes,' Jenna agreed. 'You would hope that you can trust your nearest and dearest but sadly, it doesn't always seem to work out that way.'

Harvey stirred himself and put a paper napkin over the biscuits. 'We're all fallible. We all make mistakes.'

Ade looked at him. Jenna felt an urge to tell Ade, heard herself say the words that would force Harvey to reveal what a true friend he'd been. What a relief it would be! Ade deserved to know what his wife had really been like. The stuff about crowdfunding and a hidden postcard only touched the surface!

'Of course I'll help you. I'm sure Harvey will too, won't you?'

'Sure. I think I'd better see to the horses now.' Usually, he'd have asked Ade if he wanted to wander over but the invitation wasn't forthcoming.

As he stood, a tall bulky man with short cornrows appeared around the side of the house.

'Oh, not again,' Ade groaned. He grew even paler. 'Have you found the murderer?'

'Good afternoon. Not yet, Mr Visser. Still investigating. I knocked on the door but there was no answer and then I heard your voices. DS Ali Carlin, Berminster police. I've come to speak to Mr Seaton.' Gazing at him with wary eyes, Ali thought they made a furtive-looking threesome. Visser didn't want the Seatons to know about his BDSM interests and they didn't want him to know that Harvey had been canoodling with Lauren. Good basis for a friendship, Ali thought.

Ade looked relieved to hear he was off the hook for now. He glanced at Harvey and then at the sergeant. 'What are you bothering Harvey for?'

'Just routine. We're talking to all the people who knew your wife.'

'Oh, I see. I'll be off, then. Thanks for the coffee. Talk later.' He walked away fast, stumbling as he turned the corner.

Harvey stood frozen to the spot, like a child playing statues. The sergeant sat without being invited in the chair that Ade had vacated. Jenna fumed. *This is how the police treat you once you've made yourself a suspect.*

'Lovely garden,' Ali said. 'Is it okay to talk here, Mr Seaton?'

Harvey scratched his eyebrow. 'I was just about to check the horses, if you want to walk over with me.' He was trying to sound relaxed.

'I'm sure Sergeant Carlin doesn't want to tramp across fields.' Jenna adjusted her seat cushion. 'We can sit here. There's coffee in the pot. You don't mind if I sit in, do you, Sergeant?'

'No skin off my nose,' Ali said, glancing at their faces. This could be interesting. They looked like rich, comfortable people who were losing their gloss and wondering where it was vanishing to.

'I'd rather you didn't,' Harvey said to her.

'I'm sure, but I'd rather I did.' Jenna sat and poured coffee for Ali, asking if he took milk and sugar.

Harvey glared at her and then sat. He took his panama hat from the table and put it on his head, pulling the brim low.

Ali took a sip of his coffee. Full-bodied, with a kick. He eyed the biscuits and put his hands under the table to resist temptation. Instead, he glanced at the Seatons. He reckoned that if he touched the air between husband and wife, he would come across a wall of ice. 'Mr Seaton, when you spoke to Inspector Drummond you explained that you'd had a close friendship with Lauren Visser.'

'A *tendresse* apparently,' Jenna said icily.

'Jenna, *please.* Don't make this any more painful. Yes, that's what I told the inspector.'

'You told us that this friendship ended by mutual consent in February.'

'Yes.'

'We've looked at your phone and retrieved data which you'd deleted. You exchanged texts with Lauren last Saturday. You agreed to meet her at Halse woods on Sunday afternoon, the day before she was killed.'

Seaton folded his arms. Looked away, then down. 'Yes, I did.'

The air seemed to quiver. 'You're such a fucking liar,' Jenna said. She shoved her chair back and it screeched on the paving. 'Such a fucking, unbelievable liar! If you told me it was raining, I'd know it was sunny.'

There was a silence. Ali copied the guv's example and let it roll.

Seaton leaned on the table, his face cupped in his hands. 'If you've looked at the texts you'll know that Lauren initiated the contact. I didn't meet her.'

'But you planned to?'

'Yes.'

'Why didn't you?'

'I can answer that,' Jenna said. 'At least you know it will be the truth. I wanted to go for a ride. Wanted to spend some *quality* time with my husband. So we set out after lunch and we didn't get back until five. Sorry to spoil your little tryst in the woods, darling.'

Ali looked at her gleaming, sculpted hair and wondered how much it cost to keep in that condition. Polly's was always scrunched flat and tied back. She said it never quite lost the smell of cooking, no matter how often she washed it. He liked the homely scent of it because it reminded him of his granny's kitchen, but he knew better than to tell her that. 'Thank you, Mrs Seaton, that's clear. You lied to us, Mr Seaton and you tried to cover up a contact with a woman who was murdered by deleting information. That's serious.'

'I'm sorry. I just wanted it all to go away and in the end, I didn't think it was that important because I didn't actually see her on Sunday. I've no idea what she wanted.'

Jenna made a noise like a pressure cooker starting to steam.

'The texts indicate that Lauren wanted your advice about something, Mr Seaton. She was worried. Do you know what the problem was?'

'No idea. I honestly haven't had a private conversation with her since February. You've seen the texts. I kept my replies straightforward. I only agreed to meet her because she sounded so anxious. I didn't want to. I'd never have contacted her personally again. That's the absolute truth.' He directed that at his wife but she sniffed and looked away.

'And whatever was worrying Lauren, she hadn't mentioned it to you, Mrs Seaton?'

'Oh no, Sergeant. But then the little tart preferred a male confidant, didn't she? Oh, I've bloody well had enough of this!' She banged her chair back and went into the house.

'I'm sorry,' Seaton said. 'My wife is under a lot of strain.'

'That's about it, really. Oh — what colour is your horse?'

'It's a black Welsh cob. A stallion with white hooves. Why?'

'And that's the horse you were riding on Monday morning?'

'Of course, yes. Did someone see me?'

He was looking hopeful but Ali didn't feel like helping the lying bastard. Let him stew a bit longer. He was a waste of good air. 'I can't comment at present. We'll return your phone tomorrow, if you can call at the station. Thanks for your time. I'll leave you to your horses.'

* * *

There was just sea and sky. The faint hiss of the retreating tide. The quiet evening light was fading slowly, as if someone was turning a dimmer switch. The water below changed from blue to indigo to wine purple as the sun set.

Siv had the place to herself. She picked a blade of grass and chewed on it. Cliffdean Point was six miles from town, a grassy headland that looked out over the channel. Below were tall sand dunes and a stretch of shingle dotted with wading birds. She lay back on the grass and watched the high, rose-streaked clouds. She was doing okay. Day by day. Other people were responding as if she was functioning and making sense, so she must be. She'd read about impostor syndrome but never felt like it before. There were still times when she felt a creeping numbness and had to fight it. She hadn't talked to Ed for a couple of nights. Was that a good sign? She thought it must be. Maybe she'd just been too tired.

This case, these dead. She sifted through what she knew and it didn't amount to much. Now that Visser and Seaton had alibis, there were so many questions. Mason Granger didn't own a car and hadn't hired one. She closed her eyes and saw the child's face, eager to please the photographer. She lay there until the sky darkened, and then roused herself and drove home.

She'd bought a bottle of wine for Corran and Paul by way of thanks for her supper and free firewood. As she approached their door, she heard angry raised voices from inside.

I haven't had time, Corran! It's all right for you, working at home, suiting yourself what you do and when you do it!

I was only asking, no need to bite my head off. And I have my own pressures here, you know.

What, whether or not the goats are content? I'm knackered. Just want to chill out and have a bath. I'm not up to conversation so get off my case.

I am entitled to talk. I've been on my own all day. I look forward to you coming home.

Don't start fucking guilt tripping me. I'm talked out.

It's not a guilt trip . . .

She placed the bottle quietly by the door and walked back to her car on shaky legs. Paul had sounded so vicious. She'd never have thought that he and Corran would row like that. They seemed so peaceable, in tune. She realized that she'd already spun a little story about their domestic harmony, one to suit her needs. She and Ed had never had a row. One of them might be snappy occasionally but they'd never got into a deep disagreement. They'd laughed themselves out of any tensions. She realized that was probably rare. She knew what she'd lost.

She locked her door and went straight into her routine: on with Ed's sweatshirt and then a glass of akvavit. She opened all the windows. The river was quiet tonight, just the odd splash from an animal. It was too warm to light the stove. She made cheese on toast and ate at the fold-down table. Then she fetched the section of sculpture she was working on and sat until almost 2 a.m., topping up her glass of cold spirit, checking her diagram and measurements, lost in minute paper folds.

CHAPTER TWENTY-ONE

'He's not a bad bloke at heart and I sort of miss him now,' Lynda Rochford said. She was dressed in tight, skimpy shorts and a sleeveless vest and was resting back with her feet on a low stool. It was mid-afternoon and she had a large glass of wine to hand. She seemed pleased to have Patrick's company.

He found himself mesmerized by the sweep of her false eyelashes. 'Was Mr Rochford ever violent towards you?'

'Not as such. He gave me a push once but then I shoved him, so fair dibs. He got to be really shouty, that's what did my head in. His voice used to grate. It's been peaceful since I've been on my own. Bit too peaceful. It gets lonely at times but I've got the two kids so once they're home, the noise kicks off. Are you married?'

'No, still waiting for the right woman. What was the shouting about?'

She made a rubbing motion with her fingers. She still wore her wedding ring. 'Dosh. Si used to work at the Hind hotel in town. It was good money but he got stressed out. Long hours, lots of responsibility. Weddings and parties to cater for. He'd get awful headaches and his blood pressure was high. We hardly got any time together. So he took the job at Caterpillar Corner. Nice cushy number but a drop in pay. I suppose we'd got used to a better standard of living and then we had to be more careful with money. So you know, there were arguments. Some of them ding-dongs. That was when nosy Nora next door called your lot. I wish people would mind their own business. It all went downhill after that. Si never laid a finger on me though. I told those officers who came here at the time.'

'Has Mr Rochford ever mentioned a Lauren Visser to you?'

She took a drink. 'Don't think so.' Her tone sharpened. 'Hang on, isn't she the woman found at the river?'

'That's right. She worked at Caterpillar Corner.'

'Crumbs, you don't think Si did it?'

'We're making lots of enquiries, talking to everyone.'

'Si wouldn't do anything like that. He just gets a bit chippy but he wouldn't harm anyone.'

That's what the wives and girlfriends nearly always say, Patrick thought as she showed him out.

At the door she asked, 'Are you seeing Si as well?'

'Yes, I'll be contacting him.'

'Remind him he's got the kids on Sunday. If he wants to stop for a bite of lunch that's okay with me.'

Patrick found Simon Rochford sitting in a deckchair on the balcony of his ground-floor flat, his legs propped on the railing, listening to a cricket match on the radio and drinking beer. Their conversation was punctuated by the thwack of bat on ball and bursts of applause. Rochford told him much the same story as his ex-wife had, but with his own slant.

'Lynda persuaded me to take a less stressful job and then she complained I wasn't earning as much. I couldn't win. All I got was her whingeing on about us not having enough money. We used to have the odd row like any couple but it got a lot worse. We gave each other hell. I suppose the woman next door was right to report us if it worried her, but we could have done without her sticking her oar in and bringing the police to the door.' He gave a nostalgic sigh. 'Sometimes I miss the ups and downs, having a good shouting match. Now I've no one to yell at but myself.'

'Did you ever see Lauren Visser outside of work?'

Rochford turned the radio off and drew himself up. 'No, I didn't. I can spot you coming a mile away. Just because Lynda and me had some rows, you're thinking I might have been violent. Well, I wasn't.'

'We're asking a lot of people these questions.'

'I've already told your DI Drummond that Lauren nagged me about my menus. I take pride in my work and I spend a lot of time scheduling balanced meals at the nursery, sourcing free-range meat and eggs and local organic produce. Jenna doesn't stint on the budget for that. Mind you, it's reflected in the fees. I put up good, tasty meals and I get lots of positive feedback from the parents. I even arrange taster sessions for them a couple of times a year when I'm trying out new recipes. Lauren was a po-faced moaner who gave me earache but that was no reason to murder her. Maybe her husband did it. I can imagine that I might have contemplated it if I'd been married to her. That's a joke in poor taste, I know, but I don't like you coming here asking me stuff I've already answered, just because a neighbour overheard our personal business.'

'Thanks for your time, Mr Rochford. I'd like to take a look at your car. Just the outside.'

'Oh, feel free. It's parked around the corner in front of the garages. The grey Toyota. Tax and insurance all up to date.'

'I'll see myself out. Lynda said you can stay for lunch on Sunday if you like.' Patrick felt foolish as Rochford stared and then nodded. He had the feeling that given a nudge, these two might get together again. Maybe he should add *relationship guidance* to his Twitter profile.

He walked around the car in the heat and glare. The tyres were Pirelli and all in good nick. He reckoned Rochford had a clean slate.

* * *

The mayor had declared the May festival open. A group of women Morris dancers in red and white skirts and black tights were executing a stately dance outside the fish market at the harbour. Their clogs rang on the cobbles. Siv stood in the high sun, watching them. The bells on their straw hats jingled as they turned and dipped, waving white flags. They'd pinned fresh flowers all over their bodices and hats. They looked warm but jolly. Mutsi had once insisted that she and Rikka attend a Finnish folk dancing club in Wimbledon. *You must know about your Finnish culture, it's your heritage.* They'd had to wear scratchy long skirts with black-and-white-striped aprons. The dances had been faster and lighter than the plodding Morris type and they involved couples and groups. The dancing hadn't lasted long because they'd flitted to Biarritz, Finnish heritage abandoned for a French financier with a yacht.

There was a tap on her shoulder and Patrick was there with a man in a wheelchair.

'Hi, guv. This is my brother, Noah. Noah, my new guv.'

'Hello, Noah. I'm Siv.'

'Nice to meet you,' Noah said slowly, smiling crookedly. 'Hope Patrick's behaving.'

'Oh, I never tell tales,' Siv said, smiling back.

Noah had thick fair hair, streaked with gel. The right side of his face was askew, his mouth slanting. His electric wheelchair looked top of the range, with a joystick on the left side. His fingers rested on the arms and Siv saw that he had two words tattooed in red on the backs of his hands: *No* on the right and *Pity* on the left.

Patrick waved to one of the dancers. 'Our mum was a Morris dancer one time. Sewed the costumes as well. She used to practice steps in the garden.'

'Hate bloody folk music,' Noah grumbled. 'Fol-de-rol-de-diddly-dee. What d'you think, Siv?'

'I like it, as long as no one wants me to take part.'

'There was a big bust-up a couple of years ago.' Patrick rubbed his face briskly. 'Some women wanted to join the male Morris team and they weren't allowed. There was a campaign but I think it all fizzled out.'

Sounds like the kind of issue Lauren Visser would have got caught up in, Siv thought. 'Amazing, what gets people fired up and falling out.'

'If it escalates far enough, it brings business your way,' Noah said wryly.

'That's true. If people didn't argue, we'd be short of customers.'

'We'd better get going. Don't forget to stop by our Berminster police stand outside the fire station. We're there for two hours,' Patrick reminded her.

'Hashtag keepingberminstersafe. Patrick's the media savvy poster boy. I'm handing out community safety leaflets.' Noah attempted to wink at her but it didn't quite come off and his face twisted.

She watched them head off, Noah gliding quietly, Patrick walking beside him. They were both smartly dressed in suits. That would have taken an effort. She wondered how long it took Noah to get ready and if a carer had helped him or if Patrick had had to do it.

She wandered among the thronged streets and stalls for a while, moving between aromas and music. She was glad to see uniformed officers circulating. This jostling crowd would be heaven for pickpockets and bag snatchers. Minstergreen had a stall, bedecked with greenery, oak leaves and flower garlands. It was laden with posters and banners about climate change and the projects underway in Berminster. Dozens of teenagers flocked around, some of them signing up as volunteers. She watched Mason Granger speaking to them, gesticulating, the centre of attention. He was a showman and a minor celebrity. A couple of young women were getting close, gazing at him intently and nodding. Well, now he had a committee that would hang on his every word without an annoying dissenter on the sidelines.

She moved on, sniffing frying onions, and saw Simon Rochford standing by a burger van called Hamborghini. He was flanked by two children, a mutinous-looking girl and a younger boy who was jumping up and down, holding a bun and licking tomato ketchup from the edges.

'But I said I didn't want mustard!' the girl was wailing.

'Okay, okay, the sky hasn't fallen in but if I change it I'll have to get back in the queue and that'll take ages,' Rochford told her. 'It's too much in this heat. Here, do you want my burger and I'll eat your hot dog?'

The girl wavered and then nodded grudgingly. He sighed and swapped with her. As he sank his teeth into the hot dog, he saw Siv and nodded dourly.

'Hello. Enjoying the day?' she asked.

''Scuse the mouthful,' he said, holding a paper napkin under his chin. His colour was high, his face shiny with sweat. 'Got a day off from trying to find a murderer?' He spoke gruffly.

'Sort of. Maybe he or she is here today, you never know . . .'

The children had crossed the road to watch a conjuror, the boy still hopping on the spot. Rochford ate his hot dog quickly and efficiently, blowing on it as he reached the middle.

'You sent someone round to my ex and to my place, asking loads of questions. I didn't appreciate that. I told you about me and Lauren up front. So much for being honest with the police.'

'We irritate lots of people when we're investigating. It's how it is.'

'Yeah.' He gestured at the food van. 'Lauren certainly wouldn't have approved of meat central here. She'd probably have been trying to persuade people not to buy.'

'She got under your skin, from the sound of it.'

'Nah, not really. Not in the way you'd like to think.' He finished his hot dog and wiped his mouth and glistening brow. 'I'd best get over to my kids before you accuse me of child neglect.'

Stroppy, she thought, watching him stride away. It smelled as if the onions were burning so she walked on to the arts-and-crafts area near the museum. Corran was selling his throws and cushions, with Paul helping him. They were both small with round glasses — Corran's frames were red and Paul's bright green. Both were light on their feet. Like bookends. Paul saw her and waved and she smiled back.

It was odd, being back in a community where people knew each other and it was hard to go out without someone calling a greeting. She felt exposed after London's anonymity and thin-skinned, because it was the bank holiday and they still had no suspect in their sights for the murders.

No steps forward. The forensics on the postcard showed no prints except Lauren's and Natasha Visser's and the type of card and glue were widely available. This was a careful, thoughtful killer.

Crossing the harbour, she saw the Polska stall with white-and-red Polish flags fluttering on the awning. A small group was dancing to three men playing fiddles and an accordion. A large crowd had gathered, whooping encouragement and waving glasses of beer in the air. Betty Marshall was there on the edge of the spectators, clapping along to the music. Siv hardly recognized her out of her working clothes. She looked carefree and younger in a silky striped shirtdress and a silver necklace.

'Hello, Inspector. Such amazing weather! You know, there's an old superstition that May is an unlucky month but it doesn't look it from here. Isn't it good to see everyone out enjoying themselves?'

'Certainly is. Do you have Polish connections, or do you just like the music?'

'My friend Julia manages Polska and she's running the stall, so I'm lending a hand. She's an amazing woman, never tires. She's just popped back to fetch some more brochures. Any news about these awful murders?'

'I can't comment on that, Ms Marshall.'

'Oh do call me Betty! I was at a litter pick at the beach the other night and I missed Lauren. She always geed us up.

Her poor husband must be in pieces. I saw him down by the sea. He was sobbing.'

'It's a very hard time for him.' *Especially as he was involved in strenuous activities with another woman just hours before his wife was stabbed.*

'And of course it's an awful time for Jenna and Harvey as well. They're such close friends. Jenna was very tense the other day.' There was a certain relish and question in Betty's words. Her eyes were glinting with the story she'd been swept up in.

Siv nodded. 'As you say, it's a difficult time for anyone who was close to Lauren. I met your friend Julia this week when I visited Polska.'

'That's right. We were saying . . . ah, here she is now.'

Julia hurried up, stopping to speak quickly to the musicians and handing a pile of brochures to a man behind the stall. She was out of breath and rosy. Her tapered jeans and tailored shirt emphasized her slender bones, but the lines scored around her eyes and neck belied the youthful image.

Betty patted her friend's arm. 'Take a breather, you'll wear yourself out! We were just talking about poor Lauren.'

'And poor Matis,' Julia reminded her. She nodded to Siv. 'Hello, Inspector. Have you tried some of our sweets? I can recommend the cheesecake. Here, have a freebie.'

Siv took the light square of cake topped with raspberries. 'Lovely, thanks.'

'Has anyone recognized the photo of that little girl?' Betty was keen to pursue the subject. 'It was on the local news. I'd have thought someone would know her if she was from round here. We've had nothing from the parents at the nursery so she doesn't seem to have anything to do with work, which is a relief, to be honest.'

'We haven't heard from anyone yet,' Siv said, her mouth full of creamy cheese.

'Maybe you should put posters up around town. Not everyone watches the news or reads the paper.'

'Betty, do leave off going on about the murder. I expect the inspector is trying to enjoy her bank holiday.' Julia smiled but her tone was dry and Betty bit her lip.

'It's okay,' Siv said. 'We might do posters next week. This cheesecake is great. I'll buy some to take home.'

As Siv was waiting for her cheesecake to be boxed up, someone took her arm and before she knew what was happening, she was drawn into a fast dance. Bartel Nowak was spinning her around. Holding her lightly but firmly, he manoeuvred her through several other couples. His beard had been trimmed. The sun made it look fiery and his bald head shone in the heat. He wore a handsome dark green waistcoat and he smelled yeasty, as if he'd been at the beer.

'This is a courtship dance,' he said in her ear, hiccuping, his breath tickling. 'Really, you should be carrying a basket of flowers.'

'If only I'd known,' she said.

'Better than your English folk dancing, eh? Better than clogs going *clomp clomp clomp* and waving a pig's bladder.'

'The pig's bladder is to shake at people to urge them on, get them to make more effort.'

'Ah, but our dancing is just to kick back and have fun. It shouldn't be an effort! This is so British, making enjoyment into a competitive chore.'

She didn't know if she felt annoyed or amused at his hijacking of her. He seemed to be enjoying himself, as did the other couples. The music was insistent and fast-paced, the fiddles lively and the accordion pumping, so she let him spin her around some more. Colours flashed before her eyes and she felt a giddy lightness, almost euphoria. Then she sensed the prickling start on her scalp as the shock of a warm, sure touch that wasn't Ed's sank in. The music was muffled and seemed far off. She slowed, pressing his arms away.

'Thanks. That's enough now.'

'Thank you, *madame*. You dance well. But next time I bring a pig's bladder to urge you on.' He stepped back, staggering slightly. 'You okay, *madame*? Have I offended you?'

'No, no offence. I'm a bit too warm, that's all. Enjoy your day.'

She collected her cheesecake, flustered. She looked around, hoping that no one had seen her and then realized that the press of people had other things to focus on and she wouldn't interest anyone. The music stopped as the musicians took a quick break and the accordionist was pouring drinks from a tall jug filled with slices of cucumber and sprigs of mint. He nodded to her, wiping his brow. He had green ribbons tied around his ponytail.

'Hi,' she said. 'Lovely music. I saw you at the nursery, didn't I? In the garden. You're Jerry Wilby.'

'That's right. I spoke to your colleague, DC Hill. We're all still finding it hard to believe that Lauren's gone.'

'Yes, it's very sad. You told DC Hill about Lauren's concern that a man had stared at her when she was swimming.'

He took a sip of his drink. 'I hope you didn't mind me phoning in. I didn't want to take up police time, but everyone at work has been in such a state and I thought it might be important.'

'You were right to tell us. Have you remembered anything else that Lauren said about that incident?'

'Sorry, no.' He took another gulp of water. 'Have you any idea who might have done this? I mean, it'd be good to be able to give my colleagues an update.'

'Best to leave that to us, Mr Wilby.'

'Of course. Sorry, I'm jumping the gun. How's Lauren's husband doing?'

'He's very upset, of course.'

'Yeah.' He took an ice cube from his drink and rubbed it on his neck. 'Any luck identifying that little girl in the photo?'

'We're working away all the time. You can reassure your colleagues that we're doing our best.'

'Okay, will do.' He smiled. 'Phew! It's hard work, playing in this heat.'

'Worth it, though.'

'Thanks. We're enjoying ourselves so I hope everyone else is.'

Julia appeared with a list in her hand. 'Sorry to interrupt but can I have a word about the next set, Jerry? I just want to check my announcements are correct.'

Siv stepped away as Julia showed Jerry the list. She bought a cold fruit juice and sipped it slowly as she made her way to the police stall, where she chatted to colleagues for a while before heading home.

She'd just put the cheesecake in the fridge when Cora Laffin phoned her.

'I've been thinking about that photo of the little girl ever since you showed it to me. Thing is, I thought she looked like someone I knew but I couldn't think why.'

'And do you know her?'

'No, but I know who she looks like. She looks like Lauren when we were little. I found a photo from junior school and there's a real resemblance.'

'Okay. But Lauren didn't have any other family, did she?'

'No. Just her and her mum.'

'Had her mum possibly been married before, or had a child?'

'I'm pretty certain not. She said she'd never been married and had never wanted to and I can't see her being a woman who'd have had a child adopted.'

'Can you send me a copy of the photo you have?'

'Sure. Do you think it might help at all?'

'No idea.'

But it's not as if I've got anything else. The photo arrived within minutes. Cora had sent the full image of a class photo, and another focused in on Lauren next to Cora in the middle row. Siv pinched it to its largest on her iPad and compared it to the photo of the unknown child. She saw that Cora was right. It was the same smile and expression. The same nose. The unknown girl had darker hair and narrower eyes but there had to be a genetic link. But what was it and why did it lead someone to kill? She thought for a moment. She should have set this line of enquiry in motion before now. Visser's and Seaton's lies had absorbed her and the team. Then she emailed Cora:

Can you send me any details you have of Lauren's mother? Full name, DOB, address, any other personal stuff you remember.

*   *   *

She called at Visser's house on the way back into town. She saw him through the front window. He was in shorts and a vest, working at his laptop. When he glanced up and saw her he gave a sour look. He opened the door so abruptly that it banged back against the wall.

'Do you bother people at weekends as well?'

'Murder doesn't recognize weekends. I thought you'd be pleased, since you've given us two weeks to find the killer and you frittered time away with lies. Can I come in? It won't take long.'

She sat opposite him in the living room. 'You'll be pleased to hear that Ms Davis agreed with your account of the early hours of Monday.'

'Good.' He couldn't meet her eyes.

'I need information from you. Do you have any photograph albums with pictures of Lauren's mother, or any personal information that Lauren kept about her?'

'Probably, somewhere around. Why do you want any of that?'

'It's just a line of enquiry. Could you have a look now? Then I could take it with me.'

He sighed heavily and left the room. Siv heard the sound of a loft ladder being lowered. She sat back and read an email from Cora, giving details of Lauren's mother:

Sue Farthing. Don't know her DOB but she was fifty-three when she died. They lived at 22 Broad Street. Sue had always lived here. Her parents were dead and they'd left her the house. She had no siblings that she ever mentioned. I remember Lauren saying she'd have liked to have

219

aunts, uncles or cousins like everyone else. I think her mum worked at Monkmere garage before she had Lauren. I once asked Lauren how her mum could afford not to work and she said that her grandparents had left her some money. That's all I know. Kids aren't that interested in their friends' parents.

Visser came back after ten minutes with one photo album and an A4 brown envelope. 'I've found these. Lauren sold her mother's house after we married and invested the money in this property. It was a small terraced place near the harbour. I think a lot of stuff was just cleared out but Lauren put these in a box marked "Mum." I think it's all there was.'

'Thanks. I'll return them when I've had a look. Do you want a receipt for them?'

'No. I know where to find you.'

She shook her head. 'I'm not the enemy, Mr Visser. I know you're embarrassed about Ms Davis but that's your problem, not mine.'

'I don't need any homilies. Is that all?'

'That's it. Don't bother getting up. I know where the door is.'

CHAPTER TWENTY-TWO

She glanced at her watch as she got in the car and saw that she was going to be late. She was supposed to be at Nutmeg to meet Ali and co. She'd been steeling herself for this all day. She wanted to be there about as much as Ade Visser had wanted to talk to her. Best to get it over with. Even so, she drove slowly and took her time finding a parking spot. The restaurant was in the conservation area, half a dozen or so streets that backed up from the harbour. She sat in the car park, making unnecessary tweaks to her hair and pointlessly trying to smooth creases in her cotton top. She felt all edges and angles and loitered on the pavement across from the restaurant for a few minutes, fighting the urge to bolt. Then she told herself that this was ridiculous and that if Ali had seen her through the window and she vanished, she'd hurt his feelings. She crossed the road and had to breathe deeply as she opened the door. The buzz of conversation hit her.

'Hi!' Ali looked up as soon as she entered and came over to greet her. He led her to a table where Patrick and Noah were sitting with a group of other colleagues from the station. She took a chair next to Noah and accepted a glass of wine from Ali, admiring his glowing skin.

'You look as if you've been out in the sun.'

'I went for a long bike ride.' He patted his stomach. 'Trying to keep the weight down. Only trouble is, exercise makes me hungry. I got home and made a triple-decker sandwich. Polly was already here at work so I could get away with it.'

'Does she monitor your diet?'

'She tries to. Did you, with your husband?'

'Not much. But he was a skinny-bones. Not that I'm casting aspersions on your weight.'

'Cast away. I know I'm way too lardy.'

She smiled. He was one of those people whose girth suited them and made them seem approachable. It was handy, having a sergeant who radiated a bloke-ish ease. 'Did you have a wander round the festival?' she asked.

'Aye, I had a wee look. It was cracking but I found it all a bit manufactured. I don't remember that much being made of May back in Derry. My great-uncle once told me that his gran used to wash her face in dew on May the first because it was supposed to make her beautiful for the following year. But she had to do it secretly because her dad didn't approve of such foolishness.'

'Well, the sun's out and people are relaxing and possibly being a bit foolish. That's the main thing.'

'And are you relaxing?'

She flinched, thinking of Nowak whirling her around in the dance and reached for her phone. 'Never mind me. Just two minutes about work, then I'll shut up.' She told him about Cora Laffin's information and her visit to Visser. He looked at the photos Cora had sent.

'I get it, but lots of young kids look alike. There's loads of little girls with big smiles and bunches. I see them everywhere I go.'

'I give you that but there's more there — the expression and the nose. Cora saw it and she grew up with Lauren.'

Ali shrugged. 'I dunno. This is an entirely new direction, guv. You really think it's something to do with the mother? Seems unlikely to me. Could be a real time-waster.'

'Visser and Seaton were time-wasters. Look, Mason Granger has no alibi but there's no clear motive and nothing to place him at Lock Lane. Simon Rochford has no alibi but no real form and his car checked out. We've no forensics. This is the only direction available right now. Have you got a better suggestion?'

'Well . . . no.'

'Exactly, so we'll go with this and see where it leads.'

Ali continued to look dubious. 'How was Mortimer when you saw him?'

'So-so. Abrupt.'

'Look, guv . . . I've been wondering whether or not to tell you this but Mortimer had his eye on someone for the vacancy you filled. A protégé of his, Tommy Castles. He'd been mentoring Tommy and I reckon he thought he'd be able to get him in but then you came along. Mortimer had a face like a wet week after you were appointed.'

She took a gulp of wine. 'And where's Tommy now?'

'He went off to Kent, got a promotion there. So . . . you know . . . it might be worth oiling the wheels a bit with Mortimer. He can be difficult, sometimes I think just because he can, and he's a man to hold a grudge.'

'Right. Thanks for letting me know, I appreciate it. I'm not eating, by the way. I'll just have this drink and then I'll head off.'

He looked disappointed. 'Polly's a great chef. You don't know what you're missing.'

If you only knew what an effort it took just to come here. 'Another time. Do go ahead and order if you want.'

Noah turned to her as Ali picked up a menu. 'I think I remember you from school. Did you go to Newton High?'

'That's right.'

'And you made that beautiful paper spiral that sat on a table in the foyer?'

'Yes. I'd forgotten that. It took me weeks. Sorry, I don't remember you.'

'You wouldn't. I was five years below you. I used to see you around and you fascinated me because you looked a bit formidable.'

She laughed. 'Don't tell anyone but that's the look I adopt when I'm thinking or when I'm nervous. My sister Rik was the truly formidable one, but she'd have left by the time you joined the school.'

'That spiral inspired me to take up origami. I thought it was so lovely. I'd never have thought paper could have energy. I used to pop into the foyer at break times to look at it. I touched it once and that old dragon Ms Walker told me off. So then I thought I'd try my own folding at home. I used to fold when the mood took me until I had the stroke. Haven't got the coordination now.'

'That's tough.'

'Nah. Going to the toilet's tough. And having a conversation, cause I talk so slow. I see people's eyes glazing over, wondering if I'll ever get to the point. Things take on a different perspective when life throws you a wobbly.'

He was right. She wasn't sure what her perspective was any more. Out of focus, blurred.

He dabbed his mouth with a napkin. 'Thanks for listening to the end of my long drawn-out sentences and not interrupting.'

'You don't have to thank me for that.'

'You reckon? Do you still fold?'

'Yes. I'm making something now. I've always done it, off and on, and more so in recent months.'

Noah had a straw in his pale red cocktail. He sipped and then asked matter-of-factly, 'How did you come by the scar? I wanted to ask you at school but I didn't dare. Now I'm disinhibited because of my stroke and I'm two negronis in, so I can ask people all kinds of personal questions and they can't take offence. There have to be some perks to being part vegetable.'

She realized she'd been touching the ridge of scar because she was tense. 'My mother was pushing me on a swing when I was a toddler. She hadn't fastened the bars properly. She gave me a push, turned away to talk to her gentleman friend and I fell out and cut my eye.'

'Bad momma.' He leaned forward, slurped through his straw and then beckoned her closer. 'I'm a bad bro. Patrick shouldn't have to look after me. It's not right. He's got a demanding job and me hanging around just puts pressure on him.'

Why are you telling me? Because I'm his boss and he's told you the guv leaned on him? Do you want me to give him special consideration? 'Perhaps he wants to look after you.'

'Not the same thing. It's not fair. I tire him out. I see him getting worn down instead of living his life. Just because mine's been smashed doesn't mean his should be too.'

She wasn't sure she was fit to deal with anyone else's emotions but there was something in Noah's voice, an appeal. She felt bad for doubting his motives. That was one of the problems with being a practised detective. You were in the habit of never taking anyone at face value. She heard Ed's voice. *Why are you asking me so many questions and giving me that look? I'm not in custody!* She spoke quietly. 'My husband was killed in an accident last year. If he'd been left badly injured, I'd have wanted to look after him.'

'Yeah, I get that, but you were married. You'd made promises. Not the same with brothers.'

'Why not, Noah? Love's a promise in itself, isn't it?'

His eyebrows went up. 'Food for thought but it still doesn't get me off the hook.'

Patrick was waving a wine bottle at her but she covered her glass and said she had to go. Ali walked her to the bar and a bosomy, flushed woman in chef whites hurried out from the kitchen. Ali introduced her to Siv, who nodded and chatted, barely aware of what she was saying, only that the clamour of voices around her was making her jittery. The muscles in her calves spasmed. She longed to be in the quiet of her home, wrapped in Ed's sweatshirt.

Once she had escaped from the restaurant, she ran to her car, opened all the windows and drove home too fast, mouth dry, her scalp contracting. The sky was clear, the moon bright and high. A fox darted at the side of the verge, eyes glinting. The headlights picked out foaming white hawthorn blossom. She went over what Ali had said about Mortimer. There was nothing she could do about his dashed hopes for his protégé but it added an angle to station politics that she could have done without. It proved that her instincts about Ali were right. She could trust him.

She switched on the radio and listened to a poetry programme. Her heart eased. If only there was a magic potion to heal it.

* * *

It was a glorious, still evening. Alan Vine had walked Monty to the stretch of river nearest to his home, nowhere near the crime scene. The dog was sniffing around the reeds while Vine sat on the grass, watching him. Blackbirds, jays and crows were busy. A flowering currant scented the air. Creamy yellow wild primroses were scattered around.

Vine leaned back on his elbows. Things were shaping up. He'd had several pints and a long chat with Mike Shelton, who was already nicely oiled by the time Vine got to the pub. Mike had filled in some gaps about a little girl called Sophie. Despite the booze, he had an amazing memory. The alcohol had made Vine so sleepy that when he got home he'd snoozed the afternoon away on the sofa. The late-afternoon sun had woken him, beating on his eyes. He'd roused himself and found that he'd been drooling on the cushion. He'd splashed his face with water, got out his old phone book and found the name and number easily enough. He thought about what he'd say over his fish and chips, and when he'd washed up he dialled the number.

They'd spoken for about ten minutes and the information he gave certainly created interest. He was gratified that his call was being taken seriously and treated with courtesy and respect. A meeting had been arranged and he'd agreed to keep it confidential for now because of the sensitive nature of the matter.

The business had energized him. It was good to have something different from the usual run-of-the-mill stuff to think about.

He called to the dog and set off for home, a spring in his step. *Life in the old dog yet,* he thought.

* * *

For once, Siv had slept in. She came to slowly, and saw that it was almost 9 a.m. She panicked for a moment and then remembered it was a bank holiday. She lay for a few minutes, listening to the silence. Even the river was quiet. No dreams about Ed last night.

It might be a public holiday but the team would be working. She showered, made tea and toast and carried her breakfast outside. She could see Corran and Paul busy in their vegetable garden. While she ate, she opened the envelope Visser had given her and worked through the scant documents it contained. A birth certificate for Susan Nicola Farthing, born in Berminster in 1962 to Harold Farthing and Marie Sampson. Death certificates for Harold and Marie in 1972 and 1983 respectively. So just like her daughter, Susan had been left on her own at a comparatively young age. A handful of exam certificates showing O Level passes, a first-aid certificate from the Red Cross, notification of a degree awarded from the Open University in 1995 — a BA in Modern History and a Sorry You're Leaving card with balloons on the front and half a dozen signatures inside. No family letters. Nothing about Lauren's father.

She opened the photo album. There were a couple of pages of black-and-white photos showing a solemn-looking girl, presumably Susan with her parents. Harold had a denim shirt and Marie sported a beehive hairdo and a dress with a mandarin collar. The sixties had knocked on Berminster's door. Then colour started to creep in with some photos of Susan on her own, her long mousy hair gradually becoming shorter and her puppy fat disappearing. She'd certainly grown into her looks and by the time she was an adult she was a pretty, shy-looking woman. A couple of photos of Susan holding a baby — who had taken those? — and then images almost exclusively of Lauren. A mixture of school shots and others in a back garden. One with her mother sitting under trees on a tartan rug with a picnic basket and some on what could be Cliffdean Point with the wide sky behind her. Judging by the size and colour shades, quite a few may have been taken with an Instamatic. Lauren shared her mother's serious expression but she'd never had puppy fat.

Siv finished her tea, now cold, and watched Paul trundle a wheelbarrow. The sun was hot in the cloudless sky and he stopped to don a peaked cap. She looked up Monkmere garage and checked the opening times, then washed up and tidied the kitchen, which took all of five minutes.

She arrived at the garage as it opened at 10.30 a.m. It was a sprawling site on the outskirts of town with a huge showroom and repair centre. A young man was polishing the already gleaming cars on the forecourt and directed her to an office inside the showroom, telling her she needed to speak to Mark Lamport.

He was in his sixties, spruce in a suit that was on the big side and warm-looking for the day. 'Is it just me or are detectives getting younger?' he asked jovially, waving her to a cushioned chrome chair.

'Just you, I should think.' Maybe she should have changed into one of her suits, rather than wearing jeans and a shirt. 'I'm making enquiries about a Susan Farthing and her daughter, Lauren. I understand that Susan used to work here, over twenty years ago.'

He linked his broad fingers together in front of his chest. He had hairy knuckles and raised blue veins. 'Indeed she did. Long time ago, though. Haven't seen Sue in years.'

'What did she do here?' Siv asked.

'Book keeping, invoices, all the routine paperwork. She was like my right arm. I didn't want to lose her but she wouldn't stay.'

'Why not?'

He made a circular motion over his stomach. 'She got preggers. I was taken aback, I can tell you. She worked until she was about six months gone, then she handed in her notice. She wasn't married so I wondered what was going on and how she'd manage for money, but she never talked about personal stuff.'

'She never mentioned the father?'

'Nope. I was kind of shocked, to be honest. Not because she wasn't married or anything like that but she was a quiet, buttoned-down type, thoughtful and hard-working. Never saw her flirting with anyone. She'd never come for a drink with the others, just one spritzer at Christmas. I'd have thought she'd have wanted a ring on her finger before she had a child, but maybe it was just one of those things.'

'So you didn't think that the father might be someone who worked here?' *Or maybe even you.*

His bushy eyebrows shot up. 'Never crossed my mind. Sue arrived sharp at nine in the morning and left at five on the dot. And as I said, she very much kept herself to herself.'

'Did you see her again after she left?'

'Just the once. She called in with the baby. Little girl. Very proud mum, I can tell you!'

'Did anyone else here keep in touch with her?' Siv asked.

'Doubt it. She was the only girl, and you know blokes . . . we're not ones for knit and natter. How is Sue? What's this all about anyway?'

'She died five years ago. Her daughter, Lauren Visser, was murdered last Monday.'

He rocked back in his chair. 'Oh my God! I saw the news about that on the telly. Never realized there was a connection. That's terrible!'

229

'Yes, it is. I was hoping you or someone else here might know more about Susan's personal life.'

He raised his hands and dropped them. 'Sorry. I know it sounds awful, because Sue worked here for more than ten years, but she wasn't one for talking about herself, and that was fine with me because I prefer just getting on with the work. Before Sue came here, we had a girl called Tracey who never shut up, bonked most of the staff and was always taking days off. Now, if you'd told me she'd got preggers at work I'd have believed you. It's busy here so I need people who keep their heads down and graft.'

He was glancing over her shoulder at the forecourt and she took the hint and left. There was a thought worrying at the corner of her mind. She wasn't sure if it was something she'd seen or heard. She was thinking of driving to the beach for a walk when an urgent call from the station changed the shape of the day.

* * *

Kitty Fairway both loved and loathed bank holidays. It was good to see people getting out into the fresh air and enjoying nature. But so many of them didn't know how to behave in these ancient and beautiful woods. They left litter, allowed their dogs off the lead, threw food to wild birds, picked wild flowers, used barbecues and let their children paddle in the wildlife ponds. Secretly, she wished that the car park and that bloody ice-cream van with its tinny rendering of 'Greensleeves' could be removed, so that the woods wouldn't be a destination for day-trippers. Let them go to the beach or the park. But that would be doing herself out of a job, and Kitty loved her job and felt lucky to have it.

She loved the woods most in the early morning and late evening, when the visitors had gone and she could roam around, observing the badger sett, listening to the wood pigeons and smiling at the stupidity of the pheasants. Most evenings found her in the secluded northern boundary of the woods, among the dappled shade and soft fronds of the ferns. A palette of every shade of green lay at her feet. She'd researched ferns for her degree in environmental studies and was monitoring the growth and health of a variety of the plants beneath the canopy of oak trees. Their cool greens entranced her, the way the dim light played through them, some lacy, some fan-like or tongue-shaped, others leathery or tapering. In this growing season, she was keeping an eye on the bracken in case she needed to remove some to prevent it dominating the more delicate plants.

She sat for fifteen minutes with Dan and Mia, discussing the activities they were running between eleven and three. Dan was organizing Nature Tots and butterfly-themed face painting and Mia was in charge of the obstacle course in the adventure playground and the stick-whittling. Satisfied that they were on top of things, she headed to the log store and filled a wheelbarrow with wood to take to the frog pond, intending to place the logs around the edges to provide shade and shelter. She navigated past two small boys using sticks as swords and took the path to the pond.

Once she was among the trees, she looked up at the bursting leaves. The days were opening out and stretching, the nights growing soft and warm. The fox cubs would be weaned by now. She felt a surge of joy and vigour. She took off her gilet, threw it on top of the wheelbarrow and trundled on.

It was quiet at the pond, with most children attracted to the activities in the play cabins at the car park. Later, Dan would bring the Nature Tots group here to look at tadpoles. There was a woman and two small children at the far end, peering down into the water, the woman pointing. She noticed that one of the children had a net. She'd have a word about that in a minute. She placed logs at intervals, securing them into the silt. She worked along the edge of the pond, lifting and stooping, saving the last chunks of wood for the area by the thick, tall bulrushes, heavy with their fat catkins.

She took the last of the logs, stepped towards the bulrushes ready to position them, and froze.

There was a man there, covered in blood, and she knew his rigid, contorted face. He was lying in the strap-shaped leaves and supported by them, as if he had made a bed in the strong, grey green foliage. But he wasn't going to wake.

CHAPTER TWENTY-THREE

The car park at Halse woods was full when Siv arrived, the area teeming with families having a sunny bank holiday outing and participating in the activities. Children were darting and yelling, kicking footballs and swarming in the adventure playground. Ali turned up while she was instructing uniform colleagues to clear the woods and car park, get everyone's name and address before allowing them to go, and then lock the gates.

'This is a nightmare,' Ali said, 'people trampling everywhere. Forensics are on their way. No Steve, he's in France.'

They donned protective gear and took the path through beech trees to the pond. It was surrounded for half its circumference by a raised, decked walkway from where visitors could survey the wildlife. The body was just beyond the end of the walkway where dense hazel and holly hedging formed a border. Alan Vine lay amid a mass of bulrushes, cradled by them and half concealed by the arching green leaves. He was face up, his expression a grimace, his neck and chest torn and bloody.

'Rigor has started in the face.' Siv looked at the gashes. 'A knife or scissors.'

'Same killer then.'

'I think we work with that for now. He'd found something out, or our killer thought he had.'

Dr Anand and his team were arriving. Siv and Ali moved out of the way and walked back to where Kitty Fairway was sitting at the base of a vast oak tree that rested on a root like a doorstep. Siv and Ali sat on either side of her. Her wellies were covered in dried mud and there were damp patches on her jeans. Her face was drained, with the dramatic paleness of a redhead's skin, but she was composed, her voice just a touch unsteady.

'Thank goodness I found the body and not one of the children. There's a group of little ones coming up here later. That would have been terrible.'

'Are you okay to talk to us?' Siv asked.

'Yes, of course.'

Siv nodded. 'That's good. Were you here last night?'

'Yes, I locked the gates at ten.'

'Was anyone still here?'

'Not that I know of. There could have been people around, I suppose, but the car park was empty.'

'Did you see or hear anything suspicious before you left?' Siv asked.

'No. It got really quiet after about eight-ish.'

'Take us through what happened from when you arrived here today,' Siv said. 'Were there any cars around here this morning?'

'I was the first one here at seven fifteen and I unlocked the gates. I didn't see any cars. Dan and Mia, my colleagues who are working with me today, arrived at half seven. It's busy on bank holidays so we have extra people on shift. I made a pot of coffee when I got here and then filled the bird feeders and did some prep for the day with Dan and Mia. We're running kids' activities as part of the May festival. People started arriving soon after I did. We get the early-morning walkers and joggers, or people who just like to be here before it gets crowded. Families don't usually start arriving until around half ten. I came up here around half eleven to check the frogspawn and the hatching tadpoles. Sometimes people try to take some and we discourage that, so I like to keep an eye open. I was stacking logs along the edge for the developing frogs.'

'Was anyone around?'

'A woman and two little ones. Luckily, they were at the other end of the pond. I was carrying logs past the bulrushes when I glanced down and saw him. Mr Vine.' She brushed a hand across her face.

'How did you know him?'

'He lives nearby. He walks his dog here sometimes, and he was interested in talking about our plans and the different areas we cultivate. I thought he was a bit lonely. It was hard to close the conversation at times. I haven't seen his dog, so I don't think that's why he was here.'

'Did you see Mr Vine come into the woods?'

'No. You could ask my colleagues.'

'You can access the woods on foot at any time, right?' Ali said.

'Yes. The gates are really about access to and from the car park. We don't want people trying to stay overnight. There are paths across the fields and of course the bridleway. So at least five other ways in.' She pressed her hands together. Her fingers were mucky, the nails ingrained with soil. 'That poor man. I wonder if he has any family.'

'We'll find out.'

'That's three murders in a week, isn't it?' She stared at Siv. 'And in peaceful places that should be safe and restful. Places of sanctuary.'

'I'm afraid so. I'm afraid also that we'll have to disturb your pond in a search for the murder weapon. You can go now,' Siv said. 'We won't be allowing anyone near here for the time being. You should take the afternoon off. Do you need a lift?'

'No, thanks. I have my bike. I need to be on my own for a bit.'

'What about when you get home?'

'I'm in a flat share in town. It's okay, I won't be on my own for long.'

They watched her walk back towards the warden's office, a slight figure with bent head.

'Poor wee thing, she's in shock,' Ali said.

'I'm not surprised. And she's right. Murder is always a desecration but the killings at the river and here — it seems worse, somehow.'

They approached Rey Anand, who was on one knee by the edge of the bulrushes. He rose when he heard them, peering over his glasses.

'Rigor is established throughout the body, so I would estimate that he died late last night. The stab wounds have been made with a thinner blade than that used at Lock Lane. There are some defence wounds this time, on the palm of the right hand and right forearm. That's all I can say for now.'

'Vine had been in the army, he'd have tried to defend himself,' Siv said as they walked back to the car park. 'He must have arrived here by foot, as did his killer.'

'Do you still think this is linked to Lauren's mum in some way? We've found no connection between her and Vine,' Ali said.

She looked at him. 'I have absolutely no idea, not the foggiest. Remind me, the background checks into Vine didn't bring up anything of concern, did they?'

'Nope. Ex-army, then worked at the Tesco in Bere Place until he retired. Nothing to indicate he'd ever crossed paths with Lauren or Rimas, and he's never been married or had a child.'

'Okay. I'm going to go and check out Vine's home, see if there's anyone who might be missing him. The rest of the team are coming into the office, so can you get them organized, have some of them here? I want Vine's description publicized. Ask if anyone saw him or anything suspicious in Halse woods last night. And can you talk to Kitty's two colleagues and the woman she saw at the pond earlier?'

He nodded. He was supposed to be taking Polly for a late lunch in a gastropub near Cliffdean Point but it looked as if that wasn't going to happen. Just one more apologetic call to add to the dozens he'd made to her over the years, but at least it meant a few less calories in his day.

* * *

In the stifling afternoon heat, Siv let herself into Alan Vine's bungalow. The next-door neighbour Daisy had given her a key and was now watching from her doorway. Daisy had informed her that Alan Vine had no family. She'd seemed more concerned about the dog than at hearing that her neighbour was dead.

'I got back from my daughter's around noon and I've heard Monty barking on and off. Alan's car is there, so if he didn't stop, I was going to knock on the door before long. Don't like to think of an animal fretting.'

It didn't seem to have occurred to her that the barking might have meant that her elderly neighbour was on the floor incapacitated. 'Mr Vine never had a partner?'

'Not in my time and I've been here twenty-five years. He always said he was a confirmed bachelor — doesn't that usually mean gay these days? I don't think he was though — gay, that is. Never saw any gentlemen callers, nor female ones either come to that.'

'Have you spoken to him in the last couple of days, or did you notice if he had any visitors recently?'

'Alan kept himself to himself. We said hello now and again and that was about it. I haven't seen him to talk to for a couple of weeks, but he goes out regular with the dog. Monty will need feeding and walking.'

'Can you have him for now?'

'Me? Oh, I'm not sure about that.' She stepped back.

Siv gave her a full beam smile. 'I can see that you're a good neighbour and very concerned. Just overnight, until we can sort something out. It would be such a help. I can bring food over from Mr Vine's.'

'Well . . . I suppose. I can get my Cherie to walk him later. Yeah, okay, she'll like that.'

As Siv stepped into the hall, the dog came rushing towards her. He skidded to a stop when he saw her. Unsure. She went to the kitchen, found his lead and a box of food and took him to Daisy. He was barking loudly as Daisy closed her door. If dogs could express indignation, that's what he was doing.

The bungalow was a basic, four-roomed building with a living room, one bedroom, a tiny bathroom and a kitchen with a pine table and two chairs. It was shady in the heat but also gloomy and smelled faintly of antiseptic. The living room had one two-seater sofa, a TV and a stack of newspapers on a low table. No landline but a well-thumbed phone book lay on top of the newspapers. The kitchen was neat with a frying pan and saucepan drying on the rack by the sink, with one plate, a knife and fork and a dessert spoon. She looked in the bin and saw an empty egg box and a tin that had held creamed rice. A pack of medication lay on the counter — Ranexa 375 mg. She recalled that Vine had angina. She saw a lined notepad on the table, with a biro alongside it. Written at the top of the page, she saw "*Sophie*." She took the notepad and bagged it. That was it. There was nothing else lying around. The man must have cleared everything up as he went.

A search of the bedroom and kitchen drawers provided nothing of interest: bank and utility statements, birth certificate and army discharge. There was one black-and-white framed photo on the bedroom wall of Vine as a young man in army uniform, posed against a backdrop of jungle. A clock ticked on the bedside table. Siv felt drowsy in the warmth and stillness and had an urge to lie down on the neatly made single bed. It looked so inviting. She could hear Monty's monotonous barking from next door, punctuated by the occasional high-pitched whine.

There was nothing here except for the name Sophie, which could mean anything or nothing. She was hoping that Vine's phone would be found on his body but suspected that it would be missing. This killer covered the bases.

She rang Daisy's bell again and Monty rushed to the door, throwing himself against it. There was the sound of Daisy shushing him and an internal door slamming. The barking receded.

'Sorry to disturb you again, but do you know if Mr Vine knew anyone called Sophie? Did he ever mention her to you?'

Daisy scratched her head. 'Doesn't mean anything to me, and there's no Sophies that I know of around here. Bit of a posh name for this street. I can't have that dog any longer than tonight. He's driving me bonkers with his barking.'

'I'll get someone to sort it first thing tomorrow — or this evening if that's possible. Thanks for being so helpful, I appreciate it.'

Daisy had a lightbulb moment. She raised a finger. 'Can you put me on Twitter? You know, how I've helped you out in your investigation.'

'Of course. Not by name, but I'll get you a mention.'

'Great! I'll tell my daughter. She'll be dead envious.'

Siv smiled. Whatever it took to keep the public on side. As she unlocked her car, Monty was howling pitifully.

CHAPTER TWENTY-FOUR

Siv had trudged upstairs to Mortimer to discuss this third murder.

'There's a lot of interest in these murders both locally and beyond,' he'd said. 'Yet you don't seem to have much.'

'We've ruled suspects out, which is important. And we have more than yesterday, sir. We might have the name of the child in the photo.'

'Might. Yes.' He'd looked at her shrewdly. 'Some of these people have been running rings around you. Don't let that happen again.'

'I can't stop people lying.'

'Maybe you need to change up a gear. I know it's hard when you've been off work for a while, but this is important. I need to know I've got the right DI for the job. I'd like results soon. Make sure you maximize everyone's time.'

She couldn't protest. They had so little. She felt as if this case was slipping through her fingers.

Now they were holding a meeting, going over everything from the beginning. She sat on the edge of a table at the front of the room, gripping the edge and summarizing the chronology so far. She looked out at the faces and the appraising eyes staring at her and thought she'd never sounded so unsure.

'We work on the basis that this latest murder is connected to the other two. It's possible that the child in that photo is called Sophie. We need to get new publicity done with that suggestion.'

Steve Wooton was back from France, his cold long gone and looking energized, and he swung into his report. 'The post-mortem on Alan Vine showed that he was killed with a thirteen-centimetre serrated kitchen knife. As yet, no sign of the weapon. He died on the edge of the pond and fell there. His killer had rolled him over the edge and into the bulrushes. No phone has been found. Quite a few hairs, other traces of DNA and scraps of fabric were gathered from the hedges in the area.'

Siv nodded. 'According to Kitty Fairway, children played around the pond and in and out of the greenery all the time so that was to be expected.'

'Sure. The ground was dry and there were no distinctive footprints. It looks as if Vine's killer waited in the hedges but there are lots of broken twigs and branches because kids mess around there, so it's hard to say anything definitive,' he told them.

'I spoke to Nick Shelton again,' Ali reported. 'He confirmed that Alan Vine had no family. He had a sister but she emigrated to Melbourne and died years ago. He said he hadn't spoken to Vine since last Monday, when they talked about the events at Lock Lane. He knew that Vine walked his dog regularly at Halse woods. He'd never heard of a Sophie.'

Siv gave instructions for a door-to-door to be organized along Vine's street to ask if anyone had spoken to him or seen him recently, and if they knew of a Sophie. Also to go through the list of people who had been at Halse woods when Vine was found and make sure they'd all been spoken to. She looked at Ali, who was eating what looked like dried apricots from a plastic tub. Patrick seemed wired. His foot was tapping today instead of his fingers, pattering a rhythm on the floor. He was still on a high over the number of people who'd stopped by the police stall over the weekend to ask about the detective on Twitter.

She stood, trying to sound decisive. 'I think that Alan Vine had spoken on the phone about that photo to whoever killed him. They agreed to meet in Halse woods and that's why his phone's been taken. He must have known something. We keep digging. A couple of you ring around all the members of the angling club again, ask if any of them had spoken to Vine in the past week or knew a Sophie.'

'What about the angle on Lauren's mother?' Ali asked.

'I'll pursue that. I want to go through the stuff Visser gave me again.'

She drove home, skirting the edge of the harbour. A huge clean-up was still going on after the weekend's festivities. A fresh southerly breeze had blown in, setting the bunting flapping. On the deck of a small yacht, a man lay on a lounger, reading a book. She stopped for a couple of minutes and wound down the window so that she could sniff the salt air and listen to the creak of boat masts.

At home, a case of akvavit had been delivered and was sitting on the bottom step. She was relieved because she'd finished her last bottle the previous night. The rooms were stuffy, holding the heat of the day. She had a dull headache over her eyes. She left the door ajar and unpacked the dark green bottles. She opened one and poured a glass, adding ice because it was warm from the sun. This was a different brand and had strong citrus notes.

She took her drink down to the river where she wandered along the bank, treading through cow parsley and watching the ripples and eddies of the water. When she got back, she folded for an hour to calm and clear her mind. She started on a new icosahedron, putting the crease pattern into the paper. Her hands were sticky in the heat and she had to rinse her fingers under cold water several times.

In the evening, she returned to the photo album Visser had given her and went through it again. She paused at one of the photos of Lauren and her mother under some trees on a tartan rug. Lauren looked about two years old and was standing leaning against her mother and holding one hand up with a daisy in it. She wore a pretty lilac and white dress and white sandals. Sue looked proud and a little defiant. They were posed among the remains of a picnic. Sandwiches rested on a paper plate to one side, with a carton of fruit juice. At the edge of the rug, just visible, was the corner of a sectioned Perspex box with brightly coloured shapes inside. She brought a lamp close and peered at the grainy image of the box, thinking about childhood walks along riverbanks and wondering. She took a photo on her phone and emailed it, then waited a few minutes before she phoned Nick Shelton.

'Apologies for disturbing you at this time of night, Mr Shelton. I'm very sorry about Mr Vine.'

'Yes. I can't credit it. We've been in shock here. Alan wouldn't have hurt a fly. Why would someone want to do that to him? Is what happened to Alan connected to Lauren Visser in some way?'

'Possibly. I was hoping that you might be able to help me with something. I've just sent you a photo and wondered if you could open the attachment.'

'Okay. Give me a minute.'

She could hear a TV being turned down, some murmurs and then he was back on the line.

'Okay, I've got it. Who am I looking at? I don't know them.'

'That's Lauren Visser as a young child with her mother. Just by the edge of the tartan rug in that photo, there's a box. Can you make it out?'

'Hang on, I'm just enlarging it. Yes, I can see it now.'

'Do you know what it is?'

He made a little clicking noise with his tongue and then confirmed what she'd been thinking. 'I'd say it could be a box of fishing lures. I wouldn't want to swear to it but that's definitely what it looks like to me. Those look like sinking lures at the near edge.'

'That's very helpful, thank you.'

'Where was that photo taken?' he asked.

'I don't know. I hope to find out. Thanks so much. Enjoy the rest of your evening.'

She poured a fresh drink and sat on the steps of the wagon. The air was warm and dense. Paul was playing his tin whistle, a plaintive air that drifted faintly across the meadow and made her shiver with pleasure and regret. The goats were calling and she heard the clank of a bucket from their shed, the noise carrying in the stillness. If Lauren's absent father had taken that photo, it seemed that the man had had a connection to angling, which was an odd coincidence in the circumstances. But the photographer might not have been her father and the photo wasn't necessarily taken in Berminster. Those trees could have been anywhere. And of course, none of this might be anything to do with three murders.

It was a tease and a possibility and she wasn't sure if it got her any further along the road.

* * *

Patrick came to see her the following afternoon. He looked clear-eyed, as if he'd caught up on some sleep.

'Guv, we've got a result on the door-to-door in Spring Gardens. We've had a call from a Yasmin Jerwood who lives at number twenty-six. She says she saw a man going into Lauren's house the Sunday before she died, the twenty-eighth, around lunchtime. She was driving back from the supermarket. She didn't recognize him but then she was at the festival over the weekend and she visited the Minstergreen stall and saw Mason Granger. She says he was the guy she saw at Lauren's.'

'Why has it taken her over a week to tell us she saw someone?'

'Her daughter's just had a baby and she went to Chichester to stay with her last Monday, so she said she's been "a tad distracted and not in the loop." Fair enough.'

'Very generous of you. Tell Ali I need him.' She knew he was in because ten minutes ago she'd heard his "Danny Boy" ring tone.

Within seconds, Ali was leaning against her door, hands in pockets. 'Shall we bring Granger in, guv?'

She stretched and ran her fingers through her hair, touching a thin patch below the crown. She was certain it wasn't as bare as it used to be. 'No. Let's go round there. We can ask his permission to search his flat at the same time. I'm not sure we've got enough for a search warrant, and if he's nothing to hide he'll maybe give us the go-ahead.'

Half an hour later, they were at Mason Granger's flat. He opened the door dressed in shorts and a singlet and wearing a black leather belt bag. He looked taken aback.

'I was just about to go for a run,' he said.

'That will have to wait. Can we come in? This is Sergeant Carlin.'

'Don't you usually make an appointment?'

'It depends. We need to talk to you urgently. If you don't want to talk here, you can come to the station.'

'Right. You'd better come in.'

'Let's sit at the table today,' Siv said. She didn't intend to look at the view and Granger's profile again.

The table was long, made from recycled oak planks with a white trestle base. They sat opposite Granger while he fiddled with his watch, resetting something. Siv waited while Ali sneaked a glance out of the window.

'What's this about then?' Granger asked, settling his forearms on the table.

'When I spoke to you, you told me that you last saw Lauren at your committee meeting the Tuesday before she died.'

'That's right.'

'We have information from a witness that indicates you saw her after that, on Sunday the twenty-eighth, the day before she was killed.'

Granger swallowed. 'Who told you that?'

'That's for us to know, and you to explain' Ali came in sharply. 'Quit messing about and answer the inspector.'

'There's no need to take that tone.' Granger bridled but he was looking worried.

'I think there is,' Siv said. 'We don't like it when people lie to us, especially in murder investigations.'

'I'm not sure I want to answer,' he hedged.

'Well, of course you can choose to go down that route. Then I might have to arrest you for questioning and organize an ID session with our witness. It's much better for you and less invasive if you just speak to us now.' Siv shook her head at him. 'You have no alibi for the morning of Lauren's murder and of course another person was killed around the same time. As I say, up to you.'

'For God's sake! I didn't kill Lauren or anyone else!'

'Then there's no reason not to be straight with us.'

He took his glasses off and rubbed his eyes. The left one was inflamed, with mucus in the corner. He took a small bottle from his waist bag, tilted his head back and dispensed drops into each eye, blinking rapidly. Ali tutted impatiently. Siv waited, rubbing her finger in a sunken knot in the oak.

'Blepharitis. I get eye irritation from staring at a screen too much,' Granger said. 'Okay, I did see Lauren on the Sunday. I didn't say because I thought it wouldn't look good, and you'd make more out of it than it was.'

'Tell us about it. Did you arrange it?' she asked.

'I rang her about half ten that morning. I wanted to talk to her about our difference of opinion over strategy. I thought if we could speak outside of a meeting, I might get her to see my point of view. She said okay and to come round about half twelve. I walked round to hers.'

'What happened?'

'We sat in the kitchen and talked. I went through the vision I had for our work and how we needed to develop and engage more people. It was pointless, she just banged on about focus and getting the job done. She got quite unpleasant, saying I wanted to use Minstergreen to big myself up. Whatever I said, she argued back. I left after about half an hour. I could see I was getting nowhere. That was it.'

'So you had a stand-off and bad feeling.'

'Not as such. In the end, I just said the committee would see that she was trying to hold us back with her narrow views. I left her and walked home. I wouldn't have hurt Lauren. We might not have seen eye to eye, but ultimately we were devoting ourselves to the same cause.'

'Did Lauren mention that she was going swimming at Lock Lane the following morning?'

He looked perplexed. 'No. It wasn't a social chat.'

There wasn't much to go on here, unless there was a blood-stained pair of scissors, shoe covers or any other evidence to be found in this flat. 'We'd like to search your flat, Mr Granger,' Siv said. 'We need your permission to do that without a warrant.'

He rolled his eyes. 'I suppose if I don't agree, you'll get a warrant and come clumping in here anyway, and the neighbours will know.'

'Well, you have to weigh that up for yourself.'

He frowned and then shrugged. 'Fill your boots. I've nothing to hide. Is it okay if I do some work while you're looking?'

'No problem. If you just stay sitting, we'll get started.'

He opened his laptop and they started their search, moving from the living room to the bedroom, kitchen and bathroom. The bedroom was a mess — drawers stuffed to bursting, a wardrobe crammed with shoes and boxes of Minstergreen pamphlets and a linen basket spilling over with dirty laundry. It took time to sift through all the strewn clothes and belongings. It proved fruitless. The only scissors was a small pair of nail scissors in the bathroom cabinet.

'He's not bothered,' Siv said to Ali in the bedroom. 'He looks relaxed, absorbed in what he's doing, printing stuff from his laptop.'

'He's a wee liar and that's all we have on him. I think Lauren was right, he does like to big himself up.'

Ali was looking at a pinboard on the wall, covered with photos of Granger taken in TV and radio studios, talking to journalists in the street and photocopies of his newspaper columns.

'Having a fat head isn't a crime. He might have had motive but there's no evidence of any kind against him. We might as well let him go out for his run.'

On the way back to the car, Ali asked drily, 'Nothing come from checking out Lauren's mum then? Wild goose chase?' He had an *I told you so* look.

She shrugged. He could be smart at her expense if he wanted. She still thought there was something about Sue Farthing, sitting on a tartan rug, that was yet to be explained, but she'd keep that to herself for now.

CHAPTER TWENTY-FIVE

Siv sat looking at the incident board, drinking coffee and thinking about Alan Vine. The man had no family but he must have had some social life apart from walking his dog, fishing and bossing people about at Lock Lane. She rang Nick Shelton, spoke to him for a few minutes and then glanced at her watch. She rarely went to pubs at lunchtime but today she'd make an exception.

She hadn't slept well, waking at three from a vivid dream of Ed and then remaining restless until dawn. In the pub bathroom, she splashed her face with water and patted it with a paper towel. Her reflection in the wide mirror looked drained, her lips dry and her scar seeming to stand out. She lifted her hair and craned her neck to look at the back of her head. Her hair was definitely thicker than before, but there was still some way to go. She thought she had a cold sore coming at the edge of her bottom lip, she felt it itching. She must remember to stop at a chemist and get antiviral cream. She took a tube of moisturiser from her bag and rubbed the lotion all over her face, trying to restore some colour. Better — sort of.

The Boar's Head was small, warm and filled with the aromas of spirits and roasting meat. *You'll find him at the round table to the right of the bar*, Nick Shelton had told her. She approached an elderly man who was reading the *Daily Telegraph* and eating a huge roast beef lunch. A Yorkshire pudding the size of a tea plate was drowning in a well of dark gravy. The newspaper was propped precariously against a menu card, the top folding dangerously towards the food.

'Mr Shelton? Mike Shelton?'

'That's me. Who's asking?' He peered at her, narrowing his pale blue eyes to focus.

'I'm Detective Inspector Drummond. Your son told me I'd find you here. I'd like a chat. Can I buy you a drink?'

'Now you're talking. Pint of Bombardier, thanks.'

She bought his pint and an orange juice and took them to the table. She waited while he chewed a mouthful of beef, nodding his thanks. Behind him was a photo of a merry-looking woman, raising her glass. The caption below said, *In memory of Monica Reed who always sat just here*. Shelton finished his pint and put the empty glass on the next table.

'Another one bites the dust. I've never had a good-looking lady DI buy me a drink before. My day's looking up.'

'Make the most of it, it might never happen again.'

He laughed, his shoulders shaking, and speared a carrot with a mound of mashed potato. He had yellowing teeth, thinning hair, a deeply lined face and a slight stoop but he seemed feisty. His prominent pot belly attested to his liking for beer and roast dinners. 'There must be a reason for your generosity. Hoping I'll spill the beans?' He spattered flecks of food over the table when he spoke, and she felt one land on her cheek.

'That's the idea, if you've got any beans to spill. I'm here because of Alan Vine.'

His mouth drooped. 'Terrible, that. Poor old Viney. You're after whoever did it?'

'That's right, and you might be able to help me.' He had a spot of gravy on his chin. She wanted to dab it away. 'When did you last talk to Alan?'

'That's easy. Last Friday. He came in about this time. We had a good old chat, in fact. I didn't roll home until after three.'

He picked the Yorkshire pudding up in his fingers and ate it as if it was toast. She could barely see his face behind it. 'How was Alan that day?'

'Fine. Upset, of course, because he'd found those bodies. He loved that bit of the river and he said it was like a personal insult, what had happened. He told me about you lot and your questions. Said he'd given a DNA sample.' He put the half-eaten Yorkshire back on the plate. 'Food in here's tasty but between you and me, that's not the best Yorkshire I've ever had. Not crisp enough. Don't tell them I said so, though. Mum's the word.'

'Mum it is. What else did you talk about?'

'This and that. Bit of a trip down memory lane, I suppose. Chatted about the club back in the day, when I ran things. When I got to seventy, I'd had enough and handed it all over to Nick. Let him do the worrying for a change. Viney was very interested in a chap who used to fish with us occasionally, years ago, wanted to know a bit more about him.'

'Who was this man?'

'James Stenning, his name was. It was all very sad. This was back in the nineties. He wasn't a full member because he lived in Kent somewhere but he liked the fishing in that stretch of river. He paid half-rates for about three years.'

'Why come from Kent to fish? Isn't that a bit of a trek?'

'He was a financial advisor and he had some clients in this area, so I suppose it was easy enough to go to the river here. He left suddenly. Had a bereavement. His little girl died in an accident.'

'What was his little girl's name?'

'Sophie.'

Siv took a breath. 'Did Alan Vine know about this little girl?'

'Oh, yes. Viney knew a bit, but he didn't know why Stenning left the club or what had happened.' He tapped his glass. 'This is looking a tad empty.'

She knew he could tell her more, and that he wouldn't be hurried. He liked having an audience and a bit of chat that made the hours go by. She bought him another pint and a packet of peanuts for herself. The salt in them made her lip tingle.

'I think I might have apple crumble and custard, then I can just have cheese and crackers tonight. As long as there's no cinnamon in it. Can't abide the stuff.' He called across to the barman who confirmed that the crumble was cinnamon free.

'Tell me about James and Sophie Stenning,' Siv said.

'I only knew James a little. Met him once or twice at the river. He gave me a few tips about investments. He never came to club meetings because of not being a local. He rang me one day to say he was cancelling his membership. Just said that his little girl Sophie had died in an accident and he was giving up. I remember her name because I'd just been watching a film with Sophia Loren so it sort of stuck.'

'He didn't give you any more details?' she asked.

'That was it. I didn't really know him, so to speak. I gave my condolences. Never spoke to him again.'

'Did you ever meet Sophie?'

'No, just her dad.'

'Do you remember when this happened?'

'Not exactly, just that it was early nineties. Funny, this is like a replay of the chat I had with Viney.'

A bowl of apple crumble arrived with a separate jug of custard. 'Did Mr Vine say why he was interested in James Stenning?'

'Can't say he did. We just got talking. At our age, you suddenly recall random things. They come from nowhere and flit away again.'

'How did he react when you told him about Stenning and what had happened to Sophie?'

Shelton poured his custard slowly over his bowl. 'Not sure, really. Can't recall anything in particular. What's this all about anyway?'

'Just part of our enquiries. You have no idea where Stenning lived?'

'No. The club must have had his address at some point I suppose, but I wasn't much of a record keeper back then and I had a big clear-out when I moved house in ninety-five. Once Viney took over, things were much more organized. If you wanted anything knocked into shape, Viney was your man. Poor bloke. What a way to go. This is a terrific pud. Nothing sets you up like a crumble.'

He spooned it up happily. She wondered if he might find it less palatable if he knew that she suspected the information he had given Viney had led directly to the man's death.

Back in the car, she looked at her face in the mirror and picked flecks of chewed carrot from her right cheek.

* * *

At the station, she closed her office door and started an internet search. A James Stenning of Aldmarsh had died in January 2017, aged fifty-eight. Aldmarsh was a large village about twelve miles from Berminster. The address wasn't in Kent but he was the right kind of age and he'd been a financial advisor with his own company. She looked up the company address, which was the same as his home. When she delved further she saw that he'd lived at the Aldmarsh address since 2001. Then she searched for Sophie Stenning and sat back to read the news article dated 6 April 1993.

A three-year-old Ashford girl died in tragic circumstances last Friday night. Sophie Stenning fell from a rolling chair in her father's home office while reaching for a pair of scissors. The chair moved on its castors as Sophie attempted to take the fatal blades from a shelf. She lost her balance and the sharp blades of the scissors were plunged into her neck. Sophie was rushed to hospital but sadly, she died on the way. There will be a coroner's inquest.

Okay, she thought, *we're inching nearer.* She rang Ashford police and asked for the records for 1993. While she waited for an email to arrive, she stood at her window, looking down onto the car park as Patrick drove in fast and parked. He got out of his car, phone pressed to his ear, and jogged up and down on the spot while he was speaking. Then he took a can from the car and sprayed its contents around his torso before heading into the building. *Strange*.

She heard the ping of an incoming email, sighed as she read the grim report made in April 1993, and saw the full names. *All this time and it was right in front of us if we'd known where to look.* There were photos of Sophie Stenning, one in life and several post-mortem. She looked again at the parents' names. She'd recently met someone with that first name who looked the right kind of age. She checked for a current address. As she'd expected, she saw that it was in Aldmarsh.

Ali was at his desk and came through when she called him. She recounted her discussion with Mike Shelton and showed him what she'd found.

'So Vine lied to us, he did recognize the kid's photo.'

'Perhaps not intentionally at first or he wasn't sure, which is why he went to talk to Mike Shelton. Vine must have met her at Lock Lane with her father at some point. We've found the child in the photo but apart from death by scissors, we still don't know what links her to Lauren Visser. But at least now we know who to ask. Sophie was two years older than Lauren Visser. James Stenning worked in this area and must have got to know people. We have to consider if he was Lauren's father. And if he was, did his wife know?'

They talked tactics for a few minutes. Then Siv made a phone call but put the receiver down as soon as it was answered.

'She's at home. We'll have to tread carefully. We've no forensics and only a tyre imprint to go on, which is hardly robust evidence. No pithy comments, okay?'

Ali was eating sultanas that he'd magicked from his pocket. 'Gotcha, guv.'

* * *

It was a detached stone cottage, double-fronted with shutters at the windows and set on a bank with winding steps to the front door. The front garden was paved, with a bench and a cast-iron sundial. There was no car outside but there was a stand-alone garage at the side of the house. Siv tapped the heavy knocker twice, loudly.

She opened the door wearing a blue apron patterned with red tulips, her hair tied back. Her eyes darted between Siv and Ali. 'Inspector Drummond. What brings you this way?'

'We'd like to talk to you, Mrs Stenning.'

'Of course. Do come in.'

She led them into a living room with dark beams on the ceiling, waxed floorboards and chairs covered in green linen. There was a partly completed jigsaw on a coffee table. It was shaded and felt peaceful. She took her apron off and asked them to sit down.

'I just need to rinse my hands and turn the oven off. I've been baking for the church festival. I won't be a moment.'

Siv rose as soon as she left the room and stood watching the hallway. Ali looked at the photos on the wide mantelpiece. *None of the child*, he mouthed.

Mrs Stenning came back from the kitchen, smiling. 'Did you enjoy your cheesecake, Inspector?'

'I did, yes.'

She sat opposite them near the door, loosening her hair and slipping the elastic grip over her wrist. 'We sold out quickly. You were lucky to come along when you did. I've just made another batch if you'd like some before I put it in the freezer. Blueberry topping this time.'

'This isn't a social call, Mrs Stenning.'

'Oh, I see. Sorry to witter on about the baking in that case.'

She knew, behind the polite pretence. When cornered, some people were surly or aggressive or mute with fear. Others like Julia Stenning used their social skills to help them tread water. 'Sergeant Carlin would like to show you a photo again, Mrs Stenning. You have seen it before, at Polska, but I'd like you to take another look.'

Ali took the photo of Sophie Stenning from his pocket and handed it to her mother. Julia stared down at it. Her bony hand trembled.

'Do you recognize that little girl?' Siv asked. 'She died in a tragic accident in 1993 in Ashford. I think you do know her.'

Julia gripped the photo. 'How do you know about the accident?'

'Through asking questions and reading the police report. Is that Sophie?'

'Yes. This is Sophie.'

'Your daughter Sophie?'

'Yes.'

'When I showed you the photo previously at Polska, you said you didn't know this child.'

Julia held the photo in her palm and traced a finger across it. 'I was taken aback, shocked. I didn't know what to say.'

'But the photo had been left at a murder scene. You must have realized that it was crucial information. I made it clear that I needed to know the little girl's identity.'

'Yes, you did. I'm sorry. I was appalled, you see. How did anyone get hold of Sophie's photo, and why would they leave it where people had been murdered?'

'You didn't look shocked or appalled when I showed you the photo. You held it up to the light and replied perfectly calmly.'

Julia looked down at her feet. They were aligned neatly together. She wore sandals and her toes were narrow and straight. Her sleeveless shirt revealed well-honed arms. Siv had a sense of enormous self-control. She must work hard at staying so fit and lean.

'I can't explain it. How can one explain that kind of terrible shock?'

Siv shook her head. 'No, I don't understand. I saw you subsequently at the festival and you looked quite well and relaxed. You offered me cake. You didn't think to mention it then, or to phone me once you'd recovered from your shock?'

'Sorry, no. I was trying hard not to think about it because it's so painful. I know it sounds odd and hard to credit but to me, it's as if Sophie died yesterday, not years ago. She was everything to us. A bright, bubbly girl with such an engaging personality. We were entranced by the way she turned our lives upside down. We called her the rocket because she never stopped moving and chattering. I'd gone out that evening, you see. I hardly ever went out but that night there was a talk in the church hall I wanted to attend and James, my husband, urged me to go. He was in his office over the garage with Sophie. He took a phone call and while he was talking and looking something up, she climbed on to his chair and reached for a pair of scissors. The chair rolled from under her and she fell. The scissors went into her neck.' She drew her fingers slowly down her own neck, pressing them into the side. 'Such a savage thing to happen to a little girl. I never spoke to her again. She was unconscious and she died in the ambulance. It was so quiet afterwards. I couldn't get used to the quiet.'

'I'm sorry, Mrs Stenning.'

'Yes. You get a lot of sympathy from people. James kept telling me he was sorry and how guilty he felt. I was angry with him for a long time. I did blame him and then I felt bad for blaming him. It almost split us apart. We couldn't bear to have any more children, to tempt fate again. We moved house eventually, came here to get away from the memories. Inspector, I know you find my silence hard to believe but when you told me about the photo, it was as if someone had desecrated Sophie's memory. I think I just blanked it out because I didn't want to think about it. People tell you that time heals but it doesn't. Grief doesn't fade, you see. It squats in the corner of your mind and speaks to you every day.'

She raised tear-filled eyes. Siv found the pain in her face unbearable. She tried to speak but her voice was trapped in her throat.

Ali glanced at her white face. Both women looked agonized. He fiddled with his shirt cuff for a moment and then spoke softly. 'Mrs Stenning, do you have a car in your garage?'

She wiped a tear from her cheek, focused on him slowly. 'I'm sorry, I hate crying. Yes, I have a car.'

'Do you mind if I take a look at it?'

'Ahm . . . no, of course not. The garage is open. The door catches a bit. You have to slam it hard when you close it.'

Ali left the room. Siv recovered, embarrassed that he'd spotted her distress but glad of his intervention. She watched him go past the front window and down the steps. Julia watched him too. Siv believed this woman's grief but not her evasions. 'Mrs Stenning, what was the connection between Sophie and Lauren?'

But Julia had had time to recover as well. 'I don't know. I just don't know. There isn't one. How could there be?'

'Yet they both died from scissor wounds, and Sophie's photo was at the scene.'

Julia shook her head.

'Did you put a card through Lauren's door that had a scissor shape pasted on it and a threatening message?'

'Of course not! Why on earth would I do such a thing? I didn't know her, just of her!'

'Do you have family members or friends who would have a photo of Sophie or have access to one?'

The question obviously threw her and she stammered, 'I . . . I don't think so.'

'Where was that photo taken?'

'In the back garden in Ashford. James took it. It was his favourite photo of Sophie. He *claimed* he treasured it. He always had a framed copy on his bedside cabinet.'

There was something dark surging in her voice as she said that. She'd taken a tissue from her pocket and was pressing it to her lips. Within seconds her expression had shifted from misery to a set, hard look. Siv heard the garage door clang shut. Julia glanced towards the window, half rising from her chair. An ear-shattering noise suddenly filled the air, making Siv jump.

'Smoke alarm!' Julia Stenning dashed through the door and was gone towards the kitchen.

Siv went after her, the insistent bleeping reverberating. The dense smoke filling the kitchen stung her eyes and confused her for a moment. The smoke billowed from a pan on the cooker, the gas flame burning full beneath it. She flicked the knob on the cooker and then saw that the back door was wide open. Julia Stenning had gone. Siv ran out and saw her jumping the low wall at the bottom of the garden and racing across the field at the back of the cottages. She took off after her. The grass in the field was short, cropped by sheep that were now panicking and scattering, bleating harshly to their lambs. Their droppings were everywhere, small pellets covering the ground that was dry and hard from days of heat. She saw Julia slow at the edge of the field by a barred gate, and caught her breath. The hot air shimmered around Julia, catching the glowing highlights in her hair. She raised an arm, there was a flash in the sunlight and she fell to the ground.

As Siv reached her she saw what Julia had done, saw the rush of blood. She threw herself to her knees beside her, wrenched her jacket off and pressed it to the pumping wound on the side of her neck. She could hear Ali thudding up behind her, hear his *Ach, God, no!* He fumbled for his phone and called an ambulance.

The blood was soaking through the jacket, onto her hands. She pressed harder to try to stem the flow. The woman below her was white and silent.

The long, sharp scissors she had used lay inches away, their gleam dulled by blood.

CHAPTER TWENTY-SIX

Julia Stenning was conscious but not yet well enough to speak to them. Ali brought Patrick up to speed while the guv spoke to Betty Marshall.

'Julia Stenning was quick thinking. After we arrived she must have put the saucepan over the full flame when she said she was going to the kitchen to turn off the oven. She'd dropped butter in the saucepan. The smoke was bitter. I suppose she left the scissors ready by the back door.'

'We still don't know if she killed them, then.'

'Her car tyres are all Dunlop and the front left looked fine to me. That's all we've got until we search the house and forensics check the car and look at the scissors. The guv couldn't get any link to Lauren from her.'

'Why would she try to top herself though, and using the same method? It has to have been her or she wouldn't have run.'

'I dunno. The guv was soaked in blood. It was a grim one. Mortimer called her in. I reckon she got a roasting, judging by her face afterwards. It's not good when a suspect tries to top herself while you're interviewing her.'

'You could hardly have seen that coming,' Patrick said.

'No. But it doesn't work like that, does it? I hope the guv stood up for herself.'

'I reckon she would've. She's no pushover, and she hasn't exactly been slacking since she walked through the door. I bet she stood her ground.'

'Hope so, but you know what a wee bastard Mortimer can be when he feels like it.'

* * *

Betty Marshall was sobbing. Siv had given her a cup of tea and a box of tissues and was waiting until she gained control. Siv could still taste smoke. It would be a while before she ate butter. Mortimer had been curt and sarcastic, saying that what had happened was very bad publicity.

'Makes us look incompetent, DI Drummond.'

She wanted to say that she could see it wouldn't play well on Twitter. 'I don't see why, sir. We could hardly have suspected what Julia Stenning was planning.'

'She gave no indication at all?'

'None.'

'So did she carry out these killings?'

'I don't know. We didn't get that far, but once we can question her I hope to find out more.'

He'd scratched his face. 'Don't let the doctors pussyfoot around over that. You know what they're like, wanting to protect their patients.'

'I do, yes. I'm okay, by the way and so is Sergeant Carlin. I've washed off the blood but my suit won't survive.'

'Oh . . . yes. Good. Of course, I'm relieved that neither of you sustained any injury.'

Thanks for the concern, she'd muttered, closing his door a tad too forcefully. Now she focused on Betty, who had a pile of soggy tissues in front of her but was calming down.

'Drink some tea, Betty. The best thing you can do to help your friend now is tell me about her. We haven't been able to find any next of kin and I need to know what you can tell me. How long have you known Julia?'

Betty swallowed hot tea and crumpled another tissue in her hand. 'Not that long. We met in that café at the beach — Horizon — early last year. We just got chatting. It was a chilly day and we were the only people in there. I asked Julia if she'd finished with the paper. We hit it off straight away, ended up sitting for hours over coffee and cake. We exchanged numbers and we've seen each other pretty much every week since, and talked on the phone in between. It was lovely to find a new friend like that, and we're both single so we could meet when we liked. Julia filled a real gap in my life, I can tell you. I don't understand why she'd do a thing like that. Try to take her own life. She never seemed that way inclined at all. The glass was always half full with her. When can I see her?'

'I don't know. That will be up to the hospital staff. She's no longer critical but she's still in intensive care. Did you know that Julia had a daughter who died?'

Betty's mouth dropped. 'No! When was that?'

'In 1993. There was a terrible accident at their home in Ashford. Sophie, the little girl, died. She was three.'

'But . . . no, that can't be right! Really, it can't! You must have made a terrible mistake.'

'It's true. Julia confirmed it to me. Why do you find it so hard to believe?'

'Because . . . because I told Julia that I had a little girl who died. My daughter, Erica, died of a brain tumour when she was almost four. Julia was so kind when I talked about it. I told her that day when we first met in the café. Minster Beach always reminds me of Erica because we took her there all the time and it would have been her birthday the following week. Her twenty-seventh. I was feeling sad. I didn't even realize how sad until I started talking about her. I was tearful and Julia put her arm around me. That was such a comfort. I explained to Julia that we couldn't have any more children, and then my husband Terry left me for someone else and started a family with her.' She sniffed and cleared her throat. 'Surely Julia would have told me if that had happened to her as well? It would be a natural thing, wouldn't it, because we had that in common? She gave me the impression that she'd never had children. I just don't understand. Why didn't she tell me?' She looked up beseechingly.

'I don't know. Betty, the photo of the little girl I showed you when we talked at the nursery — that was Sophie Stenning, Julia's daughter.'

Betty sat, muddling her way through this news. 'But you found that photo at the murders, didn't you?'

'That's right. I showed it to Julia when I first met her. She denied knowing the child.'

Betty shook her head and took another tissue. 'I just can't understand any of this. It doesn't make sense at all. Why would Julia have said she didn't know her own child?'

Siv looked at her blotched face and was moved by her distress. She'd have much more to come if Siv's suspicions proved correct. She thought that Betty had been the lonelier of the two women and the more trusting, needy friend. That might dawn on her at some point. Then she would feel hurt and foolish. 'You haven't known Julia that long, despite the warmth of your friendship. Maybe she had her reasons for not wanting to talk about Sophie.'

'I suppose. I don't know what to think. Julia's my closest friend these days, someone I can rely on. I wish she could have told me about her little girl. I hope she will when I get a chance to see her.'

Siv regretted having to push the knife deeper but it was necessary. 'Did you know that Julia moved from Ashford to Aldmarsh with her husband about eighteen years ago?'

Betty gave a dull shake of her head.

'Has Julia ever talked to you about her husband?'

'A bit. She told me he died suddenly of a heart attack and she'd had to learn to cope without him. That was about all, really. He worked in finance, something like that. I got the impression she was okay for money but not as okay as she thought she was going to be. She did say there were a few muddles to work through after he died.'

'Did it sound like a happy marriage?'

'Yes, I'd say so. Julia said she missed him. She is going to be all right, isn't she?'

'It looks that way.' *Depends what you mean by all right.* 'Julia has never mentioned any other family to you?'

'No. She came from somewhere in the Midlands, but she said it was a while since she'd been back there. I got the impression there was no one else anywhere near. Gosh, it's warm in here.' Betty took a tissue and patted her face and neck.

The mid-afternoon sun shone full beam on the window and the small fan in the corner wasn't having much effect on the climbing temperature. 'I've opened the window as far as it will go. I won't be much longer.' Siv waited. She wanted Betty to concentrate on the next questions. 'Has Julia ever discussed Lauren Visser with you?'

'Lauren? We . . . we talked about Lauren now and again. I'd helped her with her nursery qualification so I told Julia a bit about that, and of course about our work in Minstergreen. Julia thought she might join at one point but then she decided she was already too busy with her other commitments.'

'And your suspicion that Lauren might have been having an affair — did you mention that to Julia?'

Betty bit her lip. 'Yes, just the once. Julia's the kind of friend you can confide in, share a burden with.'

'What was Julia's take on that?'

'She said that I needed to be careful because I had no proof. She thought that if it was true, it showed that some people didn't know when they were well off. Like me, she disapproved of affairs and nonsense that broke up marriages.'

'Did Julia mention to you that Lauren had visited Polska and put up a poster there about a campaign she was crowd-funding for?'

'I don't think so, no. What campaign?'

'It doesn't matter. Would you have mentioned Lauren's swimming to Julia?'

'I might have done, yes. Just in passing. I don't understand these questions. Julia didn't know Lauren. Why are you asking about her and Lauren?'

'I'm trying to build up a picture of Julia, I want to understand why she panicked and harmed herself when I was about to speak to her.' Siv was going through a timeline in her head and thought she already understood some of it. Now it was a matter of evidence and details.

* * *

Ali was waiting for her at her office when she'd finished with Betty.

'Guv, Steve Wooton says they've finished the search of Julia Stenning's house. No evidence of anything to connect her to our deaths. Her front car tyre is a Dunlop. By the look of it, she hasn't had it replaced recently. The scissors she stuck in herself have slimmer blades than the ones used on the Lock Lane victims. But they did find this in her filing cabinet, and Steve dropped it in. It's written by the dead husband and it's quite a read.'

He handed Siv a typed, undated letter. She waved him to a seat and read:

Dear Julia,

This is a coward's letter and I've agonized over whether or not to write it. I've done you a terrible injustice and I can't face you and tell you. If I die before you, you should know about what I did. When you've read this, no doubt you'll think badly of me and maybe you won't mourn me. Well, I expect that's what I deserve. There are things I need to explain.

I have a daughter, Lauren Visser. She's married and lives in Berminster. She was born a while after Sophie died. I have no excuses. I met her mother, Sue, when I called at the garage where she was working. I didn't intend to deceive you. I was grieving and a mess and we were cold to each other. I only saw Sue a couple of times before I ended our affair.

I didn't know she was pregnant. Sue contacted me years after Lauren was born to tell me about her. She'd had an attack of conscience, I suppose, and a friend who worked in health had told her she should find out what she could about my family and medical history, for Lauren's sake. She only allowed me to see Lauren once and I agreed because I felt so guilty and agonized. I knew I didn't deserve to get a second chance at being a father. I've never seen either of them since.

I wanted to tell you but how could I after all the pain we'd gone through? Sue didn't want to accept anything from me but I have given her money towards our daughter over the years. I thought it was only fair and I hope you think that too. I gave her a lump sum when Lauren was eighteen, as that seemed right, and Lauren might have needed it for higher education or other hurdles or opportunities life might bring. I'm glad I did, as I saw that Sue died a couple of years ago and that Lauren had then married.

You'll know by now that I changed my will without your knowledge and that will have made you angry. I'm sorry that I've left you rather less than you expected but you have the house. I know I promised you that I'd leave money to Frankie but in the end, I had to reconsider as my expenses over the years regarding Lauren had had quite an impact. I couldn't tell you because then I'd have had to reveal the whole truth and as I started by admitting, I'm a coward.

I didn't set out to hurt you. I'm sorry I couldn't protect our little girl as I should have done. If it's any comfort to you, I haven't had a day's peace since she died, and knowing that Lauren was in the world was extremely painful as well as joyous. Maybe you will find it in your heart to forgive me.

I'm so sorry. James.

Siv looked at Ali, puffing her cheeks out. 'Dynamite. Julia must have been shattered when she found this.'

'He was such a coward, wasn't he?' Ali said. 'Farewell wifey and by the way, there's a wee girl you need to know about that I've spent our money on, on the q.t. He'd have done better to hold his tongue.'

'Confession's a powerful urge, especially if you're not going to be around to suffer the consequences. That was his fishing gear on the rug in the photo I found in Sue Farthing's album. The one time he was allowed to meet his daughter. No doubt fishing was his alibi for being out for the day.'

Ali took some mints from his pocket and offered her one. It was silky on her tongue.

'Are you supposed to eat these?'

He looked furtive. 'One or two's okay, as long as I ration them.'

She couldn't imagine Ali rationing anything successfully. It wasn't in his expansive, addictive nature. She knew from Ed that it was hard work, helping your body against a daily battle. They sat in silence for a few moments. Siv realized that someone in the outer office was staring at her blankly while he talked on the phone.

'Pull those bloody blinds shut, will you?' she said to Ali. 'I feel like a sex worker in Amsterdam displaying my goods.'

He gave an embarrassed laugh, reached behind him and turned the rod. 'Who's Frankie when he's at home?' he asked.

'Or maybe she. It can be a female diminutive. Julia could tell us if she wanted but I'm not hanging around until she's well enough.' She related what Betty Marshall had told her. 'I wonder whether Julia didn't tell Betty about her dead daughter because she was already thinking of killing Lauren and didn't want to divulge anything too personal. Certainly, she got information about Lauren from Betty. Maybe she engineered the meeting and the friendship.'

'We don't know when Julia found that letter, though, or where she found it. If Stenning left it with his solicitor, she'd have received it soon after he died.'

'That would have been in early 2017. Can you phone the hospital and check on how she's doing? I'm going to have a look around her house. By the way, I've been generous. I haven't said *I told you so*.'

Ali stopped at the door, eyebrows raised. 'About what?'

'About Lauren's mother. She is part of the story. My hunch was right.'

'Yeah . . . well . . . ach, have another mint as you're so clever.'

'Thank you, Sergeant, very gracious.' She sucked her second mint but it wasn't as good as the hit of the first. *Frankie.* She'd seen or heard that name somewhere. She'd mull it over on the drive to Aldmarsh.

* * *

She spent an hour in Julia's house. The forensic team had finished, so she was able to look around uninterrupted. The kitchen had been aired but was still smoky, so she opened a window before going through to the living room and looking through the drawers and shelves. She flicked through several photo albums. None of the photos was recent. She guessed that Julia and James had stopped taking any after Sophie died. Their lives hadn't been worth recording after that. There were plenty of the little girl from baby to three years old — Sophie doing somersaults and headstands, splashing in a paddling pool, skipping, dancing and perched on a climbing frame. Her scant three birthdays and Christmases were marked. She was always smiling. The ones taken with her parents showed them looking thrilled, leaning in towards their child, glowing with love. She found herself moved by them.

Upstairs she found two bedrooms, one on either side of the landing. Julia's bedroom was neat, slightly clinical even, and she found nothing of interest. The second, smaller bedroom was used as an office. She looked through the filing cabinet where the letter had been found. Everything was secured in alphabetical pockets — bank statements, church activities, gym membership, health, insurances, work. The bank statements showed that Julia had healthy savings and a couple of thousand in her current account. She found a copy of Julia's will filed in an envelope under "W." It was short and had been drawn up just over a year ago. She noted the contents, her brain whirring, a tingle of excitement up the back of her neck, and photographed it before returning it to its pocket.

She rang the number of the solicitor who had drawn up the will. After a few minutes she spoke to a Ms Perbright who confirmed that she had also acted on behalf of Mrs Stenning with regards to probate on Mr Stenning's will, and that his papers had not included a letter for his wife. She confirmed that Mr Stenning had made a new will in 2011, but that one had been drawn up through another solicitor in Ashford. Mr Stenning had left everything to his wife. *But I wonder how much less than she and Frankie had been expecting, and all because of a secret daughter.*

She closed the cabinet drawers. Which pocket had Julia put the letter from her husband in? C for cheat or L for liar? As she pulled the front door shut, she saw an older man hovering at the bottom of the steps. It wasn't raining but he was using a large folded umbrella with a curved handle as a stick. He looked anxious.

'Are you from the police?' he asked.

'That's right. DI Drummond.'

'I saw you go in. I was hoping to catch you. I wondered how Julia is doing. I'm Peter Bacon, her neighbour from across the way.'

'She's Okay, still very ill. Do you know Julia well?'

'Pretty well, yes. We've been neighbours since she and James moved here. And she's a good neighbour. She was so kind to me when my wife died. This has been a dreadful shock.'

Siv looked down into his kindly, concerned eyes. 'Could you spare me a glass of water, Mr Bacon?'

'Of course, come on in. I'm sure I can run to a tea or coffee if you'd prefer.'

She followed him across the narrow lane and into his tiny two-up, two-down cottage. It had a majestic wisteria inching across the front and heading for the top windows. She was expecting clutter and old-world charm but the living room was updated, with neutral colours and white wood shelving in the alcoves. The fireplace held a wood burner similar to her own.

'My daughter had the place done up for me last year as a surprise,' Bacon told her. 'I felt like I was in one of those TV makeover programmes. I went away for a week and when I came back, it was like this. I thought I was going to die of shock, killed with kindness. I felt quite ill for a couple of weeks. I'd get up and think I was in the wrong house. I still can't find some of my things but I have to pretend I like it because my daughter went to so much trouble. Do take a seat.' He stood in the doorway, a hand against the frame. 'Someone said that Julia tried to kill herself. Surely that can't be right?'

'I can't comment on that for now,' Siv said.

'I see. Well . . . I won't be long.'

Siv waited, feeling as if she was skiving off school, being given afternoon tea while the others were busy. She imagined what Mortimer would say if he saw her. No doubt Tommy Castles wouldn't waste time taking tea with the elderly neighbour. She'd formed a mental image of Castles — beefy and cocky, a mansplainer and manspreader. She had the reckless thought that Mortimer could say and do what he liked. The worst that could happen to her already had. Everything else was small detail.

She heard Mr Bacon coming back, breathing wheezily, with two large mugs of tea and a plate of scones with butter and strawberry jam in a pretty glass bowl.

'I make these myself, a batch every week. I always give some to Julia. She does the jam. Oh dear, I can't take in what's happened at all.'

Siv sliced a scone and spread jam on it. She wasn't hungry but she did have an appetite for information, and Mr Bacon looked like a man who'd know what went on around his manor. A wealth of small details would accompany the day-to-day neighbourly trading of scones and jam. 'This is delicious. Full of fruit. Does Julia have any family around here?'

'Well, of course her husband died a few years ago. Out like a light as he was watching TV. That's the way I'd prefer to go, but of course we don't get a say in the matter, do we?'

'Not usually. Unless we go to a Swiss clinic for an injection.'

'Goodness . . . I see you have a macabre sense of humour. Did you have that before you joined the police, or has it developed with the job?'

'Bit of both, Mr Bacon.'

'I imagine it helps you deal with the kinds of things you must deal with. The Stennings didn't have any children and I think James's family hailed from Cambridgeshire. Julia used to go off sometimes and visit her parents in Derby but they both died. I never saw any family visit them and Julia never talked about anyone. They were both very active, always out and about and involved in things. James was a keen angler.'

'Was there anyone else close to the Stennings?'

Mr Bacon scooped up jam on a spoon and held it mid-air for a moment. 'I don't think so. There was a chap who visited Julia one day last year. I think she said he was her godson. I only saw him in passing. You don't hear much of godparents these days, do you? I don't think many children have them anymore. It was a big thing when I was a little boy. I had two godfathers and one godmother. They always gave me money on my birthdays, though I don't think God or religion came into it much.'

'I think it's a custom that's dying out a bit. I don't remember having any.' Siv picked up her tea and sipped it. It was weak, and made with UHT milk, but she swallowed it gamely and sat back, smiling at him. 'Tell me about this visitor last year. Can you describe him to me?'

'I'm not sure I remember him that well. It was just after I came home to this "surprise" and I wasn't feeling too good.'

She listened as Mr Bacon half closed his eyes to summon up the man he'd seen. She forgot the stale milky taste in her mouth as she heard his description.

CHAPTER TWENTY-SEVEN

The ward staff reported that Julia Stenning had had no visitor requests. Betty Marshall, the vicar of the church in Aldmarsh, a Mr Bacon and someone from Polska had phoned to enquire about her.

The nurse pulled the curtains around her bed, and Siv and Ali sat on either side of her. She was attached to a drip and her neck was swathed in dressings. She'd insisted that she wanted to speak to them and they'd been granted fifteen minutes.

'We found the letter your husband left for you. We know about Lauren and his altered will,' Siv said. 'That must have come as a terrible shock to you.'

Julia nodded. She spoke slowly and hoarsely. 'He left it for me in one of his old jackets. He knew I always went through pockets carefully. I found it months after he died when I was sorting through things to take to the charity shop. I was stunned when I found out he'd made a new will without telling me. I couldn't understand it, or why he'd left a lot less than I expected. Then when I found that despicable letter, it all fell into place.'

'Why did you try to kill yourself?' Siv asked.

Ali looked at her. She could see he was surprised that she wasn't just cutting to the chase about the murders. She hadn't told him yet about the will she'd found, or her conversation with Peter Bacon and the possibility she'd been considering. She needed to draw Julia out, not deliver any hammer blows, and she'd told him to take it easy.

Julia ran her tongue over her lips. Her long face looked sunken, the skin tight below her cheekbones. 'After Sophie died we agreed we wouldn't have any more children. We said we couldn't bear to tempt fate again. So we slowly rebuilt a life and we did that thing that childless people do, we took up interests and activities. We were never really close again but we muddled through. We were kind to each other. Or so I thought. Eventually we moved away from Ashford and the memories there. James was keen on Aldmarsh, said he knew it from his work, so I agreed to settle there. Once I'd read the letter I knew he steered us there to be near Berminster. Near his daughter. Such cruel deception. And he . . . he was on the phone and distracted while Sophie reached for those scissors. It was his fault, yet I forgave him. And then he did that to me.' She stared ahead, stony and cold. 'I wished he'd had a painful, more drawn-out death.'

'Did you get to know Lauren?' Siv asked.

Julia looked contemptuous. 'No. Why would I have wanted to know *her*?'

'Who's Frankie?' Ali asked impatiently.

'Frankie?'

'Yes. Your husband said he was sorry he couldn't leave anything to Frankie.'

'That's irrelevant,' Julia said.

Why do you have to rush in, Ali? We would have got her to Frankie. Siv swallowed her annoyance. 'I don't think so,' she said. 'I think Frankie is relevant and you need to tell us about him.'

Wincing, Julia pushed herself up a little and looked Siv straight in the eye, unblinking. 'I killed Lauren and that other man, Rimas, and I killed Alan Vine. That's why you're here, so that I can tell you. I put that postcard of the scissors though Lauren's door. I wanted her to feel the terror that my poor Sophie would have known as the blades cut her beautiful skin. I began having dreams about killing her the night I found James's letter. I couldn't bear the thought that she was alive when my daughter was dead. I killed her to get my revenge on my husband who betrayed me and allowed our little girl to die.' She swallowed, pressing her fingers to the base of her throat. 'I didn't plan to kill the two men. They got in the way. Vine rang me, talking about Sophie's photo and James, asking questions. I couldn't let him live. That sounds callous but it's just how it was. I have thought about killing myself so many times since Sophie died. Once I realized it was only a matter of time before you found out I killed them, I decided it was the only way out. And yet here I am. Now do whatever you have to do. I'll make a full statement.'

'Before we get to that, tell me how you killed Alan Vine,' Siv said.

'James had taken Sophie with him to go fishing at the river, Vine had been there. He remembered and worked out she was my daughter. Sounded very pleased with himself. I said I'd meet him in Halse woods at the frog pond. I waited in the bushes. I killed him with a kitchen knife. I couldn't afford to let him bumble around in case he led you to me. You'll find the knife and the protective clothing I wore in a plastic bag, shoved into a tree hollow just outside Aldmarsh at the start of the footpath towards Clayfield. His phone's in there too. I threw the scissors I used at Lock Lane and Lauren's rucksack into the sea at the far end of Minster Beach.'

Ali was looking delighted. He opened his mouth to speak, but Siv silenced him with a *shut up* look. 'I see. Tell me why you left Sophie's photo at the murder scene.'

'My Sophie was gone. We had promised each other we would never have another child. Yet, while I was deprived of any other child, James betrayed my trust and fathered her. He took away my future, so I took away his.'

'But he was dead,' Ali said.

Do you have to be so literal? Siv suppressed her mounting impatience. But Julia was explaining anyway.

'Of course, but his genes can never be passed on, so his line is truly ended. It gave me great satisfaction to do that.' Her voice was fading and she was even paler now.

Siv leaned in to her. 'Mrs Stenning, where exactly did you leave Sophie's photo?'

Julia looked puzzled. 'Pardon?'

'The photo. Where at Lock Lane did you leave it?'

Her eyes flickered. 'Just . . . just beside Lauren. Yes, by her hand.'

'At her side, by her hand.'

'Yes,' she said hesitantly, looking anxiously at Siv as if she might read the correct answer from her face. 'That's where I left it.'

'Which side?'

Another hesitation. 'Her right.'

Siv wanted to ask her who she was protecting and why, but they'd already gone over time and there was someone else they needed to find in a hurry. She stood as she spoke. 'Julia Stenning, I'm arresting you on suspicion of the murder of Alan Vine.' She issued a caution, while Ali stared at the distressed woman in the bed.

Julia pushed herself up, gasping. 'But no! You need to arrest me for three murders. I'm confessing to all three. Don't you see?'

Siv had never heard anyone pleading to be arrested for a triple killing before. 'No, not three murders. Just the one. From now on while you're in hospital, you'll be in custody.'

Ali arranged round the clock police cover on Julia Stenning while Siv explained the situation to an ITU manager. Until further notice, Julia was not allowed any visitors and if anyone contacted them saying they were family, the police should be notified. Then she called Patrick with orders to get to Aldmarsh with colleagues and search for the evidence. Outside in the corridor, she looked for a bookmarked page she'd saved on her phone. Ali hurried ahead, returning with a coffee and holding one out to her.

'Here. I figured you needed one too. Why's she insisting she killed Lauren and Rimas? Is she protecting someone?'

'Yes, I think so. Here, look at this.' She showed him the page on her phone. 'Mason Granger's an animator. When I was looking him up before I met him, I noticed that he runs a website with guides to animation and tips about developing the skills. I didn't read it in any depth but when I was at Julia's house, I remembered something I'd seen.'

Ali scanned the page. '*Squiggle Animation* by Frankie Granger.'

'That's right. His full name is Mason Francis Granger. He's Julia's godson. He's also named as sole beneficiary in her will.'

'Why would he call himself Frankie?'

'I don't know, but people do employ name variations for different aspects of their lives. Maybe it's a family pet name. When I visited Julia's, I talked to a neighbour. He told me that he'd seen Julia's godson visiting last year and he was called Frankie. He described him and it fitted Granger.'

'You think he carried out the Lock Lane murders?' Ali said.

'We've got nothing at present to link him to them. She didn't want to talk about Frankie just then. That might be significant. She clearly didn't kill Lauren and Rimas. A photo might have fallen down off Lauren's chest but it could hardly fall upwards from the ground.'

'Unless Vine lied to us and moved it when he was having a look.'

'But then his fingerprints would have been on it. That morning was warm and he wasn't wearing gloves. Anyway, we can't ask him now, but we do need to ask Granger some questions. He hasn't been in touch with the hospital, so either he doesn't know what's happened or he's lying low. I think that if he's around, it means he doesn't know.'

But there was no answer when they rang the bell to his flat. Siv was debating whether to phone him when a woman arrived with a bag of shopping.

'Do you know if Mr Granger is around?' Siv asked.

'I saw him about half an hour ago on his bike. He said he was going to Halse woods. Something about a hedgerow survey.'

'He can only just have got there,' Ali said to her as they headed back to the car. 'And if he's in the woods the warden should know where he is.'

'Put your foot down,' she said. 'I'll feel happier when he's in my sights. When we find him, he's coming to the station. I'm not risking any more attempts at self-harm.'

'But what if he—?'

Siv held up a hand. 'Quiet now, and by the way, sometimes a more gradual approach works better with suspects, especially when they're in intensive care, rather than full on barnstorming.'

'Oh. Right. I just thought, as we didn't have much time with her, we needed to get answers fast.'

Siv ignored him. At some point she'd arrange for him to go on interview training but she hadn't time for that now. 'I'm thinking aloud. Granger has no alibi for the Monday morning. He'd had disagreements with Lauren. She was blocking his grand plans for Minstergreen and generally irritating him. He lied about when he'd last seen her. If he'd expected to inherit money from James Stenning, he was disappointed. And if he then discovered that the money had gone to Lauren instead, that would add to his dislike of her. If he knew James was Lauren's father, only Julia could have told him.'

'You think they planned Lauren's murder together?'

'That's still to determine. But if he did it, where's the car he used? I hope we don't have to scour miles of woodland for him.'

Ali swung sharply into the car park at Halse woods. It was after five p.m. and there were just a few cars still parked and several bikes in the cycle ramp. The sky was cloudless, the sun intense. They headed for the warden's office. Siv pushed the door open without knocking. Half a dozen people including Granger sat around the table, with Kitty Fairway at the head of it, her hand on a large map. They all looked up when Siv stepped in.

'Sorry about the intrusion,' Siv said. 'I need a word with Mr Granger.'

'Can't it wait? I'm about to photograph an important survey for publicity,' Granger said testily.

'No, it can't wait. I have important news about your family. Perhaps we can talk in the car.'

He looked nonplussed. Ali had moved near to where he was sitting.

'It's okay, Mason,' Kitty said. 'You need to go if it's about family. We can catch up with the rest of this later.'

He muttered something and then stood, grabbing his rucksack. Ali walked behind him while Siv led the way outside.

'What's this about?' Granger asked.

'Let's sit in the car. We don't want to discuss private matters in public.'

He muttered again but went with them. Ali sat in the front of the car and Siv got in the back with Granger. Despite being parked in the shade, the car was warm and Ali opened the front windows. Granger was wearing a peaked cap. He pushed it back and folded his arms.

'Well?'

'I'd like you to come with us to the station to discuss some important matters,' Siv told him.

'What matters?'

'Various. It would be better at the station.'

'Better for whom? What's this about? I don't want to come to the station, thanks. Whatever it is, we can talk about it here or you can bugger off and let me get back to my work.' He was starting to shout.

'Oh, wind your neck in, big man. We're not impressed with your blather,' Ali told him.

That rendered Granger temporarily speechless, and Siv seized the chance.

'Look, Mr Granger — or shall I call you Frankie? What we have to discuss includes what's happened to your godmother.'

'You what?'

'Julia Stenning. Your godmother. She calls you Frankie, I understand. She's in intensive care in Berminster General at the moment.'

He frowned. 'What's the matter with Julia?'

'I'm afraid she tried to kill herself. With scissors.'

'Christ. How is she?' His shoulders twitched. It was hard to read his reactions behind the smoky lenses.

'She'll be okay. Seems odd that she hasn't asked for you, given that you live nearby.'

He stayed silent, shaking his head.

'Difficult news for you,' Ali said. 'Shall we head off now and talk somewhere cooler and more comfortable?'

'What about my bike?'

'We can arrange that for you.'

'Just a minute. What are these "matters" you want to talk about?'

'At the station,' Siv said firmly. 'I can arrest you now if you like, or you can agree to answer some questions.'

He thought about it, fiddling with the strap of his rucksack. 'I'll come with you.'

'Good. Now let's enjoy the drive. Ali, put some music on — something classical and soothing.'

* * *

On the way to the interview room, Patrick called to say the plastic bag had been found at Aldmarsh, stuffed deep into the base of a tree. It had gone to forensics. Granger sat at the table with his cap still on, sipping tea. He looked relaxed. Ali took the lead. *We give him nothing, no advantage*, Siv had instructed.

Ali rolled up his shirtsleeves. His skin was smooth and dimpled around the elbows, his forearms covered in fine dark hair. 'Can you confirm that you know Ms Julia Stenning and that she's your godmother?'

'That's right.'

'Tell us about your relationship with Julia and her husband,' Ali said.

Granger shrugged. 'It's been more of a distant friendship, to be honest. My mum was Julia's friend. Mum was a traditionalist, wanted a godparent for me. I can't say it's ever meant much to me and I'm not religious. My dad died in a car crash when I was a toddler and then Mum died when I was thirteen. I lived with my gran in Ashford after that. Julia used to send me a card and money for my birthday, that sort of thing.'

Ali nodded. 'Do you know what happened to Sophie, Julia's daughter?'

'Yeah, my mum told me. I was a baby when it happened. Crap for them. Poor little kid. It was a terrible way to die. It was a bit of a taboo subject, not to be mentioned. Like *don't talk about the war.*'

'When did you move to Berminster?'

'Couple of years ago.'

'Why here? Was it to be nearer your godmother?' Ali asked.

'Not really. My gran had to go into a home. I'd visited Julia once or twice over the years and I liked the town. Wanted to be near the sea, and the rents are affordable here as well.'

'Have you seen much of Julia?'

'Now and then. I went to James's — her husband's — funeral. She's not a relative as such so, you know. It was just the odd contact.'

'When did you last see her?'

Granger pursed his lips. 'Let's think. Last year. I'd been for a cycle and I called by. Had a cuppa and a chat. She was in good form. She supports Minstergreen's work, so we talked about that a bit.'

Siv shifted her notepad. 'Did Julia talk to you about her husband's betrayal?'

'No. What betrayal?'

'He'd had an affair and fathered a child in Berminster,' she said. 'He left Julia a letter that she found after his death, informing her. It came as a terrible shock.'

'Wow! I can imagine! I'd never have thought James was the type. Seemed very straightforward, a bit boring even. I suppose you never can tell, though. Julia never mentioned it. But you know, we're not close like that and I suppose maybe she was embarrassed. What a bastard, doing that to her!'

'So you didn't know about the child, or who she was?' Siv said.

'No.'

He was calm and confident, the answers coming easily. Siv tried looping back. 'When I first met you, I showed you a photo of Sophie. You said you didn't recognize her.'

'Like I said, I was a babe in arms when she died. I don't think I've even seen any photos of her.'

'How well did you know James Stenning?' Siv asked.

'A bit. Never met him more than a couple of times.'

'Yet he mentioned you in the letter he left for Julia. Said he was sorry he hadn't left Frankie anything in his will.'

'Oh, right. Well, I didn't know anything about his will and I hadn't expected him to leave me anything.'

'It seems odd that Julia wouldn't have mentioned that to you,' Siv said. 'The way the letter was written, it sounded as if they'd discussed it and she'd expected him to leave you some money. She has no close family nearby, and usually if you've thought of naming someone as a beneficiary in your will, it indicates some level of fondness.'

'You'd have to ask her. Sorry, I can't help you.'

'So you don't know the reason why Mr Stenning had altered his will and not left you anything?'

'No. Shame. The money would have come in handy, but as I had no expectations I don't know what I missed, do I?'

'Are you named in Julia's will?' she asked.

He laughed, folding his arms. Nothing so far had discomfited him. 'How would I know? It's not the kind of thing

281

you ask someone. At least, I wouldn't. It would sound as if you were only interested in them for their money.'

'But Julia might have told you,' Siv said.

'Well, she hasn't, so I've no idea.'

'Why do you think Julia would try to kill herself with scissors?'

'I haven't a clue. She isn't the kind of person I'd expect to feel suicidal. She's always seemed very strong and capable. Look, where is all this going? I'm not sure what you're after with these questions. I've had very little to do with my god-mother. I'd like to visit her, though, now that I know what's happened.'

'James Stenning's child, the one Julia didn't know about, was Lauren Visser.'

He put his lips together in a soundless whistle. 'Oh, wow! That's amazing. So . . . hang on, did Julia ever meet Lauren?'

Siv ignored the question and left a pause. His surprise seemed genuine. Whatever had gone on between them, the next bit of information should get a reaction. 'Julia Stenning has confessed to murder.'

His head jerked forwards. 'What? Oh, come on. No way!'

'It's true. And we've found the evidence she told us about. She's been arrested and charged.'

'But . . . Julia could never harm anyone. She's a good person. Who is she saying she's murdered?'

'I can't give you that information right now,' she said.

'What . . . hang on, is it those recent murders? Is she saying she murdered Lauren and that guy?'

'I can't comment on that. Mr Granger, you lied about your last contact with Lauren Visser and you have no one to verify where you were on the morning of the twenty-ninth of April. Do you know anything about the murders of Lauren Visser and Matis Rimas?'

He held his hands up. 'Of course I don't! We've been over this. I explained why I didn't tell you about my visit to her. If I'd wanted to murder her, I could have done it there and then, when she was home alone. Much easier than loitering around a river. I was working at home, earning a living, not killing people at Lock Lane.'

She stared at him. 'I don't believe you. I think you do know something.'

'Really? What's your evidence? If you had anything to go on apart from a distant friendship between Julia and me, you'd have arrested me. So I'm known as Frankie to some people, Julia's my godmother and James cut me out of a will I didn't even know about. I knew nothing about Lauren being James's child. You can think what you like. I'm fed up with this. I've tried to help you and I want to go now. Any more questions, I want a solicitor.'

This was going nowhere. Siv was frustrated and tired. Granger was spot on, she didn't have enough to arrest him. 'I want to ask you again — do you have a car or have use of one?'

'No. I used to drive, I had a courier job when I was a student to make ends meet, but I've never owned a car and I use a bike. That clear enough for you?'

'Wait there for now, Mr Granger. I'll let you know what's going to happen shortly. You won't be able to see your godmother just yet. I can pass on a message if you wish. Do you want more tea? A coffee?'

'No. I want to go home.'

They left the room and Siv headed for the door that led to the courtyard garden. As they stepped outside into the dusk, Ali was already lighting a Gitanes. There were half a dozen lights placed around the paving, casting a silver glow. A bat swooped across, a fleeting shadow.

'Where do we go from here?' Ali asked.

'We have to let him go. There's no grounds for detaining him. We've found nothing in his flat and no trace of a car. He goes home and we have to talk to Julia again. She knows what happened. If they planned the first two murders between them, they must have made contact, so we focus on that. We scrutinize Julia's mobile and landline and ask around Aldmarsh and Polska for any sightings of the two of them together. And we talk to Granger's neighbours and the members of Minstergreen, check again if anyone's ever seen him driving a car or saw him on that Monday morning.'

They glanced at each other in the greyish light. Siv felt drained. *Look at us, one grieving, slightly crazed detective and one diabetic chain smoker with a coffee stain on his shirt.* She suppressed a smile.

'Meeting first thing in the morning. We'll get there,' she said with a confidence she didn't feel.

CHAPTER TWENTY-EIGHT

Siv couldn't sleep, worried by the lack of progress. She gave up at five and, as dawn broke, went for a walk by the river. The sky was streaked with red and gold. Ripples broke on the surface of the calm, clear water and a flotilla of ducks glided upriver, pausing now and then to investigate the sedge and reeds. This was the peaceful time of day, a time when Lauren might have been preparing for a swim, Matis putting his fishing gear in the boot of a borrowed car, Alan Vine walking his dog. She thought about an anxious family in Krosna, waiting to hear that the English detectives had brought their Matis's murderer to justice.

When she'd made tea and toast, she checked her emails and saw that she'd had one from her mother.

Horrible of you not to reply to me. I don't understand why you're so unkind to me. I suppose your father poisoned you against me years ago. My life wasn't easy at times, you know, and I had my own battles to fight. I have so many happy memories of when you were little and I hope you do too. Anyway, I'm so unhappy, Sivvi. I've been living with Ernst for a year but he's decided to go back to his wife. I'm devastated as I really thought we were long term and I'm not getting any younger. You know that song — men grow cold as girls grow old — and I don't even have any diamonds to comfort me. I think I've had enough of being in Turku. Everyone knows your business, and the people here can be terrible gossips. So I have to put my thinking cap on.

Do send some news. Love from your Mutsi.

She shook her head and ran her fingers over her scar. She missed Ed so much right now. On the rare occasions when they'd seen Mutsi, he'd acted as a protective bulwark against her. She'd been at their wedding, flirting with all the men, and had visited them twice in Greenwich. Ed was gallant with her but also steely, allowing her just so near and no further. Mutsi had flirted with him too, of course, stroking his arm and being girlish in a way that made Siv want to puke. And Ed had absorbed and deflected it all, allowing Siv to breathe. *She's a monster*, he'd said after their wedding, *but a sad sort of monster.*

She checked the time before she rang Betty Marshall. 'I hope this isn't too early.'

'No, I'm just finishing my breakfast. Any news of Julia? I rang but they said no visitors.'

She didn't want to give the news she had over the phone, and she wanted to see if Betty could tell her anything more about her friend. 'Could I call round and see you now, before you go to work?'

Betty lived in a small semi on a modern estate called Spinney Dale. It had a front garden planted with runner beans, peas, tomatoes and spinach. Betty saw her looking.

'I got the idea from Lauren. I used to have flowers growing at the front but she suggested it made more sense to grow my own vegetables there as well as at the back, especially as the front faces south. She reckoned if more people did that, we'd be using less of the planet's resources and of course, she was right. So I'm almost self-sufficient now.'

Siv thought of Lauren's own manicured, vegetable-free garden and thought that she didn't walk the walk. But maybe she was being unfair and Visser had laid down the law about what they planted.

She sat in Betty's kitchen and accepted a cup of tea. There was an aroma of frying bacon and eggs. The house had a dated look, all the fixtures and fittings from thirty-odd years ago. The kitchen was done out in pine and there was a gas cooker with an overhanging grill. It was comfortable, and Siv could see spring cabbages through the back window. Washed dishes were stacked at the side of the sink. They were dark blue ceramic patterned with orange flowers. She had a memory of similar plates at a friend's house when she was a teenager. She'd used to loiter there when she truanted from school, until her father found out and told her that if she wanted to carry on missing her education that was her choice, but she could do it living at her mother's. A terrifying but effective threat and the only time she had known her father be so assertive.

Betty was already dressed in her work tabard, cotton trousers and sensible shoes. 'Tell me how Julia is.'

'Julia's doing okay.'

'Why won't they let me see her then?'

'They can't. I'm afraid I have some more difficult news for you. Julia's been charged with the murder of a man called Alan Vine. She confessed to it yesterday.'

Betty had been lifting a cup to her lips but she set it down again with a clatter. 'Murder? What on earth? Who's Alan Vine?'

Siv explained, watching perspiration funnel down Betty's cheeks. 'In fact, Julia has confessed to three murders in total, including that of Lauren. Lauren was James Stenning's daughter, the result of an affair with a woman in town. Julia didn't find out until after her husband died. She says she murdered Lauren because she had no right to live when Sophie was dead.'

Betty reached for a gingham tea towel and held it to her face. She pulled roughly at the neck of her tabard as if she was choking and then got up and wrenched the back door open. She stood there, drinking in the air.

Siv sat, letting the cool air wash over her and sipping her tea. She glanced at her watch. 'I'm so sorry to have to tell you this about your friend.'

'My friend!' Betty's voice was faint. She sat down heavily, pushing her tea away. 'Was she getting information from me about Lauren so that she could — you know — plan all this?'

'I'm not sure. Some of the time maybe. Did Julia ever talk to you about a godson called Frankie?'

A slow shake of the head. 'No. Right now I wouldn't be surprised if you told me she had a dozen children I'd never heard of.'

'Frankie is a name used by Mason Granger, the chair of Minstergreen. He's Julia's godson. You never saw them together or heard him refer to her?'

'No. Julia said that after James died, she didn't have anyone close, which was why it was so good . . . so good to have met me.'

'That could have been true,' Siv said. 'Mr Granger says they weren't close. I have to be on my way. If you think of anything else Julia told you, anything personal, please contact me. I'll let you know when she can see visitors.'

Betty stood, cleared the cups and put them in the sink. She was suppressing tears. 'Don't bother, Inspector. I don't think I want to visit Julia now.'

* * *

Siv stopped at Berminster General next and spoke to Julia. A staff change-over was taking place and there was a quiet bustle on the ward. Julia looked pale but determined. A bruise on her right temple seemed darker this morning.

'Back again, Inspector?'

'You'll be seeing plenty of me, so you'd better get used to it. I've spoken to your godson, Mason Granger, known as Frankie. He claims he didn't know that Lauren was James's daughter and that he knows nothing about the murders of Lauren Visser and Matis Rimas.'

Julia waved a weary hand. 'He doesn't. I never told him about James's by-blow. Leave Frankie alone. I've told you, I killed them.'

'No, you didn't. You gave me the wrong location for where you'd placed Sophie's photo.'

Julia's eyes were tired. The eyelids drooped but there was a gleam of intelligence there. 'I'm so confused. I can't actually remember exactly where I put the photo. So much has happened and I'm exhausted. There's no point in asking me about it. I killed them, so you can arrest me and then you'll have sorted everything out.' She closed her eyes and turned her head aside.

'That would all be very neat and tidy, I agree. Neat and tidy and wrong.' Siv waited a moment, then tried a different line. 'I've also talked to your friend Betty. Why hadn't you mentioned Sophie's death or your connection with Frankie to her? You knew she volunteered with Minstergreen which Frankie chairs, but you never told her that he's your godson. Pretty odd. Come to that, you didn't confide in her about your husband's letter nor the rage and bitterness you felt. You're close friends, you meet every week. She told you about her bereavement and how her husband left her but you omitted big chunks of your history. That seems strange to me.'

Julia turned her head back, her eyes half open. 'I'm fond of Betty and she's been a good friend but she's an emotional woman. I didn't want to encourage drama or expressions of sisterly solidarity. Not everyone wants to wear their heart on their sleeve. Betty tends to. That's not my style. Some things are private and best left undiscussed.' Her steady, challenging look said, *and you can't prove otherwise.*

'I think Frankie possibly carried out the first two murders. You could have planned it between you. You both had motives. You both had your own reasons for disliking Lauren and you shared a common bond of anger at James for frittering money away on her, leaving nothing for Frankie and much less for you than you'd expected. So much deception and disloyalty on his part. And I think that you didn't reveal any details about Frankie or James's betrayal to Betty because you were already planning murder when you met her, so you had to play your cards close to your chest. Was the meeting with Betty random, or did you engineer it because it was part of getting to know about Lauren?'

Julia smiled faintly. 'Now you're engaging in flights of fancy, Inspector. I've confessed. I can't say any more.'

'Mason Granger is the sole beneficiary of your will. Why is that?'

'Quite simply, he's the only person left. I have no close family. I was terribly fond of Ava, Frankie's mother. She was kind to me after Sophie died, and she gave me a lot of quiet support. Frankie had a difficult time, losing his father when he was young and then Ava when he was just a teenager. He was an affectionate little boy and he was the first child I could bring myself to hug after Sophie's death. He brought me some small comfort when I was mad with grief. I've been fond of him over the years and for Ava's sake, I wanted to know he'd be okay in the future. Then at least some good will have come out of all this pain and loss.' Her voice was insistent, her cheeks flushed with the toll this was taking.

'So, let me get this right. You have no close family, you're fond of Frankie and have left him everything, yet you've chosen not to give the hospital staff his details, and he had no idea that you were in here until we told him. That too seems peculiar. It suggests that you're trying to keep a distance from him so that we don't ask too many questions.'

'I didn't want to worry Frankie. I'd have asked the staff to contact him as soon as I had the strength.'

'Julia, you have answers for everything. I can see that you've planned carefully and that you want your godson to walk away from it all. Many of your answers sound plausible and I admire your forethought, but we're going to examine every detail of your and Frankie's lives and we'll get to the truth.'

Julia clasped her hands across her chest, fingers linked as if she was an effigy on a tomb. 'Be my guest. Did you ever play that game when you were a child where you tell someone they're hot or cold in finding a clue? Well, you're very, very cold, Inspector. I know you're just doing your job but please go away now. You don't need to make life so hard for yourself, you know, battling on when there's no need.' There was a taunting glance, a little smile at the corners of her lips. 'But of course I can't stop you. We can't stop people being stupid, charging about and doing what they want. I've certainly found that out.'

* * *

Back at the station, Siv checked the updated information and called a meeting with all officers. She was buzzing now, her brain sharp. She felt almost back on form. She was going to rise to Julia's challenge. She walked up and down at the front of the room, sipping coffee.

'We've found Alan Vine's phone and the knife and protective gear that Julia Stenning used to kill him. The knife has his blood on it and her DNA has been retrieved from the hood of the coverall. Their phones have calls between them on the day before he died. We know that Julia Stenning can't have killed Lauren and Rimas. For one thing, there's her incorrect statement about the photo. She doesn't know where it was positioned. She claims to have thrown the weapon and Lauren's rucksack very conveniently into the sea. Polska opens at 8.30 a.m. and the cleaner confirms that Julia arrived at 7.45 on Monday 29th. CCTV shows her car on the road from Aldmarsh into town at 7.30 but there's no sign of her before then and no trace of her car around Lock Lane that morning. Working within those times, she can't have carried out the first two murders. I've spoken to her again but she's not budging. She might be protecting her godson. It's as if she's decided to sacrifice herself and it's giving her a kind of satisfaction. I've never seen a woman so keen to be charged. She seems desperate for Granger to be okay, to walk away and eventually inherit her estate. Ali, have you been in touch with the hospital?'

'Julia Stenning was moved from Intensive Care to a High Dependency ward last night. They're arranging a psychiatric assessment now she's stronger and can mobilize. Granger has been ringing twice a day, asking to see her. When they've refused, he's asked if he can speak to her on the phone. According to the ward he's being very persistent. He turned up there last night and got antsy when they refused to let him in. Laid it on thick about being her only family. The copper on duty sent him away sharpish.'

'Signs of desperation. Good. So, we crawl over every inch of Mason Granger's life. Julia's landline and mobile show no trace of any contact with him in the last six months, but they must have been in touch somehow. Ali, you can delegate who and where but I want you and one of our team to speak to all the members of Minstergreen to find out if they've ever seen Granger with a car or with Julia. Patrick, I want you and one other officer to speak to all staff and regular members at Polska, asking the same questions. I want Polska's phone records checked for any calls to Granger's number. The other two officers are to trawl Julia's friends and networks in Aldmarsh, asking if they've seen her with Granger. I'm going to see the other people who live in Granger's house, find out if he has friends in town or around that we don't know of. Have I missed anything?'

The room was silent but she sensed an energy there, as if they were picking up on her renewed vigour. Maybe Mortimer had a point and she hadn't been pushing hard enough. 'Okay. There's a car somewhere and we need to find it.'

* * *

There were three other flats in Granger's house. She tried them all that evening, showing the occupants Julia's photo. None of them had seen her or seen Granger with a car. As she was leaving, Granger rode up on his bike. He ignored her as he bent and folded it and carried it into the house. He slammed the door, humming loudly.

CHAPTER TWENTY-NINE

Two days later and they still had no results. That morning, a neighbour had reported seeing a back window broken at Julia Stenning's house. Patrick had gone to look and reported that there was no major damage. Just the broken kitchen window and signs that someone had gone through drawers and cupboards downstairs. Forensics had been out but couldn't find any fingerprints bar Julia's. Siv was in her office at eight p.m. going over all the information and interviews again, when Bartel Nowak rang her.

'Good evening, Madame. A DC Flore left me a message today, asking me about Julia Stenning and someone called Granger, whether I'd seen her with him. I just finished work and picked it up. I don't think I know this Granger. Is there a problem?'

'Are you still in Pevensey?'

'Still here, working away. Got another couple of weeks in this job.'

'So I presume you haven't heard about Julia Stenning.' She gave him a brief outline.

'Mrs Stenning killed someone? But she's a real lady.'

'That's very old-fashioned of you. Have you called because you can help?'

293

'Yes. But it's also good to hear your voice.'

She took a breath. 'Mr Nowak, I'm investigating three murders. Do you have information? Have you seen Julia with this young man at all?'

'I'm not sure. I might have.' He sounded deflated. 'I saw Julia a couple of weeks ago, talking to a man at the back of the centre, where there's a little service road and bins. I was making a phone call one night and there's a poor signal in the centre so I went to the back door.'

'Did you recognize the man?'

'No. That is, I thought there was something familiar about him but I can't be sure. He had his back to me and it was dark. I'd had quite a few beers and shots so it's all a bit hazy. I thought he was just someone who calls in there. He was tall, quite slim, jeans and a shirt.'

'Young?'

'Hmm . . . I think so. He had longish fair hair and he was carrying something in a black case. Well — more like a square box. I was pretty pissed you know and they were in the shadows.'

Long, fair hair. That didn't sound like Granger. His was short, dark. 'Did this man have a bicycle?'

'Don't think so.'

'Can you remember when this was?'

'Not exactly. Before I started this job, so say mid-April. Probably a Tuesday because I always try to go on a Tuesday. I play backgammon. You might like it.'

'Did Julia and this man seem friendly?'

'He kissed her cheek when he was going. Julia gave him something. I'm pretty sure it was some keys.'

She wanted to kiss him now. 'She gave him keys? How do you know? You said it was dark.'

'She held them up and they were glinting. He put them in his pocket, then walked off. Does that help?'

'Yes, it does. Thank you.'

'Good. Don't forget we're going to have a cup of tea sometime.'

She sat for a few minutes, thinking about Nowak's description of the man Julia had been talking to. She'd been so certain that Granger had played a part in these murders. Well, if Nowak was right, she had to do a rapid gear change and rethink the whole thing. *If* he was right and hadn't been so drunk that he couldn't see straight. Bloody hell. Okay, then, she'd push Granger to the back burner for now.

She closed her eyes, remembering dancing in the sunshine with Nowak's arm around her waist. As she whirled around, people's faces had passed in a blur. In the shifting crowd, the musicians had been visible and then obscured as they swayed to the rhythm of the music. She could feel the heat again and Nowak's sturdy hand pressed against her back. A case like a square box. She concentrated and saw a face that she'd come across in another context in the last few weeks.

Her scalp prickled but this time the feeling was good. She brought up the investigation records and scrutinized them, looking at names and addresses and cross-referencing them. She traced the details about the man she was looking for and then sat back and thought about the break-in at Julia's. Such incidents did happen if it became known that a property was empty, but it had seemed a strange coincidence. Now she thought she might know who had broken in and why. When Julia had told her she was very cold in pursuing Granger, she'd thought the woman was taunting and double bluffing her. Maybe she'd been telling the truth.

She rang Patrick and talked to him for a couple of minutes, going over information and background searches with him and asking him about his interview with the man she now had in her sights.

'Do you want him to come in?'

'No,' she said thoughtfully. 'Not yet.' She still needed to join the dots.

She phoned Betty Marshall then and asked her some questions. Betty sounded low and distant but her information added to Siv's tiny flickers of hope.

She fingered the mass of soft hair that was growing in at the back of her scalp, and then went to look again at all the names on the incident board. The keys that Julia had handed to the man might have been for a car. She had come to hate her husband after his death and derived pleasure from taking revenge on him. How about the killer using his car to find and murder his daughter? She thought it would have provided Julia with a perverse satisfaction. The question was worth asking.

She hurried out of the station and drove to Aldmarsh, hoping that Peter Bacon wasn't one of those older people who went to bed early. She was relieved to see the lights shining behind his curtains and an external lamp on over the door. He welcomed her in, offering tea, saying he hadn't baked for a couple of days but he had biscuits.

'No, that's fine, Mr Bacon.' Although she hadn't eaten since a sandwich at lunchtime, and could have devoured one of his scones.

He fussed around in the sitting room, switching the TV off and turning lamps on before sinking into his recliner chair.

'One of your officers called on me yesterday, and asked me again about Julia's godson and whether he'd been driving a car. I said I'd told you what I know.'

'Yes, that's fine, thanks. That's not why I'm here.'

'Oh, I see. How's Julia?'

'She's improving. Mr Bacon, I've come to talk to you about James Stenning. He drove a car?'

'Oh yes, a Volkswagen Golf. He'd bought it not long before he died. He liked his cars, did James. Traded up regularly.'

Julia's was a Nissan. 'What happened to the car after he died?'

Bacon puffed his cheeks out. 'Well, I really have no idea. I suppose Julia sold it. I haven't seen it, put it that way.'

'So did James keep his car on the road or in their garage? There's only room for one in there.'

'It varied, really. I think they took turns. But when they went on holiday, James left his at the Galloway place.'

'Where would that be?'

'Couple of miles away. James originally agreed it with Sammy Galloway but he died. Joan, Sammy's mother, is still there, running their animal feeds place, or trying to. I think she's struggling with it on her own. Not getting any younger, like myself.' He tapped his forehead. 'I heard that her memory's not as good as it used to be. Now, can I put the kettle on?'

'Thank you, but I don't have time now. You've been very helpful, but I have to go.'

In the car, she googled Galloway and saw that there was a smallholding off the main road back towards Berminster, on Stowe Hill. She rang Ali as she drove there. He answered, voice muffled, saying he was at the cinema with Polly.

'Sorry, but you're going to miss the end of the film. I need you to meet me at Aldmarsh. Get Patrick out here too.' She gave him a quick summary and then slowed, not wanting to miss the turning for Stowe Hill.

She turned off the road by a tatty sign saying Galloway's Feeds. The night was dark and clear with a full moon. The house was down at heel, a wide bungalow with straggling flowers in baskets by the door. She could see a number of outbuildings. She knocked on the bungalow door. There was no answer and no light on. She knocked again and then walked around the side, past broken pots and a smelly drain blocked with leaves. A light shone from the kitchen window and as she looked through, she saw a slender, white-haired woman in a fleecy dressing gown asleep in a chair with a TV flickering in front of her. It was so loud she could hear it outside. She tapped on the door and the window until she saw the woman's head lift and she looked around groggily. Siv tapped on the window again and got her ID ready while the woman struggled from the chair and crossed to the door.

'Mrs Galloway, I'm DI Drummond from Berminster police. I need to talk to you.'

'The police? Is something wrong?' Her hair was in an old-fashioned net and she'd removed her front dentures for the night.

'You don't need to worry. I just want to check a few things with you.' She stepped inside, taking in the mess of the kitchen. Boxes of hen food, birdseed and dog biscuits jostled on the table with the remains of beans on toast and empty yogurt pots.

'What time is it?' Mrs Galloway asked, looking around the walls as if expecting to see a clock.

'Ten fifteen. I'm sorry to wake you.'

'I made a hot drink. Not sure where I put it now. Maybe it's in the living room.'

There was a smell in the kitchen, similar to the one coming from the drain outside. 'Can we sit down for a moment? Some more detectives will be arriving soon. I'll just switch off the TV, so we can talk.'

She pressed the remote and there was a wonderful silence. Mrs Galloway rested back in her chair. Her eyes were large, distant, blank.

'Mrs Galloway, did you know James Stenning?'

'James. Yes . . . he died. He helped out with the money one time. Gave my Sammy advice.'

'He was a financial advisor, that's right. Did James sometimes keep his car here?'

'His car?' She frowned and looked around. 'I think Sammy said he could. Time to time, like. Think he paid a bit. I left all that sort of thing to Sammy. Cancer got him.'

'I'm sorry. How long has Sammy been gone?'

'I'm not sure. A while, anyway.'

'Whereabouts did Mr Stenning put the car when he brought it here?'

'In one of the small sheds, I suppose. The field at the back. I've not been down there since Sammy died.'

'Have you noticed anyone else going down there recently?'

'Why would anyone be going there?'

You could have driven a tank past the house and Mrs Galloway wouldn't notice. 'Do you have keys to the sheds?' Siv asked.

'Not sure. I'd have to look. They might be in Sammy's room.'

'Could you look for me? It's important.'

Siv waited while she pottered out of the room. She heard Ali's car and went out to meet him. He'd brought Patrick, and she led them to the back door.

'Jesus H. Christ, this place is minging!' Ali said, turning around slowly on the spot. 'But, hey, guv, this guy hasn't been on our radar. Did we miss a trick earlier on?'

Patrick was looking twitchy, scuffing the filthy floor with the toe of his shoe.

'I don't know. I don't think so. There were no flags for him and it's still tenuous. Joan Galloway lives here. Her son's dead and I suspect the place has been disintegrating around her since.'

Patrick surveyed the kitchen. 'Wow. What's the smell?'

'Drains, I think. Nothing worse, I hope. It sounds as if Stenning had an arrangement with the son to leave his car here sometimes. A lock up. I'm hoping it's here and that it has a front left tyre with a worn tread. Mrs Galloway's looking for the shed keys.'

Mrs Galloway came back with a set of keys. 'I don't know if these are the ones. I can't find any others.' Taking no notice of Ali and Patrick, she went to switch the kettle on.

'We'll just have a look then, Mrs Galloway,' Siv said, but the woman didn't respond. She reached for a tea caddy.

Ali took a torch from his pocket and they stepped over a broken fence beyond the bungalow. The torch picked out a rutted track leading towards the outbuildings. They made their way in silence past two long sheds and then saw three smaller metal structures. As they approached the nearest, Siv saw that the door was slightly ajar.

'Switch the torch off, I think someone's in there,' she whispered to Ali.

Patrick stepped forward, caught at the edge of the door and pulled it back sharply. A tall, bearded man with his long hair drawn back in a ponytail and wearing a head torch was in there, looking in the boot of the Volkswagen. The man Siv had seen supervising the children in the garden at the nursery and playing his accordion at the May festival. He started up.

'What do you want?' he asked, sounding alarmed.

'Berminster police. We were looking for this car. You being here is an added bonus,' Ali said, sweeping his torch around the shed, and then bending to look at the front tyres.

'Step away from the car, Mr Wilby, don't touch it again,' Siv ordered.

He stepped back. 'No need to make a fuss. I'm just taking care of it for Julia Stenning. She asked me to help out.'

Siv moved forward. 'Really? Since admission to hospital, she's had no visitors and no calls from you. How did she ask you to come here and how did you get the keys for the shed and the car?'

He opened and closed his mouth. Siv always liked it when a suspect did the goldfish impression.

Ali raised a thumb. 'Michelin with an interesting tread front left,' he told her.

That was all she needed for now. 'Jeremy Wilby, you are under arrest on suspicion of the murders of Lauren Visser and Matis Rimas on Monday twenty-ninth of April. Also on suspicion of breaking and entering Julia Stenning's home.'

Patrick handcuffed him while she finished the caution. Wilby was silent, dazed-looking. Siv told him to sit on an old stool at the back of the shed and wait. She called for a car to take him away and then phoned forensics, stressing that she needed teams urgently, both at the shed and at Wilby's home.

'Patrick, you escort Wilby to the station and we'll wait for forensics. Sorry about your film, Ali. Was it any good?'

'I'm not missing much, put it that way. But I was looking forward to the meal afterwards. My stomach thinks my throat's been cut. I'm going to step outside and have a fag, take my mind off it. Still, happy days, eh guv?'

Her own stomach was grumbling. Patrick touched her arm, spoke softly.

'Hope I haven't let you down, guv. When I talked to him, there was nothing to raise concern and none came up later either.'

'It's okay, Patrick. We can talk later. We followed every lead. It looks as if Visser was on the right track after all. He said the murderer was connected to the nursery.' She looked back at Wilby, who was staring at the floor, his lips moving. He glanced up and beckoned her with a toss of his head.

'I didn't mean to kill the young man. I panicked. I was just leaving when I saw him walking down to the river and I couldn't get past him, back to the car. I felt trapped. I had to get away. I was hoping he wouldn't be long. He caught a fish and put his rod down and I thought he was going. But then he walked up to where she was . . . near where I was hiding and he was staring at her. I didn't have time to think. I just came at him and then he was on the ground. I'm so sorry about him. Tell his family I'm sorry.' He was trembling, his voice reedy.

'What about Lauren Visser's husband? Do you want me to say sorry to him?'

He looked past her. 'If it will make any difference. It was hard to like Lauren. She was so full of herself, always preaching about food and the environment, lording it over the rest of us. Thought she was God's gift at work. She'd give me patronizing little tips about how to handle the children, as if I didn't know my own job. She might not have realized it but she caused a lot of unhappiness and heartache. Talk to Julia, then you'll understand. Julia's the person who's really suffered. That woman's been to hell and back.'

'I have talked to Julia. She's confessed to killing Alan Vine at Halse woods. Did you know about that?'

'What? No! I haven't talked to her since . . . who's Alan Vine? I don't understand.'

'Just another person who got in the way because he knew something. Julia was worried he'd trap her. So she stabbed him with a knife. Three dead now. You've been keeping bad company.'

He gave her a look of pure misery. 'Julia wanted me to use the scissors. She insisted it had to be scissors. I understood but I thought maybe a knife would have been less painful. Quicker, like.'

She found it hard to believe what she was hearing. 'Is that supposed to make me feel as if you were trying to be kind-hearted? Give me a break! I don't want to hear any more out of you until the formal interview.'

His eyes clouded and his head slumped again. She reckoned he'd be dying to get it all off his chest.

CHAPTER THIRTY

It was two in the morning before Siv fell into bed. She lay sleepless for a while, from a mixture of relief and anxiety. She wondered how Julia and Wilby had met and what had driven him to plan a murder with her. She'd visit Julia on her way to the station, she decided as she finally drifted off, to see her reaction to Wilby's arrest.

At six, her phone woke her from a deep sleep.

'Ma'am, it's PC Beaumont at Berminster General. Julia Stenning's dead.'

She sat up, muddle-headed. 'Christ's sake! How did that happen?'

'She deteriorated suddenly around four a.m. with a blood infection, and was rushed back to the ITU. She died twenty minutes ago. Sorry, ma'am.'

She slumped back on the pillow. Her eyes were full of grit. No chance now of working on Julia with the new evidence. She rang Ali while she put the kettle on.

'Bloody hell! She's made the final escape!'

His voice was so loud she had to hold the phone away from her ear. 'Hospitals can be dangerous places when you're sick.'

He sighed. 'Tricky in life, tricky in death.'

'Yep. I'm heading to the station now. I'm hoping forensics will get some results this morning.'

'I'll arrange for someone to tell Granger about Julia.'

She took a quick shower to wake herself up. She thought about Julia while she dried herself, her life and death. She'd been a killer but she felt sad for the woman and the tragedy and deception she'd endured. It had soured her life, made her bitter and vengeful. Siv swiped moisturiser across her face and her lip stung. She'd forgotten to buy medication for her cold sore. It was looking angrier against her washed-out skin. She stopped at Gusto for coffee and a ham croissant, devouring the food on the way into the building. She drank the hot coffee from one side of her mouth to avoid her sore lip and splashed some on the desk, but missed her shirt.

She called a quick team meeting at 8.30 and updated them.

'When Bartel Nowak told me about the man he'd seen, it rang bells with me. I'd seen Jerry Wilby in the garden at the nursery and he was playing the accordion by the Polska stall on the May bank holiday. I remembered the square box for his instrument stacked on a table with violin cases by the side of the stall. We spoke briefly. He'd come up squeaky clean in the background searches, and when Patrick interviewed him. I think we can be sure that his story regarding Lauren having concerns about a man by the river was a fiction. He just wanted to see if he could weasel out any information about how the investigation was progressing. He had no connection to Lauren outside of work and no apparent disagreements with her. But he lives in Marton, a village near Aldmarsh. When I spoke to Betty Marshall, she confirmed that Julia knew Wilby because he'd played at a Christmas concert at the church in Aldmarsh, and that's how she'd booked him for the festival. Betty didn't know anything else but she did tell me that when Lauren got her promotion at the nursery, Wilby was the other candidate. She said he'd been very disappointed at not securing the post.'

'He must have had more reason than that for killing Lauren,' Ali said.

'I hope so. We have confirmation at least that Matis Rimas was just unfortunate because he strayed into a murder scene. Wilby must have been involved in some way with Julia. We'll hear more about that when we interview him. Now that we have the car and his DNA, we'll hopefully find forensic evidence. Wilby has a small council house and lives on his own. Forensics are there now. He has a sister two doors down. Apart from Ali and Patrick, I want you all out at Marton, door knocking, asking if anyone saw him with Julia and interviewing the sister. Patrick, start digging again on Wilby, go over everything and talk to Jenna Seaton.'

Mid-morning, she and Ali were preparing to interview Wilby with his solicitor. Patrick knocked on her door. He was smiling.

'Forensics called, guv. The Volkswagen tyres are the same as the tracks found near the river. Overshoes, scissors and coverall in the boot. Traces of carpet fibre in the boot of the car same as the material used on the overshoes. Also, a speck of Lauren's blood on the gear stick of the car. Plenty of Wilby's DNA around the driver's seat, on the gear stick and in the boot. And best of all, one of Rimas's hairs on the outer rim of Wilby's washing machine in his house. They've found other fibres but haven't processed those yet.'

She leaned back against the wall, relief washing through her. Ali took a small round tin from his pocket and offered her a sweet.

'Mango drops,' he said. 'Sugar-free, of course.'

'What happened to the mints? I liked those.'

'Polly banned them and bought me these instead. She keeps on my case where the sugar's concerned. They're okay. You can get used to anything if you try.' He popped one in his mouth, sounding unconvinced.

'It's not bad. I can taste the mango,' Siv lied.

* * *

After they'd charged Wilby, Siv sat with Mortimer, watching him tidy his cuticles. Wilby's bewildered sister and a neighbour said that they'd seen Julia visit him at his house. No one had a bad word to say about him. He was apparently an all-round nice man, dedicated to his job and a good accordionist. A bit like the reports of Lauren, Siv thought. She could see why Wilby had that reputation. He was softly spoken, apparently unassuming, with a quiet manner. Patrick said that he'd been the same when he interviewed him.

'Should we have spotted him sooner?' Mortimer asked.

'I don't see how we could have, and I have no issues with DC Hill's initial interview with him at the nursery, his contact in a subsequent phone call or with our background checks. Wilby was under the radar in every way and appeared to be genuinely helpful and concerned. No previous police involvement, no debt, no apparent issues with Lauren or connection to Julia Stenning, no history of violence. He met Julia the Christmas not long after she'd found out what Stenning had done. Wilby played the accordion at the church fete and they had mulled wine at her house afterwards. He told Julia that his father had died and he'd recently discovered that the man had been a bigamist with three other children. Wilby's family is still full of bitterness about that. They never refer to the father. His sister told us that when they found out, only a couple of weeks after the funeral, Wilby removed his father's headstone from the grave and smashed it up. That resonated with Julia. She wasn't a woman to spill out her troubles but hearing about that betrayal must have struck a chord.

'So, over the mulled wine she told Wilby about Sophie's death and Lauren being Stenning's daughter. He realized it was the Lauren he worked with. He's a good listener, I'd say. Empathetic, with a kindly manner. That's why he's good with kids. He felt deeply sorry for Julia and her suffering. He told her he worked at the nursery with Lauren and that she'd got promotion over him despite the fact he'd been there longer. He had a real, slow-building resentment about that. Their phone records show lots of contacts in the following

306

months, then it stops. She'd go to his house to make plans. He claims that it took a long time before Julia could persuade him to kill Lauren, that she was the driving force behind it all. She wanted scissors used, and Sophie's photo left there. Given their personalities, I think I buy that.'

'So his motives for killing were resentment about his own father, sympathy for Mrs Stenning and not getting a job?' Mortimer looked dubious.

'Not quite. True, he didn't think that Lauren was as effective as he was at work and the more he talked about her the more his dislike showed. No — his real motive was money. Julia was going to pay him once it had all died down. Twenty thousand. He had ambitions to set up a proper business, promote his own folk group. A nursery job doesn't pay much. He'd already started talking to a couple of musicians about it.'

'Old-fashioned blood money, then.'

'Yes. Julia had earmarked a portion of the inheritance she received from her husband. She apparently liked the symmetry of his money being used to erase Lauren, just as she liked the thought of his car being used as transport for the murder. Wilby and Julia knew about Lauren's wild swimming and they'd decided it would provide the opportunity for him to kill her. Julia gave him the keys to the shed and the car and he organized the rest. Then at lunch on the Friday, Lauren mentioned to Wilby that she was going to swim at Lock Lane on the Monday morning. He phoned Julia from a callbox in Berminster on the Friday evening and they agreed that he'd stab her then. They arranged that he'd pick up James Stenning's car early on Monday morning. He walked across the fields from Marton to collect it.'

'Matis Rimas was an unfortunate extra casualty.'

'Yes, wrong place, wrong time. Wilby panicked because he couldn't get past him without being seen. After the murders, Wilby drove the car back to Galloway's, put the overshoes, coverall and scissors in the boot and left the keys under a stone outside the shed. The plan was for Julia to get rid of it. When Wilby heard that Julia was in intensive care, he got anxious. He didn't know what was wrong with her and couldn't find out. Apart from anything else, he thought she might die and he wouldn't be paid. It was all getting too complicated and he worried that if she was very ill, she might start to feel remorseful and tell us about his role in the murders. He thought he'd better check to see if she'd disposed of the car and take it away if it was still there. He went back to the shed, but the keys weren't under the stone. That's why he broke into Julia's house. He says he knew nothing about Alan Vine's murder and there's nothing to connect him with that.'

Mortimer's phone rang. He picked it up, listened and thanked the caller. 'That was the CPS. They agree that the case has passed the evidence threshold. Good result. I'm pleased to see you can think on your feet. It meant that you caught Wilby at the car. Although of course, it's best to do things carefully and by the book.'

She stood. He was so mealy-mouthed. 'Do you read the *Journal of Homicide Investigation*, sir?'

He looked taken aback. 'At times. Why?'

'There's an interesting article in volume nine about using flair and independent thinking in major crime investigation, as well as following the rules. It concludes that there's room for both. I can send you a link if you like.'

He drew his brows together. 'That won't be necessary. I can look for myself.'

'Thank you, sir. Oh, by the way, is it okay if Patrick puts this success on Twitter?'

'Yes, it is, after Mr Visser's been told.'

She opened her mouth then closed it again. She might as well leave Mortimer's office while the going was good.

* * *

That evening, she sat folding at the kitchen table, a glass of akvavit to hand. Exhaustion and relief flowed through her. It was hard to relax and concentrate on the paper after so many hours of tension.

Wilby's sister had come into the station, pale with horror at the charges against her brother. Siv had spoken to her briefly before she gave a statement.

'I can't believe this,' she'd said. 'Jerry's always been a sensitive, kind man. How could he do that to two people? I know he was fed up when Lauren Visser got the job he wanted and he was terribly upset when he found out about our dad. He was angry and unbalanced for quite a while. I was ever so worried about him. I thought he should see the doctor but he wouldn't. Do you think that had anything to do with it?'

'I don't know. Only he can say.' *Don't go making excuses for him. It still came down to ten thousand pounds per life.*

Her phone rang. Ali. He'd been on a high all day, restless and chain smoking, singing snatches of "I Fought the Law." He and Patrick had been to tell Visser the news and had come back indignant, saying he hadn't even thanked them. She'd been glad to get away from him and come home.

'Guv, want to come out for a drink?'

'Not tonight, I'm done in. Take Polly to the cinema.'

'She's working. What did Mortimer say?'

'Oh, you know. Grudging acknowledgement. He did manage to say that the team had worked hard.'

She suspected that Mortimer had been a bit disappointed that she'd achieved an arrest. It didn't feel good, knowing that he'd wanted her to fail, but she had to leave that problem to one side for now. 'I suppose Patrick's been busy on Twitter.'

'Yeah, no doubt. He'll wear his thumb down. Well . . . I'm cream-crackered myself but it's too early to go to bed and there's nothing on telly. I might wander over to Nutmeg and have a snack. Sure you won't join me?'

Ed's sweatshirt was cosy, the akvavit slipping down nicely. 'Thanks, but no. I'll buy the team a round of drinks tomorrow. Give my best to Polly.'

She checked Patrick's Twitter feed and smiled.

@DCBerminsterPolice. Man arrested and charged with recent murders at Lock Lane. Great teamwork, great result. Big thank you to members of public who gave information. We always need your help. #keepingberminstersafe.

She was in the bathroom, putting cream on her cold sore, when she heard a soft knock at the door. Maybe Ali had driven over after all to bother her, or Corran had baked too many potatoes again. She opened the door as Mutsi was raising her hand to knock a second time.

'Sivvi, darling! What on earth are you wearing? Did you get it in a jumble sale? And what's that stuff on your face?'

Her stomach lurched. She saw a car parked on the lane, saw that it was full of suitcases. She managed to speak. 'What are you doing here?'

'I've moved back, thought I'd look at settling here, near my family. You did see my emails? I said I was thinking of leaving Turku. People there can be so petty and nasty. You just wouldn't believe the cruel gossip and the cold shoulders. Can I come in? This looks so much nicer than in the photo. I was worried that you'd ended up in a dump.'

She stared. Mutsi's hair was strawberry blonde and just touching her shoulders. She was in a pink linen trouser suit with a gold belt cinching in her still slim waist. Four thin gold bracelets encircled her left wrist. Her skin was youthful and glowing. A warm floral scent wafted from her. She looked like one of those mature, well-preserved Bond girls who popped up in interviews now and again. The sight of her made Siv feel ancient. She was suddenly conscious of her bald patches, worried that any might be on view.

'I thought you reckoned this was a hick town.'

'I was probably a little hasty. I'm sure it has its good points. I stopped at the harbour and there was so much colour in the sunlight. It looked pretty and lively, almost Mediterranean!'

'It won't look anything like that on a wet day, and you're not staying with me.'

'Gracious as always, Sivvi. I don't want to stay in your little raggle-taggle gypsy caravan. Honestly, I half expected to find you in a sequin headdress, wearing huge earrings and telling fortunes! I've booked a hotel room in town while I take a look around. After all, with your father and poor Ed passed over and Rikka on the other side of the world, we're all that's left of the family. I suppose you might invite your Mutsi in for a drink after her long journey. I'm sure you have a bottle of akvavit in the fridge. You do have a fridge?'

And then she was through the door and sitting on the sofa, sipping akvavit and slipping her patent shoes off. She waved her glass. '*Kippis*, Sivvi. Here's to us!'

'What "us" would that be?'

She gave a little practised sigh, one that Siv knew well, the kind that means *I don't know why you're being unkind to me.* 'I see you still play with your paper, Sivvi. Isn't that a bit childish?' She was leaning across and fingering the design on the kitchen table. Probably leaving greasy finger marks on it.

Siv glared at her. 'When I was nine, I got home from school one day to that flat we had in Camden Town. You'd left a note on the door, telling Rik and me to come to an address in Bayswater. Luckily, Rik had just enough for the bus fares and a kindly conductor told us which routes we needed. We had to look up an A to Z in a shop to locate you.'

Mutsi smoothed a strand of hair. 'That was such a difficult time for me and I had to find somewhere in a hurry.'

'You moved home without telling us. You left some of my favourite toys and books behind and I never saw them again. We were off school for a fortnight before you could blag us into yet another one.'

'Well, goodness, that's all water under the bridge now. It was a long time ago. I know things were a bit difficult now and again but it wasn't easy being a single parent with two girls to raise. Anyway, there's so much to catch up on! Tell me what's been happening. Have you met anyone nice? I do hope so but you look rather tired and worn. You were never clever at making the best of yourself, even though I tried to set you an example. At least your hair's cut well, although it's a bit short. Not very feminine. Ed would want you to be happy, you know. Although I don't know how you'd be able to invite a beau back here. It has a certain rustic charm but it's a little . . . basic.'

Siv sat with her drink. She heard the goats calling in the dusk and the clank of Corran's bucket. If Ed was here now, he'd be stepping in, expertly diverting Mutsi and offering, with a hand below her elbow, to help her to her hotel. Signalling that he wouldn't take no for an answer. *You and your fucking bike, Ed!*

Now she had to face her solitary, vulnerable self all over again. The buttons on her mother's pink jacket shimmered in the light and her bracelets chimed as she lifted the akvavit and topped up her glass.

She felt like a butterfly caught in a net.

END

FREE KINDLE BOOKS

Please join our mailing list for free Kindle books and new releases, including crime thrillers, mysteries, romance and more.

www.joffebooks.com

Thank you for reading this book. If you enjoyed it please leave feedback on Amazon or Goodreads, and if there is anything we missed or you have a question about then please get in touch. The author and publishing team appreciate your feedback and time reading this book.

We're very grateful to eagle-eyed readers who take the time to contact us. Please send any errors you find to corrections@joffebooks.com

Printed in Great Britain
by Amazon